NEW YORK REVIEW BOOKS
CLASSICS

AN ERMINE IN CZERNOPOL

GREGOR VON REZZORI (1914–1998) was born in Czernowitz (now Chernivtsi, Ukraine), Bukovina, then part of the Austro-Hungarian Empire. He later described his childhood in a family of declining fortunes as one "spent among slightly mad and dislocated personalities in a period that also was mad and dislocated and filled with unrest." After studying at the University of Vienna, Rezzori moved to Bucharest and enlisted in the Romanian army. During World War II, he lived in Berlin, where he worked as a radio broadcaster and published his first novel. In West Germany after the war, he wrote for both radio and film and began publishing books at a rapid rate, including the four-volume *Idiot's Guide to German Society*. From the late 1950s on, Rezzori had parts in several French and West German films, including one directed by his friend Louis Malle. In 1967, after spending years classified as a stateless person, Rezzori settled in a fifteenth-century farmhouse outside of Florence with his wife, gallery owner Beatrice Monte della Corte. There he produced some of his best-known works, among them *Memoirs of an Anti-Semite* and the memoir *The Snows of Yesteryear: Portraits for an Autobiography* (both published by NYRB Classics).

PHILIP BOEHM has translated numerous works from German and Polish by writers including Ingeborg Bachmann, Franz Kafka, and Stefan Chwin. For the theater he has written plays such as *Mixtitlan*, *The Death of Atahualpa*, and *Return of the Bedbug*. He has received awards from the American Translators Association, the U.K. Society of Authors, the NEA, PEN

America, the Austrian Ministry of Culture, the Mexican-American Fund for Culture, and the Texas Institute of Letters. Currently he is translating Herta Müller's *The Hunger Angel*. He lives in St. Louis, where he is the artistic director of Upstream Theater.

DANIEL KEHLMANN is a widely translated German-Austrian novelist. He has won the Candide Prize, the Literature Prize of the Konrad Adenauer Foundation, the Heimito von Doderer Literature Award, the Kleist Prize, the WELT Literature Prize, and the Thomas Mann Prize. He is a prolific author of fiction and criticism, and three of his novels—*Me and Kaminski*, *Measuring the World*, and *Fame*—have been translated into English.

AN ERMINE IN CZERNOPOL

GREGOR VON REZZORI

Translated from the German by

PHILIP BOEHM

Introduction by

DANIEL KEHLMANN

NEW YORK REVIEW BOOKS

New York

THIS IS A NEW YORK REVIEW BOOK
PUBLISHED BY THE NEW YORK REVIEW OF BOOKS
435 Hudson Street, New York, NY 10014
www.nyrb.com

The translation of this work was supported by a grant from the Goethe-Institute, funded by the German Ministry of Foreign Affairs.

Library of Congress Cataloging-in-Publication Data
Rezzori, Gregor von.
[Hermelin in Tschernopol. English]
An ermine in Czernopol / by Gregor von Rezzori ; translated by Philip Boehm.
p. cm. — (New York review books classics)
ISBN 978-1-59017-341-1 (alk. paper)
I. Boehm, Philip. II. Title.
PT2635.E98H413 2011
833'.912—dc22

2011013386

ISBN 978-1-59017-341-1

Printed in the United States of America on acid-free paper.
10 9 8 7 6 5 4 3 2 1

CONTENTS

INTRODUCTION

1.

Gregor von Rezzori was the first writer I got to know by sight, but that wasn't due to his fame as an author so much as it was to an Austrian TV show called *Jolly Joker* that ran in the early 1980s. The program offered glimpses of the international jet-set and typically featured fast cars or aristocrats, or more often than not aristocrats with fast cars, along with movie stars who lived in Monaco or the south of France. It was an endearing show, without a hint of malice, in love with a vaguely antiquated idea of luxury and grand style—a series of charming, well-meaning, and inconsequential episodes that demonstrated how beautiful life could be for a few lucky souls. The single most impressive thing about it, however, was the moderator: an elegant, suntanned gentleman getting on in years who seemed to radiate health, sophistication, and wit, and who always appeared remarkably relaxed. He was often filmed standing on a beach or atop a hill, occasionally at the steering wheel of a fast car, and he always spoke with a soft accent that had just a hint of nasal elegance and was impossible to place. Later I learned that it was half that of an Austrian aristocrat and half the peculiar German of his native Bucovina.

This was the famous author Gregor von Rezzori. I could hardly believe it. Novelists didn't do that kind of thing, I thought: they didn't host TV programs about aristocrats and movie stars, and in the rare event they did pick up a microphone it was to warn against some nefarious political development or to help launch their latest book. But then as well as now, Rezzori's public persona hardly fit the accepted image of the distinguished writer. He had something of the grand seigneur and something of the rake; he was half aristocratic chronicler in the mold of Chateaubriand and half the enchanting trickster. As he himself put it (because even when it came to skeptical comments about himself he could put it better than anyone), he belonged to a dying breed spawned by the Austro-Hungarian Empire, "a typical, albeit anachronistic mix of high aristocrat and casino croupier."

He began early on as a writer of popular literature and serial novels for newspapers, and even after he was established he continued to write entertainingly playful books for the mass market on the side, as well as miscellaneous travel guides for German tourists and even an *Idiot's Guide to German Society.* He did this openly and mockingly and without being ashamed of the breadth of his writing; he was also fully aware of his own skill, and rightly so, for no reader of any judgment could doubt that the author of *Memoirs of an Anti-Semite* or *An Ermine in Czernopol* was one of the great writers of his time.

2.

Czernopol is of course Czernowitz, the capital of Bucovina and under the Hapsburgs a multiethnic center, a meeting place of Eastern and Western Europe, where Jews, Romanians, Germans, Ukrainians, Poles, and others lived together surprisingly peacefully. After the First World War the city was absorbed into the Kingdom of Romania; later, during the German occupation, the Jewish population was largely destroyed, and what was left of the old Austrian culture lived on only in literature—the poems of Paul Celan and the novels of Joseph Roth or Rezzori.

An Ermine in Czernopol takes place between the two world wars; it begins after the downfall of the monarchy and concludes shortly before the final catastrophe, the Nazi occupation, which forever ended the culture and way of life Rezzori describes. We are spared a depiction of the violence that followed, but we cannot read this book without feeling the history that haunts it: even in the wittiest moments of this truly witty novel we cannot forget the tragedy. Nor should we.

So why the camouflage, why change Czernowitz to Czernopol? Perhaps precisely to underscore the fact that the setting of the novel has nothing to do with the real Czernowitz, since the city Rezzori depicts has disappeared entirely into the realm of memory and fantasy. This is all the more important because Czernowitz is hardly an indifferent or coincidental location for this book. This story could happen nowhere else but in that place of diverse ethnicities, amid the constantly shifting loyalties that marked the ongoing political upheaval of the 1920s and '30s.

The concept of loyalty is crucial to *An Ermine in Czernopol*, a novel in the manner of *Don Quixote*, about a knight clinging to the outmoded code of honor of the former Austrian Empire. Major Tildy —the "ermine"—refuses to accept the new reality; he is unable to comprehend that everything in the world has become relative, and it is this staunch adherence to absolutes that leads to his ruin, when he steadfastly defends the honor of his sister-in-law, challenging everyone who insults her to a duel. His actions are all the more grotesque because this sister-in-law no longer has any honor to defend, though that hardly matters to Tildy, whose rigid code takes no account of reality—or of life and death.

Little of this, though, was clear to the narrator, who was still a child as Tildy's story unfolded, sheltered in his parents' home, where only a distant echo of events reached him. Who in fact is the narrator? Throughout the first half of the book he appears in the guise of an amorphous "we"—an atypical formal device Rezzori's novel shares with Faulkner's "A Rose for Emily" and Jeffrey Eugenides's *The Virgin Suicides.* Only later does a young man emerge from this childhood collective, and as this happens, we realize that the book is in significant part autobiographical. Yet from the start, the language of the book is not the language of the child but rather that of the mature narrator he will become, and who will look back on his childhood. From the start it is the language of the brilliant ironic stylist Gregor von Rezzori at the pinnacle of his form.

More than anything, however, the story of Major Tildy's fight for the honor of his dishonorable sister-in-law is the occasion for countless digressions, the stage for a constant stream of marginal figures and minor characters whose appearances, however brief, invariably leave a lasting impression. These include the fruit delivery man Kunzelmann, whose constant mangling of children's verses doesn't disturb him in the least but torments his listeners; or Widow Morar, who never tires of telling the story of her husband's suicide, which she watched through a keyhole; or—at the other end of the social spectrum—the worldly prefect Tarangolian, whose intelligence is only matched by his cynicism. In this way the novel captures voices from every stratum of a now vanished society, and the effect is both vital and eerie. It also preserves a no-less-vanished variety of Central European wit. In fact, Major Tildy is the only character who completely lacks a sense of humor, the only one who refuses to acknowledge and laugh at the dark side of existence. He is the only tragic figure, which is exactly why, for all his dignity, he is so ridiculous—because nothing is funnier than humorlessness.

At one point Major Tildy challenges the writer Năstase to a duel, and the latter comes up with several comical arguments for why a smart man would refuse to submit to such a contest. At the end of this speech, Năstase compliments the resolute Don Quixote for his Teutonic seriousness:

> "And last but not least, gentlemen, please convey my compliments to Major Tildy for his understanding and steadfastness of character. It's well known that his compatriots, the Germans, have to call an assembly in order to understand a joke. He, however, abandoned the attempt from the start. That compels a certain respect from me."

That itself was a joke for which the sober Germans of the 1950s had little appreciation. Nevertheless, the German critics had high praise for Rezzori's novel: in 1959, *Der Spiegel* ran a portrait of the author on its cover, and the book was awarded the coveted Fontane Prize. Equally important was the subsequent translation into numerous languages, as that ensured that the novel would not be restricted to German readers alone. Because despite his success, in the isolated and often very provincial milieu of the *Bundesrepublik*, Rezzori always remained a bit foreign, a bit suspect. The German literary establishment, it could be said, had abandoned Rezzori from the start. And *that* compels a certain respect.

3.

Speaking of Major Tildy, Prefect Tarangolian relates: "He himself supposedly said he knows only two types of response: the *witty* one and the *just* one." The prefect's clever turn of phrase may also be applied to Rezzori's writing. He didn't intend his work to be "just," in other words clear and well-balanced, with no fluctuation in quality; he wanted his writing to be "witty"—erratic, unpredictable, enjoyable, and shimmering. He wanted to live well and make money, act in films, travel the world, be a friend of the rich and famous and a great writer on top of that. In all of this he succeeded, and because he cared so little for the just response and so much for the witty solution to things, he personified the trickster, the capricious conjurer, able to mix low vernacular and high tone like few others. Like all good novels, *An Ermine in Czernopol* is also a portrait of its maker: mischievous and fun, wise and unjust, impossible to reduce to a single formula, extraordinarily intelligent, and marked with a humor that reaches deeply into the darkness of things.

—DANIEL KEHLMANN
Translated by Philip Boehm

TRANSLATOR'S NOTE

WITH *An Ermine in Czernopol*, Gregor von Rezzori conjures a world we cannot inhabit except in fiction. The once-upon-a-time city of Czernowitz becomes the invented city of Czernopol. The voices in the book are real, though the names have been changed to protect the guilty.

Nowhere but Czernopol could such a story take place. And no one but Rezzori could call this city to life, with its variety and mix of languages, its range of characters, its register of voices... And he does this with words. Words that tug and stretch at the German language, playfully, mockingly. Words that must find a new home in English.

Nor is that the only challenge facing the translator. Rezzori's prowess as a raconteur hardly eclipses the depth of his philosophical inquiry or the breadth of his erudition, and the text contains layers of style and levels of thought that go beyond the recounting of personal experience, ranging from journalistic reporting on social movements to Proustian ruminations on memory—all tinged with melancholy—not only for the passing of childhood but for the loss of all that ended with the Second World War.

In the translation I have made certain stylistic choices to help bring readers into the world of the novel without burdening them with too much "foreignness." Spellings of names and places that were "Germanized" in the original appear here in their proper Romanian (or other) form. Passages cited in another language are translated in the text or, in very few instances, with a footnote.

Many people have helped see this project through. I am particularly grateful to Beatrice Monte della Corte for her generosity at Santa

Maddalena, where I had access to the author's handwritten corrections to the novel (Rezzori frequently edited and emended texts long after their publication). For their careful editing I would like to thank Edward Cohen, Edwin Frank, Sara Kramer, and Helen Graves. Special thanks to Joana Ocros-Ritter for her keen ear and careful reading across so many languages. As always, I am especially grateful to my family for their encouragement and ongoing forbearance. For any and all lapses I can only hope that they, as well as the readers, show the same leniency as the citizens of Czernopol, where "lowliness was never a fault."

—Philip Boehm

AN ERMINE IN CZERNOPOL

The ermine will die should her coat become soiled.
—from the *Physiologus*

THERE are other realities besides and beyond our own, which is the only one we know, and therefore the only one we think exists.

A man staggers out of the howling recesses of some seedy dive into the uncertain gray of dawn.

His movements reveal the combination of bold daring and practiced confidence that mark a habitual drinker—the deadly serious parody of a clown.

His face is the crater field of some lost satellite.

His senses are seething with impulses: the din of the tavern, philological disputes, pride, humiliation, love, quotations, dirty jokes, hate, loneliness, faith, purity, despair—

He doesn't know his way home.

So he sleepwalks to the next intersection, where the tram tracks cross the street—two dully glistening snakes.

Keeping his head aloft as though he were blind, he taps and tests the ground with his cane, then he pokes it into one of the rail grooves, and lets himself be led as if tethered to a pole.

The tip of his cane sails through the groove, raising a bow wave of moldy leaves and trash, gravel, dirt and muck; his shoes splash through puddles, wrench his ankle on the uneven cobblestones, trip over track ties, churn through gravel, dig through dust. The fog slaps his face like wet cotton wool. Wind tears at the strands of hair that dangle onto his forehead from below the edge of his hat; dew settles on his lips, giving them a salty taste, and collects in tickling drops inside the two creases on either side of his mouth: his pulpy, oily cheeks do not absorb the moisture. He mumbles to himself, occasionally blurts something out loud, launches into a song, interrupts himself, laughs, goes silent, resumes his mumbling. His eyes are wide open and fixed unblinkingly ahead, like those of a blind man, like those of the gods.

In this manner he travels from one end of the city to the other.

The city lies somewhere in the godforsaken southeastern part of Europe and is called Czernopol.

He knows nothing of its reality:

He doesn't perceive its awakening, doesn't notice the hanging pearls of the arc lamps, garish against the pallid sky, as they expire with a crackling hiss, or the spaces that come looming up around the buildings on both sides of the street, hoisting the city out of the darkness and into the morning; he doesn't see the waxy bright rectangles of lighted windows as they emerge randomly amid the interlocking jumble of boxes—one here, one there, one over yonder. He doesn't see the Jewish bakers rolling their wagons out of the dark side streets, doesn't smell the heavy, hot aroma of freshly baked bread, doesn't hear the rattle of the farmers' carts wending toward the market, one by one, or the clatter of their small, emaciated horses, poked and prodded down the long melancholy roads from the flatland far away. He is as oblivious to the laughter of the passing late-night revelers as he is to the brutish barking of the policeman who fails to recognize him—a new, and obviously uninitiated, recruit. He knows nothing of the shadowy figures breaking out of the black caves of the building entranceways, wandering the streets toward unknown destinations, nothing of the sulfurous sky rising over the treetops in the Volksgarten, like Heaven on the Day of Judgment, and nothing, too, of the discordant screech of the first streetcar as it leaves the loop to join "the line," and which is heading straight in his direction—

All anyone ever does is head toward death.

And so he fails to hear the plaintive, wistful call of the trains in the distance as they depart the city of Czernopol one by one and race off into the forlorn countryside, toward a separate, sovereign reality—lonely and lost and full of yearning.

For each is lost in a solitude all his own—people as well as cities.

I

Concerning the Phenomenology of the City of Czernopol

IF YOU were to ask me to explain in no more words than I have fingers on one hand what elevated Czernopol above other cities of the earth, I would have to say: Lowliness was never a fault.

After all, there were rich people and there were poor people, just like everywhere else. And the rich were neither richer nor grander nor more hard-hearted than elsewhere. But the poor inhabited a poverty that you, happy child of socially hygienic circumstances, cannot possibly imagine. There were beggars in Czernopol—swarms of beggars—with pustules and abscesses in colors that would have astounded even Matthias Grünewald, men whose mutilations and malformations would have caused Hieronymus Bosch to question his own sanity, and they appeared, as I said, en masse, or, to put it more precisely, in hordes that crept and crawled, slithered and slid right beside you, so as to encircle you, cling to you, clamber on top of you—as if to drag you down to their lowly level, encrusted with filth and swarming with lice, as though you had stepped on one of their nests and stirred up the entire colony. Hardly a pleasant sight, to be sure. But not a single soul in Czernopol felt moved to undertake any action, as common parlance significantly puts it, either for or against—and the two are hard to separate.

No, on the contrary, if we had been deprived of this daily spectacle we would undoubtedly have sensed that something was missing. In some medieval way it belonged to our picture of the world, a world in which God was assigned not only—I'm tempted to say *not merely*—the role of gentle Creator. So for us it went without saying that whoever wasn't quick enough to avoid being accosted in the first place would strike back and kick away without mercy at the festering stumps and the torsos ridden with painful lesions; in any case this was a far more customary reaction than presuming to implement some sweeping welfare program in the name of humanitarianism, or just plain humanity. In Czernopol, aesthetic considerations were lowest on the list.

You will be tempted to call that cynical, and I have no intention of contradicting you. I could of course counter that Czernopol, like everywhere else, had its share of bad people, and I'm quite sure there were good people as well. In all probability the bad ones were not much more wicked or depraved than anywhere else; as for the good people, they may have once included in their midst someone as pure as a saint—what am I saying!—an angel. But I never heard of any angels in Czernopol, except perhaps for Herr Perko, he who was called "the angel of the emigrants," and where Herr Perko is concerned, I'd rather you judge for yourself, later on. Of course there were also the common souls, who were neither good nor evil but simply lowly—there were plenty of those, whole swarms and colonies. Yet you can probably no more imagine their lowliness than you can envision the godforsaken misery of the poor. To continue: Nor was it customary to kiss these beggars on the forehead in blessing, as Dostoyevsky envisioned, or to bow down before them, as if their extreme lowliness were a sign of their being chosen. Oh no. One simply kicked their shins, or their vastly more sensitive body parts, whenever the opportunity presented itself—but at least one spared their *face*, and that, please understand me correctly, meant they were free within their lowliness. Naturally they didn't feel particularly elevated, but at least they had no cause to stoop any lower. They were the way they were, but they were that way without blame or fault.

I realize that all this likely infringes on your good taste. But once again: taste was not a consideration in Czernopol. Those who struggled to maintain fictions of that sort were at best viewed with the ironic bemusement reserved for the bizarre, and stared at like some outlandish foreigner. More often they were shrugged off as being out of touch with reality, dismissed as extravagantly eccentric, or left as easy marks for the local wits and wags, who always found listeners eager to laugh. Meanwhile, the poor souls truly born with such a discriminating personality simply perished, without fanfare or flourish: they didn't even have the laughers on their side.

And that's saying something. Because if I had to name a second distinguishing feature about Czernopol, it would be its humor, or, more precisely, its laughter. Because laughter was everywhere, part of the air we breathed, a crackling tension in the atmosphere, always ready to erupt in showers of sparks, or to discharge itself in great thunderous peals. Its full range of nuance and timbre and tone lies somewhere beyond description. In this regard, at least, the city was quite cultured, although the culture was a very specific one, for laughter in Czernopol had been elevated to an art form, a folk art of unparalleled authenticity, stemming from a broad tradition, and widely cultivated to a degree of finesse, sophistication, and extraordinary piquancy—an art form understood and appreciated by all, drawing as it did from everyday life, and well endowed with the most vivid references, not to mention all manner of innuendoes. Nowhere but Czernopol could you find such an infallible sense of style, which could take a single laugh emitted in a large throng—a small group, a quartet, a trio, or a duet—and develop it into an elaborate interplay of voice and chorus, like Gregorian chant, and which resonated with the architecture until finally reaching its conclusion.

Just so there's no misunderstanding: I'm not talking about catharsis or some other purifying process. It's true that, every now and then, somewhere in Czernopol you might hear a simpleminded side-splitting guffaw, and then you would incline your ears to listen—after all, as I said, laughter was truly an art, so it was only natural that it should wind up both its own object and its own proximate cause. And for us there was nothing more laughable than those laughers whose hearty booming aspired to liberation. We had countless ways of laughing, but nothing of that sort. We laughed skillfully, artistically, indecently—but without the faintest intent of finding relief for, or release from, our compulsion. As a result, our laughter defied the words most often used to denote its various shadings—we did not roar, bellow, whinny, bleat, or blat, but rather performed a kind of smirk or sneer for which our language has, sadly, no expression (just as it has no way to convey true *human* laughter, for which it mistakenly borrows terms from zoology instead): a quick exhale dispatched through the nose, with scarcely sound or grimace. Because while Czernopol may not have been a good or beautiful city, it was, without doubt, an extraordinarily intelligent one.

This should not be construed to mean we had lost all vestige of loftier transcendence, however. It's well known that some types of silliness can verge on the sublime: short-circuited connections that spark back and forth for ages without producing any perceptible phenomena—except for the sharp trace of ozone they leave in the air. A rabbi joke, to take one example, or some top-rate prank, might strike us as inspirational, even uplifting.

As a result, Czernopolites had a particular soft spot for stupidity, since they placed a certain value on anything exotic, which they viewed with a tender, heartfelt irony. The city's top fools never failed to elicit fresh enthusiasm, happy astonishment, wide eyes, gaping mouths, and gleeful shouts of amazement—like grotesque monsters in the retinue of some Oriental envoy, bearing fabulous presents from distant potentates to the ruler of the world. Except our fools were part of the public domain: they belonged to the general populace, and commanded the same affection as city mascots. They had nicknames, too, that had arisen with the leavening of satire, such as those of enormous bells—"Big Ben" or "Old Pummerin"—whose sound and legend are known to every child because they have grown up with the city and shared its fate. Or like an especially powerful cannon from a regiment of Landsknecht soldiers.

The last comparison is probably more apt, because Czernopol was animated by a similar spirit—not exactly soldierly, mind you, but more reminiscent of those earlier mercenaries, with all their train and baggage. Herr Tarangolian, who as Prefect of Tescovina was the province's highest official, as well as one of the keenest analysts of its capital city—presumably because he was its most fervent admirer—enjoyed discoursing extensively on the subject.

"The world we inhabit," as he used to say, "is a world of such contradictions that it makes America look like a nation of materialistic bumbleheads. We, for our part, have been forced to become true cosmopolitans—and in the most extreme and dangerous manner, namely through our inexhaustible tolerance. But please don't call us nihilists. There is nothing we reject, absolutely nothing, and that's exactly the point. So if it's also true that there's nothing we accept—and I mean *nothing*—it's simply because we accept everything. We live amidst so many contradictions that we scarcely can find anything to hold against anybody. So what about order, you ask. I beg you, what city could possibly have more faith in order than our own? Czernopol is governed by a rigid bureaucracy, which, having inherited the most ossified system in the history of the world—in other words, the Austrian one that we supplanted—now sports its own brand of narrow nationalism, although under no circumstances is it willing to admit this. That it continues to be inefficient as well as ineffective is due only in small part to the long-established and well-honed system of bribery people are always fussing about. A far greater cause is the utter lack of resistance, the general compliance of the governed, which verges on the miraculous. This not only takes the sting out of every rule and regulation, but also dampens any impulse or momentum. In this matter Gandhi's followers could learn something from us—namely, irony. After all, even the most passive resistance is still resistance. But what can you do with a city that laughs at everything? What can you make of a world in which a rabbi capable of working wonders yields the sidewalk to some double-breasted dandy of a cavalry lieutenant, closing his eyes *so as not to be tempted by the beauty of the man's clothes.* Or where the citizens resort almost to violence in protesting the dismissal of a crooked public official, *because his deceit was too blatantly obvious to deserve punishment*! You probably consider this an Oriental practice, but let me assure you: it is completely European, Baroque to be exact, and not merely because it is so vividly explicit, but rather because of the unconditional belief in the necessity of *form*—and, consequently, in order of all kinds—along with the equally unconditional need to poke fun at same. Naturally this is bound to lead to catastrophe. But let's be fair: What else is left for us? In a world that has too many claims to validity, too many equivalences, too many relativities, a world that fashions life out of the grotesque and converts life into the grotesque—isn't such an appreciation of the comic, the droll, a physiological necessity, something analogous to the internal pressure in our bodies that allows us to withstand the weight of the atmosphere? Hah!

"Hah!" said Herr Tarangolian, giving his delicate, heavily ringed, hand, with the nails filed into yellow, almond-shaped claws, a casually elegant flip—like a magician who, having performed his amazing trick, would now like to demonstrate that such speed and dexterity, while not exactly witchcraft, clearly approach limits where rational laws do not apply. "Hah! I tell you, we are modern—modern to the point of having no history. Because the sequence of pogroms, in which we will ultimately let our various tensions play out—or perhaps I should say when we will kill them off—is unlikely to produce any history. Or, rather, it will not produce any *more* history. We have too much history already—inside us, behind us. This city is officially less than three hundred years old and yet you can find anything and everything under its roofs, whatever each new mass migration deposited on our shores, from the Aeolian invasions in Pella to the Brusilov Offensive. My guess is that about one-third of our population is illiterate, and the other two-thirds are clearly unlettered and ignorant: in fact only one in ten thousand could qualify as educated. That said, we do have coursing through our veins a spiritual inheritance that runs from Euclid to Einstein, from Thales to Sigmund Freud. I know of no other city that is more alert, more aware. Here you can find a dozen of the most disparate nationalities and at least half a dozen bitterly feuding faiths—all living in the cynical harmony that is built on mutual aversion and common business dealings. Nowhere are the fanatics more tolerant, and nowhere are tolerant people more dangerous, than here in Czernopol. Nowhere is there less sense of shame and nowhere are people less naïve. I tell you, we are modern to the point of living in the future. Because if you live in a world so full of disdain and contempt, armed with nothing but your own scorned existence, then you are bound to develop a certain insouciance where your only loyalty is to yourself. A present moment that denies both past and future, but is completely committed to the here and now. This is far more than what you might call *amor fati*. Just look around and you'll see that our city, this permanent settlement of nomads—to coin an oxymoron—has less in common with the pioneer spirit than with what might be called 'the recklessness of saints.'"

2

The Landscape of Tescovina; Herr Tarangolian the Prefect

AS I TELL you the following story, you'll have to permit me to mention myself now and then, because its hero and central character is inextricably bound to our—that is to say, my and my siblings'—childhood. By the same token, it would be impossible to sift out the people who told me about these contexts and connections, and my storytelling would suffer if you were to insist I keep myself entirely out of the tale like a good narrator. Besides, please bear in mind that no one with anything to say ever said anything about anybody but himself.

As I have mentioned, we spent a portion of our childhood in Czernopol. Actually we spent the greater part of every year in the country, though not in the wholesome way in which people tend to imagine this way of life. We wound up there entirely by chance: at one point someone from our family came into a bit of land—the measurements weren't very exact; it was simply part of the landscape whose expanse was generally accepted as beyond estimation—and we didn't consider the property particularly worthy of mention. Nor was agriculture a family passion, whereby character and essence might take root and in turn find reinforcement, a pursuit that lends staunchness of character and an enviable steadiness of spirit. We were happy to leave farming to the people we considered had been called to that way of life, namely the farmers, and if some of our family did tarry in the country nevertheless, it was for reasons, or should I say excuses: because the fathers were so keen on hunting, for example, or because the fresh air and good milk were healthy for the children, or else, as was unfortunately the case with us, because shoddy household management and constant debts didn't permit anything better. As it was, we tried not to extend these stays too long, and eagerly returned to the city at the first opportunity.

Nevertheless, this was the same countryside that looked to Czernopol as its capital, and a few things in my story might be clearer if I offer you a brief description.

"The Province of Tescovina, which is comprised of Tertiary Hill country rich in loess, has no natural eastern defenses and lies exposed to the Podolian Steppe, so that for thousands of years the land was subject to the invasions of barbarian nomads." That was the sentence we had to commit to memory as one of our first lessons in local history and geography under Herr Alexianu, who worked for a while as our private tutor—one part of our very checkered and highly unsystematic education. The purpose was to acquaint us with the idea that running through our veins was the blood of Dacians, Romans, Gepids, Avars, Pechenegs, Cumans, Slavs, Magyars, Turks, Greeks, Poles, and Russians: "a strong mix of ethnicities" was how the book described Tescovina. In the fourteenth century some landed gentry, whose names struck our ears like the curses we were always hearing—Bogdan Siktirbey, for example—founded small states, known as "voivodates," which soon came under Turkish rule. In 1775 the Sublime Porte ceded our homeland to Austria, which first annexed Tescovina to Galicia, and later declared it an independent Crown Land. Herr Alexianu spoke about this historical episode with the greatest reluctance.

And yet that chapter had irrevocably shaped the face of the country—at least for the time we lived there. The late-summer sunsets still reflected the glory of the sunken Austro-Hungarian Empire. Broad, tranquil country roads still cut through the vast expanses, bulwarks of official sobriety restraining a landscape drunk with melancholy, "roads from the time of marching and express post," straight as an arrow, drenched with sweat and powdered with dust "like ribbons of military twill"... roads lined with mighty poplars, where falcons perched in treetops flickering in the wind—the gasps of a gigantic breath that refused to be checked by a few silly barriers recently sprung up along the border... roads quietly bending in the distance, toward faraway places yearned for by the plaintive, minor tones of the shepherds' pipes.

In the small market towns the bleached black-and-yellow of the

Dual Monarchy still lingered on the tollhouses and state monopoly signs, conjuring echoes of the high-pitched calls of the garrison bugle, long since faded, floating over the colorful rural hustle and bustle as a reminder of the transience of worldly power, like the symbol of imperial sovereignty on a Flemish painting of a census. Even in its deteriorated state this former grandeur was easy to see and hard to forget, not yet fully surrendered to the garish colors of the new rulers, with all their overheated drama. As it turned out, these new rulers, too, succumbed to the charms of a grand imperial waltz, just like their predecessors, and in its blissful thrall let all the overheated drama dissipate in the plot twists of *Countess Maritza.*

But landscapes are like people, and inside every face marked by the life already lived lurks another face, which has always been there, and which is destined to reveal itself in time: the face of their future.

And so the passing seasons brought startling changes to the face of Tescovina. The first gusts of snow blew in unexpectedly from the east, smacking of Asia, and fell on the magnificently protracted blue-and-gold autumn like the hordes of Pechenegs once must have descended upon a Byzantine palace whose columned halls shimmered with cloisonné. Faster and faster it fell, its fury rising into a biting storm that raged for weeks, rending the land to reveal an expanse indescribably more vast than the one veiled behind the tender yellow-and-violet late-summer sunsets, and which promised sparkling cities that towered like Montsalvat, mountains like those of Altdorfer, and happily smiling shores. The new face of the land gaped open like a monstrous yawn; its pull was powerful and sapped at the marrow.

We experienced it most directly through the change we noticed in our beloved Herr Tarangolian, during his occasional visits to our parents. In the summer these were always very pleasant occasions: the prefect would arrive in a coach accompanied by a pair of pretty Dalmatians that ran between the rear wheels. Herr Tarangolian was only moderately tall, but portly, and there was something undeniably imposing about him, especially when he stepped out of his shiny lacquered Victoria coach. He would lean on the shoulder of the batman who escorted him everywhere like a bodyguard, and as he shifted his weight, the carriage springs would first squeeze precariously low, then snap back up when his foot, in a shoe as shiny and black as the carriage, stepped off the foot-iron. But the official pageantry of his first appearance quickly evaporated, erased by an oddly passé foppishness and ridiculously exaggerated manners. The prefect dyed his mustache and his bushy eyebrows coal black, and, in contrast to the gray, close-shorn stubble on his head, they looked as if they had been pasted on, which gave him the rather implausible appearance of a stage magician. His pearly, perfectly regular teeth seemed so obviously false we were always afraid he might lose them, or, even worse, that they would declare themselves independent and start snapping of their own malicious accord while he was kissing some lady's hand, which he did freely and with great frequency. But they were genuine, as were his eyebrows, which moved independently back and forth on his forehead, like two fuzzy black caterpillars, lending elegance to his expressions. At least their thickness was genuine, and undoubtedly their color had once been genuine as well. His blackened mustache was no less authentic, for although its delicate ends were teased out with unbelievable meticulousness, they were spun from the strong hair that really did grow from under his bulbous nose.

In fact, everything genuine and fraudulent about Herr Tarangolian seemed transposed in an amusing, if rather unsettling way, so that what was fake seemed convincingly real, and what was real smacked unpleasantly of fraud. Perhaps this had something to do with his mesmerizing histrionic talent. He could mimic a person or a common personality type with a mere shift of countenance; he was fluent in all languages, reproducing dialects to perfection, and he neither hoarded nor squandered these talents, but utilized them judiciously to further enliven his sparkling conversation without the slightest embarrassment. He was a master of banter and wit and possessed a brilliant mind; his descriptions were striking and his logic compelling, and we loved to hear him talk, even if back then we didn't understand half of what he was saying. He also enjoyed having us children nearby, and was always very attentive and caring, pampering us with presents and winning us over by treating us on an equal footing, as grown-ups.

Perhaps the prefect's overstated politeness, his exaggerated attentiveness, and his general fussiness, which at times bordered on the ridiculous, might incline you to underestimate him. Nothing could be further off the mark.

I still recall exactly how he smiled as he once held forth on the subject of understanding human nature. "We turn to psychology in the hope of recovering what we've lost in the way of direct observation of our nearest and dearest. But the way we go about applying the concepts of this science, it's as if instead of using everyday knives and forks, we set our table with forceps and surgical scalpels. No wonder we cut our own lips... Someone was recently explaining the theory of *compensation* to me, which reduces ambition to the manifestation of a secret inferiority, thereby diminishing any aspiration to greatness. But what if the opposite is true? What about someone who is utterly and unquestioningly convinced of his superiority, but comes to the logical conclusion that if he is to live with others he cannot advertise how superior a being he is—would that be an example of what we call *Christian humility*?... I don't think so," said Herr Tarangolian, and his smile became theatrically diabolic behind the mask formed by his mustache and eyebrows—three thick black lines above his perfect teeth and heavy eyes. "No, that would be a heathen way of reasoning. In a Christian world such a realization has to *camouflage* itself, hide behind the ambiguous pose of the fool or the clown, so it can be passed off without provocation. Dealing with people, my friends, is really nothing more than a question of the price that one is willing to pay. The better you understand life, the more capital you build."

I'm certain that Herr Tarangolian wasn't thinking about himself when he said that, although he was far too profound not to realize—and let show—how much actually applied to him and how much didn't. In any case, it was entirely in his nature to hand us the key to restricted areas he may not have intended to enter himself. And never was he more dangerous. He left it entirely up to us to decide which was Bluebeard's secret chamber. And so, when all was said and done, the contradictions inherent in his character were impossible to interpret. For just as his mincingly affected manners and general foppishness suited neither his intelligence nor the gravity of his position as statesman—far more significant posts than the prefecture of Tescovina would later be entrusted to him—at the same time they could not be separated from his peculiar personality, so his empathy, his capacity for sincere friendship, or even affectionate devotion, moving as it often was, came coupled with an extreme unreliability. Behind his permanently unclouded kindness he could be dangerously moody, and everyone who had good reason to consider himself a close confidant of the prefect learned sooner or later that Herr Tarangolian had made a scathing remark about him behind his back.

I will no doubt sound naïve if I say that his unreliable traits never showed in the summer. In reality they were just as visible then as at any other time, but their relationship to his other traits was different—the distribution of weight, if that's what it might be called, was different. The change showed chiefly in his dress; after all, it's an irrefutable fact that despite the equalizing effects of convention, our clothes remain a very telltale expression of character and even affect the wearer, so that, for instance, someone who fancies a tweedy suit of gray, yellow, and blotting-paper-pink, cut in the English style, instinctively imagining himself as one of the aloof sons of Albion touring the Continent, is bound to feel some of their stiff upper lip and dispassionate interest, while the same person wearing krakowiak boots and a corded tunic would unquestionably show a fiery disposition.

Herr Tarangolian's own summer dress was distinctly Mediterranean. His cream-colored suit of raw silk, and particularly his broad raffia-like woven belt with the sewn leather pockets, connected by a thread-like golden watch chain with a double drape, gave him a casual, holiday air that called to mind Adriatic promenades and siestas on hotel terraces in the shade of dusty agaves: a restrained exoticism that tempts one to accept certain things and even reinterpret them. Accordingly, his gallant clichés and charming nonsense seemed, if not natural, then at least in the right place—something like the tinselly polish of a former dragoman of the Sublime Porte enjoying the permanent holiday of the retired Levantine civil servant, a man of some means sitting in front of a street café, staring at the women with the jaundiced, heavy eyes of the liver-diseased, rolling cigarettes with delicious-smelling tobacco drawn from a silver niello case, sporting a freshly bedewed rose boutonnière to match his panama hat and his ebony cane with the ivory handle.

In winter, on the other hand, Herr Tarangolian looked like a colossal, menacing elemental force. Only then did you notice the rough cut of his face, with its strong cheekbones that seemed lifted by the enormous bear collar of his sledding fur, glowing in the cold like a hot samovar. In this season his protruding stomach, which the summer belt had gently and healthfully kept in check, nearly burst his heavy coat, turning it into an unmanageable hide, thick and prickly, while his white shirt, very spruce and stylish, with stiff collar and starched cuffs, and his glistening shoes with bright felt spats flashed deceivingly from underneath, with the waxy perfection of a horse chestnut glistening through a cracked shell—a tree, by the way, that thrived in our part of the world, and which has remained my favorite, perhaps because the prickly balls encapsulate what always struck our childlike imagination as autumn's most compressed form, like a pearl; or perhaps because the drumbeat of their falling announces a yearly parting that leaves more behind than merely another summer; or else perhaps because there was something exceedingly human in this downpour of fruit, in the sheer extravagance of flinging these beautiful things to the mercy of a frosty wasteland. I can't really say why, but then you don't always have to be able to say why it is you love.

Along with his sledding fur, Herr Tarangolian wore a creased, melon-shaped cap with ear flaps that were pulled halfway up and stood out like a pair of wings. There was something architectural about it—an odd mixture of cupola and pagoda that called to mind the baked-mud palaces of Samarkand, and Mongols in quilted robes hunched against the icy wind, driving their yaks and camels across the high plains, only instead of a face smooth as soapstone and old as the grave mounds of Tibet, the prefect's martial mustache and devilishly black eyebrows gazed upon us in strict and terrible judgment.

The prettily spotted Dalmatians stayed at home; Herr Tarangolian arrived in a sled. Wrapped in his driving fur, the coachman sat enthroned on the box, massive and shaggy, towering overhead like a mammoth. The pitiful batman, by contrast, was blue with cold in his pathetically thin uniform coat. He kept his arms crossed over his chest and his hands buried inside his cuffs, with his shoulders tensed in a high shrug and a scarf wound tightly around his chin and ears. Like some primeval bird, he peeked forlornly out from under his turned-up collar; the brass buttons of his coat had frosted over and had lost their gleam. The humble gratitude with which he accepted a glass of brandy was moving; he seemed not to have had a decent bite to eat for weeks. Whenever we heard about the suffering of the emperor's great army, which had gone down in the ice of the steppes—about the glorious regiments scattered as food for the ravens, while a small train of the defeated trudged off to distant forests, doubled over against the wind—we always called to mind the prefect's batman, who even in summer brought us a whiff of martial excitement, with his gleaming spiked helmet. And in that way the tragedy of that campaign always struck us as the victory of gray-white colorlessness over the jubilation of color whose symbols, the flags with their soaring eagles, were left behind, buried in snow and bleached by the icy winds.

Herr Tarangolian appeared even more massive than his enormous coachman within a veritable bear's den of furs, foot-muffs, and blankets, which the batman hastily tried to peel off. But the prefect made little headway, since his fingers were so stiff from the cold, and in his frustration he fell into a desperate rage and set upon the furs as if he were attempting to flay the skin off a dead animal. Once he was halfway free, Herr Tarangolian strained to pull himself up and, giving an ice age–like groan of satisfaction at the frosty landscape, set his richly ringed hand on the man's shoulder for support and stepped off the sled, his enormous weight appearing to press the man deep into the snow. We watched this scene through little peepholes we had revealed with our warm breath in the window of our children's room; the pane was feathered over with frosty patterns, so that the entire event seemed to take place in a wondrous forest of glittering palm fronds and acanthus thickets, ornamented like the tendrils of an illuminated manuscript, where reality was raised to the realm of fable, and everything seemed sharper, brighter, and more intense: *A powerful and mighty man leaning on his beggarly servant*... As far as we were concerned, the sheer fact that this servant was a soldier had a ring of biblical righteousness, and that canceled the sacrilege he had committed in our eyes by wrapping a tattered woman's shawl around his face and chin, as if he had a toothache. What we saw taught us how merciless and unfair the world could be, though none of us could have explained exactly how or in what way. As a result, our eager anticipation of the prefect's arrival was tempered with a certain apprehension, however captivating we found the man himself.

Nor were we wrong in our assessment, although the cause for our misgivings proved different than we had imagined, having less to do with our old friend himself and more with what he left behind—the emptiness that followed his visits. Certainly the dandyish elegance that burst out at us, dapper and dazzling, like a chestnut freshly released from its Siberian shell, was so exaggerated that we became increasingly suspicious it was really a kind of disguise he used to sneak into places, or, even worse, to feign sophistication in order to conceal something menacing. Consequently his banter and compliments, his general bowing and scraping, seemed all the more trite and provincial, especially given his very serious and deliberate delivery—though this might have been attributable to the cold numbing his cheeks and mouth. And so his genuine gravitas, his perspicacity and his prodigious mind, acquired something dangerously devious and inscrutable. But that would have hardly frightened us children. We loved the prefect, and whenever certain of his more dubious traits happened to surface, we were always ready to view them as play-acting—and his willingness to play in that way only made us appreciate him all the more. He was, furthermore, willing to break the rules, and bribed us with huge boxes of sweet-smelling hydrangea-colored Polish fondants in a mix of matte and pomaded hues, and once, to our delight, and even awe, he brought a curly-haired mechanical doll of dreamlike beauty, dressed in luxuriant lace who held a bird cage stiffly in front of her, with a tiny, slender green oriole that twittered and chirped restlessly about, while the doll turned her head this way and that, her round fairy-tale eyes opening and closing at regular intervals, and her left hand beckoning with a very subtle arrangement of fingers, in the best-mannered way of attracting attention.

Herr Tarangolian always took the long sled ride in the late morning. He only traveled to closer acquaintances, where he never extended his stays beyond what was considered appropriate: he would stop in for an hour or so for tea, but never stay for a meal. After politely imbibing a little liqueur he always took his leave, and once again we peeped through the frosty tendrils on the windowpane as he leaned on his batman and wrapped himself up in his furs and blankets. Then the giant coachman would instantly bring the horses to a quick trot with a slight tensing of the reins and a quick touch of the whip, and, melting into a rainbow of colors, the sled would glide across the icy twines on the window, into the glittering palm fronds and acanthus thickets, and the gray, yawning silence of the snowy countryside would close over the fading sound of the sleigh bells. The batman was taken along like a prisoner, and nothing remained of the prefect's visit except the imperturbably beautiful and exemplarily well-bred lace puppet, with her oriole chirping restlessly in his cage.

Incidentally, back then it wasn't unusual for us to be afraid, since our hearts were still burdened with the memory of the war: houses destroyed by shells, soldiers' graves scattered across the country, and dead horses with hideously bloated bodies, limbs jutting out stiff as wood, ants trickling through their eye sockets like red tears. Tescovina had been the site of heavy fighting, and the city of Czernopol could make the peculiar claim of having been vanquished and retaken six times in four years.

"My dear little lambs," Herr Tarangolian once said, "they simply want to please everybody. And by doing that they are completely true to themselves...When the commanding general threw his last contingent of reserves against the enemy—that time *we* had the honor of being this enemy—the fighting lasted no more than half an hour. Afterwards the prisoners were marched back into town escorted by Cossacks; women and old men lined the route to watch the long, sad columns pass. All of a sudden a cheery voice rang out from the ranks of the defeated soldiers: "*Riffke, look—I'm back!*"

People laughed hard at the joke, but later it caused someone to observe that the prefect was very witty and entertaining, no doubt about it, but fundamentally banal.

3
Description of the City of Czernopol

AFTER all I've said up to now, it shouldn't be too difficult for you to form a picture of the city of Czernopol. Just like all living things, cities are a mix of mind and matter, and their precise interaction is what gives each city its distinctive character. Whether we choose to present one by portraying the other—or vice versa—in order to reclaim an impression of a city's atmosphere and the nature of its inhabitants is strictly a question of artistic preference.

Czernopol lay perched on a chain of hills that fell off steeply toward the river Volodiak, whose muddy currents and brooding lagoons furnished the city with abundant stenches and stinging gnats. A double-track tramline ran from the train station near the large bridge up to the Ringplatz, surmounting an incline that, according to the repeated testimony of technical experts, was the steepest that could be managed without cogs. The cars were painted the color of rose hips and emblazoned with the city's coat of arms—a Good Shepherd against a field of blue. They stemmed from the Austrian era and were hardly ever repaired under the new regime, and so occasionally one of these trams, crammed to the point of bursting, with passengers often clustered on the running boards and bumpers, would overpower its run-down brakes and go tearing down the slope, forward or backward, wreaking bloody havoc among the horse-drawn hackneys, oxcarts, Galician ice cream vendors, stray dogs, farmers with poultry baskets swung over their shoulders, Jews, Lipovan Old Believers, mounted Hutzuls, ethnic Germans, and Gypsies.

Approaching the city from the east, down this steep incline toward the Volodiak Valley, the tin roofs cut a rather desolate silhouette out of the enormous sky looming over the steppe, sharply serrated at its highest point by the Moorish battlements of the Metropolitan's Palace, which towered over the tops of old acacias to crown the dome of the hill. Toward the south and west, the terrain gradually descended, ultimately losing itself in the vastness of the great plain, while to the north the chain of hills continued and became increasingly forested, although there too the landscape simply stretched away without any clear demarcation. And now and then, in the raw eastern dusk, when the strings of streetlights blazed away in the pallid darkness, this unsightly city, so bleakly situated in a violent landscape, seemed once more beautiful and beckoning, full of promise and adventure.

Even though the residents of Czernopol were a polyglot assortment of motley races, they nonetheless exhibited a certain uniformity. In the flat countryside, the different nationalities, languages, and modes of dress lived together more or less agreeably, but they were clearly separate and distinguishable; here, however, they were stripped of their individual colors, mixed and mashed together, and subjected to a civilizing fermentation. The city was famous far beyond the province for its knife-wielding *matchyorniks*—a particularly strong-willed type of amateur procurer—as well as for its unusually resistant strain of gonococcus, and for being the setting for most of the Jewish jokes circulating between Riga and the Levant. As I have mentioned, it was the capital of the province. A monument on the Ringplatz—renamed Piața Unirii—commemorated Romanian "union" following liberation from the Austrian yoke; a line of hackney cabs could usually be found in its shade, with emaciated horses and rapacious coachmen dozing away. The bronze sculpture depicted an aurochs—the heraldic symbol of Tescovina—lowering its horns in threat, with both forehooves braced against the ruffled and trampled eagle of the Dual Monarchy. Witty night revelers would occasionally equip the aurochs with a feed bag, and once a drunken soldier was arrested in broad daylight when he climbed the base of the statue and attempted to milk the beast.

The plaza was long and narrow. At the top stood the town hall: a typical provincial administrative building with a banal façade, fronted by a pitiful esplanade where ragged newspaper boys scuffled on cobblestones copiously sprinkled with the spat husks of sunflower seeds, like the feathers of a guinea hen. The streetcar station kiosk across from the monument served as a gathering place for loafers and layabouts; every half hour a policeman in a chocolate-brown uniform would drive them away, but within minutes they would be right back in their groups, jabbering away without restraint. Next to them, a row of shoeshine boys hammered their caked-up brushes against their boxes. Over the roofs of the far row of buildings, the dome of the great synagogue—a version of Solomon's Temple that reflected the Orientalist taste of the fin de siècle—towered melodramatically into the sky. On the near side, at ground level, were two credit-and-exchange banks, a cinema, several haberdasheries, and three kosher eating houses, as well as Kucharczyk's Café and Confectionary, where, as soon as the weather turned warm, the tables and chairs were set up on the sidewalk outside the mirrored window displays. Enclosed by a number of potted oleanders, this preserve was the meeting place of Czernopol's elegant society, the egress and turning place of the daily procession that brought half the city into motion in the early midday and evening hours.

If you allowed yourself to be carried off by this daily current, you would find the streetcar, or "line," as it was generally known, off to your right, cutting straight up the main street as it ascended, clambering past the shops, bars, credit-and-exchange banks, cinemas, and kosher eating houses, until it reached a small park outside the buildings of the provincial government at the peak of the rise. Long after the collapse of the monarchy, that place still exuded the subdued and self-assured official elegance that was projected by the governmental buildings from the time of Joseph II, as strongholds of proper order. The line continued for another few hundred yards: under the canopies of mighty chestnut trees, past the high iron pickets of the fence designed to protect the basilica of St. Miron of Czernowitz—a jewel of ancient Slavonic church building filled with the most magnificent frescoes—from destruction and desecration. Then the red streetcars came rattling out of the green shade of the trees, vigorously ringing their bells as they sped into the harsh glare and reentered the traffic of a main road leading out of town, ultimately coming to a stop in front of the stepped terrace of the officers' casino, opposite the entrance to the Volksgarten. There the line narrowed to a single track which ran, interrupted by two turnouts, toward the terminal at the southern edge of town, where the playing fields of the ethnically aligned sports clubs Mircea Doboş, Turnvater Jahn, and Makkabi adjoined the broad grounds of the cavalry barracks, and where, off to the side, isolated behind a solid wall, stood the gray building of the municipal asylum.

For years it was our passionate wish to be allowed to ride one of these red cars, even for just a short stretch, but we had to wait patiently until this wish was fulfilled—I no longer remember when. Because, as is so often the case, by the time our wish was granted, our desire had lost much of its fervor, and unfortunately its achievement had lost much of its worth—though by no means all. Incidentally, the reason for this ban was not due to any particular danger associated with using the streetcar—which really only would have applied to the steep section from the Ringplatz to the bridge over the Volodiak—but rather because of a near-manic fear of infection harbored by our governess, an Englishwoman by the name of Miss Rappaport.

Actually no one in our household really believed she was British, even if in some respects she was so Anglo-Saxon it verged on caricature. And it's true: she was not born on the Isles themselves but rather on Gibraltar, the daughter of a Mr. Rappaport in the shipping business and a woman classified as an Anglo-Spaniard, but despite that she was every bit the clichéd colorless, gaunt, and prognathous English governess anyone could wish for. Naturally the story of her clearly complicated and scarcely typical background could not escape the attention of those who claimed to see through her all too well, so that in our family circle she was simply called "the Jewess," and as such was never mistaken for anyone else, which was rather amazing, considering God only knows how easily that could have happened in Czernopol. People also took care to see that she did not come into contact with the dogs, who were very pure breeds, and for whom she felt a genuine British love. On the other hand, she was given nearly absolute control over our education. She placed great value in honing our English pronunciation into what she referred to as "the King's English," always with a respectful tremble that elicited ironic glances among the adults who happened to be present, as if her monarchic convictions amounted to a typical Jewish presumptuousness. Her method was the simplest and best: she had us repeat the same sentence for hours, and I will never forget the nuances she was able to detect and coax out of the simple construction: "Herbert was murdered." From a tone of extreme indignation, such as only an English governess is capable of, through one of matter-of-fact declaration, up to a positively gleeful communication, we ran through the entire gamut of emotional possibilities under her inexhaustibly patient instructions, with all the gentle vocal variations and shadings of the vowels that merely hint at the *r* rather than let it be heard, and I am convinced that no language instruction was suited to convey the English character so purely as one that places the student in a position to pronounce, with fresh, bright-eyed assurance: "*Heh-bet wahz meh-dedd.*"

By the way, I mention Miss Rappaport not merely for the sake of it, but rather to show that Czernopol did have neighborhoods where an English governess didn't stick out as a great eccentricity. I am talking about the villa district that ran along the northwest edge of the Volksgarten, where our town house was located. To be sure, most of the households there preferred French women, and more often than the Anglo-Saxon sounds you could hear a concerned cry coming through the pretty gardens such as *Jacquot, Jacquot, qu'est-ce que tu fais?* answered by an obedient little voice: *Je joue avec les Rochlitzerkinder, mademoiselle!* Of course Miss Rappaport didn't let us out of her sight for even a minute, and if she did let us into the garden on cold days to "take our exercise"—she herself stayed inside, as sunny Gibraltar had made her sensitive to chilly weather—then we had to pull little wagons after us, the wheels of which creaked so loudly that she knew exactly where we were and that we were in constant motion.

But let us return to the Ringplatz, where I left you in front of the Kucharczyk Café, in the grip of the restless strolling, carried off to the left by the swirling procession, down the former Herrengasse, now renamed Iancu Topor Avenue, after a hero whose accomplishment was so obscure as to cause anyone to rack his brains. There you could feast your eyes on bona fide Jewish maidens as beautiful as Esther, Judith, or Salome, women whose lines were drawn by Beardsley and whose flesh was painted by Ingres; on Polish girls with catlike faces, watery blond hair, and small pinched lips glowing with passion; on almond-eyed Armenians with nobly drawn desert profiles, proudly swaying their heads on their beautiful smooth necks like camels in unruffled trot; or on Romanians whose apple-like freshness was covered by a soft down that the shadows made even more enticing. The marvelous mix of races—which in every case infused the soul, if not the blood—worked its charms. There were young men exhibiting the noble male proportions of Antinoös next to effeminate, angel-headed youths with magnificent luxurious jet-black curls framing their translucent pre-Raphaelite faces, but each and every one, male and female alike, spoke the same raw-throated, and agonizingly vulgar dialect that colored every language spoken in Czernopol, and whose only musical justification, if I may call it that, lay in the deadpan delivery of witty anecdotes or in springing the punch line to dirty jokes.

If you belonged to the local *jeunesse dorée*, you wouldn't be left alone very long but would find yourself in the company of your peers in front of, say, the White Eagle Hotel or the Lucullus sandwich shop for a casual meet-up, called a *patchka*. These were truly ephemeral friendships, and although they displayed an intricate range of fine social distinctions, they fulfilled no other function than the twice daily common stroll up and down Iancu Topor Avenue. In the mornings, these groups of young idlers—students who studied everything and nothing, children of the well-to-do, spongers, dandies, and the doll-like lieutenants of the garrison—would exhaust themselves in a short saunter and then disperse, splitting up for a "bite" of slivovitz as a snack, or to eat some ice cream or drink a glass of fruit sorbet at

Kucharczyk's. In the evening, the pack lounged under the bright archway of lights of the Trocadero, next to the display windows with the photos of the current Argentine, French, or Russian dancing stars. There they watched the procession along the Herrengasse that ebbed and flowed with tidal regularity, noting with casual expertise what the collective unrest had driven out of the houses and onto the street, and then moved on, chatting and joking through the dove-blue twilight. Later these hunting parties broke into groups of two and three and set off sniffing in pursuit of the pretty game that they spotted earlier.

Iancu Topor Avenue first cut away from the line in a sharp angle, but then swung back toward it in a gentle bend, rejoining the tracks at the officers' casino. Here the procession turned around. Whoever was in the mood for stronger fare could continue the hunting and venture into the Volksgarten, whose broad main avenue served as promenade for the mass of plebeians. There the crowds were bigger, the milling about more robust. Now and then the traffic stalled against a row of six Ruthenian girls locked arm in arm, dressed in traditional skirts that seemed to spray color, briskly walking in step and plowing through the crowd like the Colchis oxen under Jason's firm hand; at other times the current split the girls apart amid a general tumult, shrieking and hitting. Whoever the main avenue couldn't hold, or who was looking for solitude, got lost in the extensive network of side paths in the darkness of high hedges.

In the middle of the park a military band gave concerts inside a pavilion mobbed by gawkers. Myriads of beetles and moths buzzed and fluttered around the harshly bright arc lamps, whose white dusty glare made the surrounding darkness deeper and turned the foliage of the chestnut trees, where they were hung, into islands of bright transparent green cut out against a backdrop of black iron. Regular soldiers strolled in pairs, linking the thick fingers of their heavy peasant hands like frightened sisters, following the corporals with wishful respect, full of admiration for the down-to-earth way these men—accustomed as they were to giving orders—had with the girls, and hummed their melancholy tunes while chewing on a carnation stem or sticking the flame-colored flower under their cap behind their ear. From the bushes came tender sighing. At that time the city of Czernopol housed around a hundred thousand souls, of whom a not insignificant number undoubtedly owed their existence to the dense plantings of mock orange and lilacs inside this amply landscaped and generously administered public park.

So much for the setting of the events I'd like to tell you about. After all of this, it will doubtless come as a surprise to hear that they were set off by an event more likely to occur any place else but here—namely, by a challenge to a serious duel, with army pistols at fifteen paces. In a typical display of linguistic prowess, local parlance expressed the incongruity of such an occurrence with unparalleled brevity—with a turn of phrase that said everything and nothing: *In Czernopol, of all places!*

4
First Encounter with the Hussar; Tamara Tildy and Widow Morar

THE EXTRAORDINARY hero and initiator of this duel to the death—which, incidentally, never came to pass—was a certain Tildy, or more precisely, a Major Nikolaus Tildy de Szalonta et Vörösháza, of Hungarian background, as the name indicates. His story strikes me as worth a few pages, because he belonged to a nearly extinct class of humans: those who mold their destiny. Destinies have become as rare as people with character, and they are becoming harder and harder to find, the more we insist on replacing the concept of *character* with that of *personality*.

Major Tildy, however, was a man of character, and an extremely aloof and stubborn one at that. Unshakable in his principles, and with the absolute conviction of a religious zealot, he abstained from any and all participation in that which is commonly understood or misunderstood as humor. In the context of Czernopol, however, this meant that among the hundred thousand blameworthy citizens, he alone was righteous. To quote Herr Tarangolian: "A white raven—well, it's a freak of nature, no matter how you look at it. And in a world such as ours he was bound to fall victim to ridicule..."

You will see that I am a very biased portraitist of our hero: I must confess that I've never been able to see him in any way other than transfigured by that first great boyish adoration, which is one of the purest emotions we are capable of. This was my only case of love at first sight, although where this came from is a mystery. Because whether we are attracted to what most resembles us, or, as they say, our exact opposite—whether we give shape to our own innate image or whether images shape the preferences we then rediscover in other images—this will forever remain a mystery. Nothing can explain the passionate admiration that we as children secretly—because it cannot be communicated—bestow on a person, a person who has never said a word to us; and no experience, not even time, is capable of destroying this childhood adoration. One day we caught sight of a hussar on a horse, we knew him, and we loved him.

We saw him, as is indelibly engraved in my memory, on the same day we returned to our house in the city for the first time after the Great War. But that is undoubtedly a delusion. Too much speaks against our having seen him so early, so soon after the end of the war; first of all, our familiarity with the house and the garden—we were scarcely born when they took us to live in the country—and then the notion that it was winter when he first rode past us, whereas the fact is, we had moved back to the city early in the summer. But I am happy to stick to this delusion, because it expresses the idea that the memory of that house and garden, a memory I hold dear, is completely inseparable from the first time we surrendered to a vision of perfection, and much of the painful delight we feel when we call to mind certain pictures from our childhood stems from this delusion.

The garden was protected from the street by an iron fence. A sandstone plinth extended out on either side of a small gatehouse—which we called the *dvornik*'s hut—up to the hedges of the neighboring properties. Tall, slender pickets rose out of this base and were connected by two long ribs; their pointed-leaf finials presented a straight row of beautiful lances whose form and order delighted us immensely. To this day I can physically sense the powerful magic that emerged out of the absolute symmetry of those lance-leafed finials, pulling us into its spell. And I don't just mean the unbearable craving to heft and wield one of those spears, which were more perfect and more genuine than all those we had carved for play, but a desire that was unquestionably erotic, an urgency that was intensified by its sheer unattainability, similar to and no less pressing than the yearning felt later in life after possessing a woman we loved, and which despite the physical stilling—which always remains superficial—never achieves its true goal. But we were even more taken with the equilibrium this fence presented, the sparkling symmetry of picket upon picket, all coming together to form a single decisive perspective. And just as when we played inside we never tired of arranging our lead soldiers or other toy figures into the same undeviatingly square formations, so as to discover in their repeated regularity a magical geometrical essence that corresponded to mysterious structures within ourselves, so we were drawn outside to what was undoubtedly a very ordinary iron fence, with an emotion that verged on the sacred, because we sensed or suspected something in that line of pickets, something possibly close to the wellspring of ornament and dance and ritual.

Incidentally, even back then we must have been consciously prepared for beauty. Because the day we spotted the hussar had been preceded by another notable day, when Herr Tarangolian was walking through the garden and picked up a maple leaf that had decomposed into an enchanting filigree of delicate ribs and tiny veins. As he held it up to the light for us, the prefect declaimed with pathos: "But what is this? Art—art! And what has wrought it? Destruction. Ah, let me tell you, my young friends, learn to love destruction!"

Thus we had already seen what kind of artist winter can be in populated areas, for we loved winter in the city, especially in the gardens that skirted our street. And particularly the heart of winter, January, which brought Christmas, according to the reckoning of the Orthodox Church. We loved its dryness and severity, its veiled light in the frost, when the snow that had blanketed the entire landscape and erased all shapes finally subsided, and the contours emerged crisp and clear out of the immaculate white—no longer tinged with gray or yellow like on the days weighted with snow clouds—and were finally covered with a brittle, icy down like a tender mildew, lending a fragility to the hard surfaces and muting the colors that still shone through here and there—such as the dark brick red of the neighboring home, which we could now see, as if through a filter that simultaneously softened shapes and heightened them. Things then spoke to us with a more serious purpose, they gained deeper meaning, acquired a timeless symbolism. Nothing captured winter's adamantine quality better than the beautiful Christmas carol that Miss Rappaport taught us:

"...earth stood hard as iron, / water like a stone." It was as if the world's breath had stopped, and this rigidity struck us as a foretaste of eternity, when nothing would move or breathe anymore—only frightening at first glance, and festive as death at the second. We were completely taken by the white splendor, so full of promise, so powerful that it could turn any drop of water into a frozen star, that we asked ourselves whether a Christian who had never known winter would be capable of understanding why the Lord was born at this time of year and not in spring. Because in winter the world clearly became wider and freer; the horizons burst open. Bushes, trees, and shrubs that when in leaf merely simulated the depth of the landscape, like a forest backdrop on a stage, now turned transparent, while the gossamer branches and twigs, as spare as those inked on a Japanese brush-drawing, preserved the intact forms—just like the delicate spiderweb ribs of the maple leaf—and indeed it was this bareness that first brought the forms to light, by opening a view to the distance, from where, tinted orange as if in an eternal dawn, the heavens ascended.

On such days we weren't allowed to stay outside for more than a short time, on account of the fierce cold. We played our way to the lance-leaf fence, gleefully drawing out the anticipation, as children so masterfully do, averting our eyes until the last possible minute in order to take in the sight of the slender row of shafts that enclosed our garden like a temple grove. And when we raised our eyes and looked through the veil of frost, woven with gold, we saw the hussar.

He was riding alongside a sleigh in which a woman was seated, wrapped in furs. His horse was beautiful: small, sinewy and stocky like Vernet's Arabian stallions—so intensely portrayed in works such as *The Lion Hunt*, which we never tired of looking at—its eyes agape as if in horrified fury, revealing two white half-moons beside the soft, deep, black orbs, to create twin dangers, glassy and blinking, while its mane and tail fluttered luxuriantly frontward across the mirror-smooth chestnut brown of crest and neck and flank, as if artificially brushed for a *coup de vent*—swishing black hair, firm and silky and shiny, whipped forward in ample waves and wind-tasseled locks full of pathos and teasing drama—a beautiful picture of the equestrian art, of channeling the full power of the horse into the reins and into the hands of the rider... the wild mares of Diomedes must have been like that: the same theatrically bold pose in the face of the utmost horror, the fourfold drumming of hooves, rearing up at the shaft of the chariot as it plowed through the human corpses like the prow of a light ship.

The hussar sat very erect. He seemed no more than of medium height, in good proportion to his horse. His cornflower-blue uniform, with the wheat ears and gold braid, fit snugly. The high shako—which can give the impression of a slovenly, undisciplined, irresponsible band of soldiers more than any other head covering if it is crooked or tilted back over the forehead—was cut flat following the French fashion, and sat straight and square over his eyes, imparting a seriousness and severity that was reinforced by the short dark line of his trimmed mustache. This is not to say he had a severe *countenance*; in fact, his face was practically devoid of expression; I'm tempted to say it was artificially emptied. The result was an impassive, profoundly cool elegance that would have seemed dandyish had it not displayed a compelling inner resoluteness—the manly ideal from a supposedly bygone epoch, a world that had vanished—admittedly just yesterday, but all the more irrevocably!—a world of casually practiced elegant conventions, where female beauty was wrapped and bedded in billowy expanses of crinkly cloth, like the stiff tissue paper florists use on long-stemmed flowers, their hair pulled back into a calyx, from which jutted a tropical fantasy of dove and egret plumes glittering with clasps... the epoch of monosyllabic manly politeness, curt to the point of being almost contemptuous, of poses maintained with true sangfroid even in the face of death... Alongside his horse ran a pack of smooth-haired fox terriers, one with a limp that only showed at every other bound, as if the dog were too distracted to worry about his hind legs—presumably an example of the peculiar hysteria this long-unfashionable breed is susceptible to.

The woman in the sleigh had turned away from us, so we couldn't see her face. But we weren't curious about her face. We did not allow ourselves to be astonished or amazed, because what we saw—hussar, horse, dogs, and the woman in the sled with her face turned away, took place before our eyes, for no rhyme or reason, its splendor unique to the vision itself. In this way the scene was removed from time: it was pure image, and therefore a symbol—one we would never succeed in fully interpreting, of no importance, perhaps, except in the instance of its manifestation, when the mirrors of our souls were positioned to reflect it in a mystical, kaleidoscopic symmetry, like those rare moments when the sun appears at just the right angle and its rays break through the colorful rose window of a church and the monstrance glows with illumination. This is what I mean when I said that we *knew* the hussar. It only applied to this first sighting. The love that followed was an echo, just as all our love is basically a continued search for the fading echo of a call of secret recognition.

We very soon found out his name as well, because from then on we saw him over and over, although the empty days in which we were denied the joy of his sight often stretched out unbearably. Please don't consider this exaggerated and extravagant. I think that every childhood has such secret passions, images in which we lose ourselves completely, with all our unbridled emotion, whether we encounter them in a person, a landscape, a book, or some object we may desire—and the chance of subsequent encounters lies outside our power. Perhaps life uses these images as lessons—to help us realize that the fulfillment of desire is not a matter of will, and to show us how much we are at the mercy of fate—or whatever other truths might be derived from the sheer power of incontrovertible truisms. In any case, back then we viewed our encounters with the hussar as the fervently longed-for proof of our special understanding with secret life powers, which, though it could only be established for a few moments, nonetheless consistently reinforced our belief in a higher reality of life; and the interludes between encounters, when our beautiful, courageous impatience gradually fermented into patience, seemed designed to lead us to insights, which, like all precocious knowledge, was filled with a sadness that shaped the foundation of our souls forever.

Never again would we encounter the same mythological procession of rider and lady, the sumptuously Baroque order, the sleigh gliding silently ahead alongside the whirling bustle of the dogs; the woman in the sled was no longer there, and in her place we most often saw his orderly, and so the days when the hussar rode by were tinged with a special light that lifted them out of the chain of the otherwise uneventful hours of those childhood days—idly frittered away, I'm tempted to say—and preserved their memory as sharply focused individual images in an otherwise inscrutable photograph. Undoubtedly it is always encounters like that, or rather the reencounters, which illuminate certain situations in all detail, like a flashlight, so that what we call memory is really just the recurrence of a few basic motifs, be they images or moods, in constantly changing configurations. Perhaps our soul is capable of little more than tracing the secret essence of these basic motifs through everything it encounters.

As I mentioned, we soon knew our hussar's name, that he was Nikolaus Tildy, and that he was an officer in one of the cavalry regiments that had moved into the old, former Austrian cavalry barracks on the other side of the Volksgarten, following the occupation of our homeland. We were further delighted to learn that he lived nearby. Now and then we saw his orderly leading a horse into the barracks. We didn't see the woman in the sled again until later, and then under distressing circumstances.

Meanwhile, something arose between our everyday existence and the world that had produced Tildy, which for us was automatically exotic and full of wonder—something that we interpreted as a secret connection.

In those days, our country's elaborate, unwieldy approach to managing the economy kept a great many people busy. This was not because this system made our lives any more comfortable; rather it was due to a simple inability to think or even act economically—a failing, by the way, which despite all disadvantages did make our lives unforgettably rich in a way that has since disappeared from the earth entirely. For example, if a man offered his services without specifying precisely what these services might be, perhaps by boasting that he was strong enough to lift heavy objects, then no one questioned whether he was really needed but instead went about finding tasks for him to perform, once he had indeed demonstrated that he was as strong as he claimed. A maidservant was hired because she had made a nice and honest impression with her fresh red cheeks, her clean folk blouse, and her neatly combed hair—despite the fact that we by no means lacked for maids already. Another man found a position as a gardener because his face, bright with a simpleminded cheer and sunny to the point of saintliness, along with his gentle manner of speech, seemed clear proof of a green thumb. He was soon unmasked as an escaped convict and a particularly unscrupulous thief and was handed over to the police—much to our regret, incidentally, because we loved him dearly and wound up losing a great friend.

But such gaps were soon filled. And nothing could shake the attraction we felt for these people who contributed little in the way of service to our household but rather used it as a refuge and a playground for their peculiar idiosyncrasies—just like our poultry yard, which was filled with completely useless ornamental breeds of chickens and ducks, peacocks and pheasants—and we were rewarded with an abundance of experiences and exposed to a rich gallery of people, as colorful and aromatic as a bouquet of grasses and fresh meadow flowers.

Thus had we won the affection of a certain Widow Morar, a person of revolting, virtually monstrous ugliness, who was occasionally hired to help on the big laundry days, although she undoubtedly hindered more than helped with her boundless chatter. But she was a widow with three sons, and people generally pitied her. Everyone was in complete and unquestioning accord that she should be supported, and this had become a permanent arrangement, notwithstanding the fact that her sons were long grown up and gainfully employed—one even as a streetcar conductor—and that she was spending everything she earned on senselessly replacing some of her healthy natural teeth with gold dentures. Her husband, a drunkard, had shot himself.

Driven by a pathological need to communicate, she recounted this drama to us over and over, even bringing as evidence a chromolithograph of Christ, at once unsettling and profound, where a bullet had bored a perfectly circular hole the size of a coin right in the sealing-wax-red heart of the savior—his first shot, which had missed. Herr Morar had shot himself when he was in his cups, and spent a long time clumsily positioning his long military-issue rifle. He was unable to hold the gun with outstretched arms up to his temple. As a result, various projectiles had gone into the walls and ceiling, with him falling down each time in the process. Not until he placed the muzzle of his weapon in his mouth—"like a bottle" is how Widow Morar put it—while lying on his back, and using his big toe to squeeze the trigger, did he manage to kill himself. He had locked his wife and children in the next room; they were able to follow the proceedings through the keyhole.

This ghastly experience, which she could portray to few others so often and in such detail—and which appeared to have left her with an affinity for similarly shattering incidents, because she knew of further gruesome accidents, incurable diseases, and bloody crimes to relate—this experience made Widow Morar so attractive in our eyes that every time she showed up we would sneak away from whoever was watching us in order to get near her. Then she would treat us to macabre depictions that, far from repelling us, absolutely enthralled us, because they dealt with life's darkest and least comprehensible riddle—death, which even in childhood seemed so close it verged on horror. But her attraction became utterly irresistible when we learned that Widow Morar also helped out at Tildy's home. What's more: she could boast of being a close confidante of Madame Tildy—to what degree this was true we will yet discover.

But back then could we have had any doubts? Everything about our hussar and the woman in the sled seemed so much like a fairy tale that we would not have been amazed at all to see these two mixed up in the strangest circumstances—and especially with a woman such as Widow Morar, whose mysterious ugliness made a mockery of any true human form, and put her in the company of djinns, ghosts, and demons from *A Thousand and One Nights*, not to mention her inner psychological connection to the eerie and the horrible.

In short, what we now heard about the woman in the sleigh, whose face we hadn't seen, hardly helped bring our fantasies to a more down-to-earth reality. Her beauty was something we took for granted: we had never expected anything else. But just to have something concrete in mind, we asked: "How beautiful is she?"

"As beautiful as your doll with the bird," said Widow Morar.

And of course we had known all along that she had some secret suffering—"a disease of the heart," as Widow Morar put it.

"Can a doctor help her?"

"No, said Widow Morar, closing her eyes and smiling knowingly, almost happily. The fire of her gold teeth transformed her amazing ugliness into the mask of a shaman. No, it was not a sickness that could be cured by any human art or wisdom: Madame Tildy was born a Paşcanu.

That was news to us, though not surprising. Who else could the woman be but a daughter of the man whose celebrated rise to immeasurable wealth had made him as legendary as his wild life and, in the end, his grotesque downfall! Naturally, at the time we still had no idea about his touchingly ridiculous and dreadful end; we only knew his name from phrases that had become nearly proverbial: "Rich as Old Paşcanu," or "a fox, a tiger, a wolf... a real Paşcanu." Or else: "A peasant, a *muzhik* with no more manners than old Paşcanu," and, finally, "as love-crazed as old Paşcanu."

He had had a mausoleum built for his wife—a certain Princess Sturdza, the mother of Madame Tildy—in a small forest at Horecea, just out of town, modeled after the Taj Mahal. People said she lay there covered with jewels. But he also buried his mistress, a strikingly beautiful peasant girl with the common name Ioana Ciornei, right next to his wife. It was on her account that Princess Sturdza had died, under somewhat mysterious circumstances. People spread all kinds of rumors about the true purpose of the devotions he used to say at night, in the presence of both coffins, while his extraordinarily mean coachman, a castrato of elephantine build, kept close watch on the building. In Romanian, "*taci mahala*" means "keep quiet, outskirts" and people found hidden meanings in the overlap of pronunciation.

"Does she see her father often?" we asked.

"Never. She hates him." Widow Morar closed her eyes and gave a gleeful smile. "She despises him. She calls him her mother's murderer."

"Does she cry much because of him?"

"Never. She never cries. She is the kindest, happiest, wittiest creature, chirps like a little bird. Only now and then she..."

"*What* now and then?"

"Now and then she locks herself inside. She reads in her books. Her rooms are full of books—books not even scholars can understand. No one understands them but her. She knows every author and every scholar, whatever language they may have written in. She can recite what they wrote word for word. They make her melancholic, and you can knock on her door and rattle the handle but she won't answer. The orderly keeps having to break down the door to make sure she's still alive, and then they find her lying on the floor, unconscious, or else she wanders out and speaks in tongues, words of deep meaning, just like the monks at the monastery where pilgrims visit, when they're in a religious rapture. When she's in that state she tells people their true names. To me she always says: *I love you, for you are marked.* And isn't it true that I was marked by suffering on the day my blessed husband rolled on the ground like an animal attacked by wasps and tried to drink his death from a rifle? We saw it all through the keyhole, my sons and I, we bruised our heads trying to see, all the while wailing and screaming..."

"And her husband—Major Tildy?"

"Oh, he is a true cavalier," said Widow Morar and opened her eyes wide, transfigured. "He stands before her like an angel dressed in armor and keeps silent. Even when she drums away at him with her fists, he stands there without moving and says nothing. Not until the devil inside her has been bested and she crumples onto the floor and whines. Then he orders what has to be done, in his calm and clear voice. And never a word afterward, never a complaint from his lips. Nothing happened. He speaks to her the way you would speak to a princess, to the Sturdza that she is. He approaches her like the imperial sword-bearer approaches the emperor, he opens doors for her and always lets her through first, he straightens the chair she sits in, and when she speaks to him, he stands at attention as if before his general, even when she's being playful and joking with him—because she really is like a little bird. He bends over to pick up her book or handkerchief, when she willfully tosses it away, picks up the pearls from her necklace that she has torn because the mood struck her—he bears it all without a word, like a soldier, all you can hear is her little twittering voice and her laughter, not a sound from him, even his spurs jingle quietly—they have thick carpets—until she shuts her ears and locks herself back inside her room."

We listen in rapt attention. For a long time, whenever we were left to ourselves, we played out the image she had depicted: the princess and her knight, *the angel dressed in armor, the imperial sword-bearer.* I was completely at the mercy of my sister, Tanya, and I hated the fact that she always insisted on playing the major.

What we learned about him on the side came from a different source. I say on the side because neither did our curiosity drive us to learn more about him than we knew, nor was it likely that our image of him could be more complete than it already was, in its unalterably memorable details. But once, when Herr Tarangolian managed to win us over with one of his jokes and unlocked our most secret thoughts, we asked him if he knew Tildy. The prefect answered right away, courteously and willingly, that he was well acquainted with the major and knew him to be a very excellent soldier and a gentleman of the first water, a worthy role model with admirable traits, above all an outstanding horseman; but then he turned to Uncle Sergei, a distant relative who lived in our house as a Russian emigrant, and switched languages, evidently forgetting that we could also understand, and called Tildy a *strange saint.* From the conversation that followed this casual remark, we were able to make out the following:

Tildy had been an officer in the Austrian service. Almost nothing was known of his background. He was not from Czernopol, and the Hungarian name suggested other roots than Tescovina. The landed gentry did not recognize him. Apparently he came from one of those noble but thoroughly impoverished families whose only achievement consisted in sacrificing themselves in the service of a banner, and as a result had acquired a certain aloof self-contentedness and a smoldering pride. We could see his ancestors arrayed before us, in miniatures and lockets: haughty, smug women with pious airs, with occasional traces of a former youthful beauty tempered rock-hard by a strict and stringent life, and swarthy men with the puckered look of the brave, whose only passion is to demonstrate their courage, some surprisingly coarse, with round skulls, massive faces, and martial mustaches, others of more noble cut that comes from the knowledge that early in life they will carry out their assignment to die a model death. One of these may have been Tildy's father.

And he himself: a childhood in unquestioning obedience; women of almost painfully solemn bearing as the object of the highest respect; perhaps a secret understanding with his mother that was never expressed, a shyly restrained tenderness; and an adolescence in iron discipline, total commitment to duty. But all within a world of splendid style that brooked no skimping: amid the grand waving of the pure flags, across the fresh expanses of the horsemen's dawn, overrun by a festive swarm of brightly colored uniforms topped by a blaze of glistening helmets.

And then came the war.

He was said to have served in an excellent regiment, albeit one which had been subjected to the harshest censure. Evidently, during the war-of-position in Galicia, after the last great cavalry battles had been fought and the war had become a troglodyte affair, an attack couldn't be carried out because one sector's officers were conducting a race behind the lines with gentlemen from the opposing regiment of Russian guards. The men were sent to the Isonzo Front. Tildy must have been still young at the time.

Whether his homeland, like ours, was occupied after the collapse of the empire, and ceded to a new state, was not clear, because no one knew for certain where he came from. In any case, the fact that a former officer of the Dual Monarchy was so quick to accept service in a different army was not seen in the best light. Despite all the presumed reasons that spoke for him—and on close inspection none spoke against him—he could not shake the odium of the renegade.

In Czernopol that would have normally counted as a sign of quick-witted flexibility and competent life skills, and commanded a certain respect rated far more highly than honor: "You know, we don't put much stock in such fiction," was how Herr Tarangolian put it. Strangely, that didn't apply to Tildy, however. There was something in his bearing that everyone—everyone without exception—found provocative.

"He has the very best, that is to say the most curt, manners," said Herr Tarangolian. "He despises polite gestures the way a very rich man holds them in disdain. In doing so he sets a high price—too high, perhaps. But he's one of those men who are more than willing to bleed to death."

Whether he was aware of this general resistance or not, Tildy did not counter it with anything except himself: his impeccable performance of duty, his cool, elegant propriety that was the tersest possible, and his deadly earnest.

"God knows, it's not that what he does is too little," sighed Herr Tarangolian. "On the contrary: it's too much—too much for Czernopol. But Czernopol is drawing the short end of the stick, if you know what I mean. Let me tell you a story: His people idolize him. Recently, however, one of his men had stayed a few days beyond his leave, and when he came back, he brought his esteemed major a chicken, not as a bribe—heaven forbid—but as a gesture, and in order to mollify him. Still, a chicken is quite a lot for a young farm boy. So what does Tildy do? He assembles the entire company and informs them of the incident. He punishes the man for staying over his leave—not too severely, but not too mildly, either. And he orders that the chicken, which a sergeant was holding next to him on a kind of tray—or was it a cushion for medals—in short, Tildy orders that the chicken be thrown into the regimental kettle. Can you believe it? One chicken in a soup for four thousand soldiers? Even a child knows that the quartermasters steal meat by the ton. But in the name of justice: a single chicken! Even his own recruits no longer take him seriously. No, no, nothing good will come of that."

Herr Tarangolian spoke with stageworthy pathos.

"And I don't mean his career as a soldier, although that, too, is doubtful. His superiors can't abide him, without exception. They respect him, to be sure, but they don't trust him. They find him odd, and, to put it frankly, disturbing. Recently someone asked me in all earnestness if he might not be an Englishman working for the secret service. Why does he trim his mustache the way he does? But all joking aside: the man will destroy himself in one way or the other. There's something Spanish about him. He is a *hidalgo*. Not a conquistador, no Cortés or Pizarro or Alvarez—he lacks their greed, he doesn't have enough plebeian blood for that. Nor is he Iñigo de Loyola, although I admit he shares the same rigor and passion for a Madonna embroidered on a flag. A shame to find such traits wasted on a cavalryman, isn't it? But, then again, would Roland and El Cid be able to conquer anything better than a heavyweight championship? For all we know a stigmatized headwaiter might soon proclaim himself lord of the world! But the *hidalgo* I mean is the other one, the knight of the sad countenance, Don Quixote. That is Tildy's character through and through. He is indeed the last knight. He is incapable of taking revenge on his own predicament, like everyone else in Czernopol, by laughing at it. Do you know that people deliberately play pranks on him and place bets on how he will react, and that every time the fellow who chooses the most humorless possibility is the one who wins! He himself supposedly said he knows only two types of response: the *witty* one and the *just* one. Yes, you heard right: the witty and the just! My God, what an alternative!... And then, on top of that," Herr Tarangolian added with faux seriousness, "on top of that, this woman..."

One day this woman stood in front of us, spoke to us, stroked our hair, kneeling down to pat Tanya—and we failed even to recognize her.

I believe that happened during the same year, on one of those late-spring days so much like lilac, under the deep mussel-blue of a sky pregnant with rain. We hadn't seen her coming, because the lance-leaf fence was overgrown, and our garden was hedged by thickets of foliage, like the upholstery of a jewel case, with spikes of blooms that had been blasted by the slow and heavy showers, which tore off the flowers and scattered the petals across the wet leaves and grass. As a result she suddenly materialized, exaggeratedly elegant and at the same time strangely untidy, with large eyes and a disconcertingly fixed gaze. Her razor-sharp aristocratic nose startled us, as if it had simply decided to appear there, and it was out of proportion to the rest of her face, which was smooth and round like a china doll's. She gave us the kind of smile that comes melting out of someone waking from a happy dream—lost and entranced. And as if she were indeed under a spell, she reached out and ran her hand above our hair, as if she didn't dare touch it. "Oh you beautiful children," she said, "you dear, happy children."

She hastily began rummaging through her pompadour, and since she evidently couldn't find what she was looking for, she broke into tears. "I don't have anything for you," she said, despairing. "I have nothing to give you, please forgive me. Forgive me..."

We understood that she'd been looking for sweets—chocolates or bonbons—for us, and we acted stiff and acquiescent—like children practiced in accepting food, to the delight of the adults, like deer in the game preserve.

But then she suddenly reached for her neck and started groping around, distraught. "Where is my necklace?" she asked, pretending dismay, with a false note in her voice that seemed to pain even her. "My necklace isn't there. I had put it on. It's gone. Gone. My necklace is gone." Her voice had become high and shrill. She looked at us in amazed disbelief, her hand on her throat, all the while repeating: "Gone. My necklace is gone."

She closed her eyes for a few seconds, rocking slightly. As the tears came streaming down her cheeks, she knelt down beside Tanya and said, "I wanted to give it to you. I had put it on to bring to you. You believe me, don't you? Of course you do. You believe me that I wanted to bring you the necklace?"

"Oh, here you are!" Miss Rappaport's English words cut into the scene like a clarinet, beckoning with her slightly sour voice.

The unknown woman sprang up, greeted our governess in the friendliest, most courteous tone, and said she had come to pay a visit. Not a single word or glance more in our direction: she had forgotten us completely.

Miss Rappaport jerked her piercingly bespectacled face a few times between her and us like an ostrich. Then she raised her hand and silently signaled us to follow her back to the house. At that the other woman gave the most gracious and ladylike hint of a bow, the fingers of her left hand delicately angled, and followed Miss Rappaport with quietly rustling, dainty steps, and her coquettishly dangling pompadour.

In a flash, Widow Morar was at our side, hissing at us through her gold mouth, and smiling through her closed eyes: "Did you see her? Did she speak to you? Isn't she like a little bird? They'll have to fetch a carriage for her..."

Only then did we realize that this was the woman in the sled, Madame Tildy, the hussar's wife. What we never would have imagined was her nose: the vulture-like beak of old Paşcanu.

We didn't have much time to be amazed, though, because Widow Morar grabbed us by the arm and said, loudly and meanly, in the direction of the gate: "What is *she* standing there staring at?"

And then we saw Frau Lyubanarov, leaning against the golden rain tree by the *dvornik*'s hut, from where she had evidently seen and heard the entire scene.

"What is *she* standing there staring at?" Widow Morar repeated, even more loudly.

"Oh, go get lost, you old washer of corpses!" said Frau Lyubanarov lazily, standing like Danaë under the shower of gold from the tree.

5
Departure of Miss Rappaport; Fräulein Iliuț, Herr Alexianu, and Năstase

I SHOULD have acquainted you earlier with the person I just mentioned. She was the wife of an unhappy man, a certain Dr. Lyubanarov, formerly a lecturer in classical languages at the University of Sofia, who was hopelessly addicted to drink. So as not to wind up on the street along with his wife and children—two girls our age who were our playmates—he had taken on the job of gatekeeper at our house, a position that was quite dispensable and consequently did not require much effort, and which originated solely from the fact that we happened to have a gate with a guardhouse, the one we called the *dvornik*'s hut. No one thought seriously of assigning Dr. Lyubanarov any real duties; to do so would have meant courting serious disappointment, because he generally slept for most of the day, and made his way to the drinking holes near the train station in the evening, to return home just before dawn, dead drunk, a staggering colossus spewing Greek and Latin quotations along with spittle and the last of whatever rot-gut he was drinking. We once ran into him on his way home like that. His expression was one of heartbreaking inner turmoil.

Later, someone told us the story of how he turned to the bottle. He came from the humblest origins, received a scholarship for talented students, and graduated with distinction. Full of enthusiasm, he began to teach. His sole passions were his love for his people, the eternally oppressed Gorals, and for classical antiquity. He was dirt poor. His one yearning was to see just once with his own eyes the glory of the temples and palaces, the figures of gods and men from that bright dawn of Europe. With a group of students he saved for years until a trip across Italy finally materialized, taking him as far as Naples. They visited Rome, they saw Herculaneum and Pompeii and Paestum. And there, after a scorching-hot day taking in the endlessly astonishing harmony of the column shafts and their crowning pediments, Professor Lyubanarov got drunk for the first time.

This didn't require much: his life had been practically ascetic up to that moment. And, besides, he was intoxicated already: by the beauty, the sunshine, his own happiness ... perhaps also by Pompeii, this city of death so horribly alive, by the ghosts of the former houses full of color and life, and the human castings—because it's not the people themselves we see there, frozen in the most convincing poses of death, but rather baked and sintered masses of calcium and silica that gradually seeped into the decaying forms, as the liquid metal for a bronze statue replaces the wax melting out of the mold—so perfect, that the jaws still have teeth and the fingers of young women still wear their rings.

And the people of Naples: Roman faces in the rags of our Americanized civilization; a girl in the lobby of the train station calling out in an inimitably melodious voice: *Claudio!*... the rickety two-wheeled vegetable carts, which the drivers would leap onto at full speed, laughing and shouting jokes over their shoulder as they steered through the commotion with mystifying skill; the horrible metal hackamore bits that insure the delicate horses are kept rearing up furiously like the steeds of a quadriga ...

They had pulled him out of the tavern where they had stopped. In the courtyard he vomited onto a half caved-in wall. Stars shone overhead, and the fragrance of mold and burning, of spices and swamp, urine and oil and wine and smoke and wind and sea, enveloped him, the desolate jumble of tavern voices and the tender humming of a wistful song and the rush and rustle of the great tranquility under the glassily transparent sky. And here, in front of a remnant of wall soaked with ammonia, between the latrine and the pigsty, he discovered antiquity. And from then on he drank desperately, in a fury of self-destruction.

We never learned what brought him to Czernopol, or how and when he met his wife. She was more beautiful than I can describe, with a peasant-like freshness in shape and stature and in her coloring, in her pitch-black curly locks and in the resplendence of her skin, colored like honey and pulsing with warmth from the sun and her own blood, and which called to mind the magnificence of a young pastoral deity. She had exceedingly clear, almond-shaped eyes—the goatlike eyes of goddesses—and a pale mouth that peaked up at the corners into a secretive smile, like an archaic head of Hermes. Her hair rested on her short forehead like a permanent wreath, with curls that dangled around her temples, then were pulled back coquettishly to reveal her delicate ears, and finally cascaded across the nape of her neck like the gentle grasp of a man's hand. And all of this rose out of a majestic pair of shoulders the color of ripe golden corn, out of the splendor of two vivacious breasts, the absolute embodiment of motherliness, and which she displayed with the most beautiful frankness whenever the opportunity arose.

Because she was anything but unapproachable. The callers she regularly received at home at dusk, as soon as Dr. Lyubanarov had shut the garden gate behind him, and who did not leave until just before he returned, namely at dawn, provided inexhaustible nourishment to the scandalous annals of our household. The fact that no male could resist her charms was something I sensed from my own example, despite my being a child. And as a result, the other women were unanimous in their hatred of her.

We weren't to learn until later that she was Tamara Tildy's half sister—the daughter of Ioana Ciornei and old Paşcanu.

Another character who will play a role in my story was a young man named Năstase. We only knew him fleetingly, by sight. Our tutor, however, Herr Alexianu, happened to be one of his close confidants.

Herr Alexianu was hired when our parents could no longer bear Miss Rappaport's sinus affliction—a kind of hay fever that always appeared in spring and afflicted her throughout the warmer months.

We were preparing to move for one more summer to the country, where we all ate together, unlike in town, where we children ate our meals with our governess. And our father's irritation, his annoyed throat-clearing, the angry looks he gave our mother, seeking help and at the same time full of reproach, and the general nerve-racking silence whenever Miss Rappaport, with the heart-rending defiance of the desperate, would surrender to one of her excessive fits of sneezing and snorting—all of that only amplified the existing tension between the adults in a perfectly unnecessary way.

I can remember tumultuous scenes that filled the house with terror, and us with excruciating fear—outbreaks of a temporary insanity that first infected individuals before affecting all and sundry—precipitated by nothing more than a muffled "Excuse me" quietly uttered by Miss Rappaport, her eyes crimson and swollen and blinded by tears. This had the effect of focusing everyone's attention on her for the fourth or fifth time during a dinner that had barely started, while she stuck her ostrich-like neck out even further than usual, her head swaying back and forth above her plate as if she had been struck blind and dumb by some enormous blow, and her buckteeth jutting out of her mouth with the expression of a dying horse, as if her skull were trying to peel itself out of its skin. As we waited for the eruption, keyed-up and anxious, Father hurled down his napkin, stood up, and left the table.

The ensuing silence was then saturated with a hostility that was not at all directed against Miss Rappaport, but rather set to spring like a trap, which anyone could trigger with the slightest clumsiness. And this tension grew into a painfully frustrated pleasure, when the compelling itch in our governess's nose proved deceptive, in other words when Miss Rappaport eventually stopped her imbecilic head movement, opened her eyes as though surprised, blindly gaped around her in amazement, and finally let out all her pent-up air in one gigantic, convulsive sigh from deep within. Then she pulled her lips back over her teeth as best she could, and as her blotting-paper red eyes reabsorbed the well of tears brimming behind her thick glasses, she resumed spooning up her soup with model manners.

A single misplaced intonation or inept movement of the hand could unleash a distressing insanity that would spread all the way to the servants' quarters, and this was most threatening and alarming when it went on behind closed doors, on the threshold of some catastrophic decision, as happens with people of unbridled temperament, who force themselves into conventional forms only to find their pent-up aggressive instinct festering into a blind rage. And even if we soon saw through the grown-ups' theatrics—and we saw through them completely, recognizing that within those conventions they were resorting to artificially exaggerated emotions in order to stimulate their capacity for experience, which had been diminished or numbed by life—we realized that their histrionics were merely a way of mourning for what was irretrievably lost, although we ourselves were not so insensitive as to consider their pathos completely false and unreal. A sentence such as "*So the only thing left for me is the pistol!*" (punctuated by a carefully timed slamming of a door) never caused us a moment's doubt as to whether the shot might be meant for Miss Rappaport and could free us from the cause of all discord, and the fear, with which we listened to the enormous silence that suddenly loomed in the house, mixed with a vague but painful sense of envy of Widow Morar's sons, whom no one had kept away from the keyhole to witness the consummation of the catastrophe. Because even back then we sensed that nothing we might ever encounter, no matter how horrible, would frighten us more than what Herr Tarangolian called *the horror of the literary existence*—the void that engulfs us when we have too little actual experience. "Bear in mind, my young friends," the prefect once told us, "that most people only know life from hearsay."

In fact we wound up not leaving the city at all that year, so that everything could have stayed the way it had been. But it's a well-known adage for the fickle-minded that the more you strive to avoid making decisions, the more likely you are to wind up with a weak alternative that—no matter how nonsensical—will become firmly entrenched, simply to release you from all other decision-making. And so a pretext was concocted, namely that our characters had had enough Anglo-Saxon development, and it was time that we acquire some solid learning to add to our knowledge that cats are able to fiddle and cows can vault the moon.

This goal was indeed achieved, although in a way that may not have been to everybody's liking. And so, over the course of the summer, Miss Rappaport was given notice and Herr Alexianu was hired to replace her.

Regrettably, a tactless error tainted our relationship with Herr Alexianu from the very start. Somehow the idea had caught on in our household that private tutors typically had sweaty feet, and as a result a fresh pair of socks was set out daily for Herr Alexianu, who had moved in with a fiberboard suitcase full of books, two shirts, a gymnastics device, and a sheaf of love letters. He was obviously able to interpret this indelicate gesture and took his revenge on us by ignoring us completely outside the predetermined hours of instruction, when he treated us with iron strictness—as if we didn't quite exist for him socially. This led to our having an abundance of free time we hadn't expected, and weren't accustomed to, and consequently to our discovering many details of the story at hand.

The main reason for this was that Herr Alexianu often spent his free time—when he was nonetheless confined to the premises—chatting with the household seamstress, Fräulein Iliuț, in her little back room, where we also liked to go. Fräulein Iliuț was a hunchback and beyond doubt the kindest and most likable character from our childhood.

The room where she sewed was always filled with a strong womanly scent, which was not the least bit unpleasant and was just as much a part of her as her legs, which seemed long in relation to her drastically shortened trunk, and her angelic head that was wedged between her shoulders. She had pretty, curly blond hair, and beautiful, remarkably lucid, eyes, and the fine-boned, somewhat emaciated face of hunchbacks—occasionally given to grimacing—as well as the delicate, spidery hands of the deformed. Apart from the hump between her shoulders everything about her was delicate, tender, and beguiling: her skin as well as her voice, her quick and quiet bustling, and the way her sadness dissipated into sunlit kindness. I clearly remember her gait, which was upright despite her humpback and in some unassuming way more determined than that of most people who had grown up straight. She was uncommonly dexterous and was a downright genius at piecing together something new from patches and remnants—just as she herself seemed fashioned from all sorts of remnants and remains of creation. She could bend her fingers—particularly her thumbs—amazingly far back at the last joint, and to our delight she would perform the "Great Mandarin of the Diamond Button," using a Chinese hand puppet she quilted together at amazing speed, which we logically interpreted, without anyone ever having mentioned it, as a parody of the prefect, our fatherly friend Herr Tarangolian.

Without taking the slightest notice of our presence, Herr Alexianu opined that this suppleness of the finger joints pointed to a generous character.

Fräulein Iliuţ gave a quiet, somewhat melancholic laugh between her piled-up shoulders, in the painfully transparent aura of those used to abstinence and self-denial.

"Don't say a word," Herr Alexianu objected resolutely. "I know what you're going to answer. But that doesn't contradict what I'm getting at. Because you can be the most generous person precisely because you are the poorest. My friend Năstase, who, if he only wanted to, could be our country's greatest writer—perhaps not as a poet, but as a novelist, or an essayist, because his insights are astounding—my friend Năstase says that the only fully convincing proof of love that he knows is cash. 'I've held many women in my arms,' he says—and he's not showing off, his triumphs in this field are common knowledge. Năstase believes that the assertion *I love you forever* is true in the throes of happiness, when the present moment merges with eternity, when time is rescinded. Are you following me? Philosophically speaking, this is extraordinarily interesting. Happiness is the equivalent of time that has been extinguished. It is in the present moment, fleeting and timeless like eternity. Practically speaking, happiness and eternity are one and the same. So for Năstase the assertion that *I love you forever* is completely true, precisely for that moment of highest happiness, when our earthly self is dissolved in the act of love, which makes this related to death, according to Năstase. But where time comes into play, so does matter. Without matter time is unthinkable, just as matter is unthinkable outside of time. Thus the only guarantee for love inside of time is through matter. Money, according to Năstase, symbolizes both matter as well as the immaterial value of happiness. Hence true proof of love is money."

Fräulein Iliuţ nodded with kind understanding, as her delicate spider hands busied themselves with sewing.

"His assertion is unassailable, except from the standpoint of a most banal, popular concept of morality," Herr Alexianu declared, countering an objection that no one had raised. "Năstase is by no means amoral, quite the contrary. He stands against every bogus and hypocritical convention. And not from the flippant position of a libertine, but rather out of a profound new morality. For instance, when he decides not to pay a bill from his tailor and tears it up with the words "what doesn't kill me makes me stronger," he is making an ironic—I'm tempted to say pedagogical—statement, *pour épater les bourgeois.* What has outlived its time must be destroyed if you are going to create something new. We are in the process of founding a newspaper, a political-literary journal. But politics for us has nothing to do with what usually passes for politics. We understand the word in its original and broadest sense, as in *polis*—the city. Our goal is to found cities. Not in a literal sense, mind you—just a metaphorical one. Because human thought is metaphoric. The image is the root of everything spiritual, of life itself. And this can be proved mathematically. All beginning is additive, Năstase says, and human beings mere masters of calculation. We are dealing with fundamentals. We have absolutely no intention of revising the world as it is. We don't believe in the value of reform. We are starting an entirely new world. We are establishing new foundations. The world consists of how we see the world, according to Năstase. Where existing forms are outdated, new ones need to be created . . . And it's obvious," added Herr Alexianu with a scornful frostiness that caught our attention, "that the reason for our program has nothing to do with class struggle. I don't need to demonstrate that we are completely unbiased in this regard. Those kinds of things take care of themselves. I have the proof."

He was conspicuously silent for a few seconds. Of course we hadn't understood a word he was saying, but we had no doubt that his last words and his silence were directed at us. We could clearly feel the effort it cost him not to look in our direction, and Fräulein Iliuţ seemed to sense it as well, because she, too, had glanced up to him instinctively, and her beautiful eyes reflected the exertion present in his own.

What he was saying was disconcerting to us in many ways—primarily because we couldn't make any overriding sense out of all the strange words and unfamiliar concepts, and whenever we thought we understood what he was getting at, we soon discovered that we were on the wrong track. Now, however, when there was no doubt that he was alluding to us, Herr Alexianu's statements were excruciating. Because we then assumed that everything else was directed toward us, and so the strain on our concentration was exacerbated by the embarrassment of our inability to understand—that bitter combination that so irritates us as children, and grinds down our beautiful curiosity.

Just as we suffered, for example, because we couldn't understand how the streetcar's bow collector could pass through the branching of the electrical wires without getting caught—we had seen it with our own eyes during our walks!—because our imagination wasn't developed enough to convince us that it didn't run above the overhead wires but rather glided along their undersides, held up by a flexible spring pressure, so we were also bothered by Herr Alexianu's inconsiderate monologues, which we couldn't understand, and which left us feeling that behind the visible and tangible phenomena of the world were hidden secrets to which we had no key, and perhaps never would. Today I'm positive that this scornful cheating of our curiosity was exactly what Herr Alexianu was after, a malicious revenge, because for children curiosity is both hunger and nourishment for life all in one, and to pique it like that and then refuse to satisfy it is tantamount to committing a psychological crime.

But Herr Alexianu seemed to actually savor his tempered-steel disdain. He went on expounding rigorously, but now with greater confidence, more commandingly:

"When I say *forms*, I mean the spiritual patterns and designs that make up the basis of how we think and perceive, of everything we undertake. But what is passed down to us no longer fits the modern human being. Năstase, however, perceives things in a truly modern way. His thesis is that modern man is far more cerebrally determined than his predecessors. Take careful note of this, because it is enormously significant. It describes in a nutshell how our existence is becoming progressively more abstract. Bear in mind the fact that man no longer has free control over his own instincts, which automatically enabled him to do whatever was necessary to maintain his existence in accord with the demands of nature. Instead he has become dependent on experience that has been handed down—in other words, on education. Until now we have relied on religions to deliver the basic substance of our life feeling. As institutions of convention, constructs that housed the oldest traditions, they were able to impart a certain body of knowledge, which, while perhaps no longer pure, did address a wealth of psychological states that human beings must experience for their well-being on earth. In other words, we are talking about plain and simple mental hygiene. Our ongoing alienation from nature, from a life filled with natural—i.e., violent—situations, causes certain mental functions to wither away. And the entire organism suffers along with the mind. The entire organism. To take a specific example: the way you sit at your work, day in, day out, means that your lungs are never sufficiently oxygenated. Consequently your psyche, too, can only atrophy due to insufficient exercise. Even if you walked upright it wouldn't help much. You need to work your lungs to the limits of their capacity, precisely what this organ experiences in the wild—during a dangerous hunt, fleeing and pursuing. You need to run, to jump, to box. You also need to be able to hold your breath, three minutes at least, though if you train correctly you can hold it for much longer. Only then—and this requires a daily regimen of gymnastics—would your body reach the natural condition it would have if you had to hunt down all your sustenance."

We tried to imagine Fräulein Iliuț hunting down her sustenance in the form of deer, hares, and all manner of wildfowl, like a hunchbacked Artemis—and it didn't strike us as outlandish at all. Despite all its gentle kindness, her face had a trace of slyness, though this was trumped by her soft eyes. But the skillfulness of her hands suggested she would be very capable at setting snares and laying traps; we also believed her legs were capable of greater speed than the shape of her back suggested. So we went on listening, full of excitement.

"To put this in medical terms," said Herr Alexianu, "you would have supplied your body with enough oxygen to truly feel well. And this applies to your mind in exactly the same way. It's not enough to simply perceive things. Now and then you have to fall into a state of rapture, of ecstasy, to force the organ of your soul to function at its highest capacity. But you also have to be capable of contemplation, of trance, of completely shutting down all mental activity. Only then will you feel yourself pulsing with the full current of those substances that place you in harmony with the world and life. But here, too, ongoing exercise is essential."

Herr Alexianu made a small, highly effective pause, during which he raised his head and closed his lips tightly. He breathed deeply through his flared nostrils, in long harmonious breaths. We could see his jaw muscles chewing away.

"Up to now, according to Năstase," he went on, "these mental gymnastics have been the province of the religious institutions. Religious exercises were devised to shape and form the soul: from the prayer mouthed without thinking but still fervently felt, to the raging self-flagellation of the fanatic. The saint, according to Năstase, was the soul's champion athlete, while the regular believer merely played in the neighborhood league. This formulation is compelling. If such a healthy, demystified concept as to the true nature of religious instruction were to take hold, the churches would fill up again right away. But the religions fail to achieve this. And why? Năstase believes it is because the soul has yielded to the brain its place as the central organ of life. It's not our souls: it's our brains that are in need of purification. Just try to imagine the consequences."

Fräulein Iliuț looked up at him with her clear gaze and an expression of soulful courage that promised she would give it her best try. The absurd growth of her hump stood around her angelic head like a halo of earthly burden.

Herr Alexianu, however, refused to be convinced and made a dismissive gesture.

"In any case, you see," he said, not without a hint of bitter sarcasm, "that we are not simply a bunch of banal rationalists. Far from denying the irrational, we accord it its place in life. Take love, for example. Something utterly irrational. In fact, Năstase calls it the paragon of irrationality. But only in its origin. Its course can be ascertained empirically; it may be observed to follow certain natural laws. And its implementation, too, may be determined rationally. Năstase's thoughts on this subject are both persuasive and very deep. He says: theoreticians of love from all times have wasted far too much time on metaphysics. True metaphysics is to be found in what is palpably obvious. Whatever the transcendental goal of love may be, we may see that it has two completely different, or actually contradictory, objectives—one to love, and the other to be loved. Not only are those two different aims, each of which requires a special theoretical treatment and, in practice, a separate implementation—in other words, its own strategy and tactics—but they are, above all, the products of two completely different emotional states, which in turn produce other mental conditions. Imagine what a clean separation of these two opposing tendencies would do for our entire mental climate. Năstase's amazing insight is that Western civilization's underlying dilemma is rooted in the fact that these two distinct motives are constantly mingled and confused. And that, he suggests, is the fundamental difference between Christianity and heathendom."

Once again Herr Alexianu made an artful pause, but it was impossible to tell if this one, too, was for rhetorical reasons or whether his mind was straining to grasp the full profundity of this discovery. He had taken the pointed end of the heavy sewing shears, which we were not allowed to play with—ostensibly because they belonged to Fräulein Iliuț, but in reality because they were too dangerous for us—and was keeping time, striking the broad looped handle against his left palm, as though to prolong the swordsman-like thrust of his, or rather Herr Năstase's, pronouncements, even beyond the silence. We found him exceedingly dislikable, but the somber glow with which he so ardently conveyed the mental capers of another person won us over, as if they were bound to inspire everyone the same way they did him. Despite his ponderous pronouncements and ludicrous seriousness, which we clearly recognized, without fully understanding what he was saying, because with heads buzzing from the bewildering, Volapük-like jargon, we paid that much more attention to his facial expressions and his gestures, and these brought us much closer to the true content of his words than if we'd succeeded in following the abstruse train of thought—yes, despite this ungainliness there was something that secretly moved us, perhaps because it was something with which we could identify: the fire of unconditional admiration. But we also perceived something phony, even creepy—what Herr Tarangolian would have called *the perils of the proselyte.* Today I'd like to think that back then I figured out one of the processes that contribute to our great spiritual tragedy: namely that no thought can be effective without expending a measure of unspent energy, and as a result no thought can ever be conveyed in pristine form. Of course this happened unconsciously and completely by coincidence—in this case all because of the nickname we bestowed on Herr Alexianu—Ali. And whoever it was that came up with the moniker "son-in-law of the prophet" had, with the amazing intuition that makes children seem like geniuses, captured both the disciple-like nature of his being as well as the second-rate nature of the disciple. Even many years later, when he came up in conversation, and someone remarked that Herr Alexianu wore a halo made of iron, that was an amusing and fit metaphor—but what really stuck was that particular nickname.

"Năstase has undertaken to cleanse the Christian view of love of its heathen elements," the son-in-law of the prophet continued. "His thesis is that Christianity has yet to be perfected. It calls itself the religion of love. But in order for this to be true in a new sense, it has to eliminate all vestiges of heathen views of love—and there are myriads of them. In their craving for political power, the Church elders wanted to reconcile the legacy of the past with the exigencies of the present, and as a result Christianity became the most complex religion around. It needs to be reformed, and this requires a resolute and unambiguous reframing. But Năstase has no intention of devoting himself to that particular task. He says that to be convincing, you have to swing the club of the plebeian. 'The way I think, and the way I express things isn't exactly popular. So I'll leave that to you'—by which he means me, as the editor-in-chief of our journal. He himself plans to take an advisory role. A critique of Christianity will be at the top of our agenda. Imagine the daring, the audacity of such an undertaking. I'm not referring to the difficulty involved. Năstase is by no means a specialist, but he has a broad, comprehensive education, and whatever specific training he may lack is more than made up for by his mental acuity and his enormous powers of comprehension. But we will have to contend with all Christian denominations, who will close ranks against us. Because what we are espousing strikes at the root of their teachings and creeds that have turned to dogma. Religious scholars, for example, will be arguing to the point of irreconcilable hatred over Năstase's views on the Mother of God—which he sees as a figure of heathen origin representing a parthogenetically renewable capacity for love, a pagan symbol that has no place in Christianity. The latest scholarly results support our theory. It's long been known that Mary was not originally accorded the significance that the Church later bestowed on her—a fact clearly demonstrated by the Savior's utterance: *Woman, what have I to do with thee!* Archaeology has uncovered some provocative correspondences between this figure and the prehistoric mother-goddesses of the matriarchal societies around the Mediterranean, including a number of symbolic details: cross, snake, crescent moon, star diadem, lilies, the blue cape, the child cradled in arms. But as Năstase says, let's leave that type of proof to the scientific bookkeepers. He offers an alternative to this heathen view of love, with its mother-of-God worship. He takes the Christian injunction *Love thy neighbor as thyself* and gives it a new meaning, or rather, he restores its original meaning. He considers the statement inherently ironic: after all, Jesus was a rabbi. It's in keeping with the tangled Jewish tradition of thought not to state a basic principle directly as an axiom, but rather to pose it as a mental problem. The solution is usually surprisingly simple. This unexpected mental shortcut is what produces the irony, the joke. Năstase interprets the command like this: *You know that love, which helps attain happiness, is something good. Therefore create in your neighbor that which can make him equally happy; lead him to the happiness of love.* More simply put: *Do not love so much as act so that you will be loved.*"

Herr Alexianu rapped the handle of the shears hard against his left palm and closed his fingers around it so tightly that his knuckles turned white. His cheek muscles contracted and released.

"Christianity, you see—and I mean the original, unspoiled version—is essentially a male religion, as we can see in the apostle Paul's hostility toward marriage. This rejection of the feminine was not, as people assume, a product of the apocalyptic mentality of the era; it comes from a moral-aesthetic system of values that ranks *acting* above *suffering*, and therefore endorses whatever we might *do*—regardless of the motive—over what simply happens to befall us, for active doing is inevitably more character-building, more personality-strengthening, than passive receiving. Acting is masculine. But for women life is something that befalls them. Duns Scotus's *potuit, decuit, ergo fecit*, which he offered as proof for the Immaculate Conception, speaks volumes. *Her son* the Mother of God *befell*: the loftiest symbol of the feminine. Anyone inclined to doubt the biological possibility of the fact is faced with God's utmost masculinity: yes, he could do it, it was fitting, he did it. To act is divine; to suffer is earthly. What in us is divine, acts. This is our manly part. What is earthly in us, suffers. The earth is feminine."

"So does that mean the Savior's crucifixion wasn't divine?" Fräulein Iliuț dared ask.

Herr Alexianu gave a narrow smile. "I expected this objection. In fact you might say I even coaxed it out of you. The answer is obvious: No, Christ's death, his enduring of death, was not divine; that was the human fate he took upon himself. But the metaphor goes further and deeper than that. He died *out of love.* And therefore his death must also be a symbol for love. Above all, his suffering. And that is the case. Because it is true that in love, acting and suffering are transposed. He who loves, suffers love. He who is loved, produces love—and therefore acts. Christ's suffering contains a terrible warning."

"But also an example!" Fräulein Iliuț objected with a severity that seemed to be more rooted in convention than conviction.

Herr Alexianu held up his hand in a Roman gesture of dismissal. "First and foremost it is an image. An image that each can and should interpret as he will. Or would you be ready to let yourself be crucified out of love? Would you be prepared to do that?"

Fräulein Iliuț did not answer. But it was clear that she was suffering.

"Understand what I am saying!" exclaimed Herr Alexianu. He was so worked up he had turned red; his sentences, which up to now he had been drumming into Fräulein Iliuţ with clipped precision, now became hasty and frayed, tattered like flags in the hail of fire during an assault; we watched as the swarming squads of his thoughts dissolved and regrouped, in order to take a height that had been set as their objective, at great sacrifice, while Fräulein Iliuţ's face also displayed a delicate, modest blush of red.

"Understand what I am saying! I confess the idea sounds outrageous. But it contains the secret of salvation. To make yourself loved —to produce love, without falling into the passion, the guilt of love yourself—the loftiest form of being human—an extraordinary degree of dignity...We can even see a forerunner of this viewpoint in Plato —except that's insignificant, it doesn't matter where the idea comes from, and yet it holds the secret of Christ. It's absurd to imagine the Son of God as a sentimental loving person. He was extremely lucid. His powers of perception are so refined that he has nothing to do with the emotional drivel of the rabble. He rejected every outburst of emotion, just as he turned away his suffering mother. What he acknowledged was the love of Mary Magdalene. *For she loved much*—in her case that was completely unambiguous: she let herself be loved; she created love. *That* is the essential moral religion. To love—to love from within one's self, in order to experience the momentary happiness of being extinguished in eternity—that is the apotheosis of selfishness. To love, without asking for love requited, without hoping for love requited, according to Năstase, requires the lonely strength of the man in the wilderness. In actuality it means scorning and neglecting one's fellow man. Goethe's "*And if I love you, what's that to you!*" is utterly solipsistic. He was a self-confessed heathen. Christianity is the religion of the ideal society. As a continuation of Judaism—a tribal religion—it is the only faith that counts on its God loving back. Consider the role hope plays in Christian teachings. Their aim is for God to take us up into himself lovingly—in other words: to make us beloved in his sight, to make him love us. But that, too, should be understood metaphorically. Tenets of faith are the metaphors for the most earthly form of existence."

Fräulein Iliuţ looked up at him, and her tormented expression dissolved in a reflection of pure admiration. We could see that she loved him.

But Herr Alexianu stared rigidly ahead, without looking at her.

"Năstase is striving for this highest level," he said. "But his reasons for doing so are more biological than ideological. This task was assigned to him by nature. Arranging your life according to ideas is a German approach. Our own mentality, which was molded by antiquity, prefers to derive philosophy from life. Năstase is naturally predisposed to create love, despite—or perhaps precisely because of—the fact that he himself is incapable of loving. But he is anything but cold-hearted. He acknowledges love as a necessary force, for the exaltation it creates, the animation it brings to our souls, and for its role as a binding force in civilization. But he advises us to be extremely careful and cautious in its use. Just think: if love for your neighbor became truly common, it would mean the end of love as something exceptional, as a special form of affection. This can already be seen in civilized society, in the secular form of the theocratic state. In other words: Christianity is robbing itself of its core, the core of its true ethical initiative. Năstase aims to avert this danger by a rigorous scientific analysis of the subject matter."

Herr Alexianu went silent with a sullen expression. Whether he noticed how confused his speech had become, or whether he sensed some vague regret, that his ardor had somehow been displaced, perhaps because he made a careless mistake in once again referring to his great master Năstase at the most crucial moment—in any case, what he went on to say sounded bland in contrast to his earlier zeal. He had put away the shears and buried his hands in his jacket pockets. He looked off absently as he spoke, and he held his elbows pressed tightly to his side as if he were suddenly freezing.

"He really is a genius." By saying "he" instead of "Năstase" he was conveying a certain distance: the self-identification had been broken. It seemed to indicate a diminishment, a falling-off, and this made us sad, just as Herr Alexianu's voice seemed tinged with sadness. "He is the son of rich parents and became independent early on, because his parents died. He was able to live life to the fullest when others were still timid. He knows people's secrets. For example, he distinguishes between two types of women, and claims to be able to identify each at first glance: the ones for whom, in the moment of greatest happiness, the man they are holding becomes only a male—in other words the ones who betray him, just when he is at the peak of his masculinity, with all other men of this world, and the others, who always mean this particular man they are holding and receiving and no one else, and who thus create the image of the male of the species in a mosaic-like fashion. He calls them the scientists, in contrast to the first group, the philosophically inclined women. But this is a deeper thought as well: the loving individual always loses sight of the loved one as individual and only seeks that which is generic, only submits to the general ideal, just as we submit to the most general of all ideals—death..."

For a while no one spoke.

"He talks about all this, and similar such things, in front of women without the slightest embarrassment," said Herr Alexianu, and looked at Fräulein Iliuț as if he had been frightened by his first original thought of the afternoon. "And they love him. They all love him." He took up the shears. "But as far as he himself is concerned, he refrains from any kind of reciprocity in love. And he does this consciously and intentionally. He calls it his form of monastic asceticism. It is part of his purity, his chastity, not to love. He despises the idea of *si vis amari, ama*. He says, and correctly, that it is the expression of a half-intellectual, an amateur poet courting the favor of the masses. No, not to love in order to create love, but to conjure love, to arouse love without getting mired in sentimentality—that is the noblesse of a new caste of Brahmins, and Năstase is one of them."

Fräulein Iliuț's cheeks had turned a deeper shade of red. She now looked doggedly at her sewing, and we sensed what she, too, must have understood from Herr Alexianu's peculiar lecture—and presumably from that alone: his secret penchant for cruelty, which drove him to seek chastisement. And although we loved her, and were filled with nothing but loathing for our tutor—the same deep-seated loathing we felt when he insisted on showing up our admittedly inadequate gymnastic attempts by dispassionately performing some acrobatic feat, ignoring the fact that he would stretch his tendons to the point of tearing or scrape his hands to the verge of bleeding—even though we were fully aware that he was behaving in a base and perfidious manner, that he was using a person who was utterly defenseless to still his desire, we were completely enthralled and took care not to diminish the spectacle by any slackening of our own undisguised curiosity. Because even if we were wrong in thinking that Herr Alexianu's words were directed against us, we weren't altogether mistaken, since our presence had undoubtedly provoked him to make a display of himself. Among the various experiences we had that summer—and not all were particularly happy ones—we learned that the best way of getting someone to reveal his true colors is to provoke him into showing his concealed disdain.

And so life started to become an adventure, in a way we had never known before. In fact, Miss Rappaport's properly stiff and slightly sour departure—and we never saw her again—contained a grievance and a warning that was all too prescient. Because as the reliably tight and firmly established ring of obligations and activities, with which she had kept our attention focused on a few simple things, loosened, our sudden, unanticipated freedom finally opened the protective enclosure of our garden and released us on the city, bringing us in contact with its people and its spirit. And so Czernopol took possession of us. Once again it was only later that we realized what deep meaning may often reside in a chance nickname, and we had ample cause to regret the departure of our "Rock of Gibraltar."

Still, the new experiences were not entirely without benefit for us. Because even if it was in many ways risky for us, at our age, to be made witnesses to the kind of dialogue that transpires behind a conversation—and what was behind Herr Alexianu's words was clearly an act of rape—we were also repeatedly able to store away treasures within the cave of childhood that immensely enriched our imagination. The sayings we overheard, the whimsical sentences, the amazing word formations all burst into glowing colors when touched by the magical light of association, something well beyond the logic that Miss Rappaport had insisted on with her determined patience. It was like a star dropping from the sky if one of my siblings actually used in speech one of the words that had so excited us—for instance, when Tanya spoke of a *leap of great capacity*—and if we were able to trace it back, not to the gymnastic exercises which Herr Alexianu had also described as a kind of *capacity*, but to a name—in this case that of a certain Fräulein Kapralik. Of course we had never laid eyes on her, but people said she gave Italian lessons. In any event, beyond our associations with *capers* and *capricious*—expressions our father liked to use in reference to us—her name called to mind a jaunty Capricorn. A similar wealth of associations opened up when a chance overlap in pronunciation created the miracle of fused meanings; for instance, when we heard the newly experienced word *ekstase*—ecstasy—in the name Năstase, which right away seemed to capture this young man's tango-like essence.

For it was mostly names that provided our education with its richest nourishment, by lending essence to whatever ideas they were connected to, and thereby equipping various concepts with content. Our world was constructed from the names of people, landscapes, places, and buildings, and the words that surrounded them, and just as Herr Alexianu, following his grand master Năstase, had claimed, images were at the root of meaning and life. Nor were we ready for any degree of abstraction apart from thinking in images—which is what makes childhood expression so poetic—thus Tanya, inspired by Herr Alexianu's lecture to speak in aphorisms, said: "*The world is a door, and I am the keyhole.*"

Encountering such images, we felt like the prince in the fairy tale who eats a special herb or a bit of snake and suddenly understands the language of animals—in our case, we felt we understood an abundance of references to the most sublime things. It was as if we ourselves had thought up such splendor and carried its truth within us: we casually appropriated it and forgot where it came from. This happened very differently from the way we learned abstract expressions from Herr Alexianu and, later, from a man named Adamowski, who was an editor: the enormous effort and strain it took to achieve a precision so hyper-sharp it seemed brittle and therefore ambiguous was absolute torture for us. That manner of retaining sentences and entire conversations made us uneasy; we thought of mistletoe lodging itself onto the branch where a desperate bird had been scraping its beak, and where it continued its parasitic existence, the way these expressions stayed in our memory against our will, a tangle of tendrils that bears no fruit but still contributes a certain ornamental charm, just like the filigreed balls of leaves growing in the treetops of our garden.

"Is your friend Năstase so busy being loved that he doesn't have time to write?" asked Fräulein Iliuț quietly.

"No," said Herr Alexianu firmly. "He rejects the idea of creating a work. If artistic creation still had some value today, he would set about producing one. But his opinion is that today's consumer of culture is indifferent to the work. The only thing that interests him is the artist—as a particular way of managing one's existence. *What prompted X to write this poem, or Y to paint that picture, and how is it that Z came to compose this sonata?* are the commonplace questions. And the answers are equally shallow: *It was because of this or that painful experience!* All experiences are painful, according to Năstase. By giving artistic expression to their suffering, X, Y, and Z are playing a dishonest trick on their audience, who are inclined to view these works as acts of redemption. 'I will not publicly nail myself to the cross of my suffering,' says Năstase. 'I am not here to tend to your average bourgeois citizen before he goes to bed and after he consumes a great amount of pork and beer following a whole day of petty pleasures by providing him the liberating feeling that someone is dying for him over and over... only to be resurrected in glory on top of that. I see through the swindle of this kind of crucifixion. Works of art are the blood of martyrs—the kind of martyrs who are only too happy to spray their blood around and have no illusions what they think of the whole thing.'"

Fräulein Iliuț looked up at him, frightened, and then over to us, as if to suggest that not everything could be safely said in front of children.

We were to see this fabled Herr Năstase with our own eyes, although not until long after everything had already played out; he was already wearing the mark of Tildy's bullet—exactly like the mark of a Brahmin—on his forehead, just above his nose. For some time he was on everyone's tongue like a popular song, and not at all as the fiery genius Herr Alexianu preferred to see in him, but rather as one of the craftiest pranksters in Czernopol. He left the city soon afterward to marry the daughter of a factory owner in the country. Madame Aritonovich, whose educational institute we attended for a short time, and with whom we remained in friendly contact, sent him off with a dry kind of epitaph: "I wouldn't have even received this man in my bed, let alone in my salon."

I can no longer say with any certainty when and where we saw him. It must have been on the street, since I can't imagine where else. And it must have been one of those highly charged moments, when his name, which we had heard so often and which for so long had led its own existence inside us, suddenly coincided with a genuine person—a magical act that invariably also breaks the spell.

He was a tall young man with lanky joints, quite elegantly dressed, and very pale. His conspicuously high forehead showed a strong backward sweep. His cheeks and chin were dotted with reddish pimples. "There are skin impurities," he used to say, "that can be traced to a particularly delicate epidermis. My soul is covered with pimples." His eyes were beautiful, as were his hands and his hair, which formed a blaze of black around his forehead and temples.

Incidentally it turned out that he had for a very long time been a special protégé of Herr Tarangolian, who appreciated his sense of humor and his witty mind—and this was interpreted as further proof of some of the prefect's completely unreliable traits.

6

Report on Colonel Turturiuk's Ball

THE EVENTS that would provide such ample nourishment for the laughter of Czernopol were unleashed by a private ball hosted by the commander of the regiment in which Tildy served, a certain Colonel Turturiuk, in celebration of his birthday, which also marked forty-five years of service. The whole neighborhood took great interest in the preparations for this festivity as well as the celebrations that preceded it. Because like most of the higher officers, Turturiuk lived in our neighborhood, on a street named "*Aviator Gavril*."

This pretty residential street derived its name from a hapless young pilot who was attempting to perform a loop when his plane crashed, killing him on the spot. A small monument of crossed propeller blades marked the place where his plane had hit and shattered, and the Czernopol branch of the national student fraternity Junimea had made vociferous demands that, next to the plaque honoring the sixteen flyers who had died under similar circumstances, there should also be a plaque of shame listing the names of the commissioners who had purchased defective and obsolete material abroad and sold it at considerable profit to the nascent air force. Naturally their demand was never met: the whole matter was undoubtedly just one of the rumors that surfaced in Czernopol at every opportunity and which persisted more stubbornly than any presentation of demonstrable fact, even though no one could cite a specific source.

The little monument with the real propellers always held a powerful attraction for us. We constantly arranged to have Miss Rappaport walk us past it, and as a result we knew that part of the neighborhood and were able to imagine the festive goings-on that had caused such excitement in our servants' quarters.

The colonel's special day began with a processional trumpet serenade early in the morning, followed by a parade at the barracks grounds, a grand ceremony of congratulations, followed by a banquet that the city fathers and provincial delegates attended, and then there were untold other honors. The newspapers published his picture and reported on his brave and simple soldierly life. That evening the Mircea Doboş sports club—of which he was honorary president—conducted a torchlight parade, in which practically the entire national fraternity participated. All this extravagance served only to make the colonel extremely uneasy.

Turturiuk exemplified a type of soldier that even then was obsolete. He was just as famous for his coarseness and gruff good-naturedness as for his thick-headedness, which was extraordinary even by the standards of the cavalry—a bowlegged peasant whose mouth was the bravest thing about him. He kept his massive backside straight as a board, with his two overly long arms lunging forward; he had an enormous potbelly and an apoplectically red head of stubble, as well as a mustache that stuck out like a pair of buffalo horns. The elegant hussar uniform refused to fit him; it would burst at the seams at every one of his impetuous moves, and the gold-braided collar cut into his bull neck so much that it was unclear whether the purplish tint of his skull was really due to his temperament or perhaps to strangulation. He would unbutton it at the first opportunity, revealing the gray wool of his chest, which he would then scratch with his fingers to produce an audible rasping. With his saber dragging between his bowlegs, wearing neither cap nor gloves, which he constantly took off and immediately mislaid, only to demand in his smoke-ridden drill-sergeant's roar that they be found immediately, he looked like one of the Cossacks in Repin's famous picture. But he also had something of Balzac in his house dress with his fat neck, and indeed, his rough manner concealed a tender nature in need of love.

At an advanced age he had decided to marry a lady who, though she lived in the capital, came from a highly unsophisticated background—a step which made him quite sympathetic but was hardly beneficial to his career in an army that had to catch up in matters of prestige, as well as everything else.

The time of Repin's Cossacks, too, was nearing its end. In short, Colonel Turturiuk was standing on shaky legs in more than one sense, and he feared, not without reason, that the only reason for all the fuss was so that he could be sent off all the more quietly into retirement afterward.

As usual in Czernopol, this was a public secret, openly circulated by all and everyone. Of course the servants knew every detail of what was being provided, and how and where Madame Turturiuk had obtained the fancy food for the enormous cold buffet, and where the colonel had procured the wine and liquor—and they debated fiercely among themselves as to whether it was proper to borrow a neighbor's bathtub to keep the suckling pig on ice. Similarly, Herr Tarangolian would sit in people's living rooms and go over the list of invitees with malicious thoroughness, never stinting in his highly amusing explanations as to why each individual had been invited. The ball was staged on a scale that would give the city something to talk about for weeks and in the end did the colonel more harm than good by setting off a public guessing game concerning the source of funding.

As an active member of the national student fraternity Junimea as well as the Mircea Doboş sport club, Herr Alexianu had been among the invited, and, incidentally, this was the only known occasion when he made use of the socks that had been set out for him. He stayed through the entire affair from the very first minute to the very last, and didn't show up at home until two days later, whereupon with head still throbbing he managed a hasty hour or two of lessons before repairing to Fräulein Iliuţ's sewing room, where he delivered a detailed account of the evening.

In this way we learned more about the events that had already been rumored through the house and which had sparked our curiosity all the more because any questions were dismissed with a sentence or two.

Nor could Herr Alexianu resist whetting our curiosity to the point of torture; without paying the slightest attention to us, he turned to

Fräulein Iliuț and gave a colorful description of the ball, from the arrival of the guests to the high point of the evening, which, according to him, occurred after the military band—which played smartly enough, if a bit too briskly—was replaced by a group of Gypsies led by Gyorgyovich Ianku, who was quite famous in Czernopol at the time, and the more stilted members of the company had left. Only then, according to Herr Alexianu—in other words, only once the younger guests had won the upper hand and were able set the tone—did the fraternal and familiar atmosphere come to life such as the colonel had had in mind from the beginning. The older company lingered in the rooms on the ground floor, with the still-impressive remnants of the cold buffet. In the meantime the younger and more enterprising guests moved upstairs, where they could go on dancing, if they so desired, or spread out comfortably on the sofas to listen to the Gypsy violins in the muted light of the stained-glass lamps.

Perhaps it was on account of his headache that Herr Alexianu's report failed to show off his usual stolid gymnastic determination, and was instead tinged with something brooding, unresolved, and even agonizing. For us, however, his depiction was so powerful we never forgot it. Summoning the atmosphere of those advanced hours, when the festive lights shifted into a mystical glow, he managed to conjure the night as it rushed along, with all its tender and awkward moments stirring amid the commotion, how the surfeit of light and color blended into a golden undulating fog in the blinded eyes of the partygoers, occasionally pierced by the musical rhythms slipping in and out of perception—when the overwrought and sensitized nerves take up a life of their own within the twirling bodies, a life that proceeds like a strange and deep conversation on a skittering vehicle, remote and yet unmistakably clear, when finally, as Herr Alexianu quoted Năstase, "man in his most advanced state returns to his cave, where he transforms the horrors of the world into religion"—in other words, when the hour of drunken melancholy sets in, in which loneliness, the inner cage from which there is no escape, "turns into desire and torment and consolation..."

Herr Alexianu even allowed himself to be carried away enough to describe the Gypsy fiddlers, "whose music weeps even when it's joyful." To relieve his headache, Fräulein Iliuț had persuaded him to place a moist cloth on his forehead, so that his fanatical gymnast's eyes stared out like the feverish gaze of a wounded soldier in the field hospital.

During this phase of the festivities, he went on, Major Tildy could be seen examining a picture hanging between two tapestries, with his uniquely unmoved and arrogantly expressionless manner—what might be called his "English" face—while Năstase and his friends were sitting with a few ladies on the sofas. The picture in question was the kind of enlarged photograph they sell at fairs, with an artificial background; it showed a peasant couple in traditional dress in front of a well, framed in unfinished birch twigs that overlapped at the four corners.

People were dancing in the next room. Gyorgyovich Ianku's curly black head was visible through the open double doors, snuggled against his polished, chestnut-colored violin, rocking back and forth, utterly abandoned to the rhythmic swaying of a tango. The cimbalom player, who had a bean-sized purple-brown growth hanging from his lower lip, watched the tender intertwining of the dancing couples with olive eyes sticky with melancholy as his felted mallets raced over the strings, hammering out bewilderingly fast cascades of melody. Everyone had yielded to the magic of the very popular tango, and joined in on the refrain—"when the streetlights start to glow / and the evening shadows fall"—and consequently Tildy's aloof manner, the unseemly attention he was devoting to the family picture, seemed conspicuous and somewhat offensive.

Colonel Turturiuk, a supremely cordial host who constantly encouraged his guests to eat and drink by setting an excellent example, himself noticed Tildy's rigid and much too prolonged examination of the picture. With the tip of a napkin stuck in the opening of his full-dress uniform tunic, long since comfortably unbuttoned, carrying a full glass in his left hand and swinging a partially gnawed turkey leg in his right, he approached Tildy and addressed him, as Herr Alexianu reported, with a moving mix of good-natured annoyance and gruff reconciliation—"that kindness of character," according to Herr Alexianu, "which blithely and directly dismantles the barriers of mendacious convention that serve to divide people, which is proof that our nation is truly still a child, and an expression of its admirably unspoiled character."

I will recapitulate the small scene as related by Herr Alexianu, eyes fixed, the damp cloth clinging to his forehead, his face showing an occasional twitch of pain.

Colonel Turturiuk (approaching Tildy, raising the turkey leg above his shoulder to point at the picture): "So, you're getting a close look, eh, Tildy? Getting a good look, Niculaie, my son. But do you know what you're looking at? No, you don't. You don't know who those two people are up there. Shall I tell you? Do I, your colonel—do I, Mitică Turturiuk, dare tell you who they are?"

Tildy collected himself, very correctly and properly, in his unique, provocatively expressionless manner—his "English" face—displaying a nonchalant polish that according to Herr Alexianu would have been considered ironic coming from anyone else, but from Tildy, who was known for being incapable of irony, could only be taken as an attitude of supreme arrogance. Meanwhile the colonel continued, raising his voice:

"I want to tell you who these are, these two peasants, by the devil and all his relations with his mother. Because I am proud of them, you understand. Understand what I am telling you, Major: these are my parents, my father and my mother, legitimately joined before God by the Orthodox priest, exactly nine months before my birth. Yes sir. Not one day too early and not one hour later..."

Here the colonel paused briefly—Herr Alexianu couldn't say whether it was to reflect on the somewhat confusing time relationship, which the colonel might have expressed more precisely, or to ensure that his words had the proper effect. In any event Turturiuk immediately continued:

"Yes sir! Both parents. Father and mother of a soldier, by all the whore's churchbells. You understand, Major? Father and mother of your comrade and superior. Your colonel and your commandant. Do you understand what that means, Niculaie Tildy?"

The colonel was merely trying to dismantle the barriers that exist between people—it was a salt-of-the-earth attempt, candid and direct, but Tildy found no other way to react, according to Herr Alexianu, than to click his heels together so that his spurs gave a slight clink, ostensibly as a sign of polite respect, but one that showed the same provocatively dismissive mastery-of-military form for which he was all too well known... According to Herr Alexianu and the accounts of all those who had the opportunity to witness this scene, Tildy's gesture—at that precise moment and in that precise context—seemed cold to the point of confrontational, and caused the colonel to stop for a few seconds and stare at Tildy, shaking his head and wagging the turkey leg in disapprobation.

Turturiuk: "No, Tildy. No, you son of boyars. That's not the way to do things, understand? Not that way, Major! I ask you: Do you know who these people are up there? And I answer you: Those are my parents, in the name of the holy whorey Trinity, yes sir, my parents, the parents of Colonel Mitică Turturiuk—these two boorish peasants who couldn't read or write, photographed on the fairgrounds for three hard-earned kreuzers. But they were real people, you understand? Real people with real hearts. You aren't a real person, Major. You are a good officer, and a fair man. You wouldn't be capable of hitting a recruit. There's no other squadron like yours. But you're not a real human being. What are you, anyway? A Hungarian? I shit on the Hungarians—we're not afraid of them. Or are you a Russian? I shit on the Russians, too. Or what, then? You're a German. Or are you a human being? Tell me yourself, Niculaie—are you human? If you are, then take this glass here and drink! Drink to my parents. To these two simple peasants, the parents of your superior comrade, Colonel Mitică Turturiuk." The colonel's head, already deeply flushed, now turned a shade of purple. "To the parents of all your comrades. The parents of this country, which you have the honor of serving, with your arms and with your blood. Drink!"

With that the colonel held his glass out to Major Tildy, while his right hand held the turkey leg aloft like a club.

What followed, according to Herr Alexianu, caused the witnesses of this encounter great dismay, or even disgust, and provided proof after the fact for the legitimacy of the indescribable inner aversion people had always felt for Tildy. Because, as Năstase put it: "Coldness of heart needs to be paired with character. Then it becomes a form of being that deserves acknowledgment, a biologically correct attitude—nature is cruel—in accord with the basic precept of intelligence in dealing with one's fellow human beings: the respect we receive only grows to the degree we show disrespect for others. Coldness of heart without character, however—in other words coldness of heart that is kept within certain bounds and is coupled with sentimentality and timidity in the face of conventional institutions and ideas, grand phrases and melodramatic situations—that is nothing more than being German."

In any event Tildy, without a moment's hesitation, grabbed the glass and, standing to attention, with eyes so fixed on the photograph he failed to notice the smear marks from Turturiuk's lips, drained it in one stroke.

Even Turturiuk was so taken aback that he didn't embrace Tildy and seal the reconciliation with a brotherly kiss. "The embarrassed silence that followed," said Herr Alexianu, "was felt by all."

This awkward scene was interrupted by a fortunate coincidence that allowed for a saving exit, as Gyorgyovich Ianku finished his tango at that very moment, and Madame Turturiuk, wearing her very cosmopolitan dress, left her dancing partner, walked over to the two officers, and said: "What's going on with you two? Is this a fight or a declaration of love?"

Turturiuk (his conciliatory inclination was reemerging, under the influence of the wine): "Look here, my little woman, by all the Easter votives of the Metropolitan!" (To Tildy) "Isn't she a sweet one! You should see her when she's all undressed!" (Again to Madame Turturiuk) "Permit me, Alexandra, to introduce my comrade, Major Niculaie Tildy."

Madame Turturiuk (with a cosmopolitan smile): "We know each

other from sight, I believe. I'm very sad, Major, that your wife was unable to grace us with the pleasure of her company."

Tildy: "No one regrets that more than Tamara herself, Madame. She is ailing and hasn't been able to go out for some time."

Madame Turturiuk: "So I hear. Please give her my best regards. Unfortunately I haven't had the privilege of meeting her, but I admire her greatly. *Elle est très élégante.*"

Tildy gave a curt bow, and Madame Turturiuk burst out in hearty laughter. "You can see right away you're not from the capital. Otherwise you would have slapped me."

At that point, according to Herr Alexianu, a clear look of bewilderment registered on Tildy's otherwise expressionless face, and in a very wooden voice he asked: "Madame?"

Madame Turturiuk: "In the capital, if you tell an officer his wife is elegant, it is an insult. Because it means either that she steals her clothes or that she has a lover who pays for them. An officer never makes enough money to buy fancy clothes."

The colonel roared with laughter at the well-played joke. Still catching his breath, he gave his wife a slap on the ass and added: "Or else he has a mistress who gives him enough money."

Madame Turturiuk didn't spare her husband her own look of astonishment at his unexpected riposte. Only Tildy didn't laugh, as was to be expected.

Just then Gyorgyovich Ianku started up the tango "Drive on, Coachman." Madame Turturiuk stood there a few moments, fully expecting that Tildy would ask her to dance, as propriety demanded. But Tildy, once again master of his "English" demeanor, made no move to do so, and the situation would have become embarrassing all over, if Lieutenant Boldur hadn't saved the day by jumping up from the couch and leading the colonel's wife away. Even the colonel just stared off pensively for a moment, gave a deep sigh, and then walked off without saying another word to Tildy.

Herr Alexianu, seemingly worn out from his report, asked Fräulein Iliuț to remoisten the cloth on the side of his head. While she went to get some fresh water, he lit a cigarette, but after carefully inhaling one time he stubbed it out, with a look of torment. He took pains to avoid noticing us, and made a point of elaborately cleaning the charred tip of the cigarette before returning it to the pack. We thought we saw in his gestures a certain worldliness that he had gleaned from his exposure to wider horizons—they no longer seemed so brutally fidgety. But that could also be ascribed to his suffering. We kept quiet and remained inconspicuous until Fräulein Iliuţ returned with the newly dampened soothing cloth, which she applied with motherly tenderness on Herr Alexianu's forehead. The sight of this hunchbacked Samaritan was moving, and reminded us of the fairy tales with bewitched characters who can only regain their form after long and laborious trials. We always expected that one fine day Fräulein Iliuţ would be transformed into a radiant princess, and I was fearful that this might happen before I was old enough to declare my love to her. I often dreamt of this moment, and though there was nothing I wished more than to see it come to pass, I wondered how much she would retain of the strong and somewhat pitiable charm that naturally and effortlessly emanated from her deformity.

Incidentally, my secret love for Fräulein Iliuţ soon brought a bitter disappointment, whose source was none other than Fräulein Iliuţ herself. It had to do with a certain turn of phrase that she explained to us, and although her definition was perfectly correct, it did not satisfy our curiosity. So while we remained devoted to her with all our heart, we no longer believed she was a princess who had been bewitched.

Herr Alexianu spent several minutes regaining his composure under the moist cloth before continuing his report, at which point he uttered the phrase that immediately captured our fantasy: *he lost face.*

But first I want to recount the events that led up to that:

After the colonel had left him standing there, Tildy himself was about to turn around and leave the room. But then Năstase spoke to him, as Herr Alexianu related—

"Permit me to introduce myself, Herr Major," he said. "My name is Năstase, Vintilă Năstase, student of human nature, if you will. I come from a good family, and so may take the liberty of addressing you without incurring your immediate displeasure..."

"How may I be of service?" asked Tildy, without the slightest sign of impatience.

Năstase smiled. "You are very polite, Herr Major. Uncommonly and exceptionally polite. You know our saying: One can choke a guest with curds. By that I mean to say, that your politeness, your perfect manners, your aura of gallantry—it's all like a great arsenal of weapons. You are a knight, Herr Major, armed and prepared. They say that street curs step aside for a born cavalier: they can smell his presence. Do they step aside for you, Herr Major?

Tildy: "Up to now they have."

"Up to now. And suddenly they've stopped, Herr Major? That's a bad sign. In fact, that justifies the question I would like pose to you, if I may. You are a person of character, Herr Major. I would be insulting you if I asked whether you knew that the concept of *persona* originally comes from the masks worn by actors."

Tildy: "What would you like to ask?"

Năstase, who had earlier risen from the sofa and approached Tildy to address him, gestured around the room. "We were all witness to your conversation with our esteemed colonel, whose birthday we are celebrating. We were impressed with the elegant way you had of dealing with a truly embarrassing situation. *Chapeau bas*, Herr Major! Without diminishing your own stature in any way, you did not spare the colonel anything either—truly well played. Very well played indeed. The ladies were particularly impressed. Because even if we do love our little father Mitică, we can both agree that he is peasant through and through, can we not?"

Tildy: "Surely you don't wish to speak with me about my superior officer, who happens also to be our host, do you?"

Năstase: "Of course not, Herr Major. I simply wanted to compliment you on behalf of all of us. I only mentioned the colonel in order to convey to you the depth of our understanding and the extent of our regard for the way you comported yourself. My own interests are literary, consequently I don't stint on words, which must irritate a military man. I beg your pardon. I admire you, Herr Major—you will permit me to be so frank. There is something saintly about you. A saintliness devoid of kindness. I find that extraordinarily interesting..."

Tildy: "You wanted to ask me a question."

Năstase: "Yes, of course—presuming that you are so willing. You have a face worthy of admiration, Herr Major. I wanted to ask you: *When will you lose it?*"

Tildy: "I don't understand you. Please put it more clearly."

Năstase: "My question is quite clear: When will you lose your face, Herr Major? Of course I could phrase my question differently, like our host, the colonel, whose words you seem to have understood: When will you become a human being, Herr Major? But surely you know what I'm getting at, you must know what I mean..."

Tildy wanted to walk away without replying, but Năstase blocked his way: "You are so impeccable, Herr Major, that it strikes me—and forgive me for saying so—as a kind of tactlessness. Your irreproachable standard serves as an embarrassing reminder for your fellow human beings that they are, in essence, riffraff. But if you truly wish to crown your chivalrous qualities, for social reasons, so to speak, you need to have a weak spot, no matter how small. After all, even Achilles had a vulnerable heel. On humanitarian grounds as well as for reasons of tact. One should not resemble the gods too closely. And what about your hero Siegfried? Wasn't there a certain linden leaf? Forgive me, Herr Major, but it is precisely that small chink of vulnerability in the armor of the invulnerable that makes heroes bearable. We derive consolation from knowing that ultimately they, too, are mortal. It makes the street curs less sad. You should have a little more sympathy for the curs, Herr Major, even if you despise them beyond measure. You know nothing of their sorrow."

Tildy, after some moments of silence: "You are probably right. I assume that is all you wished to say to me."

Năstase: "Of course—but no—what else was it? Ah yes, I wanted to inquire after the health of your wife? She is ailing, as I'm told. It doesn't behoove me to ask what from or why. Just like Madame Turturiuk, I haven't had the privilege of making her acquaintance. I hear she leads a rather withdrawn life. Quite in contrast to her sister, the beautiful Ileana Lyubanarov. She is well known in this company. Or should I say... extremely well known. Ask anyone here and you will find unanimous confirmation. They say her temperament is a legacy of the Paşcanus. It's very regrettable that Madame Tildy leads such a secluded life."

At that, Tildy looked Năstase in the eye for several seconds, and Năstase withstood his gaze, then bowed to Tildy, smiling with exaggerated politeness.

"You will hear from me," said Tildy. Năstase stepped out of his way.

What happened next explained to us why Herr Alexianu had been so little engaged in his report up to that moment, as if everything he had described so far had been a long-winded but unfortunately necessary introduction. And this despite the fact that his idol Năstase was in the center of the events, which would have normally elicited a minutely detailed account and boundless commentary.

But then the following happened, and only now did the real Herr Alexianu emerge, so to speak, from behind the dampened cloth, which hung over his eyes like a partially raised visor:

When Tildy started to leave the room, Herr Alexianu happened to be standing in the doorway. And because he did not step aside quickly enough in order to let Tildy through—a gesture of respect, which, according to him, he had no special reason to show the major, based on what had transpired—Tildy gave him a resounding slap on the face, in front of everybody, taking the man so completely by surprise that Herr Alexianu had no chance to ward off the blow.

Herr Alexianu recounted this with Roman plainness, even greatness.

"Just as I am standing here with you, that man struck me. I am neither embellishing nor exaggerating. He hit me in the face. Without any cause, and quite unjustly. But that's neither here nor there. I was hit in the face."

He relit the cigarette he had previously extinguished and smoked it, albeit wincingly, one long drag after the other until he finished it.

"You can rest assured that Tildy would not have gotten that far if he hadn't caught me off guard. Consequently there's no need for me to be ashamed that he managed to hit me. Some of my friends jumped in to hold me back, but I made no move to pay him back right away. It is not my custom to fight in public. Those are peasant manners. Besides, he was in uniform and I respect the dress of honor more than some who wear it—and it has yet to be determined with what right they do so. I also said as much to Năstase, when he attempted to console me. I don't need any comfort or consolation, I told him. Others may, but not me. 'What are you going to do?' Năstase asked me. 'People will say you got your ears clipped at good old Mitică's party. All right. But you should have picked a better occasion than old Turturiuk's birthday. After all the man's about to retire.' Honestly I expected more from Năstase. And I wasn't afraid to tell him that to his face, either. With all due respect for your intelligence, I told him, your jokes are often tasteless. So maybe your intelligence isn't quite so high and mighty after all. Besides, Tildy raced out so fast it was impossible to follow him. He left the house at once. I for my part found no reason to do the same. It would have looked as though the incident mattered to me, as if I'd really taken a beating, if you know what I mean. It would have been the equivalent of confessing a bad conscience, which would have suggested that I somehow sensed I deserved to have my ears boxed—in other words, that deep inside I felt I had provoked it somehow. But none of that means anything, because it doesn't apply—as interesting as it is to speculate. You see, I'm far enough above the incident to consider it from the point of view of an outsider and not a participant. At the same time, however, I'm not so removed as to not draw any conclusions. Yesterday morning, as I have since learned, Tildy challenged Năstase to a duel by sending his seconds. I myself spent the entire day at home, without their paying me a similar visit. Evidently he wishes to avoid getting seriously involved with me. Well, well, he'll be hearing from me, this German..."

A few days passed before the excitement generated by Herr Alexianu's report wore off. And because we didn't dare tell anyone where we had learned about the events—else we would have been forbidden from paying further visits to the seamstress—Fräulein Iliuț was the only one we could discuss them with.

We asked her: "What does it mean: *to lose your face*?"

Fräulein Iliuț explained to us that it meant to fall out of one's role, to be guilty of a shameful deed, or else to let something happen that doesn't match what is expected of us.

We searched her eyes to find out what she was trying to conceal from us, but that really was all she knew, and she had no need to reassure us that was the case.

So she wasn't a bewitched princess after all. She was never going to change back from a hunchbacked seamstress into her real figure. Because bewitched people are children's allies. But she was just like everyone else; she, too, was part of the conspiracy of grown-ups bent on convincing children that words and things mean no more than what meets the eye, and that whatever they might sense and suspect beyond that meaning has no reality.

So the world was even more enigmatic than we imagined. And we were being kept from understanding it. And even Fräulein Iliuţ was part of the conspiracy.

Because what Fräulein Iliuţ told us could not possibly be everything there was behind such a phrase as *to lose your face.*

In this respect Widow Morar was much more part of our world. She had us repeat the phrase a few times, then closed her eyes and said, very slowly, her golden teeth glowing in the abysmal ugliness of her leathery, shamanic mask: "It means your face is completely extinguished. It means that something is going to happen that will wipe it away, the way a sponge wipes chalk off a slate—or someone wipes away what you've drawn on a misty windowpane."

"But can you go on living without a face?"

"No. Then you have to die."

"So how come it's only then that you become human?"

"When you wipe what you have drawn on the windowpane, then the glass is clear."

Incidentally, the next day we were informed that Herr Alexianu had been dismissed, and that we would have a few weeks' vacation before being admitted into Madame Aritonovich's institute.

7
Change in Perception of War as "Beautiful"

THE IDEA that Tildy would be considered a German struck us as so outlandish that we fretted over it for a long time—since in our childish gullibility we took everything at face value, accepting every hint of a possibility as cold hard fact—and led us to observe anything or anyone German more closely. Not without some hostile bias, it seemed at first, ultimately, though, it helped us discover positive qualities that would make it easier for us to accept the illogicalities if they ultimately proved true.

The fact that the Germans had been our comrades-in-arms during the war that had recently run its course and which very much still captivated our imagination, as well as the shared sense of defeat that weighed on our souls—not because we had to bear any consequences but because all our fervent wishing had proven powerless, and so the magical core of our faith in ourselves had been shaken—this had engendered a familial feeling for all things German, though it was not strong enough to drown out a closer kinship to our former opponents. Our family contained Italians and Russians whom we loved as Cousin Luigi or Uncle Sergei, although that didn't stop us from viewing the cockerel-feathered Bersaglieri and bearded Cossacks we knew from the photos of the war as our enemies, but neither did it bring us closer to the men in *feldgrau* who had fought shoulder to shoulder with our own, men who always struck us as slightly wooden, and who never missed an occasion to proclaim how our military prowess paled before theirs. Naturally we inherited our mother's Francophilia, which was shared by her sisters and seconded by Herr Tarangolian's own passionate admiration for the French, for their art, the beauty and richness of their language, their fashion and their cuisine, and which had hardened into one of the preconceived judgments that youth, with its penchant for absolutes, is so quick to grasp, and which despite all later reservations continue to influence our life: the prejudice, for instance, that whoever didn't speak French and wasn't familiar with the French way of life was seen as provincial and uneducated and therefore of little account. The transfiguration in the expression of the men whenever the talk turned to Paris was in no way inferior to the depth of feeling summoned by our aunts when they spoke of Reims and Chartres, or Florence and Siena, and this led us to suspect that these cities would one day become our own places of pilgrimage, similar to the one our Polish cook took every year to the Black Madonna of Częstochowa.

On top of that, Miss Rappaport never hesitated to give vent to her genuine British distaste for the hapless German kaiser, which was only seen as a further attempt to pass as more English than she was, and triggered astonishingly well-informed discourses on the significant role that Jews played in the establishment of the Bismarck Reich. But such silly remarks—which we saw through, and which even Miss Rappaport met with an obtuseness that, while hardly attesting to her intellectual powers, spoke more for her strength of character than for the groundlessness of the insinuation that she was a Jew—could not cancel the reservations we had in our feelings toward things German.

Nor did this apply to the Germans alone; our encounters with all sorts of nations came first and foremost through their soldiers. In fact, whenever we heard about nations it was in relation to wars. As we understood it, the Israelites first became a nation with the Exodus from Egypt and the destruction of Pharaoh's army in the Red Sea. We first learned of the Hellenes in front of the walls of Troy. Our own nation long ago gave up its mythic origins in favor of some bloodbath. So for us the word "nation" never failed to summon images of an army with its own colors, its own weapons and dress—which amounts to a uniform—that distinguished it from some opposing nation which had set out to attack it—or which it had prepared to defend against.

We knew, as I have mentioned, that our own Uncle Sergei was a

Russian. But for us the "Russian Nation" consisted of swarms of regiments of good-natured, misled peasant boys in long coats and stiff flat caps, armed with dangerous, triple-edged bayonets, throwing themselves against our brave ranks in such numbers that they drove our men back—despite heroic resistance—far beyond the borders of our homeland. And only in their wake, as if it constituted part of their train and baggage, could we discern the toyland world of the Russian landscape, with its colorful figures: gruff-happy troika coachmen with ruddy beards dangling over steaming tea, long-haired Orthodox priests, and apple-cheeked women in prim skirts and high-heeled morocco-leather boots—all against a backdrop of small carved wooden houses and blunted onion-domed churches with delicate three-barred crosses.

And after we expelled the martial images from our imagination—which in the innermost depth of our subconscious we never managed to do entirely—when we finally replaced the uniforms with folk costumes and added a few more essential traits—invariably as much a caricature as a display of character—what we wound up with were more or less well-founded generalizations. Considering the fact that, even today, our inner illustrated atlas of the world shows every Chinaman with a queue and every American with a bottle of medicine *cum* spot remover in his pocket and a set of false teeth in his mouth—the prejudices and biases we had back then as children may be forgiven.

We knew the Germans from the wartime illustrated journals, clopping along in marching columns, each man the same height and maintaining the same posture as the next, like so many lead soldiers, each with the same stereotypical stiff and empty seriousness—although not quite as erect and slender as their toy counterparts. Even the gauntest among them had something earthbound and heavy, something clumpish and bulbous, especially when they were weighted down with veritable mountains of war materiel like the little old mothers in the German fairy tales, doubled over under the heavy bundles of brushwood they had packed on their crooked shoulders, a symbol of how oppressed they were by need. And, indeed, our allies seemed burdened by a particular kind of poverty, an oppressive lack, the result of an ongoing and all-exhausting deprivation that was hard to square with the pictures of their homeland, with its productive landscape so rich in mountains, forests, cities, meadows, and ponds. This lent them a pathetic quality—the pathos of a righteous claim that forever remained unfulfilled—a negative dimension, like the reflection of the cathedrals in their celebrated rivers, where the mirrored towers rise high above the old-fashioned world of gabled houses. And just as the flaunted immensity of those great churches, the points and piers, the sharp teeth and deep notches, all seemed rooted in their rippled reflection, so, too, the defensive stance of our brothers-in-arms, so beset with misery, seemed to shoot up from an upside-down image of themselves, a restless delusion welling from a melancholy deep within.

I no longer remember which one of us had the idea that they should all be called *Schmalhans Küchenmeister*—Little Hans Kitchenmaster, aka Short Rations. The name seemed to lie somewhere between the world of fairy tales and the world of insects, ideally suited to express their anonymous, or really absent, character—which scared us. Because the tiny patches of face we could make out didn't seem to belong to them; they appeared borrowed and appended to the uniform, just the way the primitive heads with curly locks stamped out of colorful paper were pasted onto the cotton-wool angels at the German Christmas fairs. If you tried to look at them as human beings it only heightened the impression of estrangement and forlornness. They had evolved from being human into another, perhaps higher, form, into a pupate stage which would undergo a final, glorious metamorphosis, emerging in victory or in death. Simple being had been replaced by purpose, and consequently all character was determined by purposeful things: uniform and equipment. What appeared as ornament and decoration was also in the service of this mission—all those collar insignia and chevrons, epaulets and medals. Even the oak leaves that proliferated from the muzzles of their rifles and on their helmets as they marched off may have been placed there for functional reasons, such as camouflage or to provide a last bit of grazing.

The swarming ranks industriously and dutifully trickling onward called to mind a millipede or a column of termites. A teeming mass fused into a single organism, so that if you removed an individual you would find him tied and bound with multiple strings and bulging straps, in places roughly armored—we had been told that most of their equipment was made of paper and cardboard—or webbed together in a felt cocoon. Mess kits jutted out of the taut bulges of blankets, tents, and coats rolled and wrapped around their knapsacks, forming bumpy shields on their backs, while the stumpy cartridge pouches dangling in front of their soft bodies like rudimentary prolegs further enhanced the image. All their gear—rifles, bayonets, wire cutters, spades, satchels, canteens—was either tied down or stuck inside cases and sleeves, and as such became prickly or sagging outgrowths of the integument. The segmented rings of wound leggings bulged over huge hobnailed boots: serrated grips on the busily creeping claws. The spiked helmets had cloth coverings that made them merge with the head into something that seemed even bigger, the spike lending no more than a nascent sense of form, an embryonic physiognomy. We knew that the poor Germans had evolved to this stage in order to be *brought into action*, as the expression went, and we asked ourselves if the miraculous butterfly would emerge in the fiery, starlike blooms of bursting grenades and the fountains of glowing shots—so that in some sense they were larval fireworks, each equipped with a life of its own, firecrackers accoutered with movement and will.

We had no other way of explaining why they were so extraordinarily dangerous, and the images we saw of particularly effective units only substantiated our belief: shock troops—or, rather, what was left of them—whose heroism consisted in conquering or reconquering a section of trench, or retaking an elevation or a spectral bit of forest that was nothing more than a numbered grid on a map, in a war that had stretched across the continent, stiffening into a motionless dragon whose teeth were sunk into its own coiled tail. Not only was the landscape where this had happened pitted and perforated as if by a plague of gigantic caterpillars; there was no stem left standing, not even enough earth intact where one might sprout; barren earth yawned out of the craters of a lunar landscape; what had once been a tree lay uprooted across muddy puddles, or else its stump rose into the dead sky—defoliated, torn to shreds and shorn of bark, a withered ghost. Bits of flesh stuck on the barbed-wire thorns bore witness to the greed with which the devouring plague had fallen on the land. And as though this radical feeding had finally stilled their hunger, they now seemed close to the longed-for release from their larval state. They were in the process of breaking out of their confining husks. Their field tunics had burst open across their chest, revealing other protective membranes: shirts, undergarments, flannel warmers in the earthy colors of their reptilian existence. Their leggings had come apart, and what had once been tight and bulging now shook loose and fluttered, hollow and empty, in a universal process of peeling and flaking off.

Meanwhile, they were straining under so much military equipment that we had difficulty imagining how it could all possibly be used at one time: we figured it could only get in the way during a surprise attack. Nevertheless the long snakes of the machine guns' cartridge belts draped over their necks, the ammo pouches and the massive pistol holsters on their hips, the clusters of hand grenades in front of their bodies seemed like viscera turned inside out, entrails expelled during their metamorphosis. Everything about it was highly volatile, just a moment away from exploding: all these pouches and pockets and cases, seedpods that would soon flower into flame.

We were particularly taken by the young noncommissioned officers: slight, gangly figures so completely bloodless they might have sprung from the soil of the trenches and crater-fields instead of a mother. Their boyish faces seemed permeated with the dematerialized glow of quintessential, dreamlike obsession. Peering out from under the shading brim of their hugely oversized steel helmets, with buckled chinstraps, they stared in our direction through white, ship stoker's eyes, emaciated by unimaginable privations and filled with an ashy ecstasy, as if the white-glowing lava of horror had entered the landscape of a human face. But because we had been assured that they wrote the most beautiful poems, or at least carried the same with them in little volumes—because they fought to *purify the soul* more than merely to win the war—and hence their rather certain death was not only a casualty of enemy fire but a sanctified sacrifice on the *altar of the highest human values*, we felt obliged to somehow square this spirit with the horror. And while we agonized over these terrible impressions and tried to discover what about this spirit was so terrible it would lead men to literally ignite themselves like gigantic fireworks, our inability to understand formed a secret repulsion that combined with guilt over our own inadequacy to create a mixed emotion of respectful awe and absolute horror.

When we compared these young Germans to our own soldiers—and also to our enemies—who were really nothing more than simple soldiers, flushed peasant boys or nondescript faces in a disguise that they wore not without a degree of smugness along with the crude but understandable satisfaction that rowdiness had been made legitimate—we realized the distance that separated our German allies from the other warriors. But that only made the secret of their otherness more enigmatic than ever.

Herr Tarangolian, whom we once asked for an explanation of the German military prowess, offered the view that an attack wave of so many dumb faces had to render their enemies equally dumb. He then tried to placate us by noting that this martial superiority did not ultimately lead to the desired success that it had so reliably promised at the start—which was for us neither a comfort nor an explanation. What was truly horrifying about the exploding termite-men could not be dispelled with a joke, no matter how much it reflected the horror, and the fact that they were only bested by tremendous sacrifice and ultimately through starvation only further convinced us that the Germans were not people like everybody else.

We were particularly persuaded by the pictures of those great Germans who were said to personify the military genius of our brother nation. These stubble-headed commanders, so exaggerated, in a close-fisted way, bending over maps at the general staff headquarters or surveying the death-ridden terrain through field glasses from a protected shelter, instead of riding into battle at the head of their troops, leading the colors, had so little in common with our naïve concept of heroism that it took elaborate explanations before we were prepared to understand what was truly admirable about their achievement. But the in-sect-like machine of the German troops did make enough of an impression on us that we began to have a vague sense of what we were supposed to understand: that this war *to purify the soul* combined the highly concrete use of force with the highly abstract use of steering, planning, and projection. And if our perception struggled against the idea of giving the planners priority over the actual fighters—who although they may have rated little more than cannon fodder at least had the stigmata of the sacrificial death in their favor—we nevertheless viewed the German generals with different eyes from then on.

In other words: it was they who would change our perception of *war as beautiful.*

I'm not saying that we had thought of war to that point with the aesthetic sensibilities of a battlefield painter. We had been born into the war and to some extent were spawned by it; it was in our nerves, our nature, our blood. It lay in the world that surrounded us, a world distressed and distorted, not yet fully revived following the tumult of annihilation, a world that had been blinded and now had to grope its way back onto its old course, its former trajectory, which had been lost, broken, interrupted for a deafening period and now had to be rediscovered like a drunk finds his way back home after a night of excess. But these old paths still contained the same old ruts, the same insanity: lurking in plans for new life was a lust for new power, new hopes were laced with greed, the newborn generation stilled itself with the essence of the old sin, and the buildings that grew out of the rubble already housed their own ruins.

Everything had been consumed by the war and kept within its fury. The very landscape replayed the fighting: strong winds rushed out at dusk from the yawning, sulfurous sky, driving a vanguard of dark, rolling, leaden clouds, urging us to duck, to charge, to strike back, tearing off chests and foreheads as they beat ahead, while the steaming earth with equal power sucked up the knees and splayed hands and faces of the fallen—the mouths with their eternally unborn screams, the white teeth and gums that yearned for the moist, cool, crumbly loam—and inhaled their warm breath. The vast, melancholy flatland was drunk on the spilled blood, the orange rim of the sky showed the bright pain of wounds sawed into by the toothy lines of distant woods, and the pale-blue opal mists offered cooling, soothing, forgetting.

The beauty of the war, then, was not the same abstract beauty we might admire in a work of art, our eyes delighting in the decorative tumult, the abundance and variety of twisted and tangled movement, the display of strength, the immediacy and intensity of all expression and, finally, in the explosive contrast between life at its most unrestrained and its solemn stilling in death. The endless dazzle of colorful effects, from the glowing purity of the flags to the matting of all color in the sooty gray of gun smoke, from the dazzling brightness of explosions to the tender nuances of decomposition, did not tempt us to transmit our regard for the painterly object onto its cause. I say: we carried the war inside us, the tumult of destruction and annihilation, the addictive obliviousness it contained, the triumphant feeling of victory, of invulnerability as well as the dark terror of mutilation, the biting fear of sudden flight, the dull cutting torment of defeat—all its delight and all its deep despair lived in us in its original form, and needed no awakening or aiding.

Nor did we need to be fueled by the thought of the *just* war. For us every war was just. The spear from the Iliad, whose point smashes through the helmet of the fleeing warrior, running through the skull and coming out at the other end so that his teeth fall out of his mouth and he collapses, clattering in his armor—that was just, not because it produced gruesome beauty and certainly not because it was undertaken in the name of a *just cause*, but *because what happened, happened*, and without much in the way of reason, explanation, or rectification.

Because what were the flags other than symbols of the honor of the cause for which they waved and for which they were torn by the hail of bullets? The mere sight of them was enough—even apart from the battle, as in a signal book—to be carried away by their pathos and to know to which ones victory would attach itself. We did not choose sides based on which party was more in the right—it was, after all, a prerequisite of battle that they all believed they had right on their side—but by the persuasive ability of a particular banner, which we read as an expression of a given nation's essence, signaling great clarity and passion, or else inadequacy and false entitlement. We had seen with people that it wasn't always a question of who was right, so it didn't necessarily matter which side in the war was right, or even which was proved right. Instead, our sympathy was involuntarily drawn to the more nobly fashioned character, so that the fairness of a cause—if we had inquired—would have derived more from the fullness of the life that produced it and by which it was represented. It bothered us to keep butting up against the lawyerly evidence that the Germans constantly produced in support of their cause, as if the readiness to die on its behalf wasn't convincing enough.

The war, which had very much started as our own but was soon completely remade into "the Germans' war," had been presented to us as Siegfried's battle with the dragon. The image of dragon-slaying was convincing and left nothing to speculation. We were amazed that people felt it necessary to explain to us exactly how Siegfried felt challenged by the dragon in order to attack it *with just cause.* This *cause* struck us simply as part of his heroic nature. After all, the beauty of the dragon-slaying lay in the boldness of his attack. And even if Siegfried, as we believed, had always harbored the idea of killing a dragon, that made him even more of a hero. Nothing changed the immediacy with which the event itself happened.

But now, called upon to admire the war's mechanics and engineers, we found ourselves faced with the unreasonable demand to view Siegfried as a master planner who calculated every sword stroke—indeed, the very core of his courage and fiery zeal!—with a slide-rule. Naturally that didn't prevent what happened from happening, but it did remove us by the distance of a peep-box, and the marionette-like impression made the event into a mechanized performance, which may have not have lost any of its power to fascinate—in fact, in some respects it gained a new measure of attraction, but it did lose the immediacy of our participation. Siegfried had become a subordinate. We marveled greatly at this remotely steered springtime hero and took his side, but we no longer identified ourselves with him so unconditionally. So we watched the intellects that held him so completely by the threads and gave them our most careful attention, but not our love.

What differentiated them at first glance from the termite-men under their command were their faces, so different from the physiognomies produced in the high-pressure chamber of primal biogenetic experience. Their faces were very much their own: robust, easy to read, everyday types such as you meet in offices, even at universities, and in all kinds of higher bourgeois professions. Nor did they stand in striking contrast to the uniform; on the contrary, they managed to make their dress as bourgeois as themselves. To be sure, their features seemed more drastic, more sharply chiseled than those of their civilian counterparts, and they were doubtlessly more important. The sheer patience and constant willpower demanded by these highly determined careers, as well as the limitations they imposed, where objectives were specific, unambiguous, and easily grasped, gave them something solid, at times even monumental.

This stamp of personality, so conspicuously noticeable, set them a world apart from the anonymous swarm of their troops, whose first and obvious trait was the complete loss of individuality—in fact, their specific qualities of strike power and operational ability were derived from an aggregate renunciation of personality. This suggested an unspoken mutual relationship. It was as if all the individual elements of the uniformed men had been relinquished to the collective cause, either voluntarily or else by artificial coaxing, and had taken sanctuary in a single leader's personality, with the men offering their empty shells like molds to be filled with one will. Thus the commanders derived their impressive greatness from the sheer authority to command, and not the other way around: their greatness had not led them to command.

While that shed some light on their less-than-convincing greatness, it did not explain the mutual relationship between leaders and the led. There had to be something more that bound the leaders to their troops and made them mutually dependent—some higher principle, something we did not feel could be sufficiently caused or justified by functionality alone.

We looked for it in the idea of sacrifice.

Nothing had made such an impression on us as the German soldiers' willingness to make sacrifices: they set forth in jubilation and did not spare themselves the most dreadful hardships and deprivations. We saw from the pictures how they discarded even the most basic conditions of their humanity, in order to seek the thickest barrage—as it was plain to see—where the casualties were greatest. The thought of the Fatherland alone was not enough to effect such a renunciation of self. For that people died in simpler, less complete ways—though in no fewer numbers—as the enemy showed and ultimately our own as well. So there had to be some deeper sense at work—the same that had fashioned a termite-people into an instrument of war, and kept it functioning in this interplay of commanders and commanded. And this was what we sought to find, with a patience born of passion.

The faces of the generals and field marshals did not yield this information easily. Because when I said earlier that their greatness was not entirely convincing, what I meant was that they lacked the integrity that could have made them believable as stewards of pure principle. The lines in their cast-metal faces were etched as if by acid, but then immediately wiped away. Just as in a landscape following a flood, the furrows were deeper and the flat surfaces raised and bloated, all covered by a suspicious sheen; we saw the effects of a sudden deluge of satisfaction that had broken its everyday constraints but immediately trickled away, scattering ponds of unguarded complacency and settling in the rills of toughness and shrewdness that had finally paid off.

We could imagine them as theatrical directors, but not as the high priests of a sacrificial ceremony at the altar of the highest human values, despite the fact that the immensity of the hecatombs they had to manage lent them a macabre solemnity. But even if a terrible seriousness covered their mundane, petit bourgeois features, like the shadow of a scaffold, the bare emptiness of their faces deprived them of any grandeur.

In other words: we easily believed their determination to sacrifice their sons en masse, but not the holy passion that would have lent true greatness.

Two German field marshals they said we should particularly admire were Hindenburg and Ludendorff. We always confused one with the other, and as a result they fused into a pair of twins we called "Hindendorff and Co." or "the brothers Ludenburg." They reminded us of the uncle and nephew who made deliveries to our house and whom we could never tell apart, the owners of the large grocery store and slaughterhouse Dobrowolski & Dobrowolski, who were constantly roiled in petty jealousies and yet despite all discord were united in business. Just like the grocers, Hindendorff and Ludenburg shared the same profession, and their irksome but indissoluble partnership had made them scarcely distinguishable from each other. And just as we were never sure whether Uncle August Dobrowolski or Nephew Stefan was behind the wheel of the delivery truck that rolled through the garden gate once a week, always equipped with new, brightly colored advertisements for household items, imports, sausages, and smoked meats from Dobrowolski & Dobrowolski, or which of them was the larger one with the bell scraper and which was the pink-fleshed bald-headed one, we never succeeded in differentiating the paternal, iron sternness of the *Generalfeldmarschall*, his well-known patriarchal face troubled with the monumental pathos stemming from the harvest of lives and his eyes ringed dark with worry, from the scornful, overly competent expression in the small, budlike mouth of his chief of staff.

We observed them in profile, with stomachs protruding and knees angled forward, holding a field marshal's baton or a cigar that emitted a fine fuse of smoke, greeting the parading battalions or departing trains encrusted with troops, weapons, oak leaves, lady Samaritans serving coffee, mothers and brides, and wagons where we could make out the load capacity *6 horses or 42 men,* and over that: *Berlin–Paris*, or *Leipzig–St. Petersburg*, which we involuntarily completed with the words *and back*.

Or else the men themselves, the commanders of the army, boarding a special train, seated *en face,* their faces pressed into a stiff, double-chinned dignity, casually saluting, hands in tight nappa-leather gloves raised to the covered spiked helmet, and then presenting a staff officer frozen at attention two miserly leather fingers to be shaken in absolute obedience.

That was the pose we found most revealing, as the two men descended from the train, their short legs carefully searching for the next step, dressed in the opulently red-brocaded breeches that were gathered below the knees in bulbous leather gaiters that reminded us of the parchment wrap used for serving fried chicken legs, staring pompously ahead, necks rigid, past the troops standing at attention.

We found them colossal in a strangely buoyant, cloudy way. Their cigar-smoker stomachs didn't seem to pull them down but to propel them forward. The sight of them always brought to mind the happy silly couplet from "The Aviators' March": *In der Luft, in der Luft fliegt der Paprika / auf zum Himmel, Himmel, Himmel, hipp hurra!*—because we always expected them to suddenly float off the train step and soar over the train cars, into the cheery shrapnel-clouds of the blue sky, while the befuddled staff officers held tightly onto their helmets and gaped at them with open mouths like fairgoers surprised to see the balloon lady carried off by a gust of wind while clutching her colorful inflated cluster. Perhaps then the strained satisfaction would finally break loose and spread roguishly across their faces, merry and optimistic like the happy end of some droll fairy tale. Because as it was, when they stepped out of the train, harnessed by an iron sense of duty, shackled to the earth, they displayed a bombastic sullenness: their swollen and corseted bulges tugged against their moorings like captive hot-air balloons that make their anchor lines work all the harder the closer they come to the ground—up to the last stretch, which is accomplished through what might be called a mutual understanding about weightiness, so that the landing occurs with an impressive sense of ceremony. The caption of this particular picture reinforced this idea: *Their Excellencies were greeted by an escort.*

And once on firm ground, these balloons, which were the color of pea-sausage, churned and billowed with a mistrustful glance at the honor guard, to keep themselves at a safe distance, possibly afraid that the saw-teeth of helmet spikes and bayonets might tear open their envelopes. A platoon commander marched behind them with drawn saber, as if on guard to make sure no one had the mischievous idea of uncorking their excellencies' shoes from the leather spats so all their hot air would come hissing out.

We had to be careful not to allow the comical aspect of such impressions to distract us from the very serious side of these German field marshals. Their pomposity, which was both amplified by what was funny about their puffiness, and at the same time defused by the dozily comfortable, feather-bed-and-pillow quality of their well-padded, ponderous, and broad-hipped figures, was downright misleading.

Because we merely had to imagine this honor guard barking three *hurrahs* and then starting up one of their foot-stomping, manically clipped songs—songs that subtly drew us into their grinding rhythm, stirring us in a bad way—and right away all the horrors of this war were present once again: the swarms of iron termites awakened and jolted into action, the highly explosive larvae crawling toward us out of their trenches in the cratered fields, dangerously primed and ready for detonation at any minute, while in the background, streams of columns flowed in to fill the underground reservoir.

Then the scenery quickly darkened; the cheerful white fluffs in the sky gave way to a stormy, leaden gray that loomed overhead and threatened catastrophe—gathering towers of darkness, magically lit from beyond the black depths of the horizon, gaping wide open in the mythical drama of some primal hour. Like dark-purple cloud gods, the brothers Ludenburg climbed out of the hissing iron caterpillars of their special trains and descended to the waiting hosts, charged with an elemental voltage, their legs rooted in the Leiden jars of their spats, their hands strictly insulated in their nappa-leather gloves, as if the slightest contact with the earth might set off shocks that could destroy the world. The spikes on their helmets spewed secret codes to the lightning bolts that lay ready and waiting. Iron hailstones crackled inside their dagger scabbards. The bags under their eyes were heavy with a menacing gloom. We now knew why they were always sniffing at their mustaches with such disgust, as if they—one crimped, broad, and brushy and the other short and bristly—carried some repulsive odor: they sensed the acrid uncertainty of their existence.

And their officers were the angels that proclaimed their will to the divisions: the triple "Hurrah!" of the troops was like a trumpet blast, a signal that the larvae-men would pour over the earth by the hundred thousand, that the lightning bolts would smite the ground, thunder would roll, missiles would come raining down... This was no longer merely a struggle to overcome a foe: it was a mythical event, a violent impregnation: blinding impacts would light up for a fraction of a second, while the mole-crickets prepared the earth, sinking their teeth into it, devouring it, exploding it and themselves in giant fountains, churning it and plowing it and finally fertilizing it with their own remains in the name of the deity who had called down the iron rain.

So even in this war we found a new kind of beauty, eerie and cruel and exhausting—a different possibility of beauty, which caused us anguish, which seemed to be constructed of a more solid reality, and which positioned itself behind every other image of beauty, shining through, dissolving, distorting, and making them cruel with satire.

Later, when those images no longer carried the same weight and force, but—as with everything experienced early in life—were removed and reflected many times over, suspended, as it were, one of us made the pronouncement that everything undergoes the same transformation as our perception of the war, as if Altdorfer's *Battle of Alexander* had been repainted stroke by stroke by Breughel the younger, known as "Hell" Breughel—who would have also depicted the humor in the horror, which was always present and intensified by the dreadful surroundings.

In this way we finally stumbled onto the secret we had sought so urgently and persistently without achieving anything more than a vague intuition. I'm talking about the physical principle that kept the whole mechanism running, the interaction between the beingless larvae and their *grand leaders*—as well as its metaphysical sense. And we found it in the tension between chaos and order in that mythically monstrous picture of battle. In an instant it became clear to us that the nearly—but not quite—perfect uniformity of the advancing columns, dissolving chaotically in the clash of the fronts, reformed itself after the battle in a far more perfect form: as the utterly precise, utterly indistinguishable rows of crosses in the heroes' cemeteries, where the lines spread out into a broad perspective, moving in its spare monotony, cut at right angles and chopped in blocks, so that an absolute order was finally achieved.

And so the highly explosive iron larvae, the unreleased fire butterflies, for whom the intensity of life was compressed into the fraction of a moment before bursting into flame, and who had caused us to realize, in the strangest way, what it meant for them to *light into the enemy*, were granted one last metamorphosis toward perfection.

With that the sacrifice acquired its valid symbolism—along with its meaning. Little Hans Kitchenmaster died so as to rise again, purified, in perfect orderliness. Even his dearth and deprivation found its apotheosis in the divine acres where the crosses sprouted like seeds at measured angles.

The brothers Ludenburg, too, moved from the windy reaches between thunderhead gods and light-headed balloons into a firmer station, which did acquire a kind of high-priestly consecration—as the highest functionaries of the total order.

Nevertheless, back in the days of our childhood, we were still disinclined to fully abandon our perception of *beautiful war*, which we saw expressed in Tildy, the hussar, *pliant as a windblown sleeve* and ready to strike—exuding the aura of a bold and shiny knightly past. In him we rediscovered the grand fluttering of silken banners embroidered with gold, the flash of the saber wielded by a man's hand, the mystery of bloodletting, and a different proximity of death that made one proud and unworried, because it was fervent, full-blooded, and full of life.

Nothing we thought we knew about Tildy fit with the impression we had acquired of our German brothers-in-arms. But it was even harder for us to imagine him alongside the Germans of Czernopol.

8

The Volksdeutschen*: Professor Feuer, Herr Adamowski, and the Smirking Kunzelmann*

THE CITY of Czernopol cannot be imagined without its Germans. Franconian settlers directed to Galicia under Kaiser Joseph were among its putative founders, and their descendants comprised nearly a third of the population. Of course, they became so mixed with the original inhabitants and other migrants who arrived before or after, and their language was so corrupted, that they could hardly be considered children of the same nation as the famous stone Horseman inside the Bamberg Cathedral—though that didn't stop them from invoking him and all other good Germans as part of their crude and pushy jingoism. But today a pedigree like that is hard to believe even for the ones who stayed in Franconia, so that it's tempting to suspect some puzzling cosmic event caused one large nation in the heart of Europe to be replaced overnight with a different one, completely alien and incomparably inferior.

The head of the ethnic confessors, the honorary president of the German Men's Chorus and the Turnvater Jahn Athletic Club, a fanatically nationalistic polemicist and fervent anti-Semite, was a certain Professor Feuer, whom we called "Champagne Bottle" because of his steeply falling shoulders. I have difficulty describing him because his external traits—and undoubtedly his character as well—seem such a clichéd picture of the disciple of Wotan and the cranky high school teacher: tall and ungainly, with enormous feet in ridiculous orthopedic lace-up boots, with a cycling jacket and a broad, Odin-style slouch hat over his petit bourgeois clothes, and their stiff propriety stood in contrast to the threadbare condition they showed from everyday use. He would step along, craning his head like a madman, casting fiery glances this way and that, his long white neck jutting out of his collar like a singer preparing to deliver the highest note his vocal cords can muster. But it wasn't just his dress, bearing, and demeanor that made him seem comically operatic and anachronistic: he was one of those men whose bodies never reach their full maturity, or else skip over manhood and proceed straight to a eunuch-like old age, while they themselves remain stuck in a transitional period of development, like giant boys, who along with their laughable and pronounced erotic traits have something angelic about them. Not until later, long after we had left Czernopol, did we realize how much he looked like Strindberg: he wore the same thick, salt-and-pepper mustache, with the ends loosely brushed up and recurved like cupid's bow, and a soft, reddish, and seemingly moist little spot beneath his lower lip. Perched above his finely modeled chin like that, framing his responsive, highly elastic mouth, the beard seemed as fake as the beards donned by participants in historical pageants, the sort who reenact the Swedish siege of Rothenburg, when after everything has ended they sit down in the pub, in full costume but with none of the fun and foolishness of carnival, still ostentatiously seeking respect for the greatness of the past which they embody—while wolfing down sausage and swilling beer.

Perhaps Professor Feuer knew of his resemblance to Strindberg and deliberately cultivated it, because if I remember right, the impression was undeniable. It could be seen in his conspicuously small, nervous hands as well as in his unusually handsome forehead and his soft, defiant mouth, but above all in his eyes, their fundamental tragic crazy-headedness, which had also given the brilliant *Son of a Servant* his torn, youthful expression. We of course had never even heard of Strindberg, and had certainly no inkling of his importance, so we were unable to transfer the respect for the original onto his Czernopolite doppelgänger—in fact, later just the opposite would happen—and so Professor Feuer's exaggerated soulfulness struck us as hilarious —I can no longer remember whether on its own or if we were influenced by some ironic remark, a sardonic smile, or simply a general repudiation on the part of the grown-ups, presumably never voiced, something children always keenly sense. Because for a very strange reason, namely his strident anti-Semitism, the mere mention of his name at home evinced a silent but clearly palpable disapproval. This must seem odd, to say the least, considering the continued digs against the hapless Miss Rappaport, which were hardly evidence of an unbiased attitude toward the Jews. But in families with a strong sense of identity you frequently find the strange tendency to appropriate the most common and widespread maxims on decency, honor, virtue, or taste, as well as all manner of questionable attitudes temporarily in vogue, and consider them a kind of familial prerogative—with the result that any attempted influence by so-called outsiders is rejected as presumptuous and unseemly. Such an attitude is widely but mistakenly designated as *conservative.* While the family members usually reacted to supposed infringements of this sort with no more than raised eyebrows and a tense, oppressive silence, the servants reacted with considerably less restraint, as they considered it their privilege to keep guard over everything in the house. And in the same way that our cook, for example, felt excited that our much wealthier neighbors served game the exact same way we did, so our coachman gave us a stern lecture about how inappropriate it was for someone of Feuer's social position to broadcast his political views.

The Feuers lived in a house not far from ours at the edge of the villa district, in an overgrown garden, a house we liked very much. The properties there verged on the first fields, which were parceled off into small plots planted with cabbage and turnips, corn and potatoes with meager yet tender-colored blossoms, blossoms which, full of yearning for faraway places, bounded out into the open country as it stretched away, wave after wave, until finally lost in the promise of the horizon. The land at the town's edge was mostly in German hands. A belt of settlement connected the city to the countryside: half peasant, half small-town, it lacked the tidy, toylike quaintness of the small country towns and showed all the signs of poverty and neglect of a remote province. Even so, thanks to its lush and sprawling vegetation, it fared much better than the average proletarian outskirts, where the mangy city limits resembled the edges of a living, festering wound in the landscape. What the corrupting proximity of the city—and particularly the city of Czernopol—had done to spoil the pleasing solidity of the German farmsteads was offset by the peculiar romance of natural decay, which is entirely different from the desolate squalor spread by the wastefulness of civilization. Here weeds unfolded into their full plantlike beauty: seas of nettles broke against the walls of half-collapsed sheds and barns, their deep green stalks forming a dangerous deterrent; morning glories whose touchingly timid flowers turned their heads in shame from the matted greed of their tendrils as they angled up the rotting fences; silvery-gray thistles that had changed the acanthus of Corinthian capitals into a knightly array bristling with points, clinking and clanging, breaking out in helmet-like metallic buds with plumes waving in the breeze; and, once opened in full flower, the heraldic black-and-gold discs of sunflowers, towering overhead on succulent stalks, replicated in wrought-iron patterns as though for an altar. The unpruned fruit trees were webbed with ivy that reached into their branches. And in their shade, the fat, soft grass, knee-high and gently bent, showed runic traces of life, like spoor from a game trail, where some human had passed. All this gave the garden an enchanted, fairy-tale-like quality.

This neighborhood attracted us as powerfully as home did the prodigal son, though it wasn't until much later that we understood why, when we realized that what we were seeking in the garden was actually within ourselves, and not because it offered a world of freedom, or because it was a paradise for adventure and play—which it was, with the dense row of hazels along the silky gray weathered picket fence, the thickets of rustling cornstalks strewn with giant striped pumpkins ripening on rough, bristly vines that twined across the ground like wondrous tropical flora—and we looked on longingly every time Miss Rappaport led us past. But strangely we were most attracted by the garden when this splendor of self-sufficiency, lapsed into a run-down slovenliness, was disrobed of all of nature's magic, in the bare seasons on either side of winter, in early spring or very late fall. In other words, when the buildings scattered among the defoliated gardens and barren yards lay lonely between the muddy paths, and the gables stood forlorn against the never-ending background of empty fields striped with monotonous rows of dead stubble. The bleakness of the clay mines at the small brickyards, displaying a Chinese succinctness, seemed filled with some deep-seated meaning, one that reduced all life and the entire world into a stark formula, as did the emaciated, bony, bent-over figures of goats tethered by the edge of the path, with their swollen bellies and heavily pendulous udders, nibbling the last meager herbs. In the evening, the reddish lights of the petroleum lamps glimmered in the windows of the pitiful shops, glowing our way like the stigmata of poor people's humility, pinned at the base of the enormous sky as an admonition that despite all irreconcilable differences, and no matter how far apart our worlds might be, we were united by the same abandonment.

The Feuers' house lay exactly between this very mundane edge of town and the manicured villas masquerading as lordly manors. Their garden abutted the orchards of a man named Kunzelmann, of whom I will speak later. Only when the trees were bare could we see enough of the unusual building to satisfy our admiration. The moderately large house was covered with wooden shingles from its base to the ridge of its roof, shingles that overlapped like the scales of a dragon, and it was adorned with countless balconies and balustrades, turrets and towers topped with weather vanes, and fortified and decorated with fretsaw work like a cuckoo clock. Nothing could charm us more than this confused and overly ornate hybrid of Black Forest cottage and late-medieval castle in miniature, constructed with the carefree randomness of childlike fantasy—the ideal playhouse if a child had the manic patience to dream up every ornate detail. They said that Professor Feuer and his older children had acquired and rebuilt it without expert help. The surrounding garden was large and every bit as untended as most gardens in the neighborhood, and the house seemed enchanted, like the playful grottoes or pavilions hidden away in the remote corners of abandoned and overgrown aristocratic pleasure parks.

The house gained a special charm thanks to a saying over the entrance, burned into the wood in ornamentally entwined Gothic letters:

Wunschgott hier wohnet und Sälde selbander
niemals nahet, widrige Wichte!

(Godspeed who dwell here and fortune withal
Draw nowise nigh, ye nasty gnomes.)

Miss Rappaport was extremely disconcerted by the word *Sälde*, which she didn't know, and she finally read the complete works of Richard Wagner, with a dictionary close by, to see if she could guess it from the context. Meanwhile, she had been told that Professor Feuer himself was the author, because he had written a book, *Wälsung und Waibling*, published by the *Tescovina German Messenger* with support from the German School Association, in which he proved himself a true aficionado of alliteration and a master of poetic haziness permeated with the mystic magic of dawn that lit the primal oak forests of German fairy tales. Of course no one had any clue as to the content.

Despite our own constant curiosity, however, we were not dying to know or find out who was a *Wälsung* and who a *Waibling*, or decipher the riddle of their relationship. Nor were we anxious to hear the results of Miss Rappaport's philological investigation concerning the word *Sälde*. We loved words like that precisely because we didn't know their meaning and because the sheer sound of them, which would have evaporated the moment it was filled with some explicit meaning, not only gave our imagination almost limitless room for play, but magically opened a door for us into secret regions.

Listening to the sound of rare words with unclear meanings was one of the secret passions we pursued with a dangerous devotion. We considered them treasures, like the oddly shaped and colored things we collected and kept—potsherds, pebbles, twisted roots—not only because they provided the most vivid models for our imagination, but especially because in their fragmented state they suggested a final form that was all the more perfect; they were, for instance, *more* barrel or glass or stone or root than the usual objects of their kind. As the relics of an ideal design, they seemed to promise more information about the objects as they were meant to be. Just as an old coin long retired from circulation but of obvious fine alloy flashes unexpectedly in a handful of change, all the more promising the more its once-clear features have become blurry and worn under a patina of long disuse, and just as its value is all the more exciting because it is unknown—so rare words would occasionally pop up in everyday speech, and immediately command the high price set by our hopes for something marvelous and wonderful. And as with the money that—all too seldom—passed through our hands, nothing could compare with the glittering gold ducats and twinkling silver talers of our play chips as symbols of the most lavish wealth, precisely because these could not be tendered or traded, they were money in and of itself, and so there was nothing we craved more than words with meanings we never discovered or had lost due to a misunderstanding or mutilation—or, even better, words that had been freely invented and were thus words in and of themselves, vocabulary that no one took away from us because they were "complete and utter nonsense." Words like that were capable of harboring more than a single sense. Not that they could be given any arbitrary meaning, but their meaning could be expanded arbitrarily. Their sound alone, the rhythm of their syllables, the body of vowels curving around the framework of the consonants, contained more than just the vague outline of a presumed structure: their foggy, diffused appearance enclosed every shade of the moods they strove to inhabit. Nothing seemed more worthy of contemplation than Lewis Carroll's "nonsense" lines from "Jabberwocky":

> 'Twas brillig, and the slithy toves
> Did gyre and gimble in the wabe:
> All mimsy were the borogoves
> And the mome raths outgrabe.

Enticing and foreboding, conjuring the light and shadow of that fabled forest and the grotesque, fairy-tale-like slaying of a dragon, each and every one of these glimmering words had been made up, none of them was real, and we knew that—but the last thing we wanted to do was deny ourselves the reassurance of their pretend meanings by dismissing them as nonsense. That would have meant abandoning our secret hope that they might be part of some higher language, a special lingo for the initiated, for which there was no key, but which we expected to understand at some miraculous moment, as the apostles understand the language of all people at Pentecost. A language with an undeniable splendor all its own, with a relative absolute value like that of our play money, with no value but its own worth, which could be set as high as we wished.

So ingrained was our habit of trying to force meanings out of words we didn't know that we often had to endure Miss Rappaport's reproaches that we were too vain to admit our ignorance. But it was not a matter of childish vanity or childish pride—a pride, incidentally, that is more immediate and therefore purer than later in life—that kept us from admitting this. Nor was it our disappointing experience that the answers to our questions usually proved as unsatisfactory as what Fräulein Iliuț told us about losing face. Certainly we were reluctant to give up the free rein to play afforded by these inexhaustible possibilities. But even this playful impulse expressed a more deeply rooted unrest. We resisted fixing things unambiguously, because we ourselves were anything but fixed and unambiguous. By the same token, we looked elsewhere for reassurance—to the definite, to the set and certain, fully expecting that things would reveal themselves to us of their own accord. Consequently there was something amiss about the passionate way we listened to a name such as *Wälsung*, fully in the thrall of adventure, convinced that our urgent desire would compress the sound of the word into some shape, making our wish come true, and that the peasant-knightly traits augured by its sour-apple smell would suddenly appear—whether in the form of gnomelike dwarves or a race of Æsir. The stealth, too, with which we carried on this foolhardy game of enticement and desire also had something wicked about it; we were ready and willing to be terrified, and this made us aware that our evil invocations were as sinful and dangerous as Doctor Faust's, for we were summoning the spirit of language itself, and that brought us perilously close to falling into the hands of the devil.

But that wasn't enough to make us want to stop. We did our best to avoid Miss Rappaport's relentlessly sober explanations, and managed to cheat her out of the richness of the word *Sälde*. In this way its mystery, which kept the saying over the Feuers' door in a state of enigmatic ambiguity, reconciled us with the disappointment this house had in store for us. Precisely because it was a house we would have preferred to encounter in a game of our own imagining, in which we wielded powers that could make our boldest wishes come true—to the point of reinventing ourselves—in other words, because it appeared to come from the realm of make-believe, where we felt much more securely rooted than in the actual world, its reality bothered us. Its roof and four walls ought not to have fit so well together. An unfinished construction, or one fallen into ruin, would have been a clear sign that the place came from and belonged to the land of fantasy. But as a home serving the same banal aims as any other, connected to the municipal electrical works and sewage system, it belonged in an embarrassing way to the real world, where it merely seemed odd and bizarre. Only the saying above the door, which we never fully explained, served to dispel this everyday quality like a magical incantation, returning it to our daydreams. And at the same time its dark conjuring, which corresponded to the irrational side of everything that was magic, including the nonsense of all our count-out rhymes and witches' spells, offered us admittance to the secret essence of all things German—full of wonder, and always a little uncanny.

Sälde selbander—the words seemed to arise from the depths of the German linguistic wellspring, where the old sagas rested in a dusk twilight shimmering with a wine-colored light, like the sunken jewels of the Nibelung hoard—the sagas whose heroes, born of yearning, stood pale as birches in the den with the coiled dragon and the ranks of dwarves. Sadly, that is where most of them perished.

And as these words above the door seemed to be the true entrance to the Feuers' house, portals to its promise of magic and marvels, they also opened onto a hole as dark and deep as a well shaft, leading to the place where German wondrousness proceeds from the depths of the German demonic genius.

An air of eeriness surrounded the Feuers' house once we learned he had placed guns in his garden and set them to fire automatically, in order to scare off the countless Jewish peddlers whose favorite domain was the villa district, and who were in fact a genuine nuisance. Whenever Miss Rappaport led us past their garden and we saw Professor Feuer's swarm of reddish-blond children playing with absolutely no inhibitions among the dangerously positioned, and in our minds all-too-effective, shooting devices, we felt a timid admiration for them. Our governess hated these children, who ranged in years from bloated students of theology sporting the first dueling scars on their cheeks and heavily braided maidens unable to suppress their embarrassment at their all too generous and early-developed bosoms, down to a horde of boys and girls our ages and even younger, and there would undoubtedly have been an infant in the spidery pram that now served as a cart for shrub-fruit, if Frau Feuer hadn't died a few years earlier "in fulfillment of her maternal duties," as noted in the obituary.

Their clumsy formality, and above all the sheepish way they exchanged awkward glances in an attempt to arrive at some secret understanding, made the Feuer children unsympathetic. Even so, for a while we felt tempted to make friends with them, because our only playmates, the Lyubanarov daughters from the *dvornik*'s hut, had been sent to relatives in a vicarage in the country. But our tentative approaches were nipped in the bud by Miss Rappaport. Without ever coming into contact with them, our governess had determined that the young Feuers were insolent and uncouth, although whenever our paths crossed, the older girls never failed to curtsy, blushing as they did, while poking their younger brothers in the ribs to remind them to remove the caps from their blond heads. But a single ridiculous incident, which Miss Rappaport could not get over, confirmed her prejudice. We once ran into the entire horde of Feuers as they were chasing a field mouse through their garden and across the street. The mouse had slipped into a hole along the embankment of the ditch on the other side of the street. While the majority ran back home to fetch a spade to dig it out, one of the little girls bent over the hole and tried to coax the creature out by tenderly saying "Meow!" As far as Miss Rappaport was concerned, this innocent mistake was proof of unbounded stupidity, as well as an ingrained cruelty. From then on we were forbidden to have anything to do with the inhabitants of the miraculous house.

Every day at noon we saw Professor Feuer walking down our street after finishing his classes at the boys' lyceum. He was always in the company of another man, whose name, as we learned, was Adamowski —the chief editor of the *Tescovina German Messenger*, the third German-language newspaper in Czernopol, and the only one not edited by Jews. One of Herr Adamowski's legs was shorter, with a clubfoot, which was shod in a cork boot that was bulky but nonetheless insufficiently padded. While Professor Feuer strode ahead with his back straight as an arrow, draped in loden and wearing his slouch hat low over his handsome forehead, the much shorter Herr Adamowski tottered alongside, struggling to keep up. His dress, which was oddly thrown together, had a certain shabby elegance: along with a heavy plaid ulster with two rows of bumpy leather buttons—the kind of coat that in those days was seen only at very sportive events—he wore a very modest silk scarf, a so-called collar-saver, boldly tossed around his neck, as if he were dressed in top hat and tails, stepping from the grand opera into the pale gaslight of the Parisian night, heading straight for the Moulin Rouge. A monocle enhanced this image of the bon vivant, as well as a beret on top of his faded and straggly hair, which he combed back. The strain of firmly maintaining his monocle between eyebrow and cheekbone had frozen his otherwise labile face into a teeth-baring grimace that also formed the backdrop for a whole array of rapidly changing expressions which flitted like shadows over the fixed scenery of his face. He wore his beret slanting over his right ear, angled so that it pointed to the source of his affliction, and as he walked he would swing his short leg forward, like a pendulum, his progress punctuated by the dull thud of the cork sole. His grimacing face reflected the broken lines of this movement, which, despite all the swaying, was quite rhythmic, as he tottered alongside the erect Professor Feuer, speaking to him through bared teeth, rising at his side and then humbly descending. A bamboo cane served as a support. He always carried a bulging briefcase that was buckled and fastened with complicated locks.

Before telling about one very confusing run-in with this Herr Adamowski, I have to mention another man who also came from the German settlement at the edge of town, where he had a large garden plot with beautiful fruit that he delivered to our house. His name was

Romoald Kunzelmann. Several times a day the small cart that he called his *taradaika* came clattering up to our house, because apart from delivering fruit he helped out in all sorts of ways, as gardener, plumber, paperhanger, cartwright, hauler, and even once as a skinner when our draft horse died from colic in its stall. Although we had been forbidden to watch the sad operation, we managed to observe in detail how our coachman and Herr Kunzelmann loaded the gigantic carcass onto the *taradaika* with the help of some ingeniously constructed winches, and covered it with a few old sacks. The little Polish pony, a mare we called Kobiela and were much attached to, waited between the shafts of the *taradaika*, and the undaunted bravery with which she had dragged her fallen big brother from inside the stable, moved us as much as the lyrics of the song "Ich hatt' einen Kamerad."

From then on, Herr Kunzelmann had for us a slight air of horror, which made his irrepressible cheerfulness all the more unsettling. His creepiness was different and far more disturbing and upsetting than what we experienced when Widow Morar told her hideous stories. Because while our chatty friend with her tarnished golden smile whispered her message of death like a magnificently glistening promise, an Easter secret that the angels had proclaimed to her sternly and severely, Herr Kunzelmann seemed intent on keeping it hushed in a low-down, tricky way, and in doing so made it all the more frightening. The same day he carted off our dead horse, he came rattling down the street, sitting on the box of his *taradaika*; when he saw us at the garden fence he gave a sharp pull on the reins and brought our Kobiela, who had been trotting faithfully ahead, to a sudden stop, pointed with his whip to the load behind him, and called out to us, waving, in the harsh, coarse dialect of the Tescovina Germans: "Hey there, if you think you're smart, what's in Kunzelmann's old cart?"

We didn't have an answer, and he didn't seem to expect one. He reached under the empty sacks that a little while earlier had covered our horse's carcass and held up a limp piece of skin, which we recognized from the mane and ears as the hide of our old horse. "Little miss sees and starts to cry," he sang out, "but all that's left is horsey's hide!"

We knew that Herr Kunzelmann thought it clever to speak to us in painfully contorted rhymes loosely borrowed from Wilhelm Busch, whom he evidently considered the favorite poet of all children who understood German, or at least as a great magician of a language that was perfect for fostering an air of rascally conspiracy. Unfortunately, in our case neither assumption was correct. Nothing bothered us more than the ambiguous irony of this ostensibly smiling philosopher of the little man, whose gruesome, sentimentally internalized misanthropy not only made the all-too-catchy rhymed and illustrated stories embarrassing, but also called into question the purported moral. We were far more aware of their crudity than that of the much more drastic *Struwwelpeter*. That a child who sucked his thumb had it cut off, or was burned into a heap of ashes as a result of playing with matches, we accepted as fairy tale: it was transported to the realm of the unreal, and so, despite the lasting impression it made, it had little actual effect on our childish soul. Even at their most gruesome, the *Struwwelpeter* rhymes, in a book where cats cry, a hare shoots at a hunter, and Saint Nicholas finally shows up to punish the bad boy, were clearly cartoons. The bloody, knocked-out tooth, on the other hand, which seals Busch's utterly mean story about the boy with the peashooter, and which is described with gleeful realism, came close to making us feel physical pain and mutilation of the most brutal and direct sort, no matter how fascinated we were by the sight. And just as we had been bothered by Max and Moritz getting ground up in the mill, the death of Fips the Ape tormented us our whole life long: it was an overly enigmatic satire, in which bourgeois morality triumphed over a clever, comical, intelligent, and obviously loving animal.

Back then we didn't realize what made these craftily unfolding cautionary tales so perfidious, and at the same time so great—though very bad reading for children—at least when viewed in the light of intellectual refraction: namely, that in the world of Wilhelm Busch it is people—and petty, dumb, and vengeful people at that—who punish the wrongdoers, whereas in the more innocent moral fairy tales, the higher power of good always sends out an avenging angel, albeit often in foolish disproportion to the incident at hand. But we did feel the strange impotence of hatred that seeks to still itself in humor, thereby robbing both of any claim to purity. We felt the meanness of the souls that he created and had made to act so true to life that they were indelibly etched in our memory, equipping us with the dubious pleasures of boorish situational comedy as well as a cynical, worldly-wise attitude—the worst bastard offspring of a casually smirking worldview. A little later we were led into the morass of scornful tolerance, which attempts to placate all the indignation of a wounded sense of justice with the logic: "What do you expect? That's the way the world is. You can't change it. And would it be any better if you could? It's smarter to laugh than to cry your heart out about it." But in those early days we suffered from our inability to excuse the baseness, especially as we wanted so much to see everything resolved in pure cheerfulness—for instance in the story of the two dogs Plisch and Plum, which was utterly ruined for us because of the ending: we despised the converted boys who, like the dogs, had had their good behavior beaten into them, and their only reward was to look on happily as their beloved dogs were sold off to the eccentric Englishman.

And then there was the malicious laughter with which Herr Kunzelmann accompanied his quotations, his menacing index finger with its horny and permanently dirty nail, the bad German he spoke when making pronouncements such as "But the children start to plan again more and worse shenanigans" or "The best is written here in stone: leave what's well enough alone" in order to jokingly dissuade us from pranks we neither intended nor ever committed; and, finally, his compulsive bad habit of expanding each verse with nonsense syllables and thereby ruining it, occasionally to the point that it took us hours to reconstruct the original form—that was enough to elicit a strange antipathy mixed of disgust and attraction, both for Wilhelm Busch and his dreadful interpreter. But the unfathomable tastelessness that Herr Kunzelmann committed by showing us the hide of our dead horse, which he crowned with the concluding citation "No matter what you think or say, death is always in your way!" whereupon he once again gave the reins a lively jiggle to bring our Kobiela into motion, and drove away laughing—we considered that a desecration, and it upset and depressed us for days.

It's worth noting that years later, and ever since, I was to absolve Herr Kunzelmann of blame, thanks to a certain gesture of my sister Tanya, which freed us from any psychological burden his action might have imposed on us—if, contrary to the custom in Czernopol, we were to consider the man's lowliness a fault. This absolution was rendered without any intent on Tanya's part, simply as a result of her grace and its liberating power. I am speaking of the absolute politeness with which Tanya once took an apple from Herr Kunzelmann. It was an apple of choice beauty, an early variety we called "paper apples" because of their tender-brittle linden-colored skin. One day Herr Kunzelmann, whom we had avoided for a long time, surprised us while we were deeply engrossed in one of our games. There he was, apple in hand, out of the blue, looking us over one after the other, as if he were Paris and had to decide who deserved the apple. Finally he handed it to Tanya. And while the rest of us waited for Tanya to politely decline, she took it, completely unchallenged, her eyes focused on its immaculate beauty, then curtsied politely and turned back to us, expecting us to continue our game. She had gently crossed her legs in a pose we would later develop more thoroughly during ballet instruction at Madame Aritonovich's institute, and her slender body, already quite tall, supported her childish head with its abundance of brown hair the way the smooth stems of parrot tulips carry their full and richly feathered blossoms. In her simple play-dress she seemed as sexless as an angel. I can't say I was aware of the grace of this image back then, but I held on to it, and it returns every time I think about the majesty of a child. Such was the power of Tanya's grace that even Herr Kunzelmann lost his crude compulsion to utter something shallow; he stepped away without a word, his leather gaiters cautiously departing our field of vision. Tanya held the apple for a while, then ate it up without a glance. From that day on we no longer avoided Herr Kunzelmann. And yet even without agreeing to do so, from then on we called him, with the thin edge of our earliest derogatory irony, Schmunzelmann, or "the smirking Kunzelmann."

But now to the incident with Herr Adamowski. The sight of the ill-matched couple he formed with Professor Feuer—"a horse and a cow on the same shaft," was how our coachman put it—always brought us to the garden fence when Strindberg's doppelgänger and the hobbling journalist passed down the street around noontime. Moreover, by nodding and blinking and baring his teeth at us, Herr Adamowski had given us to understand that he well knew the cause of our curiosity. Then he would exaggerate his laborious gait, rolling his eyes and puffing out his cheeks when he rose up on his healthy leg, powerful yet still woefully short next to the tree-sized Professor Feuer, and shaking his head and letting it sink to his shoulders in distress when he then went back down on his short, crippled leg. He would look straight at us and laugh by baring his sawlike teeth and squinting through his flashing monocle. His grimaces were so sudden and darting, his expression so full of mystery and expectation, that we had the impression we were looking into a whirling wheel of fortune, from which the thick red winning number would jump out at any moment. He raised his rubber-tipped cane to his beret and lowered it again as if saluting with a sword. As with the Wilhelm Busch illustrations, we were at once fascinated and repulsed. Out of politeness we soon managed to return his greeting, which he acknowledged with a broad, obliging smile, which strangely reminded us of Widow Morar's golden mouth. But we never greeted him out loud; we bowed or curtsied in silence, out of fear that he otherwise might say something to us.

For his part, Herr Adamowski didn't seem bound by conventions that even the pushiest Jewish peddler immediately understood and respected—because no matter how bald and direct most dealings were in Czernopol, a traditional sensitivity regarding distance had survived, even if it expressed itself rather maliciously in most cases. But we still didn't understand that very well; we had spent most of our young lives in the country, where the people showed an almost holy respect for those of higher station, which is the kind of distance that we, incapable of understanding irony, thought we were experiencing in the city. Herr Kunzelmann was the first one who had blatantly disregarded that. The second was Herr Adamowski.

That said, the editor did show an almost frightening ability to empathize with our thoughts and feelings. One day he suddenly stood in front of us, knocked with his cane against the garden fence that separated us, and asked: "Lances, right?" Only then did he show us the spinning fortune-wheel of expressions, which had momentarily frozen in a grimace of astonishing authenticity—the winning number had just jumped out.

"Long-lanced and blinking blade, playful the pike but hard to hurl," echoed Professor Feuer by his side, raising his head with Odin's slouch hat against the wind that wasn't blowing. "Weak hands in wielding stiffen to stout, the fist shall be fearless and favored by Fortune."

"Wouldn't it be nice to have one?" asked Herr Adamowski with a new whirl of promise in his face, and then walked closer to the fence, alternating his swinging leg with the stamping one.

All we could do was nod, breathless with expectation.

"Come along, then!" He hobbled to the far end of the lance-leafed fence, where the raised base separated it from the neighboring garden. We had followed, still in the thrall of his insight, but also a little doubtful, irritated by his hard German, which reminded us too much of Schmunzelmann. But indeed one of the iron pickets had rusted away and was hanging by a single screw, leaning crookedly against its neighbor. Herr Adamowski easily pried it loose. He handed it through the sadly widened gap, nodded to us with bare teeth, then reached suddenly under my nose and held a candy out that he pretended to have magically conjured, which he then, equally unexpectedly, made disappear. But right away he took it out of his pocket and gave it to me. Then he saluted us again by raising his cane to his beret, and stamped off like a dinghy in a rough sea toward Professor Feuer, who had since moved slowly on.

I will never forget the feeling of disappointment and disillusionment that overcame us as we stood there holding the iron bar, which was no coveted spear but merely a ruin from the destroyed perfection of our fence, the fence that had preserved our home and garden like a temple grove, and from which now a piece had broken off, like the tooth from Wilhelm Busch's boy with the peashooter. For the very first time—I can still feel it today—we were filled with the fear that people might think we had unscrewed the piece ourselves, though we were never accused of doing anything that wasn't clearly our own doing. So great was our dread that we didn't dare tell anyone but Uncle Sergei, who commanded our unreserved affection. He listened to our story, and then consoled us, saying, "Iss no problem, my little hearts, don't think more about it. The Germans do very many strange things; we say in Russian they invented the ape. They also invented the railroad—*alors, qu'est-ce qu'on en veut!*"

The next day the picket was screwed firmly back in place. But as though our faith in the invulnerability of our house had been shaken by the possibility that even one of the lances that watched over us might fail, even if for just a moment, a secret pride began to wither inside us. We avoided approaching that remote corner of the garden fence, where the new screws stood out against their brothers. Their cheap gleam seemed to us a flaw.

I am telling about these occurrences in such detail because all the people involved still have a certain role to play in our story, and also to give a picture of the world in which it took place, especially the world to which they wanted to consign Tildy by declaring him to be a German. Their contempt in so doing was unfortunately all too obvious, although every other ethnicity might have been viewed with equal disdain, if it were to be judged by its representatives in Czernopol. In some ways the others even outdid the Germans, but they had the advantage that their reputations were not so highly developed as that of the children of Teut, and were therefore less likely to be belittled. Not that I am presuming to dismiss our German neighbors with examples of an oddball, a pseudo-genius and a surly cur. But we would later find out that in Professor Feuer, Herr Adamowski, and Schmunzelmann we had encountered three varieties of German mischief that we would continue to meet, either separately or, very often, all together. In any case, at the time we took them to be representatives of their species since we didn't know any others. We confided our anguish to Uncle Sergei and asked him how we could reconcile the repulsiveness of the Czernopol Germans with Tildy.

Uncle Sergei smiled and shook his head. "Tildy," he said, "is *cavalier.* He is gentleman. The homeland of aristocracy, of people with honor and manners, is very broad, it surpasses all nations and languages. But is very thinly populated, extremely thinly. And today this land suffers some epidemic disease, so its people are dying out..." He sighed from the bottom of his heart, but all the while beaming and smiling as if he were telling the most amusing anecdote. "*Enfin,* don't scratch your head over what one person says about another, only scratch if you have worry. Or if you have louse."

We took comfort in this oracular speech, because we loved Uncle Sergei and felt secure in confiding in him. Above all, we were convinced by what he was saying about the homeland of the noblemen throughout the world; no one seemed a more competent expert on that subject than he. If someone had asked us whom we considered the perfect cavalier—after Tildy—we would not have hesitated a second in naming Uncle Sergei, although his position in our household was not the best. We couldn't see what was so bad in what our aunts called "the bad habits of our dear cousin," especially because he had the kindest and most attentive manners, far more convincing in their unforced grace than the calculated and often seemingly artificial bonhomie of Herr Tarangolian. Nor was anyone prepared to explain to us what exactly these "bad habits" were. We knew he had a tendency to talk about gruesome things as if it gave him some joy to describe them, but we figured that he did that for fun, as play-acting, the way we felt that he exaggerated his Russian accent or his horribly off-key singing, for the amusement of himself as well as others. For a while we were troubled by a small incident with a servant girl, an otherwise easygoing creature, who once came running through the house, completely beside herself, declaring that she couldn't stay another hour under the same roof with "a man like that," and although we naturally had no idea what might have happened, we knew it had something to do with the dark goings-on that occasionally happened in the servants' quarters and with repellent regularity at Frau Lyubanarov's in the *dvornik*'s hut, and which comprised one of the great secrets the grown-ups guarded from us so jealously. No matter what the case, our Aunt Elvira always seemed to consider men to be the initiators of such incidents, and spoke about "*une crise juponière*" as though of a sporadic bout of insanity, much as Widow Morar had described the effects of amanita poisoning. We asked Miss Rappaport to translate the expression and received an almost brusque reply, delivered from a haughty arch of protruding teeth, as severe as a window of a Gothic cathedral: "Why, skirt fever, of course!"

The idea that Uncle Sergei might be particularly susceptible to this disease seemed contradicted by the fact that he was always extremely restrained toward Frau Lyubanarov—and this type of conversation came up primarily in connection with her. Moreover, we would have found it more natural that he were the one to be pitied, if that were the case, just as we found it ungenerous, and even untactful, to criticize his passion for "playing," just because he was forced to live as a poor refugee at our expense. We couldn't grasp why they would hold against Uncle Sergei what they were constantly urging in us—mostly when we were following a conversation among the grown-ups with particular interest. Then they would usually shoo us off, with a gesture we hated as the most arrogant grown-up gesture: "You look like you don't have anything to do, my dears. Don't you want to go out and *play* a little?" But when it came to Uncle Sergei, people spoke in muted tones about the sad fact of his "regrettable penchant for playing."

But from the strange, almost hostile world of the adults we had learned simply to accept certain things that didn't make much sense, including at times their crass lack of understanding—for instance, when people, in their ongoing efforts to prove Miss Rappaport a Jew, cited as evidence the fact that on an order slip for religious utensils she had misspelled the word for rosary—*Rosenkranz*—as a Jewish name: *Rosencrantz*. No one believed us when we explained that the spelling came from Rosencrantz and Guildenstern in *Hamlet*, which she had read out loud to us in batches. The stubborn assertion of preconceived opinions seemed to be one of those annoying prerogatives claimed by the grown-ups, on the basis of nothing more than an agreement concluded solely among themselves, a convention that was, unfortunately, unassailable, and the occasional vague interest they showed in our own views, always tentatively expressed, had long since demonstrated to us that we were better off keeping our thoughts to ourselves.

We had also learned, however, that there were grown-ups who defied categorization according to the arbitrarily established rules of the grown-up world, or who in fact opposed them—outlaws, or at least people like Uncle Sergei, who were not fully accepted or who had outgrown existing conventions, each in his own way, and had thus acquired the privilege of disregarding them, whether through some particular fate or sheer force of personality, such as Widow Morar or Herr Tarangolian. They participated to a lesser extent in the general conspiracy of the grown-ups who considered themselves keepers of some great seal and who were bent on protecting us from the secrets of the world. On occasion they also served as our interpreters. Not that we would have communicated to them our most intimate concerns, for childhood does not engage in communication. But in addressing the riddles that confronted us, they spoke the way we would have, if we had been equipped to do so. They helped us understand by expanding our imagination. Thus, after Uncle Sergei told us about the vast homeland of the aristocracy, we were no longer plagued by the doubt that Tildy might have some blemish because he came from the same tribe as Professor Feuer, Herr Adamowski, and Schmunzelmann. Nothing was more illuminating than the fact that he belonged to the special nation that formed the substratum of the noble qualities of all the nations, a legitimate descendant of the early-medieval knighthood, united by *one* God and *one* ideal image of itself.

Consequently, we were all the more bothered by what Widow Morar told us about Tamara Tildy. We had asked her if she thought it possible that Tildy might be killed in a duel, and whether his wife would then be unhappy. She shook her head. "She is a Paşcanu," she said. "She is not afraid of anything—only herself. Her father once told her how people in the mountains, where he came from, used to kill wolves: they would set a knife in the snow and let it freeze over so that only the blade was visible. Then they sprinkled blood on it. When the wolves came at night, they licked the blood and cut their tongues. In their greed they did not feel the pain. The taste of the fresh, warm blood coming from their tongues put them in such frenzy that they attacked each other and tore themselves apart."

9

Herr Tarangolian Reports on the Challenge to a Duel

IN THOSE days Herr Tarangolian paid regular visits to our house, for reasons that gave the most eloquent proof of his tender sensibilities, but which, given our family's constant urge to criticize, were interpreted in a less appreciative manner. He had an obvious fondness for one of our aunts, my mother's second-youngest sister. She was a delicate creature of nervous, girlish charm, with an alluring hint of something unrealized, unawakened, that came from the shadow cast by an early misfortune—a shy, tightly budded blossom that in another place, under more caring hands, might have unfolded into a tender glowing beauty. She had distinct musical talents but never developed them beyond a promising dilettantism, mostly because she suffered from a very painful and persistent ear complaint that later proved much worse than first assumed.

The prefect paid her a chivalrous attentiveness that never went beyond a tender thoughtfulness, but which struck us as all the more conspicuous, because all of us except our mother, who loved her younger sister very much, had grown used to viewing Aunt Aida's constant poor health as a conceit, and her overly inhibited and supercilious air got on our nerves. And indeed she clearly bloomed under the discreet favors of the prefect, although she had to endure relentless gibes about the age and corpulence and dandyish swagger of her prominent admirer. Although Herr Tarangolian never gave the slightest hint of such an intention, people spoke bluntly about the possibility of a union. This was clearly a case of wishful thinking, because not only did the prefect's high position win people over—he was also considered rich—but no one believed that Aunt Aida would ever find another suitor, and certainly never a more fitting one.

But as I said: Herr Tarangolian kept his attentions entirely within the bounds of warmhearted fondness and the understanding of an old family friend, and whatever tomcat-like gallantry accompanied this paternal familiarity could be ascribed either to his vanity or to a certain compassion for the unfortunate girl—and perhaps also to a genuine attraction for her faded magic, which would by no means have obliged him in any way. Unfortunately, our aunt's ear complaint broke out with a ferocity that made it necessary to send her to Vienna to be treated by the great specialist Professor Neumann. But by then it was, sadly, too late. She died half a year later of tuberculous meningitis, in indescribable pain.

There was no reason to doubt the sincerity of the prefect's grief. They said that his wreath of white camellias covered the entire grave. He asked for Aunt Aida's photograph, which he placed in his apartment, where, years later, it continued to be decorated with the same tenderly glowing, romantic flowers on every anniversary of her death.

In fact it was unfathomable how the idea could have taken hold that Herr Tarangolian took double pleasure in the role of the prematurely bereaved bridegroom: first to conceal his relief at having escaped the marriage, and second because his sentimental attachment to the deceased provided a welcome barrier against all future endangerments to his long-established bachelorhood.

During Aunt Aida's illness he had developed the habit of showing up shortly after meals for some black coffee—in other words, at an extremely unconventional hour, which suggested more than a merely casual friendship. His heartfelt expression on those occasions and his compassionately muted voice when he asked our mother, without letting go of her hand: "Do you have any news?" and later, after Aunt Aida's death, when he continued to visit, his daily exclamation of "*Ma chère!*" uttered in deep sympathy with my mother over their shared grief, while the red carnation of the old playboy flamed in his lapel and faint tinges of green and ruby could be seen in his raven-black, freshly dyed mustache—all that caused us so much wicked pleasure that the tragic death of a near and beloved relative wound up being treated as a highly amusing anecdote.

Part of this was certainly due to the fact that Herr Tarangolian's natural temperament never allowed him to display such sympathetic concern for longer than a few fitting moments. No sooner had he had his first cup of mocha, which he sipped in silent and pensive dignity, then he began to relate whatever news he had to tell, in his incomparably lively manner, full of wit and insinuation that captivated and delighted his listeners, so that in the end he sat there, completely engaged in entertaining his circle as best he could, cozily leaning back in his chair, a cigar in his comfortably perched hand, legs crossed, outdoing himself with sparkling wit, while our mother and her older sister, Elvira, sat beside him, their own grief undiminished.

"You are listening to my stories with the kind of flattering attention, Ladies," he said, with a malicious laugh, "usually reserved for indiscretions. Permit me to say that I expect this. As it happens, I am so bold as to hold my own views on the subject of discretion, and how much it is worth—or not worth."

He took a nip of his chewy brandy, gently blew a thin trail of cigar smoke from under his large Levantine nose, and again showed his overly perfect teeth. "Most people consider me to be an incorrigible gossip. Well, they are right. But they should know I have good reason to do what I can to earn this reputation, since this allows me to take the wind out of the sails of the other gossips in our city. Where nothing stays secret anyway, where rumors are entrusted to unbridled imagination, to suppressed hopes and desires, to scarcely concealed calculated lies and, finally, to a deeply ingrained craving for jokes and witty anecdotes, where—as I may safely say among friends—the press prints more and dumber lies than all the other liars put together, there has to be, ladies and gentlemen, a different source of information, one that circulates nothing but the pure facts, nothing but the unadulterated sequence of events. As you can imagine, in my position I hear practically everything there is to hear, reported to me from the most varied sides and the most diverse points of view. I know who stands to gain by presenting something in this light or that—in my position one gains a certain overview, a certain instinct for associations. I know what to add in each case and what to take away. In a word, what you learn from me is the purest, so to speak the scientifically sterilized, pasteurized news. And because objective presentations are always a little dryer than biased ones, I enhance my report with the piquancy of a confidential communication. I am indiscreet, my dear ladies, in the service of truth."

He gave us children a quick glance, screwing up his eyes in a comic way, as if his jokes were part of some conspiracy with us, then, raising one of his black, artist's eyebrows into a diabolical arch, he turned back to the grown-ups: "But in no way does that mean I wouldn't at any moment fiercely deny having said a single word of anything you might claim to have heard from me. Just in case anyone should have the unfortunate thought of citing me as a source. But I have nothing against spreading stories without using my name. I am a servant of truth, but I prefer to be an invisible servant. For you as well. And now you will have to excuse me, but I must leave ... Nothing is dearer to a poor and increasingly lonely man such as myself than these hours with your family, surrounded by such good, close friends, showered with such kindness. But—*hélas*—my burdensome everyday duties are calling once again."

He finished his brandy, stood up, took our mother's hand, looked deeply into her eyes, and said in a voice only she could hear: "*Soyons forts, ma chère!*" And with that he guided her hand quickly and fervently to his lips, turned on his heels as if overcome by painful memories, and left the room with a sad wave, his head somewhat obscured.

Most of us had a hard time restraining ourselves from bursting out in laughter—of the kind that quickly escalates into full-fledged fits capable of bringing relief to the tension that always lurks in nerve-ridden families. Once, I recall, we managed to avoid a catastrophe at the last possible second when a visiting teenage cousin pinned an enormously long mourning band onto the prefect's straw hat. Luckily the tasteless prank was discovered before it could do any harm. Otherwise Herr Tarangolian never would have entered our house again—and he would have been right not to.

But we will never know how much snickering, presumably hidden behind his back, how many quick winks and suppressed laughs and evident breaches of tact the prefect intentionally overlooked, for instance

Uncle Sergei's very indelicate habit, when our aunt was still alive, of warbling "Celeste Aida" each time he saw Herr Tarangolian, as if by chance—and off-key on top of that by whole quarter- and eighth-tones. Such gross disregard or crude violation of taste, directed against an entirely natural sensitivity, as well as against certain pardonable weaknesses—which would have been bitterly taken amiss if directed the other way around—was probably what prompted our family friend to be so sharply critical of us, as we later found out. In any event, these infractions from our side were far more worthy of blame than what we, in our arrogance, referred to as the prefect's "unreliable traits." Only our mother was spared his merciless judgment: he called her "one of the most lovable women" he had ever met, a woman "of the most tender sensibilities and equally rare stupidity."

It was Uncle Sergei who took the most interest in Tildy's case, and who persuaded Herr Tarangolian to provide us with a detailed report—or at least a more detailed report than the prefect would have provided anyway "in the service of truth"—and to keep us well informed as to any developments.

Naturally the incident at Colonel Turturiuk's and the events that followed immediately became the biggest sensation in town, and the mere possibility that a duel with real weapons might be held in Czernopol was a subject that could not be talked about enough. Uncle Sergei, as a former member of the imperial Russian *garde à cheval*, was regarded as an expert on the subject, and over the course of things came close to offering to face Tildy himself, "to give the gentleman opportunity to wash his honor clean, in the only possible manner—*nu vot, voilà*!"

"Ha!" he called out with all the ebullience of his Russian soul, which was ready to burst, overwrought with passion and underfinanced by his measly allowance—and smiled as if he were parodying himself with every word. "This is conspiracy! They are wanting to destroy this man! Murderers, *da*, dogs—but not officers! What is left for him to do if no one will shoot with him? He will need shoot himself—*nu vot*!" Uncle Sergei was beaming in the full glory of his charm. "I am telling you, is same case exactly as my fellow officer Vinogradov—he was also Nikolai: Nikolai Pavlovich Vinogradov. Nikolai Pavlovich became tangled in some affair—while playing cards—and a certain somebody says to him—as joke—after drinking, you understand—well, so this certain somebody says to him: Nikolai Pavlovich, are you sure there is nothing funny going on here?—or whatever people are saying when they are cross because they lose—he was of course a frontline officer with no manners, this certain somebody—I was always telling Nikolai Pavlovich: If you lie down with dogs you wake up with fleas—*voilà*! So, in short, Nikolai Pavlovich breaks off the game, just like that, does not touch his winnings, not one kopeck, arranges to meet the other one the next morning at seven o'clock sharp at such and such place, then he goes home and goes to sleep. They wake him up at six o'clock exactly, he eats a little bit, takes his coach, and at five minutes before seven is ready and waiting—but who is not there? The certain somebody. Nikolai Pavlovich waits one half hour, one whole hour, two, three hours—who does not come? The certain somebody. *Nu vot.* They search all over Petersburg to find him, but who has gone and disappeared? He has. So Nikolai Pavlovich goes to his best friend and says: You must shoot with me, there is no other way. This certain best friend comes up with one excuse after the other, he has just become engaged, he is afraid of his father-in-law, one doesn't simply come and ask a man to duel like that, and so forth, he has obligations—all what people say in such a situation—in short, what do you expect? Nikolai Pavlovich, he takes his pistol and shoots this certain best friend dead, and then he shoots himself. *Voilà.*" Uncle Sergei looked around the room, in a good mood, as if expecting applause for the delightfully simple and obvious way in which everything had been settled. "Fate had it that I was not in Petersburg at the time. I would have said to him: Nikolai Pavlovich, I understand your situation—of course! If you lie down with dogs you wake up with fleas—but of course! As I have said: I was unfortunately not in Petersburg. Otherwise, of course, naturally! Because what else is there for him to do, *je vous en prie*? A certain somebody offends your honor, you want satisfaction, and he—the swine—invents excuses—*nu vot*! I say if you lie down with dogs you wake up with fleas. There is nothing for him to do except shoot bullet into his own head. Nothing." He held up the palm of his hand as if presenting evidence, as if he wanted to say: Make up your own minds, you will come to the exact same conclusion, it is the only possibility. "Because what is he supposed to do if no one takes the challenge? Perhaps he should say it was nothing at all that happened—*c'était une blague*, should he say that? Then show up at the casino, or at the racetrack in the afternoon, or in the evening for *Aida* at the opera, and so on, *et ce n'était rien qu'une blague*! Ridiculous! An impossible situation. Read Lermontov. A completely impossible situation."

What had happened was absolutely predictable: both of the seconds whom Tildy had sent to challenge Năstase to a duel—with army pistols at fifteen paces—came back and reported, with a serious expression, but not without a hint of malicious pleasure, that Năstase had politely but resolutely declined to accept Tildy's challenge.

His words had been more or less as follows: "Gentlemen, please convey my thanks to Major Tildy. I am honored by his request—if that is the correct expression for such a case, though I can't really say since I have no experience in this area. I am a writer, and hence I cannot—in fact, I am not allowed to—claim that I am a gentleman. Major Tildy will presumably have the kindness to realize that I have not the slightest practice with weaponry of any kind, whether lances, sabers, pistols, rifles, machine guns, clubs, or spiked maces, or whatever else military men and gentlemen prefer to use to settle their differences of opinion. You may further advise the major that in this matter it would be difficult—by any means at all—to dispose of our difference in opinion, unless he were to dispose of himself. He feels obliged to defend the honor of his beautiful sister-in-law, but his conviction is completely at odds with the otherwise unanimous opinion that she neither possesses such honor nor would ever aspire to possess it. To the great enjoyment of all of us, as you, dear sirs, will no doubt agree. Please have the kindness to further convey to the major that I must regrettably retract my previous regrets concerning his own wife's seclusion. I have since had occasion to see her. She was in the process of using an umbrella to attack the rolling shades at the apothecary in the Wassergasse, where I had gone with a few friends to a familiar place for a morning drink. Instead of a hat she was wearing what I took to be a hot-water bottle in a crocheted cover. Her nose is very ugly. The major need have no worries concerning our curiosity to uncover a certain familial resemblance to her sister. If the major should now have the idea of taking his riding whip to me, as is the custom among gentlemen, please inform him that I would not hesitate to hire a few powerful men who would return the favor with a bullwhip. And last but not least, gentlemen, please convey my compliments to Major Tildy for his understanding and steadfastness of character. It's well known that his compatriots, the Germans, have to call an assembly in order to understand a joke. He, however, abandoned the attempt from the start. That compels a certain respect from me. Apart from that, I have nothing to offer you except for a little plum brandy, which I presume you will have to politely decline, first because it would not fit the code and second because you probably realize that I want to drink it all myself."

The two officers did indeed decline, thanked Năstase, and went back to Tildy to convey everything that had been said, as faithfully as possible, down to the intonation of every syllable.

But before Tildy had a chance to proceed to the next step, he was ordered to see his commanding officer.

Given the exertions of the previous night, it was perfectly understandable that the colonel had shown up late at the barracks the following morning—too late to prevent Tildy from sending his seconds to Năstase. In other words, it took much explaining, and much hard work to activate Turturiuk's memory, before he had any idea what the whole incident was about. But then he began to rage like a rabid buffalo.

Nor was his rage directed solely at Tildy. He roared through all the guardrooms and sleeping quarters of the vast barracks grounds, raged through the stables, inspected the ostensibly freshly groomed horses with a thoroughness that made the long-serving sergeant green with envy, and yelled until his throat hurt when he scratched a fingernail's worth of dust from just below a bad-tempered kicking horse's tailbone. Then he stormed into the arena, where a pack of hapless recruits in a hard trot on the stiffest old training mounts were having what was left of their brains pounded out of their peasant skulls, picked up a longe whip, and took over the instruction himself, until the arena looked like a witch's cauldron. When a bit of tanbark abundantly laden with horse manure landed on the colonel's shoulder, an eager corporal attempted to brush it off, whereupon Turturiuk turned around and soundly slapped the man.

Having thus worked himself into the proper mood, the colonel reminded the first-years on the parade ground of their duties, *blasting away* at them—as the proper term goes—for a good half hour from a practiced throat, and especially upbraiding them for their rampant alcoholism. After that, he meted out a few hefty punishments among the higher ranks, which were bound to set off chain reactions lower down, and then, spurs clanging, his heavy cavalry saber trailing between his Cossack legs, his collar opened down to his chest, his shako boldly shoved into his neck, he marched back into his lion's den.

There the two officers Tildy had sent to Năstase as seconds were already waiting, clearly anything but happy with that assignment. Turturiuk didn't even take the trouble to close the door behind him, but *blasted* them the moment he stepped over the threshold, using expressions the noncommissioned officers would repeat much later in the mess hall, with great awe and admiration, as if the words of a poet. After he had promised to demote them and ship them off to the Okna salt mines for a few years' forced labor, he had them present a fully detailed report on Năstase's reply, though they had to explain to him its sheer malice sentence by sentence. Finally he was ready to face Tildy one-on-one.

Whether because the colonel's anger failed him, like the excessive passion of a lover when he finally holds the object of his desires in his arms, or because Tildy's calm and correct demeanor, his inviolable "English" composure made it impossible to be *blasted*—in any event, the private conversation did not transpire as dramatically as would have been expected. On the contrary: Turturiuk's ire first changed into a sullen paternal grumbling, then into a whiny tone weakly cloaked in coarseness.

To be sure, he did try to begin things with a look that he considered so ferocious a tiger would have crawled away and hid, but which Tildy withstood with an unruffled calm that had not a hint of disdain or disregard—nothing but cool and earnest patience. So the colonel's furious stare turned more and more inward, as if that somehow helped him collect his very scattered thoughts, and swelled into a blank, animal-like gawking that was completely devoid of ideas and imagination, like the remote look of a constipated man following an explosive exertion.

Thanks to his great gift for storytelling, Herr Tarangolian was able give us a vivid recreation of events, and Uncle Sergei didn't spare his own humorous commentaries, so even though we found the incident extremely upsetting, because it concerned our secret idol, the retelling gained something daringly amusing, something fantastic—an inconsistency that placed great demands on our ability to bear the psychological tension, and certainly did nothing to strengthen our character.

I will never forget how masterfully the prefect was able to reproduce Turturiuk's expression, his bloodshot, alcohol-ridden eyes, the befuddled rage rising and dissipating into silliness, the pitiful attempt to remobilize its momentum, and, finally, his complete bewilderment, and the vague realization dawning on him that he had been doomed to lose the match from the very beginning.

Because ultimately the colonel had been forced to break off his lion-taming stare, and since he had evidently lost the connection to the events, he simply stared ahead and sighed. Then he looked at Tildy once again, and, shaking his head, said in his deepest, smokiest, most soldierly bass voice: "Tildy—you! You, Tildy, an officer, a gentleman, a man of decency and reason, a man of form and breeding, an educated man—by all Christendom's holy..." At this point Herr Tarangolian substituted the rest of Turturiuk's expression with a wave of the hand, in consideration of the ladies present. "You, Tildy, a major in one of the most renowned regiments of this country, which you have the honor of serving with your arms—you are bringing disgrace on your flag, disgrace on your comrades, on me, your commander, your fatherly superior, your oldest and only friend—you are disgracing me because you are disgracing yourself! You, whom I have fostered like a relative, defended against resentment and suspicion, you who have grown close to my heart like a mother's weakest child—by the seven church bells of..." Herr Tarangolian made another gesture that unleashed a torrent of laughter from Uncle Sergei. "You, Tildy, a serious man, go and make a fool and a buffoon of yourself in front of all the whoresons of the city, the layabouts and loafers, the procurers and drunks, the sodomites and flaneurs—you hit one of them in my home during a celebration in my honor, and you let another one entangle you in a quarrel and then you send two of your comrades-in-arms, two respectable young people who don't know any better, who don't dare contradict you—you send them to take part in your disgrace—in the disgrace of all of us! And what have we become because of you? Laughable. Or did you expect that this whoreson hack, this gigolo, this little piece of snot and filth would accept your challenge and duel with you? All you could have expected was that he would laugh in your face and mock you. Shame and disgrace, that's what you could have expected. And not just *your* shame and *your* disgrace, but the shame and disgrace of all your comrades, the entire regiment, the shame and disgrace of your colonel and superior officer, who has been like a father to you, who has taught you by his own example, who has led you and protected you!...Or have you forgotten, Tildy, that you were once our enemy? That you once shot at men who are now your comrades? That you killed many of them? If you have forgotten that, then very good, I commend you. But others haven't forgotten that you used to be with the Austrians. The ones who are just lurking in wait ready to pounce on me because I protected and promoted you, now they will have their opportunity. For forty-five years I have been carrying this uniform honorably just so that you can come along, you Austrian, and throw filth on it, and make a clown and a buffoon out of me! So that the idlers on the street can pull each other by the sleeve and say: Look there goes the colonel of the regiment whose officers break out into fisticuffs at his house and who want to have duels with us for no reason at all! Because what did he do to you, this gigolo? He told you that he knows your sister-in-law. That everyone knows her. He wasn't telling you anything but the truth. So you want to challenge a man to a duel because he tells you the truth, is that right? You want to play the knight to defend her honor, *Herr* Major? For your sister-in-law, when every rascal off the street knows that she's a harlot, and can prove it, too! Do you want to hear it from everyone, Herr Major Tildy, that your sister-in-law is a whore? All right, then hear it: your sister-in-law is a whore. There, now you've heard it, Herr Major! But that's not the end of the world, do you understand, you German fool, on the contrary: the world will go on like clockwork, because it's the pure truth that was said there, by all the... sacraments of the devil, the pure truth, and speaking the truth is doing a work that is pleasing to God. You want to shoot a man because he's doing work that is pleasing to God? Fine, Herr Major, so you can duel with me. I am screaming the truth into your face. More than that: I'm going to open this window here and shout out the truth, so that every bastard of a recruit can hear it. And if you want to, Herr Major, then you can have a shooting match with me! Your sister-in-law, do you hear, *is a whore*!"

Naturally Herr Tarangolian substituted a hand gesture for this particular expression as well. But the colonel did not, and before he could catch his breath after this denouement and continue his speech in a more dignified flow, possibly bringing it to a more conciliatory ending, Tildy had turned on his heel and left the room. One hour later, two men appeared as Tildy's seconds and delivered the major's challenge to Colonel Turturiuk.

Tildy had been downright crafty, as Herr Tarangolian assured us, in his choice of seconds. One was a major whose career on the general staff had been ruined by Turturiuk; the other was a lieutenant colonel who had his eye on succeeding Turturiuk as regimental commander. With that, the case became bitterly earnest.

Because it wasn't acceptable for an officer to deliver a direct challenge to his immediate superior, an honor court was convened, but this did not reach a verdict. Of course Tildy was temporarily dismissed from service, and it was clear that his career as an officer was over.

Uncle Sergei discoursed on the affair with cheerful expertise. He considered it a truly tragic conflict of two ethical principles: honor and obedience.

"Permit me to raise an objection," Herr Tarangolian replied. "Fundamentally you are correct. But with Tildy the matter is different: he should have gone out of his way to prevent the misunderstanding that his challenge was over the wounded honor of his sister-in-law. He could have demanded satisfaction from Năstase for, let us say, a more than insinuating remark about his wife. But not because the man had defamed his sister-in-law. Anyone who knows Colonel Turturiuk—and I appreciate his human, or I might say all-too-human, traits, but one should not overestimate his intellectual capacities on their account—should have expected him to miss this subtle difference in a chain of smug provocations. Tildy, too, should have been prepared for that. His otherwise superior calm, his model self-discipline, should have withstood the—admittedly harsh—test of Turturiuk's loutish behavior, for the clarity of the case."

"What is this clarity?" Uncle Sergei countered. "Is it not clear enough that he has to have shooting match, no matter who it is with? Take Nikolai Pavlovich Vinogradov..."

Herr Tarangolian parried with a smile. "Excuse me, dear sir, but this is a different situation, and a different epoch as well. What might suit a Lermontovian hero of nineteen years..."

"But Nikolai Pavlovich shot himself when he was twenty-one years, in 1911, and Lermontov, *je vous en prie*, was killed in 1841 in duel with Martinoff. In the Kavkaz. So what you are speaking about?"

Herr Tarangolian maintained his considerate smile. "I am speaking about Lermontov's bold young descendant. What might have redounded to the credit of a young officer of the guard in a golden era—and please believe me when I say that I mourn its passing as well, because I experienced it—what was a beautiful sign of courage and passion, in such a profaned time as ours can be read as an atavistic throwback in a mature man, a relapse into impulsive belligerence... My friend, don't forget: we live in Czernopol."

"*Eh bien, alors!* And you are not happy to find someone is here who is establishing honor and order?"

A shadow of old, wise melancholy fell across Herr Tarangolian's smile, narrowing it with a shade of irony. "I would welcome such an effort if I thought it might prove successful," he said. "Because, in this case, failure would be worse than not having attempted it at all. I understand exactly what you mean; I interpreted Tildy's actions in the same way. He is concerned with establishing order within the world he inhabits—the order that he loves so much because it is the only one he knows, the only one he knows exists... At least its appearance is essential. Maybe that would mean something, maybe that would be all that was needed, if the appearance of order were established, don't you think? If it is strong enough that someone is ready to risk his life on its behalf. I see that just as you do. He is a hussar, this strange Nikolaus Tildy. He loves bravery, style, and élan, it's in his blood. To ride out in single combat against the slovenliness of a city, of a country—that is truly a deed for hussars—beautiful and mad. But permit me to say that he did not handle it skillfully. By allowing this mix-up, by letting people think he was demanding satisfaction on behalf of his sister-in-law, by challenging his commander expressly on her account, makes the whole case a farce. With all due respect for chivalry, dueling on behalf of Madame Lyubanarov is more than quixotic: it is the act of a clown. Above all, and what strikes me as even more important, he is no longer championing a pure cause. We should not underestimate the mystical requirements of heroism—or should one simply call this an act of martyrdom? Tildy knows that he is no longer representing a pure cause. You understand me, yes? It is no longer a pure cause, and therefore he will not succeed in defending it with victory. And he knows that. He is no longer setting forth with the beautiful but painful knowledge of the hero who is bound to perish, but with a bad conscience, and therefore he is at fault. For me that is reason enough to declare him the loser. If in my capacity as prefect of this province I should have to decide for or against Tildy—I'm speaking very hypothetically, because in reality this could never occur, since these things are completely outside my sphere of influence—even so, assuming it did come to that, I can say right now without the slightest hesitation that I would decide against Tildy, that I would let him fall. And not out of a sense of justice so much as just to be on the safe side—sheer superstition, if you will. Or else belief—or whatever you choose to call it."

These words elicited an awkward general silence that was finally broken by our mother. She said: "I wrote Aida about it. The poor child follows our lives here with such interest; she wants to know everything that's happening. Perhaps you would be curious to read what she thinks about it."

She handed the prefect a letter. Herr Tarangolian took it with his fingertips like a rose petal, pulled it close to his face as if he intended to kiss the paper, knitted his eyes and scanned the lines while moving the letter farther and farther away, until it was finally at arm's length.

"You are wearing glasses when you read?" asked Uncle Sergei, curious.

"Not at all, not in the least, my vision is perfect," muttered Herr Tarangolian with the quick, defensive tone of someone embarrassed. "Although when I am moved—please forgive me but the fate of your dear sister touches my heart so much..."

Our mother took back the letter. "Here, Aida just wrote a couple lines about the matter: 'I find Major Tildy's conduct exceptionally beautiful and noble. Precisely because he chooses to stand up for L. shows him as a man of chivalrous sensibility, of the sort that seems to be extinct in this new world. Standing up for those who are lost is Christian in the noblest way. I admire Tildy as one of the last men under whose protection women can still feel secure.'"

"That is very deeply felt, and very feminine," said Herr Tarangolian, after a brief moment of emotion. "Very much Aida with her tender sensibilities. May I ask if she mentions how she is doing?"

"Only two sentences at the end of the letter: 'I am suffering indescribable pain. Pray for me!'"

Herr Tarangolian, shaken, went silent. "If only we could live our lives all over again from the beginning," he then said. He got up, came over to us children and stroked our heads. "You, in whom our wasted hopes are resurrected," he said, full of melancholy. He kissed our mother's hand and left with an elegiac wave.

Uncle Sergei played with the silk tassel of the everlasting match from his cigarette case. "*Eh bien*, a little game of piquet, *ma chère cousine*?" he asked Aunt Paulette, Mama's younger sister.

"You would be well advised to take stock of yourself," said Aunt Paulette, who flirted with him in a familial, teasing way.

"Is it really necessary for the children to be present after we have eaten?" asked our father, irritated.

"Now that Miss Rappaport is no longer with us there's hardly any alternative. After all, they can't simply be sent onto the street."

"As if that would make any difference," our father said, getting up to leave as well.

Aunt Paulette, who was twenty-one and progressive and wore her hair short, leaned so far back in her chair that her neck rested on the back, exposing the beautiful curve of her white throat. "Give me a cigarette, Sergei. And if you want, I'll play with you, but rummy, not piquet. Since we're all having such a good time... Incidentally, what is it that Madame Tildy takes? Morphine or cocaine?"

"Presumably both, my dear," said Uncle Sergei softly. "A very interesting lady."

"Presumably we should pray for Tildy as well," said Aunt Paulette, blowing her cigarette smoke up toward the ceiling. Then, with a lethargic look to the side: "But you have to shuffle the cards well and let me cut the deck three times. Otherwise I won't play with you."

A few days later, Herr Tarangolian brought the latest sensation: the honor court had been dissolved. Tildy had been ordered to report to the division commander.

Thanks to his remarkably competent sources of information, who apparently had their eyes and ears at every keyhole in town, the prefect knew the content of this conversation and did not hesitate to pass it on to us, word for word.

He began by describing General Petrescu in a few strokes, as a highly qualified, albeit very vain man, one of the youngest generals of the army, with shadowy political ambitions, a sophisticated demeanor, and the oratorical gifts of a Roman lawyer.

Petrescu's nimble ability to empathize was evident in the manner he received Tildy, who, without realizing or intending it, had done the infantry officer a great service, since the breaking scandal gave him the chance he had long been waiting for to "give that stable of studhorses a good grooming." The general chose to hold the interview informally; he approached Tildy, shook his hand, and with polished nonchalance offered Tildy one of the chairs that faced his leather-topped desk. In order to fetch a small box of cigars and a bottle of cognac he stepped upstage to the little cupboard where he kept these gentlemanly fortifications, and this maneuver allowed him to make a very effective entrance as he commenced his speech:

"Let me just say, Tildy, that I am very glad to have an occasion to meet you, regardless of the circumstances. Your outstanding reputation as an officer has made this a long-standing wish of mine. Nor am I merely paying you a compliment. In fact, I should add that I have another motivation as well. The incidents that led me to request your presence, incidents which are certainly regrettable but by no means earth-shaking, and which we will have sorted out in no time, since I'm certain we share the same opinion—these events will inevitably bring the issue of your nationality into the debate. I'd just like to say that I have the greatest possible respect for men like you, who have demonstrated enormous political understanding by placing their faith in our new government, which is both more stable and more just than its predecessor—men who may speak a different mother tongue than the people after whom our new country is named, but whose allegiance to our new state is no less steadfast, because they love the land of their birth and the people among whom they were raised. Such chosen devotion is evidence of a civic virtue that I respect far more than the chauvinist nationalism of those who maintain that merely because streets and currency have been renamed, or because police regulations, tax acts, and public warning signs have been translated into their language, they then have the right to bash away at their fellow citizens of different ethnicities. I confess quite plainly that I don't know what to make of the concept of a state built on minorities, unless we examine the question qualitatively and not quantitatively, and in my opinion the single deciding factor should be the individual commitment to upholding the state. All that by way of introduction. Please, help yourself if you'd like a cognac. The glasses are lady-sized, but as your commanding officer I order you not to draw any conclusions from that."

Shallow though it was, one would have expected Tildy to acknowledge this joke, which was clearly made with the good intention of keeping the atmosphere as casual as possible. But nothing of the sort happened. The general, meanwhile, showed great aplomb in covering up the gentle irritation he felt when he realized—unexpectedly but perhaps insightfully—how ineffective his charm was proving. With a practiced voice, whose melodious tone was ready to swell to its forensic fullness, he said:

"Let's get down to business, Tildy. The fact that I approve of your conduct—down to one or two formal errors, or let's be frank about it, clumsy mistakes—I hardly need to tell you. It is our task to bring esteem and respect to the army of this young state, from within as well as from without. It is completely natural that an officer should defend his family's reputation with a deadly determination. In other words: it should be absolutely clear that I am grateful to you for providing such an example to your comrades-in-arms. But as I mentioned: in your very understandable agitation, you managed to commit one or two clumsy mistakes. First: you should have realized that Năstase would not accept your challenge—Colonel Turturiuk is absolutely right on that account. I don't need to lecture you that not just anyone may be deemed worthy of crossing arms with an officer of our army. Even so, perhaps Năstase could be given the benefit of the doubt: he comes from a respected family, is educated, has a certain social polish. But he is young—a flaw I would happily share with him, incidentally..."

Tildy's countenance remained unchanged. The general waited a few seconds in vain for a kind remark, then brought the fingertips of his hands together—he had seated himself in an armchair across from Tildy—and went on, a little dampened, with his extremely well-turned speech:

"You should have taken this youth into account, Tildy. You should not have given Năstase the possibility of treating a challenge to a pistol duel as a trifle. You should have castigated him on the spot. Then it would have been up to him to challenge you. Had he not done so he would have passed judgment on himself. You might object that it would be unseemly to hit someone in the house of your superior. But you yourself, Tildy, rendered this argument invalid by slapping Alexianu, who was in no way involved. So up to that moment the case was a complete muddle. What saved it—and you see how open I am being with you—was your challenge to the colonel. I'm sure you realize that you will have to bear the consequences of such an action. I will take pains that they don't exceed the bounds of the routine disciplinary actions. But only because I am in complete agreement with you that this is a question of principle. The honor of an officer is sacrosanct. In that regard I am completely on your side. I will not hesitate to support you in front of all authorities including the highest. Just as a matter of principle, you understand. That is why I ordered the honor court to be dissolved for the time being. It will be reconvened at the appropriate time in a different form and given greater powers. At that time all sorts of items will be brought to the table. Until then you are to hold yourself ready. Once again: I find your conduct not in the least reprehensible, apart from the ineptitude at the beginning. As I said, it's a matter of principle. Because the idea that you would feel your honor had been wounded..." The general smiled. "*Entre nous*, Tildy—for that I consider you too smart, too superior. Because it would be a very strange place indeed to keep your honor hidden—"

At this point Herr Tarangolian interrupted his report and said that it would be impossible for him to repeat the general's joke. We children were sent out under some pretext or another.

But we soon found out what the general had said. Of course it cost my sister Tanya a golden heart with a Madonna medallion, which she used to bribe Uncle Sergei. But we had long gotten used to slipping him little pieces of jewelry, which we would then claim to have lost, and at times, too, the contents of our piggy banks, so that he could play his cards, and in this case we would have been ready to give up much more to hear the words that sealed our hussar's fate.

And so we heard them. And we also heard what followed.

The general said: "It would be a very strange place indeed to keep your honor hidden, Major Tildy—*between the legs of your sister-in-law.*"

At that, Tildy jumped up, grabbed his shako and gloves, clicked his heels together and left the room without a word.

One hour later his challenge was delivered to General Petrescu.

That same afternoon Tildy was arrested and placed under observation at the municipal asylum for the insane.

10

Birds That Dwell Above Cities: The Story of Old Paşcanu

OF ALL the birds that dwell above cities, pigeons are the serious patricians. They are linked to the Baroque, which opened and softened the craggy, narrow world of gables to provide a clifflike homeland, full of accommodating hollow nesting places and hideouts, as well as platforms, ramps, and stages where they can collect, cuddle, and strut with pigeonly self-importance. Because unlike the shy and furtive tree dwellers of the parks and gardens, who whoosh back and forth to create an abstract tapestry, as if weaving the bare wintry branches into the green leaves; unlike the tireless gulls of the ports, who glide up and down in waves that mimic the surface of the restless sea, pigeons are steady and gregarious, they like a show of fussiness, and move sprightly and coquettishly, their bodies quivering like a cluster of lilacs, their nimble feet pattering, and their small heads always bent in a tender curve.

Swallows and falcons belong to Gothic towers, creatures of a different sphere, of reverie, natives of heaven for whom diving through the boundless sky is pure ardor translated into movement. Jackdaws are the denizens of abandoned buildings, crumbling walls, and barren, defoliated treetops—oddball artists of flight, playful bohemians of the air—while the starlings form a quarrelsome proletariat that goes whirring off the rooftop gutters to scrap over a bit of straw lying in the dust. Pigeons alone display a cultured, bourgeois behavior, showing grace and circumspection in a firmly ordered world, politely stepping aside for you on the squares, where they have descended in swarms, trickling over each other, nodding their heads, cooing as they bow deeply to one another; and the slightly coarse clapping of their wings carries them to the stony saints gesticulating on the cornices, breathing gentle life into their isolation.

The pigeons above Czernopol were wild and fast: they flitted high overhead as if sweeping past inhospitable territory, in arrow-straight paths, from the range of hills along the Volodiak to the scattered oak groves of the great steppe across the river. Only a few would from time to time drop to perch in the crowns of old beeches and poplars that lined the main roads out of town, just for a brief rest. You seldom saw them by day, except when they cut across the pale, early-morning sky, or just before evening, when the heavens turned the color of their plumage, without smoke, and a first star appeared, magically, as if announced by their flight.

We always treated that first star as a mystery, a deeply mystical occurrence. We could never pin down the moment it actually emerged, in a sky that was the same sky that had passed through the day, but had taken a giant step back, so that it was now deeper by a whole heaven's breadth, and open to newer depths beyond. This star that appeared without warning twinkled with the magic of something placed in the world complete and fully formed; it was simply there, and required no becoming. And even if we told ourselves that we could discern these new reaches only because our eyes had acquired a fixed point with which to gauge the distance, the actual appearance of that star would forever remain a mystery of creation. Beyond all scientific explanations, we realized that all new creation necessarily enlarges and enriches our own world by bringing new dimensions.

For Czernopol it was the mark of a daily deliverance: a release from itself. The city awoke from its ruthless, overpowering reality, which was as glaring as the day, and which nothing could cancel except the dying day itself. The earlier waking state, so close to reality, now seemed like a daze that slowly faded, layer after layer, with every veil that evening lowered onto the streets.

Because the reality of Czernopol was the street—those wide roads that are life's thoroughfares, roads that stretch across the boundless countryside and do not end with the death of the wayfarer. It was thanks to these roads that the city had come into existence, having arisen at one of their intersections as a stowing place for those without a homeland, a collection point for those without a home—pulsing with restlessness, spurred by a consuming desire for a vague beyond, for something further, pervaded with the yeasty ferment of discontent. At the same time it was naked and unadorned in its need, burdened with hardship, with the compassionless severity of those who know life, for whom everything is fleeting, every trouble a mere phantom, and all sympathy is rendered invalid by the knowledge that all pain will pass.

Unlike in other cities, then, where life proceeds agreeably on the streets by day, and only shows its cruel and desperate side at night, and even then keeps it confined to secret niches and lairs that become visible when its veins are emptied, like rats' nests in drained sewers—unlike in these other cities, the day in Czernopol bore witness to all kinds of reality. Crass, unembellished life, the midday glare, and the street itself were one and the same in Czernopol: they were inseparable. Everything, from birth to death, took place in the open as if in the palm of a hand. Thus, by day the streets of Czernopol were the site of sheer meanness, brutal selfishness, shameless depravity. People laughed, cried, loved, robbed, and thrashed each other at the markets, coupled behind fences, died in the gutter. Purse-snatchers stole the last few coins off poor beggars; murderers fled from their pursuers; obscenities spouted from the lips of young girls.

And people loved the day and its brash reality. In Czernopol nothing remained unsaid. Nothing was concealed; nothing allowed itself to be concealed. No pretense was admitted, no keeping-up of appearances, no glossing over, no pretext was valid, no deception went undetected. Everything was left mercilessly to its own devices; nothing relied on anything else, and nothing had acquired a healthy distance. All the devices that help us imagine the dark spaces we inhabit as richer than they are—deception, delusion, embellishment—were banned from the glaring light of day. Foolishness was nothing but foolishness, intoxication was only drunkenness, despair was a door that led nowhere.

Nevertheless, the faces of the people in Czernopol were by no means banal. Their alertness was magnified to an expression of highest intelligence; it came beaming out of them as a dry, bright zeal—in their fervent, unerring gaze, in their delight of exposing things and reducing them to their proper measure—in other words, in their passion for wit, and it was this passion that gave free rein to all the others. The penchant for bluntness found its full, uninhibited expression. People laughed when a coachman took his whip to a blind man who happened to step in the way of his droshky; they laughed about a Jew who was howling because he'd been cheated out of a few coins; they laughed about a passing drunk bellowing obscene songs, while next to him a dog that had been hit by a vehicle kept spinning around his lame rear end, slobbering with pain and biting himself blindly in the flank. The children of the street laughed with the raw, tinny laugh of meanness; their agile, thieving eyes always on the lookout for new cause, and nothing escaped them, no misunderstanding and no confusion, neither torment nor terror, vice nor crime—nothing that was painful, and certainly nothing grotesque, because that was always close at hand for everyone.

Evening descended over all of that, bringing freedom and release, like the shade of a soothing hand. As its light dispersed, reality dispersed as well, gently felled: what was rude softened, what was close moved away, what was immediate became mediated and indirect. The dimension that that first star acquired for the world was that of heaven—the insight into our own extreme forlornness. The violet blue of the shadows transformed the anxiety of the lonely into another type of solitude. Those who had never escaped themselves now fell back, and by withdrawing they gained the world in its boundlessness. As the earth gradually turned from the sun, they discovered the other side of the planet, and found a place for themselves in its visibly increasing detachment. A sense of yearning permeated their glances and gestures, followed by a kind of tenderness—the tenderness that can only come from the anguish over what can never be reached or realized, and which therefore tastes so much like sorrow. It burst out in songs sung in a minor key, sought refuge in wondrous stories, shrank into amorous whispering. It made people restless, driving them on a search with no particular object or definite goal—and so the evening promenade was more than idle strolling, it was a ritual, in which the restiveness of the lost souls abated, when the raucous mood of a barnyard wedding mixed with the Maytime Devotion of the Blessed Mother.

Night in Czernopol was also beautiful, although the moonlight found no cathedrals or palaces it could infuse with reverie and transform into the charnel architecture of exquisite dreams, and only gave a shabby gleam as it hit the stepped tin roofs that rose from the area around the train station and up the steep escarpment by the Volodiak. At the top of the hill its merciless beams fell on the ugly tenements, cutting their banal silhouette out of the horizon, and exposing the battlements of the Metropolitan's Residence as the fakes they were. Then it lifted the bulbous dome of the synagogue from out of the jumble of gabled and flat-topped boxes, and, a few streets further on, the toy stone towers of the Catholic Herz-Jesu Church and St. Parachiva, which towered over the synagogue in stark pathos. The moonlight dripped down the firewalls at the Ringplatz without having any poetic effect on their plainness; it collected in a milky puddle on the filthy paved esplanade in front of the Rathaus; it cast the finely etched shadow of the basilica of St. Miron across the mangy, enclosed square of grass; and finally faded away behind the complex of provincial government buildings and the flat temple of the officers' casino, darkening into the olive tone of tarnished silver in the Volksgarten as it mingled with the foliage that was swaying in the night wind.

And yet it was as if the vast surrounding countryside had taken a blot of shame compassionately into its lap. The black forests of the Volodiak hills seemed to surge closer, having sent narrow spits and isolated islands into the wasteland of stone, tin, and mortar, each tree fanning out into the night as though by some great accord, a chalice of living darkness rich in mystery. The ring of fields closed more tightly around the town, drowning its bare ugliness in their richness, and the same wind that combed the silver ears of grain far away, carried off the gutter-like stench from the Jewish courtyards, mixing the biting odors of dishwater, rotten fish, and rancid sunflower oil, of garlic, mare's urine, and cat feces with the aroma of earth, hay, and fir resin. Puddles that by day were as brown and foamy as beer glistened like ponds, like pieces of heaven accepted into the earth, and the enormous stillness of the star-studded night lay over Czernopol—punctuated by crickets, shrouded by the sound of frogs, as soothing as a mother's lullaby, unbroken except for the occasional clatter of hooves of a droshky hack driven to exhaustion, or by the distant, forlorn howl of moonstruck dogs, baying in dismal futility.

At times like that mothers would occasionally turn to their unruly children, if they refused to go to sleep, and frighten them into silence by raising their fingers to their lips and saying: "Shhh! You hear those hooves rattling? That's old Paşcanu—and he'll come and get you if you don't stop crying."

Because at night was when Tamara Tildy's father used to set out in his old-fashioned, heavy coach, pulled by two colossal horses, to visit the mausoleum of his two wives in the little woods of Horecea.

Only little is known about the early history of the city of Czernopol. A half-day's march north, on one of the Volodiak hills, lay the ruins of an old watchtower, known as the "Zitzena Castle." According to local folklore, the name came from when the Turks destroyed the fortress. A child had been stolen and placed in the forest: it was hungry and cried for its mother's breast: "*Zitze! Zitze!*" In her desperate search the mother is said to have heard her child, and as she pressed forward, offering the source of nourishment, she kept calling out "*Na! Na!*"—which in Tescovina means, more or less, "Here you go, have at it!"—but she never found her little darling.

The legend proves little except the unreliability of folklore as a source for historical research. And as interesting as it may be to know which *voivode* had the watchtower erected, whether the Poles, the Hungarians, or the Turks themselves—what is certain is that the city of Czernopol was no more than a few hundred years old, and probably entered European consciousness far sooner owing to its fondness for anecdotes than on account of any historical significance.

The Tescovina Germans enjoyed taking group hikes to the ruins of Zitzena for their solstice celebrations and similar folkloric occasions. The Turnvater Jahn Athletic Club, the German Men's Chorus, and the German Women's Chorus would set out with their flags and beer wagons, merrily singing their way through the Ruthenian suburb at Kalitschankabach, despite the fact they always encountered a few heroes of the Romanian Mircea Doboş sports association or the Junimea fraternity who saw fit to spoil their innocent joy, and which usually led to lusty fistfights. The representative of the German minority, a certain Professor Dr. Hodelein, whose name with its unfortunate overtones the nationalistic circle around Professor Feuer jokingly romanized as "Testiculescu" because of his alacrity in accommodating the new sovereigns, would then have occasion to appear before Herr Tarangolian and submit a formal complaint.

These fights usually occurred near a pub, known to be the place where Săndrel Paşcanu first appeared among men. Widow Morar told the story best: how the pub maid had gone to the well and come back screaming, because evidently a bear or, even worse, a forest spirit known as a *djuglan* was bending over the wooden bucket to drink from it; how a few brave men had gone out, and how they, too, came back running into the house, afraid, because the giant had turned around as they approached, and he had been *without a face*—a black head without mouth or eyes, only a white beak jutting out. Then the presumed *djuglan* had raised its hands, parting its long black hair, which had fallen over his face while drinking, shoving the two halves aside like curtains, revealing a mouth after all, and a pair of glowing black, but actually gentle, eyes, and what they had thought was a beak was really his nose. They invited him to eat, and he stayed. He was young and strong as a bear and useful around the pub. But one day he up and left, to join the soldiers fighting the Turks, in the last of those wars, when the Ottomans were beaten and lost the fortress at Plevna and wound up leaving the country, or perhaps he had joined the robbers; in any case, when he returned he was a rich man and had married a princess.

If you drew a straight line from that pub across the city of Czernopol—something like the flight of a wild pigeon—directly on the other side of town you would come to a small oak forest called Horecea, where Paşcanu had built a mausoleum for his two wives, modeled after the Taj Mahal. The house where Paşcanu lived lay almost exactly on this line as well.

Later, once we had finally outgrown full-time supervision, and were occasionally able to roam through the city, we often visited this house, to see if we might catch a glimpse of something behind the windows or in the yard, some particular feature of the environment where some of the most exciting events of our childhood had taken place. It was on a crooked old little street, in the neighborhood around the so-called Turkish fountain—we had no way of knowing whether it really dated from the time of the Turkish occupation or not; things in Czernopol rapidly acquired the patina of great age. The buildings of that neighborhood had gabled fronts that faced the street, in the old-fashioned way, with a wing off to the side for stalls, just like a farmhouse. The large gates, which usually had an entrance door cut in, were made of mighty planks and covered with wood-shingle roofs. They were covered with layers of paper an inch thick: movie posters, advertisements for Passover matzoh, death announcements, slates of candidates of various parties, and wanted posters—all scribbled over with obscenities. The street descended with the escarpment; powerful streams of sewage flowed down the gutters of the bumpy cobblestone, which was only visible during the spring thaw and was otherwise covered with coarse, ankle-deep mud or else floury dust. The back boundaries of the yards ran alongside a beautiful old Jewish cemetery where birch trees shaded the slanting gravestones. We were told that most of the surrounding buildings—and especially the former stables that had been remodeled for human habitation but were in great disrepair—housed the rooms used by the neighborhood streetwalkers. Large feral cats lurked in every corner, coupling every night with loud passion, multiplying without restraint. A single lantern, completely at the mercy of the street urchins and their throwing-stones, cast a dreary light lengthwise down the ridge of the street, which curved off into the thick darkness on either side. Looking the other way you could see the five onion domes of St. Parachiva towering over the rooftops, a ridiculously atrocious construction of brightly glazed brickwork.

Paşcanu's house was larger and more solid than the ones surrounding it, and furnished with slate tiles rather than the usual tin. An ancient acacia stood in the courtyard, practically devoid of leaves. In no way did this building resemble how we imagined it ought to look—as the town house of the richest man in the province and the husband of a Princess Sturdza. The front wall had lost all its stucco except for bits around the first window, and the bare bricks gave a desolate impression indeed. In the Austrian times the gatehouse had contained a kiosk that sold tobacco, stamps, and salt from the state monopoly; the wooden shutters still bore the weathered remains of the once black-and-gold paint, in slanting stripes like on a sentry's hut. In the early 1880s this house may very well have seemed the epitome of patrician dignity and well-established tradition, at least to an adventuresome shepherd boy who had only recently emerged from the forests; the black-and-gold-striped kiosk in particular must have made an impression on him, as an institution of the state, so to speak. Incidentally, Princess Sturdza never lived there, though it was rumored that a famous Titian, a painting worth millions, which Săndrel Paşcanu had bought for her, was still hanging in the house.

Because by the time Paşcanu married the Princess Sturdza, he already owned several other houses, in the city as well as in the country, including a hunting lodge in his huge forests, where princes of royal blood had been his guests. But even at the height of his grandeur he lived in the house by the old Turkish fountain. He clung with great tenacity to that first house, which he had acquired soon after his return from the siege of Plevna, paying for it with shiny Turkish gold coins—coins of shadowy provenance, from uncovered treasure perhaps, or else from a robbery—the rumors about it abounded. And, indeed, the former owner of the house was found a little later, murdered and robbed. And while things like that were not exactly rare in Czernopol, and there was certainly never a shortage of suspects, the crime was popularly attributed to the young new arrival, though nothing could ever be proven against him.

In any event: he stayed, and multiplied his wealth—whatever its origin—by a fantastic degree. No one knew for sure exactly what business dealings he pursued in his early days—and, to some extent, in later life as well—and on that subject the rumor mill was equally active. The fact is that he could never write more than his name. In later years he would have the paper read to him by his coachman, a *scopit,* or member of a Russian religious sect that required men to undergo castration after producing two children in marriage. Săndrel Paşcanu had his business partners read his contracts out loud and immediately memorized the wording down to the tiniest detail.

His main business was lumber. The egregious purchase of entire forests, scandalous con acts, bribes, and misappropriations filled entire annals, from which Herr Tarangolian was able to recite the most amusing entries. Because anything Săndrel Paşcanu undertook had the character of a coup—and often of a caper as well. And for the longest time he enjoyed a fabulous success. Even one of his middlemen came into a sizable—and, as it turned out, more stable—fortune, and in 1916 was raised to the landed Austrian gentry: Baronet Hirsh Leib von Merores—people later spoke of the family's Spanish heritage.

The stories about his two wives, however, were far more exciting and eerily romantic: the legitimate spouse, the born Princess Sturdza, and his mistress, the beautiful peasant girl Ioana Ciornei. He had lived with both at once, and rumor had it that they died at the same time—that is to say, he killed them, or they killed each other. The motive was said to be a fabulous diamond, a single stone of unusual size and unique cut: Săndrel Paşcanu was said to have presented it to the princess the morning after their wedding night, and later to have taken it away to give to Ciornei on a similar, though less legitimate, occasion. Supposedly the two women, whom he forced to live in the same house, battled each other fiercely, and at the center of their conflict was the stone, which became a kind of a symbol, a fetish for conjuring the love of Săndrel Paşcanu.

People said that they conducted their feud with the strangest weapons. For instance, Ioana Ciornei couldn't withstand the princess's gaze and always wore a veil whenever the latter was present, so that Princess Sturdza would lie in wait, ready to reveal her eyes and force Ciornei to her knees and make her give up the stone. Meanwhile, the princess had a very delicate sense of hearing, and couldn't bear her rival's voice: so once the princess had recovered the diamond through the power of her princely gaze, Ciornei would sing peasant songs day in and day out, both happy and sad, until the princess was driven to the point of insanity and would hurl the stone at her rival's feet. In the end Paşcanu is said to have killed them both, or else they killed themselves, their hands so firmly locked onto the diamond that they had to be buried in one coffin.

Of course that was sheer fantasy. After all, we had our friend Widow Morar to thank for most of the stories.

What was true, however, was that both of Săndrel Paşcanu's wives lay buried next to each other in the little forest of Horecea. The oak grove was about a half hour's wagonride out of town and belonged to a small monastery; Paşcanu's generous donations had made the monks eager to do his bidding, and they watched over the grave of his wives like a holy shrine. Apart from that, he was accompanied on his nightly visits by his elephant-sized coachman, who despite his mutilation, which was generally understood to have a mollifying effect, was supposedly as mean and cunning as a buffalo gone wild.

We did manage to visit the mausoleum several times, though always during the day, and without being able to see whatever fantastic things were happening behind the thick tangle of barbed wire. The structure was indeed a detailed reproduction of the Taj Mahal, except for the fact it was made of the cheapest limestone and covered with plaster that had long since yellowed and partially peeled off. It was also very much scaled down in size, so the whole thing looked pretty hideous. The long reflecting pool, where we expected to see lotus flowers, was brimming with frogs and toads.

But perhaps it looked different by moonlight. Presumably the air of danger exuded by the castrated coachman prowling about while his master paid his devotions to the two coffins gave it a bizarre charm. And just as children everywhere challenge each other to venture into the cemetery at midnight, we would say: "I dare you to go to the Taj Mahal at night, to see what old Paşcanu is up to."

People said he couldn't sleep because of a terrible conscience, that that was what drove him to the coffins of his two loves, and that in his remorse he kept buying new jewels to present to the dead women, hoping for the forgiveness they could no longer grant him. The coffins were supposed to be completely covered with the most expensive gems.

But people also said he skulked around the crypt at night because he wanted his huge diamond back, and that every night he was tempted to open the coffins, but he was always held back by the horror he felt at the sight of the crypt.

Both tales were probably simply made up. But that didn't stop Săndrel Paşcanu from using the first one to his advantage, to give his last coup the aura of romantic extravagance—and thus credibility: he had some middlemen purchase a gem that was worth a fortune, then let out that he was looking for the perfect match, no matter what the price. After that, he tried to sell the same stone to the first seller, through intermediaries, for two or three times the original price.

Old Paşcanu hadn't realized that the trick was one of countless primitive scams known to every jeweler of any stature. After that he tried to dupe his middlemen—and wound up being robbed himself in the most ignominious way. It cost him all that was left of his fortune—and his life.

This all happened at the same time as the events I have already described, shortly after Major Tildy was sent to have his mental state examined at the municipal asylum.

Later people said: "And one fine night old Paşcanu rode out to his two wives for the last time." And nobody knew that it was true...

Perhaps the moon was out. Perhaps the crickets were chirping their silvery notes all across the fields and meadows of the vast countryside. Perhaps the croaking of myriad frogs in the cattails around the pools and ponds and muddy lagoons of the Volodiak hung like a veil in the starry stillness. No one paid attention to that. That last night swallowed his secret, and never surrendered it.

No one will ever find out what he really did that night, or all the nights before, in front of the coffins of his dead wives.

Perhaps when he came back there was only one star left in the pale sky—the one the wild pigeons had announced, and which they hurried after when it suddenly went out, proving themselves its loyal messengers, always at the ready.

And the colossal horses in front of Paşcanu's old-fashioned, swaying coach stamped their great hooves, raising the dust on the country road that led to the little forest of Horecea and far beyond until it lost itself in the immeasurable expanse of the countryside. What had been a pale-yellow ribbon of moonlight just a little while before, banded by black stripes from the hard shadows of the poplars, was now a melancholy trail in the morning twilight, urging the wanderer to shoulder his bundle and move on, toward that which can never be reached. A black box, framed by the silhouette of the poplars: this is how the old coach looked, coming down this road, thumping onto the planks of the ferry, which was pulled by a wire cable which workers from Frost's Steam Mill had set across the muddy water of the Volodiak arm. The colossal horses snorted down at the water, while the mammoth *scopit* seemed to sleep on his box, his head covered with a narrow-brimmed Russian cap. The water gurgled past the rusty iron drums beneath the planking, and the cable sang quietly. The ferry creaked to a landing on the opposite shore, and while the sleepy sawmill workers patiently waited in the gravel on the bank, Paşcanu's horses clattered up the escarpment and trotted hard and heavy over the wretched cobblestones of the Wassergasse, up toward the town.

On the outskirts of the city, the moonstruck dogs had stopped their baying. Columns of small farmers' carts rattled monotonously on their way to market. In the cellar bakeries of the Jewish quarter, which stretched over five-sevenths of the built-up area of Czernopol, muscular journeymen shoved long peels loaded with kosher rolls, braided challahs, and *kolatschen* pastries into heated ovens, causing the rats to flee into the rear courtyards, where snarling cats waited for them, their backs arched over the remains of fish, and where the whining and bawling of little children mixed with the sad singsong of their mothers and the groaning of their grandmothers and the abysmal coughing of the grandfathers to form a symphony from the dormitory at Saint Bridget's hospice, which was an antechamber of hell.

In front of the Trocadero, on Iancu Topor Avenue, a pack of

drunken students gathered, then went rampaging along the park past the provincial government offices, down to the main street, to paint swastikas on the warehouse belonging to Usher Brill. In the garage of the house belonging to the Baronet von Merores, the chauffeur began washing the Chrysler. Further on, beyond the Volksgarten, the buglers blew reveille on the grounds of the cavalry barracks. In their stalls, the horses snorted and ground their teeth, chains clanked, buckets rattled, and from the windows of the troops' quarters could be heard sergeants bellowing at their men, shooing the sleepy soldiers out of the stuffy, sweaty rooms, and sending them pattering into the corridors like a herd of groggy sheep. In the large loop beside the sheds, the first streetcar howled.

At the Bahnhofstrasse, the old-fashioned coach had to cross the streetcar tracks. Perhaps the sleepy *scopit* reined in his team with a loud curse, because a man was walking along the rails, his cane riding inside the groove that was leading him forward, his head aloft like that of a blind man, mumbling Latin odes to himself, occasionally laughing or launching into a song.

It was Professor Lyubanarov, coming home from a long night in the seedy dives around the train station.

The rampaging students recognized him. They danced around him a while, hooting and jeering, without his even noticing. Then they ran ahead to the Ringplatz and reset the switch at the tram stop. They roared with delight when they saw him switch tracks, with all the confidence of a sleepwalker, then let him move on in peace, turning their attention instead to the aurochs of Tescovina, which with lowered horns was trampling the breast of the eagle of the Dual Monarchy. One of the students climbed onto the primal bull, straddling its neck to work his way up to the horns, from where he pissed down onto the pavement of the esplanade in a high splashing arch. Day was breaking over Czernopol.

The coach with the faded violet silk repp curtains and the mice-infested upholstery rattled onto the bend of the narrow street at the Turkish Fountain and pulled to a stop at its crest. The coachman swung his rippling castrated corpulence off the high box and opened the gate with a massive key. Then he led the giant horses by the snaffle into the courtyard. The gate was immediately shut; a heavy bolt slid into place. Săndrel Paşcanu was alone in his home, with his mean castrated servant, his solitude, his senile pride, and his Titian.

II

On the Myth of Childhood: Madame Aritonovich's Institut d'Éducation; Blanche Schlesinger and Solly Brill

WHENEVER in later years we thought back on our childhood, painfully recalling its richness and dignity, what we had retained from our youth struck us as an inheritance acquired by devious means. It had so little to do with what we had become that we at times felt tempted to consider it the "literary existence" Herr Tarangolian had dutifully warned us against. The images from those days seem as far-removed as the untold fairy tales and legends that filled it with such wonders. Just like these stories, our childhood may be told and may even come to life in the telling, although the unmistakable quality of its reality cannot be reproduced. And even if this reality is awakened inside us for a few moments, in all its layered complexity, and speaks to us so directly and urgently that it causes us to shudder, what we then hear doesn't seem entirely our own, but rather the voice of the past itself, lamenting that which is lost, and which continues to dwindle into oblivion, with us and around us, with every passing hour.

"We are like the housing of an hourglass," Herr Tarangolian used to say, when he felt obliged to admit that his memory was beginning to deteriorate with age. "Our consciousness is its narrow waist, unable to hold on to what passes through. Only the distant filling spaces cast back a vague reflection. To perceive something in a way it won't be forgotten we have to become aware of its presence without looking at it. You have to look past something in order to see it in full."

And indeed: at times we encounter something that happens to correspond to one of those essential images we carry inside us, like iridescent refraction in old glass, so that it lights up within us, for just a heartbeat, setting off a flash of magical splendor, which is as fleeting as an echo and fully out of our control. For we cannot simply conjure at will its momentary shine in all the fullness of being perceived—the unity of color, smell, sound, and touch that absorbs all these characteristics and transmutes them into a single essential core. We are left to the mercy of a moment that resembles the moment when it first crossed the periphery of our field of vision, when we were focused on something else entirely.

This powerlessness of our will to command our perception, the discrepancy between what we believe we experience and what we truly experience, makes it difficult for us to examine our past for any fractures that could reveal to us when and how we lost our supposed paradises. Memory occasionally descends upon us with the weight of authenticity, only to vanish into the shadows, inclining us to question the world in which we have lost ourselves, since we began fobbing off our ardent yearning with cheap secondhand goods. As if we ever had any other choice! And so later on we sometimes feel tempted to attribute the loss of our blissful, dream-bound childhood to certain events, which back then—as the story of Tildy I am relating here—affected us directly. We held Czernopol accountable for awakening us to the crude banality of the world, which from then on ceased to fill us with any longing. But there was more than just one error to that logic.

Certainly our yearning was inspired by our abundant inexperience, and it was this hunger for the world that sharpened our perception. But this negative abundance was paradoxically a burden, because its pressure complicated the experience itself. What we consider basic aspects of our character—aspects that appear to us like the ruins of a large, emotionally structured composition that was never completed due to the powerlessness and carelessness of its creator, and which is now completely lost but for a few barely discernible fragments—are clearly nothing more than the moments when our desire was at its strongest, and connected to images, sounds, smells that it was not aiming for, perceptions it had *looked beyond,* as it focused on a goal that was very far away. In other words, these were the moments of our most secret torment.

No childhood is beautiful, and none is happy, and ours was no exception. The distress a child feels as he attempts to recreate the world in his playing within a reality that is proportionate to his own, springs from the consuming awareness that he himself does not possess any reality whatsoever. Just as Professor Feuer's house seemed to us the most beautiful of all, because it most resembled a play-world house, and just as we always regretted the fact that it was so real, and just as we wanted with all the power and weakness of unbridled desire to wield one of the spears of our garden fence as a play-world weapon and then were terribly disappointed, sobered, and hurt when Herr Adamowski unscrewed one and placed it in our hands, so we wanted everything to hover in some intermediate sphere of reality, balanced between expectation and readiness; in short, we wished it were all there in the same never-never land in which we ourselves lived. And that was a landscape of melancholy. What today seems to be the most reliable legacy of our childhood, and the only one truly intended for us—the sadness that was secretly mixed in with every one of our hopes—comes less from the disappointment of half and paltry fulfillment and more from the knowledge we had already acquired as to the invalidity of wishing at all.

And meanwhile the unfilled space inside us reflected the richness of images that the world contained. Because our desire focused so far into the distance, we looked past whatever was near, catching it by surprise in unguarded moments when it revealed its secret. Our childhood is the myth about ourselves, the saga from a time when we were yet an intermediate race, when we stole knowledge from the gods, insight into the essence of things. It is our magical dawn, a twilight filled with mystical happening. And every reencounter with it has the character of the numinous.

So if the memory of Czernopol includes experiences which we presumably ought to have been spared, that does not make it any less fortifying and purifying—or, in a word, any less *holy*, than whatever impressions we might have retained from some other perfectly harmonic world. On the contrary: the city's reality, with all its dubious morals and drastic goings-on, was so mercilessly close that it provided a truly mythical background, so that the heroic characters of our early years stood out in all their ambiguity, impossible to forget. But what truly infuses our memory with a sense of primal experience is not so much these remarkably distinct figures and the impression they made on us, but rather the quality of the time when these events took place, and their ever-changing symbolic effect.

Old Paşcanu's bizarre undertaking, which would lead to a grotesque and dreadful end, had a certain connection to the case of Tildy. Because hardly had the word gotten around that Tildy had been locked up in the asylum—which as usual in Czernopol took no more than a few hours—than a number of creditors approached Madame Tildy with claims that amounted to a fortune, and which had been guaranteed by nothing more than the modest, and now very questionable, pay drawn by the major. Madame Tildy dealt with the worried gentlemen exactly as one would expect from a born Paşcanu—in other words, at first she refused to receive them, but had Widow Morar, who was in those days constantly around, and who even later never left her side, show them out quite unceremoniously, while threatening to set the dogs on them if they didn't kindly leave the premises at once. Widow Morar executed this task with closed eyes and with such a gleeful smile in her golden mouth that Messrs. Fokschaner, Lipschitz, Merdinger, and Falikmann fled the house as quickly as they could.

We could never find out if Tildy himself had in fact incurred such high and risky liabilities, or whether Tamara Tildy had run the debts up behind his back—though in his name, possibly enabled by the fact that she could be considered the only legitimate heir to old Paşcanu. Even so, every child knew what the enormous sums were used for—sums well above the demands of even the most luxurious lifestyle. Nor did the press fail to take up the matter, and the leading daily, *Vocea* (The Voice), went so far as to publish a lead article under the headline "Czernopol: A Center of International Drug Trade?" which made numerous unsubtle allusions to the case of Major Tildy, though without the slightest reference to the presumed suppliers of the unfortunate lady, nor any explanation of how our city deserved such an appellation.

The possibility that a third party might be responsible for inflating the case into a public affair, and for entirely different purposes, could not be overlooked. At first only Herr Tarangolian had picked up the scent with his Levantine nose. His heavy eyes, which floated in the oily yellow veil of the liver-diseased, rolled more indolently than usual behind his thick eyelids—in his case, always a sign of extreme alertness and dangerousness. His sentences were more polished, his gestures more exaggeratedly polite: whoever knew the prefect couldn't help notice that something was going on, and that he was in his element. He spoke of General Petrescu with an almost tender irony, an affectionate attentiveness, rather like a fencing master who gently raps his opponent's blade to assess his skill, or offers a halfhearted feint suggestive of this thrust or that cut—until finally he performs a true attack entirely unexpectedly and with alarming power and efficacy.

"Don't say anything against vanity," he explained, fanning cigar smoke under his nostrils with obvious pleasure. "It is a manly trait, a romantic one, the coquettish sister of pride, whose menacing histrionics it transforms into a flowery garland of dainty grace. And it especially becomes the military man! Because is there anything more elegant than a martial bearing when it verges on coquetry? Isn't that exactly what lends his elegance its deadly earnestness? And doesn't the wish to excel in the bloodbath of a battle show a beautiful love of extravagance, a willingness to squander everything just for the glances and sighs of the young women who line the streets to greet the returning victors? There are occasions when the very traits that people point to as examples of how old-fashioned our nation is, how far behind the times, make me happy and grateful to be its child, and to live among my siblings. Isn't it delightful to watch our generals cultivating the passions and gestures of Napoleonic officers? Take, for instance, my friend Petrescu's ambitions. The political game he is pursuing so arduously is really nothing more than an expression of his warrior-like restlessness, the impatience of a knight worried that he might disgrace himself through idleness, who engages in the business of the state because he has no war in which to prove his rank among men. The *will to power*—so full of sound and fury, but we are most inclined to accept it when we realize that it's really all about the ladies on promenade in Czernopol whispering their admiration... Incidentally I will predict that the article in *Vocea* is only the first of what will become a whole series of similar pieces. And I will be paying them all the more attention as they represent the journeyman's labor, so to speak, of a young man who is not unknown to you. I'm talking about the children's former tutor, Herr Alexianu. *Vocea* has acquired his promising journalistic gifts, and he is finding it a much more suitable and fruitful place for his polemical talents than if he had followed Năstase's malicious cajoling and founded his own paper, which would no doubt have been the wittiest rag around, but for a limited readership—yes, alas, a very limited readership..."

In any event, when Tildy's case became public it acquired a certain piquancy, which the local gossips made all the more delectable. As for the major himself, no one doubted that had he been free to act on his own he would have categorically protected his wife and assumed all of her liabilities. Unfortunately, however, he was in strict isolation for the foreseeable future. Aside from that, it was unlikely he could cover any debt at all, since he was now utterly destitute. And so it would have amounted to nothing more than a beautiful gesture, which would hardly have created much of a sensation, since the character of *the last knight*—or "the dumb German"—was already widely known. As things stood, the scandal was unavoidable. Suits, demands, and seizures rained down on Tamara Tildy. The bailiff had to arrange a forced entry. The small names among the creditors gave the affair its "human interest" as Herr Tarangolian remarked sarcastically. "The case is so embarrassing," he said, "that there is nothing to do with it except turn it into a tale of the grotesque."

None of it caused old Paşcanu the slightest discomfort. On the contrary, malicious as he was, he actually gloated to see his daughter, who he was convinced hated him, and his son-in-law, who he was convinced despised him, in such a situation—and it would have given him great satisfaction to see them come begging at his doorstep. But, strangely—and Herr Tarangolian had certain suspicions concerning this as well—at about the same time the news was spreading that there was something almost deceitful about the way that Tildy—or his wife—had fallen into financial ruin, rumors started making the rounds that Săndrel Paşcanu's own finances were far from rosy. People went so far as to doubt his fabled wealth, declaring that the business with the jewels he collected for his dead wives was a fairy tale, and that even his Titian was a fake. And what followed proved these sudden doubters right. The death of Săndrel Paşcanu set off an economic catastrophe that affected the entire city. The whole lumber business—which was of incomparably greater significance for Tescovina and its capital than the drug trade—was hit very hard, and that had grave repercussions for other trades. And not only that: certain transactions involving state funds were uncovered that were more than merely dirty, and a whole gallery of public figures was exposed in the most embarrassing way. And so the terrible events that would one night turn Czernopol into a witches' cauldron, when the basest instincts ran amok, were preceded by other incidents that were disconcerting on any number of levels.

But it would be wrong to suppose that old Paşcanu was simply trying to save what he could with his childish scheme. We later overheard a conversation between our parents and Herr Tarangolian in which the prefect had his own insightful explanation ready and waiting. But Uncle Sergei would have none of it.

"You no understand what is proud man's act of desperation," he said. "Forgive me, my esteemed friend, but in this case your psychology is not enough."

"Don't call my knowledge of people and characters 'psychology,'" answered Herr Tarangolian. "That would do offense to my modesty." He closed his heavy eyelids for a moment, as if he wanted to suppress a smile. "I knew the old man very well. It's quite true that he was dumb enough to be proud—in his way. But not so dumb that he didn't know exactly what chances his maneuver really had of succeeding. Even if the swindle had gone through, the winnings would have covered just a fraction of his debt—what am I saying!—not even enough worth mentioning... No, no, it was something else entirely..."

Herr Tarangolian woke up from the idly relaxed and reflexive pose of the bon vivant. His perfect teeth flashed beneath his twitching mustache; his temperament gave wings to his hands, and they began to speak with him, forming and kneading his thoughts, sketching pictures in the air, sculpting his speech into strikingly animated forms. Animated himself, he leaned forward as he spoke, delighted by the liveliness that had taken hold of him.

"How could you possibly understand old Paşcanu! Forgive me, but to do that you have to be a child of this nation. Pride, you say. Yes—but what kind of pride? Even you, a Russian, my dear Sergei Nikiforich, overlook the mythic element. He was a force of nature, this old swindler, a true son of our Romanian soil—personal pride has no part in this. He was always half wild, I tell you: they had to pin him down to get him to wear shoes, they had to chain him, like a wild horse being shod for the first time... Have you ever wondered what his secret was, how he managed to keep it all so well hidden for so many years, the fact that he was totally bankrupt? There had to have been at least a dozen people who knew of his circumstances, and not all of them were so entangled in his shady dealings that they thought it prudent to keep their mouths shut. No, the force of his personality outweighed any such prudence. Today we know he was never as rich as everyone thought. But he had the aura of a man of unlimited wealth. You see: he knew that this aura was suddenly in danger. Not that he wouldn't have been able to slither past the catastrophe in the years still granted him. Anyone who's managed to pull it off for as long as he had can manage a little while longer. But that's not what he was after. What he was concerned about, if you will, was *saving face.* More exactly, in saving the aura that had surrounded him his entire life. Because he, too, was in danger of disgracing himself through *idleness*, like my chivalrous friend Petrescu, or like Tildy, if you follow me. It was again time for one of his strokes of genius, some fantastic, and if possible clever, coup that would have dazzled and amused everyone as much as possible. His dealings were always astonishing, witty, and sly, full of a con man's grotesque humor. He would bluntly grasp a possibility that others overlooked either due to lack of spirit or lack of brains. As a result people were inclined to immediately forgive the more disturbing aspects. As a son of this nation he knew in his blood how to best impress his brothers. Force alone is not enough. You need wit, you need satire. That is the only thing our people truly value—and their respect is absolute—because of its symbolic character, because wit is both a symbol and reflection of life. Of course . . ."

The prefect was practically glowing with joy at how vividly he had been able to summon the character of the man he claimed to know so well. "Of course, it was his pride that drove him to that act of insanity, the pride that had always been his most prominent trait—just like his nose. But it was a clown's nose, you understand, a bluff, a joke for its own sake. By the same token, his pride was not that of a gentleman; it was the vanity of a great bluffer and prankster . . . the pride of a clown. Once more, and for the last time: he was never anything else but the wild man of the woods who climbed down from the mountains to live among people: a half-child with a fairy-tale imagination, a primitive peasant with a knack for hatching devilishly cunning plots and ruses, and intricate schemes that took a long time to devise and a long time to develop. He was a man full of superstitions, given to drastic images, unbridled emotions, plagued by twisted passions, a soul as coarse and colorful as a wood-block print from a calendar, full of uncouth humor and wily schemes. Ah, I always loved him, this prankster of my homeland, this great and fundamentally humble swindler. Yes, humble. Because what we see as pride was actually his humbleness before the world that he wanted to conquer. And his fear came from this exposed humility. Săndrel Paşcanu's intended scam with the jewels was a childishly primitive attempt at saving himself from ridicule. It was his fear of being unmasked. He feared the spirit of Czernopol: the lurking vigilance so eager to reduce every claim to greatness to its true measure—to the satisfaction of all who are lowly—all in the service of one great unembellished reality. I know of no more potent form of blackmail than this spirit of watchfulness. It extorts tribute from everyone, and especially from those who have managed to deceive it for a while by giving it the run-around. It is a vicious profiteer, and whoever attempts to buy its respect winds up squandering all he possesses and sinking into debts no fortune can pay off. Whoever makes a pact with this spirit is bound to go under, just like Săndrel Paşcanu. Didn't it come to fetch old Paşcanu exactly like the devil comes to fetch a soul? He died on a great slide into the hell of ridicule, and his death was ghastly and grotesque—and thus only then did he finally achieve symbolic status... Ah..." said Herr Tarangolian, "I see that you don't understand me..." He waved his heavily ringed hand in a gesture that was almost dismissive, and then draped his hands over the back of the chair, dandy-like, so that his pretty fingers with their clawlike nails dangled in the air.

"We are trying with all our might to understand meaning of what you say," said Uncle Sergei. "But as you know: *tout comprendre, c'est tout mépriser...*"

Herr Tarangolian stared at him for a while with inscrutably melancholic eyes. "I think I understand what you mean," he said. "But is there any other way to understand something except by interpreting it through our own person, or in other words, by uncovering in it the secret we are not willing to reveal about ourselves? Be that as it may, this misunderstanding, if you care to call it that, still gives us information about ourselves. And what else is there, I ask you, *that we truly want to understand*? What I meant to say was quite simple. I found myself moved by Paşcanu's tragedy, by his figure's tragic stature. Because in essence he was anything but the conscienceless rogue, the predator that people make him out to be. Essentially he was soft and gullible and compliant, so compliant that he was all too willing to become what the world he inhabited expected of a man. He was not the vulture that his nose suggested. Quite the contrary: he was a dove—one of the wild and shy doves that live in our forests and that occasionally fly past the city of Czernopol. One could have tamed him and placed him in a garden as a kind of ornament."

At the time, we were enrolled in Madame Fiokla Aritonovich's Institute, which Uncle Sergei had recommended to our parents as an excellent educational institution. In this matter, our easygoing and charming relative found an unwavering advocate in Herr Tarangolian, much to everyone's surprise.

Madame Aritonovich was a Russian whom Uncle Sergei knew from St. Petersburg, where she had been married to a fabulously wealthy Armenian from Tbilisi and had presided over a large household.

"If I tell you," Uncle Sergei declared, turning to our father, who as a result of this description later had cause to say *of course it was all to be foreseen*—"if I tell you, a salon. Not only *société* but artists as well. Writers, intellectuals, theater, ballet, the choice is yours. She has been at university herself, Fiokla Ignatieva, she is very educated person, she knows life, is talented, *une artiste*, shc has for instance a certain *faible* for my voice, wanted me to train for the opera, *à tout prix*. She danced, as well, naturally not on the public stage, only in private circles, but for experts and connoisseurs—just ask Krupenski, ask Dolgoruki, ask any of my countrymen here, she had great talent. Legat knew her and was great fan; Cecchetti was an intimate friend: he said it was tragedy that he could not get her for the Maryinsky. She spent thousands on her collections, poets—whatever you wish. *Et une belle femme!* Her neck—I can see like today—her neck was most elegant neck in all Petersburg. *Un cou de cygne*. Nefertiti is nothing compared to her, nothing at all. A neck that makes you wish you were an executioner—*vous comprenez*?"

Herr Tarangolian completed this sketch by saying: "Fiokla Aritonovich is undoubtedly a personality. I have been her friend for years. And"—he said in English—"*she is a lady*. You will not regret your decision."

Because after the debacle with Herr Alexianu, the question of our further education had become critical. When they implored Miss Rappaport to come back she declined, saying that unfortunately she was about to accompany three charming children of an officer of the British Colonial Army to India. Apart from a postcard with a picture of the Taj Mahal, which we knew well enough anyway from the little forest at Horecea, we never heard another word from her, and because Uncle Sergei assured us that she could not possibly have been devoured by a "tyiger" because tigers despise Jewish flesh, and also even the fiercest beast would be afraid of her, we had to assume that she was grateful to have half the planet between us, and were probably correct.

Madame Aritonovich had begun her institute as a ballet school, which was then expanded to include instruction in French. The institute's popularity increased dramatically, and as a result it had very recently added all the subjects necessary to prepare students for the *gymnasium* and had—undoubtedly thanks to the prefect—been duly licensed.

When further inquiries yielded positive results, our mother and her older sister Elvira went to meet Madame Aritonovich in person. They both returned with the unreserved impression that Madame was "quite *formidable*."

"*Voilà ce que j'ai dit!*" said Uncle Sergei, triumphantly.

"Perhaps a little too much personality," Aunt Elvira dared to object.

"*But she is a lady!*" said Uncle Sergei, in English. "Don't you agree?"

"Of course, of course..."

"*She is a lady.* So what else do you want?"

With that our matriculation into the Institut d'Éducation, as it was called, was a done deal. We would have it to thank for a wealth of experiences that were both unusual and, without doubt, also educational.

I don't want to omit how much we were looking forward to the new school, and especially to our future schoolmates. We expected they would also become our playmates, that they would visit us and that we could visit them, and that we would finally be freed from the isolation we had experienced up to now. Our eagerness was immediately dampened, however, when we were told that we would never be allowed to go to school unaccompanied, but would always have to be taken to the institute and picked up later in the day. This supervision ultimately led to discoveries that caused our parents great dismay—though for no reason at all—and that sadly put a stop to our close relationship with our new friends.

Today it seems obvious that we loved Madame Aritonovich from the very first moment, and we maintained our attachment and tender admiration for years, all the way up to our final departure from Czernopol, while she in turn rewarded us with her friendly affection. This is somewhat odd, considering that we must have found the general milieu of the school, and above all Madame Aritonovich's own appearance, puzzling, even frightening.

Madame Aritonovich was very thin, almost disturbingly emaciated, and she was the first woman we ever saw in pants. The day we met her she was wearing a kind of Chinese garment—a three-quarter-length black silk jacket with wide sleeves lined with cherry-red fabric, and broad white silk pants, with high-heeled slippers. She was ghostly pale. Her thick hair was parted severely down the middle and tied in a knot at the back of her neck, so that it lay like a narrow cap of shiny black lacquer on her slender head. She was smoking a cigarette through a thin jade holder the length of her arm.

"You are a charming little flock of chickadees," she said, with a voice that was alarmingly full and deep. "You, there—come here!" She pulled my sister Tanya over, ran the tip of her fingers along my sister's dangling arms, then took her hands and raised her arms up to her shoulders. "Stand on your tiptoes!" she commanded.

Tanya obeyed. Madame Aritonovich took Tanya's right hand in her left and held it tightly by her fingers at a graceful angle over my sister's head, then spun her in a quick turn, quite firmly but also amazingly tenderly. Thus supported, Tanya performed a pirouette as if entirely on her own, one that was full of grace.

"Well, that certainly looks promising!" said Madame Aritonovich past her cigarette holder to Herr Tarangolian—the prefect had offered to introduce us. "What natural poise, don't you agree, *Coco*?" She released Tanya with another artful swing, as skillful and gentle as before.

"She reminds me of myself at that age, although I was perhaps somewhat less naïve. In any case, five or six years later my father said to me: *Si tu continueras comme ça, tu finiras dans un bordel.* To which I replied: *En tout cas ce sera un bordel de premier ordre.*"

Herr Tarangolian tossed his head back and laughed, his pearly teeth flashing beneath his dyed mustache. "That's delicious, Fiokla, delicious! And your father?"

"All he said was: *J'en doute.* But this one here could really become something, don't you think, *Coco*?"

She turned to us: "Did you understand what I said?"

We had understood everything except for the word *bordel.* But her voice was so natural and had such a winning authority, that we would have gladly confessed if we had understood it. However, we had very little interest in that, distracted as we were by the discovery that one could call the prefect, whose first name was Constantin, *Coco.* We found this absolutely delightful, because the nickname made us think of a large, intelligent, and multicolored parrot, and in this way we gained a new and very informative image that illuminated the character of the prefect, and for a long time we only referred to him as Coco.

Incidentally, Madame Aritonovich didn't leave any time for an answer. She said: "As I told your mother and her rather sour companion —what do you think, Coco, it was probably her sister, no?—anyway, as I explained to the two ladies, the most important thing a good school can teach is a small dose of cynicism. Do you know what that is?"

We said we didn't, and were very eager to learn more.

"That's the word used to differentiate smart people and dumb ones. Please take note of that, because we'll never speak about it again. Perhaps people will tell you something completely different later on. And when they do you should think of me. Or else think of the story about Queen Victoria and Prince Edward. She caught him cheating at cards. "Do you know what happens to little boys who cheat at games?" she asked, in English. To which he replied: "Yes—they win."

She turned to a young person who had witnessed this exchange with undisguised disapprobation—one of the teachers, as it later turned out.

"Be so kind as to show these little titmice the classrooms, Fräulein Zehrer. And don't let them know that from now on they are my favorite students."

As we later discovered, this was something she said in front of all her new students. But Fräulein Zehrer, who was our German teacher, made it very believable by treating us especially badly from then on.

And I remember as if it were today that we suddenly saw how beautiful Madame Aritonovich was—in an entirely different way than the somewhat shallow white-golden good looks that had been our only model for beauty up to then. She was so thin that the delicate bone structure of her skull seemed to be covered with nothing but skin—or perhaps just a layer of powder. Her face was a death mask; only her eyes were full of the splendor of life. Her mouth was large and very mobile, with thin lips. When she closed it, there was something strained or even exhausted in its expression, which immediately vanished as soon as she smiled or began to speak, and both things happened the moment she looked at you. Her neck—the same neck that caused Uncle Sergei to wish he were an executioner, really did stretch in an almost alarming fashion from her shoulders, longer than Miss Rappaport's, and incomparably more attractive. We realized that the spirit of a woman could be seen in her neck. Even later, after Madame Aritonovich had aged abruptly and hid her neck under rows of thick fake pearls—"my tortoise neck" was how she put it—it was still full of grace and poise, and ennobled by the shimmering pale-blue lines of two veins that emerged below her cheeks and ran to her collarbone—the runes of the *sangre azul*, which had given the light-skinned Goths the name "Blue-bloods."

But as much as her beauty stemmed from her innate vivacity, it derived even more from the masklike quality of her face, which had something terribly sublime—a feature we later found in only two other women, who were as different from her as they were from each other: Madame Tildy, once her addiction had destroyed her and made her into a human wreck; and a young woman who will appear later, a streetwalker named Mititika Povarchuk.

That same day we encountered beauty in another form, which if a play on words may be permitted, was not marked by the terror of the sublime but by the sublimity of terror. It was a child's face, which belonged to a girl our age, looking at us among all the other children's faces when Fräulein Zehrer introduced us to our class. Her dark eyes, her tender, pale cheeks framed by a luxurious tangle of black hair, and her almost overly expressive mouth, which seemed too experienced, too mature, showed a ready capacity for enduring all kinds of brutality—noise that was too loud, colors that were too garish, will that was too headstrong—a capacity that transformed extreme vulnerability into courage. Nothing could have shown greater contrast than the bold fearlessness, with which Madame Aritonovich *looked upon the face of the Medusa*, whereby she became its mirror image, and the brave suffering of little Blanche Schlesinger, who in her way seemed to have learned that the gaze was not to be averted, the sight of horror not to be avoided, and whose torment was amplified by the realization that she would not be able to turn to stone.

It was Fräulein Iliuţ, the hunchback, who found the right words for our schoolmate—she had also worked as a seamstress for the Schlesingers: "Looking at her, you realize," she stated, "that Jesus was a Jew."

Blanche was the first person whose friendship we sought and eventually found, although only after overcoming a great and strangely superior shyness, and unfortunately for only a very short time.

Another friendship sprung up right away and established itself with an assertiveness that was so carefree it was practically brazen—and which delighted us immensely. This new friend was a small, red-haired, freckled boy with short legs: very animated, cheeky, and intelligent. His name was Salomon Brill.

He immediately approached us as if it were the most natural thing in the world and spoke to us directly. At first we had some difficulty understanding his manner of speaking, because he pelted us with a hailstorm of questions, and we had been drilled to answer every question right away. It took us a while to catch on that he didn't expect answers to most of his questions; nevertheless, we kept ourselves ready because of our upbringing and always fell behind, so that every time he really wanted to know something, we became confused, focused as we were on all the previous questions. But that didn't matter to our new friend, who just considered us a little stupid and clumsy—which he had probably assumed anyway, and which, compared to him, was undoubtedly the case—and didn't dwell anymore on the matter. So actually it's not true when I blame our difficulty on some trait of his. There was nothing difficult about Solly Brill: his lively spirit, which was always focused on the matter at hand and never on anything personal, made everything easy; he let things glide as if on ball bearings, so to speak, and we found his company so enjoyable that it gradually became a kind of vice, a habit that was hard to break and produced a severe withdrawal when we were forced to give up our friendship with him.

The minute Fräulein Zehrer left us alone he planted himself in front of us—standing a full head shorter than me—and said, "The new arrivals, let's have a look at you. So, who are you? What are your names? You want to play with us? Or maybe you're too good for that? Maybe you want to learn something here? How old are you? Did you bring money for *kigla*? Or maybe you don't know *kigla*? Or maybe somebody's watching you the whole time? Are you enrolled in the French course or the German one?"

He showed a great and completely genuine interest in our family circumstances, the character of each person, how much they owned, and for the quality of our clothes and our satchels.

"Look at those antiques! *Nu*, you haven't heard of zippers? You can find them in our store. The latest type. The man who invented them became a millionaire overnight—in *dollars*. The dollar is worth about sixhundredthirtyfive, figure that!"

"But why should we figure that if you know the answer?" asked Tanya, puzzled.

Solly Brilly never dwelt on misunderstanding. "*Schmontses*," he said, "what kind of nonsense is that! Figure that, like . . . can you imagine? Not like go do the arithmetic. *Nu*, so you want to play *kigla*, or don't you know how?"

We found out that *kigla* were marbles. Solly's were fantastic—glass ones almost as big as your fist, with bands of color wound inside, and others that were tiny but weighed just about the same, of heavy flashing metal, like quicksilver, like Solly himself.

"Just a game," he said. "You can have some of mine. As a present. No joke. Later I'll take something of yours. Deal?"

Solly helped us understand many things—including several interesting details that belonged to the story of old Paşcanu.

It turned out that Herr Tarangolian had a much closer relationship with Madame Aritonovich and her Institut d'Éducation than we had imagined. The prefect came to the school every week, mostly when we had ballet lessons, and would spend entire afternoons there, as a connoisseur of dance, and of Madame Aritonovich's conversational gifts. Occasionally we asked ourselves how he found time for his official duties, given the number of his visits. But he typically got up very early—although he never admitted this, incidentally—and much to the horror of his subordinates, he often appeared in his offices in the provincial government building at six o'clock in the morning, and was ready to leave just before eleven. Moreover, much of the success and intelligence of the measures he enacted was undoubtedly due to his custom of donning the mask of a bon vivant and mixing, like Harun al-Rashid, among the people, thereby discovering anything of any importance that was going on, and especially what was brewing or ready to happen.

His visits allowed us to witness firsthand the inconspicuous and sly manner by which he came by his information. Naturally this meant we had to give up the exciting and somewhat ominous impression we'd formed of a man who commanded his own secret service—an impression that was reinforced whenever he revealed some amazingly detailed tidbit about a case or an event, something he never did without a specific intention. But even if we had to give up our image of shady, masked characters stealing through the night and reading secret documents by flashlight, or else disguised as lackeys and secretaries eavesdropping on conversations, our admiration for him only increased when we saw how simple and practical his methods were, how ably he could discern background, intent, and motive, and how cogently he drew the proper inferences.

Whether or not it was a passionate folly of Madame Aritonovich that she couldn't give up, ballet clearly formed an essential component of the institute's educational program, with the classes conducted by Madame herself. After we had performed our pliés to her satisfaction, we were given a short course in etiquette. The girls were taught the art of curtsying, from the court curtsy—six steps forward four back, knee bending on the fourth step—to the simple curtsy with bent knee while standing; for us boys, greeting a person of respect meant standing three steps away, giving a slight bow of the head while clicking our heels together, then approaching, giving another slight bow and accepting the hand that was offered. We practiced the various intonations of *bonjour* and *au revoir* depending on whether we were addressing a superior or someone of inferior rank—if, for instance, a *monsieur* were added to the *bonjour*, it was a clear sign that one was dealing with a subordinate. Solly Brill would shrug his shoulders when he performed these assignments and make comments such as "About as useful as a wreath on the head!" or "We're rocking dead babies here!" a phrase taken up by Madame Aritonovich and whoever happened to be visiting.

For Herr Tarangolian was not the only visitor to the Institut d'Éducation. Now and then Uncle Sergei showed up as well, to observe our practice *à la barre* and *au milieu* and to say to Madame Aritonovich something like: "That little one there, in the pink tricot—she is already fourteen?" Madame Aritonovich answered in Russian, which we didn't understand. Both laughed. "You misunderstand me completely, Fiokla Ignatieva. I am only speaking of her stiffness. How did they loosen up stiffness in the old days? By pulling or by beating?"

But usually the prefect sat alone during ballet class, his legs spread out a little in order to accommodate the bulge of his belly, his ringed fingers clasping the handle of his ebony cane so that he could rest his chin. His mustache was twirled out into two venomously black radish tails. A carnation flared in his buttonhole, and his white playboy's spats gleamed brightly over his delicate, pointed, highly polished shoes.

His dialogue with Madame Aritonovich had the same easygoing tone we knew from our own conversations with her, which were remarkably open and refreshingly accepting. And although she spoke about the most risqué things in front of us, and with a disarming naturalness that might have petrified other grown-ups, we'd grown so used to it after a few days, that no one ever thought anything of it. Nor can I remember any of her charges ever using an inappropriate tone with Madame, and there were fewer secrets, whispers, and rumors and less talk of sexual matters among the students in the Institut d'Éducation than in any of the schools we later attended.

"You are the only person, Coco," said Madame Aritonovich, with whom I associate as if I were carrying on a correspondence." She inserted a new cigarette in her long jade holder and had him light it. "Take a look at your protégée Tanya. She is truly talented. And you,

Solly," she called out to little Brill, who was trying in vain to bring his short leg up to the barre, "make a little effort. Where there's a will there's a way."

"Some people might have lots of will, but there's still no way," said Solly. Madame Aritonovich and Herr Tarangolian laughed out loud.

"Come over here, Solly," said the prefect.

"Certainly, Herr Coco." Solly planted himself unabashedly between the knees of our old friend and fingered the handle of his cane. "Ivory, yes? Well well. Genuine? What's it cost, a cane like that?"

"It belonged to my papa."

"*Nu*, so it's an antique. But what's it worth?"

"I don't know. Your papa's the one to ask that."

"He'll know for sure."

"Of course he will. And how's he doing, your papa?"

"The old man? How is he supposed to be doing? Miserable, that's how business is—so he says." Solly cocked his head ironically.

"And how's business really doing, Solly—just between us?"

Solly leaned over to whisper the answer in the prefect's ear.

"Oo! said Herr Tarangolian and raised his thick black eyebrows in comic amazement. "In the course of this one year?"

"Do you think he'd be sending his children to French institutes if not?

"Don't talk nonsense, Solly. Your papa always pampered you beyond bounds."

"Yes, of course, as a late-born child... Bubi flies into pieces every time I say *bonjour* to him, followed by a *monsieur* as to a subordinate. That's as much French as he still understands, barely a word more. He'd like to but can't, poor guy."

"But he'll end up giving his father more joy than you, you rascal."

"That's what *you* think. You should have heard the ruckus he had again with the old man last night. The whole floor was rocking and shaking." Solly snuggled up to the prefect's stomach. "Is that the chain from your watch? Gold, eh? Is it hallmarked?"

"I'll show you the watch if you show us how your brother Bubi argues with Papa."

"I see a lot of watches. Better give me ten leos."

"All right, ten leos. But you have to do it right, like in the theater."

"Deal." Solly turned to us. "Everybody stop your fussing so I can show Herr Coco here how Bubi had it out with my old man. Nonsense time! Solly Brill's Summer Theater!"

"Nonsense time!" we cheered back.

The institute had a standing policy that all instruction would stop briefly to accommodate any proposal that promised to be sufficiently entertaining.

We sat in a half-circle on the floor, blissfully awaiting the play.

"So!" said Solly, as he bustled about. "Picture for yourself, here is the shop floor, here is Mama sitting at the cash register, here is the old man, here is Bubi, wearing a trench coat he's thrown over a pair of tennis shorts, the silly guy. And the old man says to him—I'll be the old man now..."

Solly crossed to the place he had indicated for his father, and immediately underwent an almost uncanny transformation: his head sank between his shoulders, his face—that ruddy, freckled boy's face containing the preformed characteristics of an ancient race—shrank together, knitted and pursed and lined like that of an aging man. His voice, too, became hoarse and worn.

"So," he growled almost voicelessly at the imaginary Bubi Brill—whom we saw right before us in the flesh—"so, for this I—I, Usher Brill, a respectable merchant in this city—for this I have toiled with my hands my whole life long and slaved away in order that you, my flesh and blood, turn into a *parasolnik*, a peacock, a salon-knight, a kept man, a layabout? For this you studied at the lyceums and business schools at home and abroad, off my money, I should live like that, and turned into a grown man living off my money, a nice boy with red cheeks, a kind of reservist in the finest regiment, running around in a gold-braided uniform a whole expensive year and not a day with the soldiers and all at my expense—and for this you spend every evening at Schorodok's Trocadero getting drunk with the officers and whores? While I stand the whole day, with my varicose veins here on the shop floor!"

Solly paused, changed back into himself, and looked Herr Tarangolian right in the eyes with inimitable self-assurance. "Not good enough?"

"Excellent, Solly, absolutely excellent," said the prefect.

Solly pulled his head into his shoulders and wrinkled his face to look like a red-haired man who'd spent his whole life peering at burning embers. Then he marched up to the prefect, as if Herr Tarangolian were Solly's older brother, Bubi.

"For this I have davened every day, so that something like that should become of you? A dandy, a bon vivant, a fashion fop and *aesthetnik*, instead of a regular, decent hardworking honest man! For you to lounge around the ball fields instead of standing on the shop floor like your father and your mother and your little sister and working! For you to sit watching the ballerinas"—Solly was standing right in front of Herr Tarangolian—"the little children twelve and thirteen years old in their tricots..."

"That's fine, Solly!" said Herr Tarangolian, wiping his eyes and so delighted he was incapable of laughing. "You're a genius. But stick to your father and Bubi."

"Deal!" Solly said and jumped, with the dancer's agility he owed to Madame Aritonovich's instruction, to the place he had designated for Bubi. "Now I'll be Bubi."

He took on an expression of bored superiority and at once Solly disappeared and in his place we saw the snooty upstart Bubi Brill, wearing tennis shorts, quarreling with his hoarsely rasping father, who vented his spleen in rage—no, not just them: with a single gesture he also conjured his fat mother on her throne behind the cash register, unmoving as a sphinx, his sister Riffke lurking in the background, and the blasé, condescending salesmen of Brill's large department store, leaning over tables covered with samples and receipt ledgers. The scene took place in the atmosphere of relaxed and unstinting openness Jews create with one another—the intimacy of an Oriental people deeply acquainted with life.

Bubi (bored and supercilious): "All right, Papa. We know this record by heart. Please, give me part of the business so I have something to do."

Old Man Brill: "*Here* is where I do my business, here on the shop floor, *bokher*, and if you want to do business, then get to it! It's nine o'clock. Customers will be walking in at any moment. Get out of your foppish rags, and hop to it!

Bubi (haughtily): "Excuse me, Papa, but this is a *nebekhdike* way to do business, with aprons and garter straps. Forgive me if I laugh."

Old Brill (his voice cracking): "*Ja*, in this shop that's exactly how we do business, with aprons and garter straps! He can't sell half a garter, the scab, but he wants to make big deals, ten wagonloads of hazelnuts from Constantinople to Lemberg, perhaps—or hustle jewels! A lazy lounging nobody who gets drunk with officers and whores like a *goy*, with women and furs and champagne and Paris in his head. Massman in an automobile. He lets his old father with a hernia sell garter straps, while he wants to do big business. The swastika-louts that paint up on my shutters, this is how I live, they know why I have worked myself to the bone my whole life long, they know. For the *Protocols of the Elders of Zion*—that's what they say. For domination over the earth, that's what they believe. But I know the real reason why I've slaved away—*dos iz emmes*—I know. For a cavalryman, a playboy with film stars in his head. A man for whom the shop floor isn't good enough, and the city isn't big enough, not elegant enough, and the business isn't profitable enough, and the whores don't cost enough. That's why I'm standing today on the floor here with my rheumatism, so that the swastika-men just need to wait for him to take over, the fop, for that the business should go bankrupt, and for me I should wind up a poor man and in debt. And for that I—I, Usher Brill, an old man with a bad diabetes—for that I'm supposed to put up an entire fortune and risk my neck? For the *Protocols of the Elders of Zion* and for domination over the earth, when the young gentlemen will no longer be around—that's what for."

Bubi: "Excuse me, Papa, what's all this about investing? All I hear about is investing. What investments, may I ask? As far as I'm concerned you don't have to invest a thing with this deal."

Old Brill: "You think I'm going to tell it to you, *bokher*! Your little sister is a good girl, you understand. If she wants to get married, I'll tell it to her, you understand, but not you. You can go look for your deals somewhere else, that's what you can do."

Bubi: "God knows, you don't have to get so worked up, Papa. Anyway, Mama told me everything already. So I'm asking you: What investments are you talking about? First of all, isn't old Paşcanu good for the few million? Permit me to say that the way I see it it's purely a matter of brokering a deal. The profit is enough, at least for me. I leave it up to you. If you don't want to do it, then I will. Or don't you think Paşcanu is good for the money?"

Old Brill (with mock cheerfulness): "Listen to him ask the questions, the freeloader. He'll broker a deal! He'll leave it up to me! Look here, old Paşcanu's fortune is in lumber, you *meshuggener*. Here—do you ever look at a newspaper? You studied abroad. Figure it out. Old Paşcanu is as broke as—as broke as a *goy* can possibly be. That's what old Paşcanu is, you understand. I spend good money to send you abroad so that you can ask questions like a simple peasant? Old Paşcanu, I tell you, is finished, that's what old Paşcanu is."

Bubi: "Why are you getting so upset, Papa? In terms of psychology, that's very interesting. If old Paşcanu is broke, then you don't need to do the deal, right? I leave it to you."

Old Brill: "Deal! What kind of deal is that, I'd like to know? It's a better deal to go caca in the Volodiak, you understand, you *goylem*? That would be a better deal."

Bubi: "Why are you getting so riled up over nothing, Papa? In terms of psychology, that's very interesting, so why is nobody supposed to know anything if it's already dead in the cradle? By the way, there's something I want to tell you: I, too, have my information, you'll permit me—you understand. I, too, have my information, and I, too, glance at the papers now and then. Old Paşcanu isn't standing in his smock and selling garter straps—not him. Old Paşcanu is a businessman of class. He doesn't need to perform any schemes for credit or any other *shmontses*. But, as I said, I leave it to you. If you don't want to, then I will."

Old Brill: "With my money, you think? You scoundrel! I am supposed to stand here and sell garter straps, with my ailing heart, while you go do business with old Paşcanu..."

Bubi: "As I said, it's no more than brokering a deal. Pure and simple. Again: I leave it to you. By the way, with your permission, I have to go to the club. Anyway, I find it psychologically extremely interesting that you are getting so worked up over this."

Bubi—or, rather, little Solly, because he was once more himself—took his leave with an inimitably nonchalant wave. We were entranced and delighted, and, sparked by Madame Aritonovich's example, we applauded enthusiastically.

Solly went up to Herr Tarangolian. "The show is over. Curtain. That's all for this season." Turning to us, he said: "Ladies and Gentlemen, the theater is closed."

Madame Aritonovich shooed us to work. "*Allons!* Go back to your work! To the barre!"

Herr Tarangolian gave Solly a ten-leo coin. Solly looked it over carefully.

"I'll bet you know what deal your brother Bubi was talking about, don't you? Or didn't your Mama mention anything about it?"

Solly blinked at him through his carrot-colored eyelids: "Not for just a tenner, Herr Coco."

Years later, when we paid Madame Aritonovich a friendly visit, we tried to compliment her by saying that the most beautiful thing that we had learned at her school, in the woefully short time we were there, was candor. Then we attempted to double the effect of this acknowledgment by explaining what we meant—an approach that is always prone to backfire—and added that she masterfully understood how to remove the sting and thus the embarrassment from any type of indiscretion, intended as well as unintended, by taking the matter in hand and immediately making it everybody's business, as if that were the most natural thing in the world.

"How can you be so indiscreet as to tell me that!" she said to us, indignantly.

12

Aunt Paulette Calls on Madame Tildy, While Papa Brill Visits Old Paşcanu

ALTHOUGH Widow Morar had attached herself so closely to Madame Tildy that she was living with her and hardly moved from her side, she was still not entirely lost to us.

Of course all the furniture in the Tildys' house had been pawned, and the house had been acquired by another owner, but Madame Tildy kept living there for the time being. So Widow Morar stayed in our neighborhood and visited us—meaning, us children, and no one else—when Tamara Tildy was taking a nap, or when she had been sent by Madame Tildy on a mission that brought her to our house.

"I'm coming to you, my little ones," she said, with closed eyes and a golden smile, "to no one but you, because you have no part in their disgraceful behavior, trampling on my mistress and slinging mud on her and laughing cruelly because she's suffered such a fate. In all other faces I see scorn, but not in yours. We are living in an empty room, and no one will take her. She doesn't have a blanket, and she's always cold, she can't help being cold, even with the sun at its warmest, that's how refined and delicate she is. I have to take her in my arms to warm her up; I hold her like my own child. They took away her brushes, they were made of gold with the finest marten bristles, she can't use any other, her hair is as delicate as a spiderweb and any other kind of bristle tears it out and makes it stand on end and spark and burn with every stroke. This makes her cry—is her hair supposed to mat away into elflocks? So I comb it with my fingers, I put each hair in order. But my fingers are hard and tough from all the hard work I've done my entire life, a widow all alone with three sons, mouths forever hungry, a challenge for a poor woman to fill. My hands are heavy and clumsy; she frequently loses her patience and hits me. She flies into a rage and throws herself on the floor and curses the major, who plunged her into misfortune, or else she's perfectly still and holds her head at an angle as if she were listening closely and says to me: What do you think, is it nice where he is? I sense that it's a nice place, she says, that he's happy, yes I can feel that he is happy. Why does he get to go where I belong? Why is he in a place where there is peace and not me? Don't you see that he betrayed me? Now he is where I should be, among all the others who are allowed to dream, who smile at each other and don't even realize they are speaking, because they don't need any answer, they don't see whether a face returns their laughter or not, they don't see any face at all. After all, they have themselves, they enjoy hearing their own voices, as if someone else were speaking to them, and they're happy to hear that this other person says exactly what they want to hear and how they want to hear it; they have this person say happy things and bad things, let him curse and rage and are happy that he does exactly what they want; they are delighted. They ask him something and hear him ask the same question and they already know the answer, but they don't want him to know their questions and answers, and so they ask faster and faster, and still he's always quicker than they are, and they hate him and they get angry and shout and throw themselves on the floor to escape and roll around on the ground to shake him off—like your husband, Morar, when he wanted to drink death from his rifle. But you suck and suck at the cold iron muzzle and death doesn't come; in order to die you have to let go a shot that erases your face, and this is what I am afraid of—so she tells me—I don't want to be without a face, you hear, I don't even want to be dead without a face, I am afraid, you hear, it's horrible to destroy your face, even dead people need a face. I am afraid... And she clings to me and whines and yammers. That's what I came to tell you, because you asked me what it meant to lose face. She doesn't want to be without a face. I'm telling you this as a great secret, I won't talk about her with anyone else, because the others spit on her, they're full of scorn because of her misfortune, but you, you know better. I just rushed over to tell you that, because I have to get back to her, she sent me to fetch poison for the dogs she can't feed anymore and who whimper for him all day long. No other man is to have them, and because they're going crazy with worry we're going to kill them, we'll mix the poison in some ground meat and feed it to them—here, you see? The very best meat, almost four pounds. They almost chased me out at Dobrowolski's when I told them we needed it for the dogs. Nothing to eat themselves and she cheats people so she can feed her dogs with roast meat, they cried. That's the way they are—they don't know a thing. They don't know that this is the last blessing this earth has for the poor animals, and they curse you for giving it to creatures who are marked to die, because people are cruel and don't understand anything. But they go on bathing their arms in blood up to their elbows and hacking the smoking flesh into pieces. They don't know. That's what I came to tell you, not the others, who don't understand a thing."

"And what about him?" we asked. "Is it true that he is happy?"

"If she feels it then it must be true," said Widow Morar, smiling with her gold mouth. And he was. We later found out that it was true.

"You are surprised, even indignant, because they didn't release Tildy long ago," said Herr Tarangolian. "Permit me to say that for the moment it's best for him to stay where he is. You can be assured he is being treated with the utmost consideration, with great courtesy and tact. The head of the institution, Dr. Kobylanski, is an unusually reliable man. And he has found in Dr. Schlesinger someone who can attend to Tildy with great sensitivity..."

"Yes, but none of that excuses the fact that a gross injustice has been committed, that it was all completely unwarranted!" exclaimed our Aunt Elvira. "You can't just pack a man off to the asylum because he makes you feel uncomfortable."

"My dear friend, if you had to decide his case, would you send him home right now?" asked the prefect, with an ironic look.

"You don't expect us to believe that they're keeping him there out of kindness, do you?" asked Aunt Paulette, the youngest.

"I don't expect you to believe anything. I only said that he is being treated with consideration and tact."

"So he has no idea what's happening outside the walls of his confinement?"

"I don't believe so."

"But that's even more horrible, if that's possible! Isn't anybody thinking about his poor wife?" Aunt Elvira was outraged.

"On the contrary, everyone is thinking about his wife." Herr Tarangolian seemed to enjoy the general silence that followed his words.

"Permit me," he said after a while. "Could he be of any help to her?"

"That's not the question. But at least he ought to be given a chance to try."

"Unfortunately that's impossible."

"Nothing is impossible."

Herr Tarangolian shrugged his shoulders and busied himself with his cigar.

"Won't Major Tildy demand accountability when he's dismissed?" asked our mother. "A man of his character will consider this the worst thing that could be done to him, obstructing the performance of his duty."

"Demand accountability from whom?" asked Herr Tarangolian.

This time the silence proved a little embarrassing, full of hidden shoals—there was too much being unsaid. Our temperamental Aunt Paulette couldn't bear it any longer.

"I hate you, my dear old friend! Admit that you have your hand in it. And not for Tildy's sake. You're no angel. But because he's in your way somehow, because he doesn't fit into one of your intrigues. The notion that he's being spared out of consideration while he's actually being kept locked up in a nuthouse as long as possible is a perfidious hypocritical pretext. Admit it—you are a devil."

"I don't feel close enough to the beyond to say which category suits me best," said Herr Tarangolian. "The only thing I know for sure is that you, my dear young friend, look as much like an angel as a human being possibly can—although perhaps one of Lucifer's entourage..."

"A fallen angel, in other words," said Aunt Paulette drily. The comment unleashed a palpable wave of embarrassment.

Herr Tarangolian acted as if he hadn't heard her. "*Ach,* my child," he said. "Be annoyed, be indignant, wax righteous with anger, champion all that is noble and good, or else the opposite—at your age everything is beautiful."

"Do you know much about the institution?" asked Uncle Sergei, interested. "What I mean is: Do they not have methods? Straitjackets for raving madmen and such like? Or perhaps they are using certain therapies such as electrical shocks?"

"You can rest assured none of that will be applied to Major Tildy," the prefect said with enigmatic irony.

"Naturally!" exclaimed Uncle Sergei in all his disarming naiveté. "I am asking only out of curiosity, medicinally speaking, you know."

"Naturally," said Herr Tarangolian.

"I have the picture you requested of Aida's grave," our mother said. "The gravestone is up now. My relatives wrote that it turned out very nice."

"You are kindness in person," Herr Tarangolian mumbled, moved, as he kissed her hand...

Aunt Paulette reclined her bobbed hair against the seat back and stared up at the ceiling with arched eyebrows.

"You have very beautiful throat," said Uncle Sergei.

"Are you tempted to sink your teeth into it?"

"Paulette!" said our mother. "If I might ask, would you help the children with their schoolwork this afternoon—or better yet, why don't you go up right now, you'll have the whole afternoon to yourselves." She turned back to Herr Tarangolian: "It's really a terrible shame that Miss Rappaport couldn't come back..."

Aunt Paulette got up. "A terrible shame," she said. "And no one has more cause to regret it than I do."

She shooed us upstairs. "Incidentally, even when the dear departed Rappaport was with us the brood was always sent out only when it was too late."

"An excellent educational method," said Herr Tarangolian. "Children can never be corrupted early enough. On that matter I agree entirely with my friend Fiokla Aritonovich."

"Paulette, please!" said Mama.

Aunt Paulette opened the door and let us out with an ironic bow. She didn't exactly hate us, but she made no secret of her indifference toward us, and of the fact that recently we had become downright burdensome. It was also clear that it was only reluctantly that she undertook the task of helping us with our homework and otherwise standing in for the absent Miss Rappaport. But perhaps she was simply venting her general displeasure at us. She was twenty-five years old, very pretty, full of joie de vivre, and unspeakably bored in our household, which was anything but companionable. Apart from Herr Tarangolian and the occasional relative from the countryside, no one came to visit us, and it didn't occur to anyone to pursue some social connections or visit friends in town. Although the household was large and busy—we were still a large family, including the help, and we did include them, a whole tribe—nothing could hide the fact that the empty space around us was expanding to the point where we felt entirely alone and utterly isolated.

We had yet to endure the painful experience of seeing such an entity as seemingly natural as our own family dissolve and disintegrate. In later years we told ourselves that we had parted from nothing more than a beautiful delusion, that the nestlike warmth we remembered from our intact home had never truly resided between its walls but was more the product of the warming rays of our childish bodies, our liveliness and open-mindedness, and that what we experienced was therefore the only natural outcome—namely, that we grew colder, along with the world around us. But no matter how reasonably we bore that in mind, it failed to assuage our homesickness—any more than a secret suspicion we shared that none of us would ever be capable of erecting anything as solid, sheltering, and warm as our childhood home.

Or should we already have had some feeling, some premonition, of what it was that made Madame Tildy so cold?

Meanwhile, Uncle Sergei seemed to show more understanding than might be expected from the implacably cheerful and charming countenance of an unreformed rogue. The accidental silence lasted for several minutes and at one point suddenly became palpably oppressive, without anyone being able to say why. Then Uncle Sergei blew a few rings from his cigarette in faux contemplation, puckering his lips in a kind of artful parody and sending the smoke off into the past, while quoting: "He who doesn't build a house today will never build; and he who is alone will so remain . . ." He reached his hand out to Aunt Paulette, who was resting her head against the back of the chair and staring at the ceiling, and said with exaggerated sentimentality: "Give me your hand, *ma chère cousine*, in order to warm me."

Aunt Paulette didn't move. Uncle Sergei raised his eyebrows very high and then sang, as mellifluously as a tender Pierrot, and bone-chillingly off-key, "*Là ci darem la mano*," then sighed and got up. We knew he was going to play cards. Our mother stood up with him and left the room under some pretext. We knew that she would slip him a little money outside.

It may have been a mood like that which led Aunt Paulette to go and visit Tamara Tildy. She hadn't told anyone her intention, and we didn't learn of the visit until a few days later, and then quite by coincidence.

The conversation proceeded the same as most of the conversations that took place in our house did, and exactly the way, strangely enough, we would recall later on: assembled in the so-called *salon,* drinking black coffee after dinner, a group of people sitting motionless, silent, and fossilized. The only thing that occasionally enlivened this group was the presence of Herr Tarangolian, but after Aunt Aida's death his visits grew less and less frequent, and finally, after a difference in opinion that had become all too clear, they ceased almost entirely. We were always inclined to think that this increasing stiffness in the lifeless room didn't start until after Miss Rappaport had left us—which is proof of how much we are prey to optical illusions whenever we look back at the past.

The conversation was trivial and disjointed. Sentences such as "Will you have some more coffee, Sergei?" and "Thank you so much, Cousin Elvira!" floated randomly on the surface of a sluggish silence. Aunt Paulette, her head resting on the back of her chair as usual—which earned the undisguised disapproval of her older sisters—interjected: "Do tell me if you should ever win anything at cards, Sergei. I'd like to borrow some money from you."

"You know, my angel, I never win. Alas."

"It might happen yet. If you cheat as cleverly as you do when you play rummy with me..."

"Why do you need money, *moye serdtse*? A woman who has your beauty has everything."

Aunt Paulette said nothing.

"I understand," said Uncle Sergei after a while. "She is not doing well? She is always hungry?"

"Yes, she is hungry."

"Oh-là-là," said Uncle Sergei. "But this hunger is very hard to still. Very expensive. The games I play are for kopecks."

"You sometimes see a doctor, by the name of Zablonski or some such?"

"You are speaking of Madame Tildy?" our mother said, not without a certain edge. "Have you seen her?"

"Yes, I went to visit her," said Aunt Paulette with unabashed nonchalance.

"To visit her?"

"Yes, the day before yesterday. There was already someone else there as well. A certain Herr Adamowski, an editor from what I understood. He was performing magic tricks."

"He was doing what?"

"Magic tricks. He pulled a sugar-egg out of his nose, and other unappetizing and boring things. Card tricks, too. You should avoid him, Sergei, if you run into him in one of her circles. He's better at it than you. You can recognize him by the fact he has a clubfoot. And a monocle. Both are hard to miss. Incidentally, Tamara Tildy seemed to be thoroughly amused by the man. She was practically bubbly, witty and charming. And the old Morar woman was lurking like a spider. When you look at her she closes her eyes and smiles. Her gold teeth are so bright you have the impression the sun is rising."

"She waits on her, from what I hear," our mother said.

"I think they sleep in one bed, if you can call what I saw a bed."

"It's horrible," our mother said. "By the way, children, you haven't been outside all day. Go play in the garden until Aunt Paulette calls you in to do your homework."

If someone had told us back then that Aunt Paulette would wind up marrying Herr Adamowski, and then only after she'd been his mistress for a long time and under circumstances very embarrassing for all of us, we would have considered it the product of an unsound mind. We once spoke about it with Madame Aritonovich.

"What's so hard for you to understand," she said, "about your aunt falling for this man? Tamara Tildy fell for him as well."

"And?"

Madame Aritonovich smiled. "Didn't you ever notice how fascinated Paulette was by Tamara Tildy, from the very beginning, the same way you were fascinated by Tildy?" Except she was fascinated the way one woman is by another, through constant secret comparison, relentlessly lying in wait for the moment when she might emerge triumphant. She was younger and more beautiful, and that made her envy all the more bitter—that gives it an edge right away... You understand what I mean, Tanya, don't you?"

Tanya didn't answer.

"Of course," the rest of us said. "And we could have understood it if she had taken Tildy away from her when he came back. But not this clubfoot, this salon-buffoon."

"Tildy!" said Madame Aritonovich, almost disdainfully. She looked at Tanya. "You know what I mean, yes?"

Tanya still said nothing.

"Wait until you are twenty-five," said Madame Aritonovich. "Live with relatives when you are young, beautiful, and at the peak of vitality but unable to move freely. Your expectations from life have been curtailed. Meet a man you find repulsive in every way—physically, mentally—but who has conquered the woman who makes you uneasy, because you sense that you have something in common, if nothing more, or nothing less, than a seed of the same despair. What will you do? You take revenge for this despair that she has beaten you to. You will want to hit her where it hurts the most, on account of your own despair... I don't expect you to approve, I only expect you to understand... Ah, but sadly you weren't in my school long enough, you little titmice, back then."

The platitude that "You never can tell" could be aptly applied to the short time we spent in Madame Aritonovich's Institut d'Éducation, and we could count ourselves lucky that we didn't know back then how soon we would leave it. Because we were happy there, apart from a few very mundane childish worries—minor aches that later struck us as ridiculously trivial, though at the time they seemed as bitter as any sorrow yet to come.

One of those early pains, which I alone experienced, was responsible for our friendship with Blanche Schlesinger.

For a few weeks we had tried in vain to get to know her. But she was as retiring and shy toward us as she was toward all the others, and, moreover, we felt awkward and embarrassed by our attempts to approach her, and especially by our poorly feigned casualness. This was a technique we had picked up from Solly Brill, and to us it seemed a wonderful way to overcome embarrassment. But while such spontaneity was second nature to him, we were never to fully master it, not even later on. Nor did it work in the least bit with little Blanche. When her large, knowing eyes met our own, when we saw her sad smile that seemed to say "Don't try to disguise anything, don't put on an act, tell me what you want from me and I'll do it if I can, if it isn't too loud or garish," we were stopped in our tracks, succumbing instantly to a sensitivity against everything garish, loud, or direct. For we had seen, often enough, how just one excessively familiar word or overly intimate gesture could cut to the quick, wounding a person where he was at his most vulnerable, at the core of his personality. And having to watch Blanche's eyes grow a shade darker, or her smile turn more sadder, while knowing that whenever things remained unsaid that should have been stated hardly helped us overcome our shyness—well, it only made things worse.

I feel a little embarrassed when I say "little Blanche," for although she was probably younger than we were, we never had the feeling that we had to patronize her, or that we even could. She was superior to us in every respect. Just like Solly Brill, and for the same reason: she was thousands of years ahead of us—the superiority of an older race.

We had no reservations when it came to treating Solly, who was a head shorter than we were and almost two years younger, as a superior being. His verdict on Blanche was, incidentally, absolutely matter-of-fact: "A whimsical creature, the Schlesinger girl"—and here he was right—"but intellectually anemic. Not worth talking about."

So we contented ourselves with greeting her from afar, with a short nod and a quick glance, both conveyed in embarrassment, leaving us even more embarrassed because we knew that she was still observing us with her big eyes. And then the day came when she spoke to us.

It was during Fräulein Zehrer's German class, which usually passed sluggishly, unless it was fraught with the kind of tension that made us refractory and unleashed all the bad habits children are capable of when pressed into a stupid and unenlightened educational mold, although it should be noted that Fräulein Zehrer was hardly the fossilized schoolmarm people are inclined to blame for the shortcomings and taxing boredom of school. She was healthy and red-cheeked, relatively young, blond, even bright. But her unconcealed disapproval of Madame Aritonovich's pedagogical views and methods—which were never presented as a program but simply derived from her unique personality—made her contrary, and thereby inept. She taught in protest, and her protest was as much against Madame Aritonovich as it was against ourselves. Alone among the teachers employed at the Institut d'Éducation—mostly mousy old spinsters or kind, grubby old men—she had trained for her profession and had fallen victim to various modern ideas. Her ideal was most likely a German *Waldschulheim*—a boarding school in the woods with lots of sun, enormous windows, where the walls were adorned with the students' artwork and where the children sat outside in a meadow, singing chorales in a circle—the idyll, in a word, of a kindergarten teacher. The very building that housed the Institut d'Éducation, a dilapidated private home where the only equipment was the barre in the ballet room, must have been repugnant to her. Her revenge took the form of teaching us with a matter-of-factness and thoroughness that suffocated us with boredom. My guess is that Madame Aritonovich probably realized all this, but kept her—or possibly even hired her—for pedagogical reasons, namely to provide contrast, following the only principle she ever did put into words: *Children should not be spared anything.*

We were practicing what was called the "spoken essay." My assignment consisted of retelling the fairy tale of Sleeping Beauty. I did my best, and when I came to the place where the prince reaches the castle surrounded by thorns, I said: "...and the prince saw before him a sleeping castle, covered with layers and layers of briars..."

"*What* was sleeping?" Fräulein Zehrer interrupted. "The castle?" She turned to the class: "Did you hear that? Have any of you ever seen a castle sleep?"

The class howled with laughter, with Fräulein Zehrer laughing along at full volume. "The people in the castle were sleeping, you *dummkopf*—Sleeping Beauty in the attic chamber, the king on his throne, and next to him the queen, her pages on the steps and the guards on the balconies and over the gate, even the cook, who was in the process of giving his apprentice a slap on the face, and the court dog on his chain and the cat at the hearth—but *not* the castle!"

I stood there close to tears, overcome with shame. What hurt me the most was the betrayal of my friends: Solly Brill next to me had thrown his arms over the table and laid down his head, which was red from so much laughing. And although I knew that he wasn't laughing so much at my mistake—which I couldn't consider a mistake—as much as expressing his relief from the deadly-dull torment, which would have made me every bit as cruel if someone else had been in my place, I did feel the stabbing pain of having been utterly and despicably abandoned.

"Now take your seat and think about whether a building can sleep," said Fräulein Zehrer. "But don't go dozing off on me, you sleepyhead!"

Solly Brill grabbed his protruding ears as if his head were about to fall off. "A sleeping castle! Who ever heard of that! You have words for that, all right! Go to sleep, sleepyhead!"

I was as if blinded.

But when the class was over, Blanche Schlesinger came up to me. "What you said didn't make me laugh at all," she said. "I thought it was exactly right, and very poetic, a beautiful shortcut that said all that was needed."

My sister Tanya joined us. "You have a very nice dress," said Blanche, briefly turning a little red, as if the compliment seemed a little empty. "And very pretty hair," she added, as a kind of compensation, "and pretty eyes. I'd like to be friends with both of you. Do you want to trade some books?"

We brought her Dickens's *A Christmas Carol,* which she already knew, but was happy to have because of Rackham's beautiful illustrations, and she in turn gave us a very strange book, *God's Conic Sections* by someone named Sir Galahad, who Blanche said was actually a woman. We didn't understand a word of it, but when we came across it years later it seemed like a revelation, and it took us another ten years to get over it.

Because we realized the imbalance of this literary exchange, we next brought her Agnes Günther's *The Saint and Her Fool,* which our Aunt Elvira had found very moving, and which we begged her for, supposedly so we could take it to Fräulein Zehrer. We felt that Blanche was the spitting image of the "little soul" in the book—a misunderstanding that later proved to be quite cruel. That must have led her to judge us for what we were. Her next gift to us was Kipling's *Jungle Book.*

But that wasn't all. She gave us Mörike, in homeopathic doses, then Thackeray's *Pendennis,* which to this day remains one of our favorites, and, finally, a volume of selected poems by Goethe, and after that Longus's *Daphnis and Chloë,* in all naïveté and undoubtedly only because of its beauty. We loved her more and more with every book.

I don't know what was more exciting for us back then: the events concerning Tildy, his wife and her father, old Paşcanu, who were often the subject of conversation first at home and ultimately throughout the entire city—or our friendship with Blanche Schlesinger and the other world that she opened for us, the marvelous wonder-world of literature, this real place of refuge for those who have need to flee.

"Come visit us sometime," we asked her. "We have a big garden."

She smiled sadly. "I don't think that's possible."

"Then we'll come visit you, and you can show us all your books and your father's as well."

"That won't work, either," she said quietly.

We were inclined to consider her very elegant, because she was kept so isolated. So there she was at last, our bewitched princess, who remained beautiful and noble even though a terrible curse had deprived her of her crown and her rule over her subjects. I loved her, and I loved her name, which I expanded into the name of Parsifal's love: Blanchefleur.

Later, after our friendship had been sundered in the most horrible way and she and her father had left Czernopol, she sent one last book: Disraeli's *Tancred.* As a dedication she had inscribed a few lines from Verlaine:

Vous connaissez tout cela, tout cela,
Et que je suis plus pauvre que personne,
Vous connaissez tout cela, tout cela,
Mais ce que j'ai, mon Dieu, je vous le donne.

In the meantime, while we were so absorbed in our immediate concerns, things were happening that would have a far greater impact on us. Czernopol was weaving the background for our myth.

In this city, where whatever didn't take place on the street was indiscriminately dragged into the open, the events that led to the animated conversation between Bubi Brill and his father, which Solly had so masterfully reenacted for us, did not remain hidden for long.

People said that Usher Brill looked up old Paşcanu in order to propose a daring business deal with him. But that wasn't so: old Paşcanu had summoned him.

People knew everything, down to the smallest detail:

On the morning before the night when he paid his last visit to his dead wives in Horecea, Săndrel Paşcanu appeared in the stairwell of his house. He hadn't slept. He stood there, nearly six feet tall and despite his eighty years—or more, since he didn't know his exact age—quite erect, although admittedly one hand was leaning on a rough cane, while the other, as horny and clawlike as the talon of a gigantic bird, rested on the dirty handrail of the wooden staircase, scaring the cockroaches into the cracks. He was wearing the trousers and vest of a suit made of the finest material, of a cut that a dying breed of London tailors is taking to the grave. His shoes, too, with their suede uppers fastened from the side, were almost dandy-like in their elegance. Instead of a jacket, however, he had put on a sleeveless sheepskin, a so-called *cojoc*, which after decades of use hid a fleece that had worn down to a few moldy remnants with the brownish sheen of old bacon rind. His nose was bold, prominent, and vulture-like, and his mustache was white as snow and soft as silk and covered his mouth completely. His black eyes glowed beneath his bushy eyebrows. They were set close together, like those of a lurking boar, wily and dangerous. He was unshaved—white stubble covered his gaunt cheeks. A tall, pointed lambskin cap crowned his skull, which was completely bare; he never took it off, no matter what the season or occasion. He called for his coachman. His voice had retained the power of his youth and betrayed the full tone used by the speech-happy Latins.

He called out three times: "Miron!" Then, louder and louder: "Miron! Miron!"

The *scopit*, who had the same name as Czernopol's patron saint, came waddling on flat feet across the yard. The eunuch's fat rolled up the stairs and was still in motion when its owner came to a stop. Old Paşcanu, who hadn't taken his angry eyes off his coachman, turned around without a word and walked into the next room, rapping his cane against the floor. The coachman followed. The room was in disrepair, with ugly plush-covered furniture, almost entirely darkened by the heavy curtains in front of the small windows. A covered picture hung on the wall—the Titian. Beside it stood a large iron antique safe.

Old Paşcanu stepped into the center of the room and turned around. The coachman had stayed by the door. He was even taller than his master, and his back was so enormous it could have supplied five times the flesh the other had on his bones. When he was behind the two colossal horses, up on the box of the hulking old carriage, he looked natural enough, but on his own two legs he looked like a human mountain. The street boys of Czernopol called him *Gogeamite*, which was derived from the name of the giant boxer Gogea Mitu. His spongelike neck was covered with a network of delicate, sharply etched grooves, as if the skin of the oldest Indian temple-elephant had acquired the rosy color and the tenderness of a suckling pig. His body was shaped like a roller, and was wrapped around several times with a purple sash that must been miles long. His back was like a whale's, beckoning to be harpooned.

Old Paşcanu was clearly tempted to vent his feelings with his cane on that very back. He yelled at the coachman:

"You're sleeping, Miron! You sleep day and night, in the stable and on the coachbox. You sleep in your shoes. You just hang there in your pants and sleep like a pumpkin in a sack."

"I'm not asleep, sir, I'm awake," the man said in a fluting voice that spilled out of his throat like some clear oil.

"You were sleeping while I was on my knees praying next to my wives' coffins!"

Miron didn't answer. Old Paşcanu looked him in the eye. His mustache was twitching.

"Praying, you understand!"

"Praying, sir," the angelic voice echoed.

"Now go to the Jew Brill, you elephant without balls. Go to his house. Tell him to come here right away, before he closes up his shop. Right this minute. I want to speak with him. Tell him to bring his magnifying glass. You wait for him and bring him here. Tell him you've been instructed to go to another Jew if he keeps you waiting. Bring him here. Then, while he's with me, drive out to the Jew Perko..."

"He's not a Jew, sir," the eunuch objected gently.

"Are you contradicting me? Go to the Jew Perko, I say. Bring him here as well, and keep him waiting until the other has gone. They're not to see each other. Now go!"

"I'm going, sir," said the voice from the whale, with heavenly unction.

He rolled out the door. Old Paşcanu waited until he'd closed the door behind him, then pulled a bunch of keys from his pocket, went to the safe, and opened it. He bent over, panting, leaning on his cane, and plunged his arm up to his shoulder into the deepest place of the safe. He rummaged around a while, finally withdrawing his talon, which now clutched a fist-sized ball of newspaper. He unfolded the paper. A small box appeared. He pressed his calloused thumb against it, as if testing it, and then deposited the box in his vest pocket. With the fussiness of an old man he then relocked the safe, tucked the keys in his pocket, walked to the desk, banging his cane hard against the floorboards, and sat down on one of the plush-covered armchairs. In this way he waited, in the half-slumber of a very old man, slightly bent forward, lightly nodding with his upper body, with half-closed eyes and an occasionally twitching mustache. As soon as steps could be heard on the stairs, however, his eyes reopened, and his entire life force, sinister and incalculable like a violent force of nature, seemed to flow back into him through the crafty slits beneath his white eyebrows. Only his eyelids opened, nothing else moved. Tilting forward, he lurked like a huge forest creature crouching in the damp coolness of the deep leafy shade, awake and ready to spring out of the underbrush, dangerous, wreaking havoc, dominant. He was very striking. A narrow, dense band of light fell through a slit in the curtain at a slant in front of him.

The castrato led in the merchant Usher Brill.

"We want to be alone," ordered Săndrel Paşcanu, without reacting to the Jew's greeting.

"Alone, sir!" Miron fluted, then rolled out the door and pulled it shut. Brill was breathing quietly, his calm as profound as a well. Jews are heroes.

"Did you bring your glass?" asked old Paşcanu.

"I did," answered Brill from the depths of inexhaustible patience.

"Here!" said Paşcanu, and reached into his vest pocket. He had stiff cuffs on his sleeves, clamped together with enormous barbaric cuff links that betrayed his background: lumps of gold studded with rubies. One of these caught on his watch chain. He fumbled with it, then impatiently tugged it off. His movements remained animated after he pulled the small box from his pocket. He tossed it onto the table so brusquely that it bounced. Something rolled out and onto the ground. Brill bent over to pick it up.

When he stood back up he almost bumped into old Paşcanu, who had risen and was looming menacingly above him, his vulture's nose jutting forward as if ready to hack something to pieces, his white mustache fluffed out, his claws digging into the back of the armchair. Brill glanced at him with sad, cyclamen-colored eyes behind eyelashes that had faded to a colorless stubble. The old man sat back down.

The diamond Brill had picked up was as big as a dove's egg. He turned it in his short fingers. The backs of his hands were covered with reddish hair, his skin spotted like the belly of a salamander. Steadying the stone in two fingers, he held it in the thick, dusty ray of light. The stone flashed blue and fire-red.

Brill examined it at arm's length, then brought it right up to his eyes, stroked the facets and edges with the tips of his fingers, finally took his jeweler's loupe from his pocket, wedged it under his eyebrow, and continued his examination long and thoroughly. Finally he removed his glass, set the brilliant back on the table, and gave a deep, melancholy sigh.

"Speak!" said old Paşcanu.

"A beautiful stone," said Brill, slowly, as if recalling a distant memory. "Very much a beautiful stone. A stone with hardly a cloud, hardly a spot of coal..."

"You're lying!" snorted Paşcanu. "It's perfectly pure. I paid five million for it."

"You were cheated, Herr Paşcanu," said Brill, troubled. "You should have bought from people you can trust, like Usher Brill."

"What you sell are whipcords," said Paşcanu, disdainfully. "And bad ones at that."

"I have seen much in my life, Herr Paşcanu. Some of it thanks to you. And one time a remarkable diamond."

"Not one like this."

Brill rocked his bleached head back and forth. "You want to sell, Herr Paşcanu?"

"I want you to tell me what this stone is worth."

"*Nu*, five million. You said yourself."

"I bought it before the war," said Paşcanu.

Brill nodded, resigned, with closed eyes. The lie was transparent.

"What's it worth today?"

Brill sighed. "What it's worth is from me my whole life, and from you a good laugh, Herr Paşcanu, that's what it's worth. Because you are a rich man, Herr Paşcanu, and I am a poor man. But if you ask me what it should cost... It should cost a fortune for whoever buys it, and bring a fortune for whoever sells it. But it's another story again if you ask me what it'll bring... *Nu*, Herr Paşcanu, it's a beautiful stone, a big stone, hardly a blemish, so, what will it bring? What it will bring—there aren't many stones like that on the market today..."

"No," old Paşcanu interrupted, vigilantly. "There's not another one like it with the same cut. It has a name. I won't tell you, because I gave it another one. Now it's called Ice Heart."

"A beautiful name, Herr Paşcanu. But sad. Why don't you just rename it the Paşcanu Diamond? People don't want to hear sad things."

"Just tell me what it's worth."

"Why me, Herr Paşcanu? A stone like this has an international reputation. Why don't you simply send a telegram to the bourse in Amsterdam: 'Wire back estimated value Paşcanu diamond." You want to sell, you make an auction. Rothschild makes a bid, Morgan makes a bid, the Prince of Linz or Wels or whoever, your friends, rich people, they bang with the gavel, going once, going twice, sold. All very simple. What need do you have for Usher Brill?"

"What would you give me for it as a lump sum?"

Brill swallowed. "A man can't give what he doesn't have, Herr Paşcanu."

"All I'm after is security. I mean to entrust this stone to you. Then you'll buy for me a second one. One exactly like this. I need two." He made a small, meaningful pause. "That one I'll call Fire Heart. You'll buy it for me. Never mind the cost. You understand?"

Usher Brill looked back down at the diamond for the first time since he had examined it. He swallowed once again. He made a movement with his hands, as if to pick up the stone, but then let his arms drop. Once again he closed his eyes and rocked his head from side to side, as he said:

"When I was twelve years old, Herr Paşcanu, I had a dream. I saw old Herr Paşcanu coming to me and saying, 'Usher my boy, here is a diamond, a diamond so big as a cannonball. Take it and go and buy me another cannonball just like it.' *Nu*, that was the dream I had when I was twelve . . . I am an old man, Herr Paşcanu. God forbid, not as old as you, and yet not everyone has your health, Herr Paşcanu, may God preserve it for you. My business is getting along moderately well. My oldest boy is a *parasolnik*, a nobody, a *nebekh* who plays at being a cavalry officer with tennis racquets and goes drinking at the Trocadero like a *goy*—you'll excuse me, Herr Paşcanu, as we're old friends. But I have a little daughter, may God protect her, a nice reasonable girl, and she's going to marry a sensible man, and I have another boy, a good smart *yingl*, God's blessing on our old age, by the name of Solly. They will take over the shop with the whipcords, and maybe even go a little further. But I am an old man, Herr Paşcanu. If I still dream it's only about the men who come painting swastikas on the shutters at night. Not about great deals with profits in the hundred-thousand range. I have the tax man on my back enough already."

Paşcanu said nothing.

"Besides," Brill went on after another deep sigh, "if you'll permit me to repeat myself, Herr Paşcanu: Why do you need me? What need do you have of Usher Brill? What you need is a telegram sent to Amsterdam: 'Obtain identical piece Paşcanu Diamond same size form any price stop Paşcanu.' If they don't find one, well, at the worst they'll cut a new one to match. They have enough raw diamonds in all sizes and good for all kinds of cuts. You don't have to get personally involved, you have people here on the square with excellent connections. But me, I don't deal much with stones anymore, Herr Paşcanu. I have my shop with whipcords, like you say, it's getting along, may God protect it, it's known better days, but I'm an old man, what more do I need, grow up poor and poor you stay . . . You have experts right here on the square. You have Merdinger & Lipschitz, you have Gottesmann & Rubel, you have Falikmann & Company. And if you don't want to deal with them, you have Merores. An old acquaintance, Herr

Paşcanu. What's wrong with him? Is he suddenly too high class not to need a few hundred thousand? Maybe the boy, growing up with all those millions. But the old man?"

Herr Paşcanu didn't move.

Brill looked past the diamond, concentrated. "I am an old man, Herr Paşcanu, of over sixty years," he said. "You knew me in younger days. Back then, whenever you said to me, 'Brill, I have some deal, this thing or that, it's difficult, it calls for discretion, we have to be careful but it's a good deal,' well, did I hesitate, Herr Paşcanu? Tell me yourself—did I hesitate, Herr Paşcanu? No I didn't, Herr Paşcanu. Today I am an old man. I have my business, yes, with whipcords, but there is a crisis in the whole world, and not everyone can take advantage of a situation like you can, and take refuge in stones, but in those days, when you said to me, 'Brill, I have serious difficulties with the business, avoid making a fuss, a matter of trust'—you tell me! I hear lumber isn't doing so well, but you are a chosen one, Herr Paşcanu, may God preserve whatever other businesses you may have, I'm always telling my Bubi, my oldest, look at old Herr Paşcanu, I say, the way he climbed down from the mountaintops and didn't have a shoe on his foot, you'll excuse me, Herr Paşcanu, but, you know, that's how people talk, and for the young people it's an example. So I say to my Bubi: 'Look at him, this chosen man, who climbed down barefoot from the mountains and now he's a *meylekh*, a king among the lumber merchants.' But he prefers to go the *kurvehs* at Schorodok's. So permit me, Herr Paşcanu, but it will be a very expensive purchase. You'll have to pay in Dutch guldens, and the exchange today is nearly sixty-five to one—not just another order of net stockings, Herr Paşcanu, it will cost millions. And you will kindly permit me to ask: What kind of security are you offering, Herr Paşcanu?"

"You have the stone, you ass! You take it with you, to London or Amsterdam, and show it, so that the other stone will be exactly like this one. You want me to give you some security for putting a stone in your Jew fingers? *You* need to leave the security here for *me*, understand? Not that I mean to cheat you, but you shouldn't be able to cheat me, either."

Usher Brill rested his hand on his heart and smiled forgivingly with closed eyes. When he opened his eyes again they focused on the diamond on the table, and widened of their own accord. "You are a good man, Herr Paşcanu," he said. "People can say what they want, but I say you are a good man. A hard man, but a good man. I have earned well by you. I've earned better by other people, just for your information, in terms of percentage. You are a hard man. Nevertheless, many people have risen high because of you. And the more you wanted them to grow, the bigger they grew. Why, I ask you, Herr Paşcanu, do you suddenly want to make the small people as big as the big people, and not, for instance, make the big people a little bit bigger? Aren't you more in contact with Merores, Herr Paşcanu? Is Merores suddenly too high-class for a deal like this, now that he's become a *chevalier*? Just between us, are there many noblemen these days who wouldn't give their eyetooth for a deal like this? Merores wouldn't? Don't take me wrong, Herr Paşcanu, but what for do you need Brill?"

"Miron!" old Paşcanu shouted so loud the room shook. He banged his cane impatiently against the floorboards and repeated: "Miron! Miron!"

"It's a very confidential business, Herr Paşcanu," said Brill. "Better don't tell me anything. Diamonds you could use to find like crumbs of shabbos-cake on Monday under the table, but these days it's not so easy. There are different people involved: officials, detectives, what do I know. Everything is written down. Buying a raw diamond as big as a ball will come out very expensive, if you can find one before it comes up for auction. It will be extremely difficult to have it cut in this extravagant form, please understand, without it being talked around for whom and why. You don't want to give your money out for costume jewelry, Herr Paşcanu, I'm guessing. It will be an expensive business, Herr Paşcanu, and a difficult one for whoever does it for you. More than one person will have to go to London or Amsterdam, not just one, and serious people, no *bokher* or *nebbokhanten* like my son Bubi. And you won't want to leave the stone rolling around inside some foreign safe, Herr Paşcanu. You will want it back. But the import duty on stones is high, Herr Paşcanu, and the export is no simple matter. Do you want to give gifts to the customs inspectors, Herr Paşcanu? I don't imagine you do. You'll need reliable people to take the stone abroad and bring it back, along with the second one as well. The commission will be high, very high. All in all, it would be a matter of twenty or twenty-five million, maybe more, for certain. It's an investment that calls for more than just one personal fortune, Herr Paşcanu. I can't shake the impression that we're rocking a dead baby here. You are a well-known man, so I beg your pardon, but please permit me to ask again, Herr Paşcanu: What kind of security are you offering?"

"Miron!"

The castrato appeared in the door.

"Throw the Jew out," said old Paşcanu.

Brill stayed where he was.

"Throw him out or else I'll smash his head in, and yours as well!"

Brill started to leave, anxiously burdened by all the misunderstanding and the futility of explaining himself. Just before reaching the door he turned around, resigned to one last attempt. He shrugged his shoulders and lifted his blotchy, red-haired hands, opening his palms up as if he were presenting his case to old Paşcanu one last time, as if he were weighing his arguments for the tough old man one last time, for his own good, so that Paşcanu would see how serious and at the same time how clearly simple the matter was. And what he was offering in those open palms was none other than himself, Usher Brill, a man trapped by fate, unable to do otherwise... His wise, despairing gaze attempted to force this stubborn old man to show a little understanding. It was an urgent gesture, tragic and ridiculous and very human, full of the frailty of the human desire to make oneself understood. He sighed, nodded sadly, and dropped his arms. The castrato towered next to him, his flabby, masklike Mongolian face showed no expression: eyes, mouth, and nose carved out of a moonlit pumpkin.

"God is just. May he protect you, Herr Paşcanu," said Usher Brill and walked away, disheartened.

A few minutes later Miron led a man in who barely reached his belt, and who sauntered into the room with overwhelming casualness, his hat tilted back on his neck, his hands in his pockets, and his shirt billowing out of his open jacket, like the clown in a tragedy.

Without ado he plopped down in one of the plush chairs across from old Paşcanu and smartly crossed his short legs, showing off his elegant, orange-colored shoes.

"*Salut*, esteemed prince!" he squawked. "What a fine morning! Well, is he going to take it on or not?"

"He is," said old Paşcanu.

"Perfect, very excellent, *wunderbar*! You have not drink for me: shorbet, soda water, orange juice—*sans* alcohol? Because it's heating up outside, *bozhe moi*!"

It was Herr Perko, "the angel of the emigrants."

He had earned this epithet with some daring undertakings in Russia during and after the revolution, smuggling packs of refugees across the border—not without having first relieved them of the last valuables they had on them. A certain Prince Krupenski, a fanatical connoisseur and breeder of roses, for which he had had mile-long greenhouses constructed on his vast estate, was one of his victims: on market days he could be seen on the cobblestones at the Theaterplatz, where he helped a small garden stall sell radishes—a man of seventy. Now and then he came to the villa district, where we lived, to work in a garden. One exaggeratedly tactful lady, who had heard his name whispered about, had a tray taken out to him with a ham sandwich and a glass of sherry during a break in the work. He thanked her kindly but requested to be treated as what he was, namely, a day laborer.

Herr Perko was also associated with the shady story involving the rescue of a purported daughter of the tsar, who through some miracle supposedly survived when the ruling family was shot. It was a proven fact that he had saved the lives of other members of the high nobility—and thereby acquired fabulous jewels. Uncle Sergei was of the opinion there was no point in hanging him, because the noose would refuse to touch his neck.

13
Ephraim Perko; Old Brill Visits the Baronet von Merores

NO ONE will ever know exactly how old Paşcanu planned to carry out his swindle, because he never managed to pull it off. His intentions had made the rounds in Czernopol before the business ever really started. Bubi Brill, who had been crazy enough to get involved in the deal, was arrested as a diamond smuggler at the Dutch border just a few hours after leaving Amsterdam, and although the stone could not be found on his person, he spent a half year in jail, and was ultimately sentenced to pay an outrageous fine, which he avoided, but only because his father paid bribes amounting to nearly as much as the fine itself.

Herr Perko, meanwhile, had disappeared, along with the diamond.

It will also forever remain a secret how Paşcanu ever managed to come up with enough money to buy the diamond and smuggle it into the country in the first place. At his one and only hearing, which was conducted following the arrest of Bubi Brill, he was informed of the charges that would be brought against him: attempted fraud, smuggling, tax evasion, bribery, embezzlement, and other similar crimes, but he scarcely said a word. That same evening he was dead.

Nor did he betray Ephraim Perko. No one understood what might have motivated him to forego this final—and, one would think, justifiable—act of revenge. People said he was simply a broken man.

The opposite sounds more convincing: he was anything but broken, anything but ready to resign what was clearly the game of his life. And so, presumably, he said nothing so as to be able to exact his revenge in a far more thorough manner later, without incriminating himself by showing his hand now.

The word among the Russian emigrants was that the old man had succumbed to the unique charm and the astonishing powers of persuasion of Ephraim Perko just like everyone else. But that, too, is highly unlikely. Săndrel Paşcanu was not the man to be fleeced by a brazen scoundrel like Perko, who was as brash as a blowfly. Paşcanu did not feel the aristocratic constraint that required having a creature like that on hand to take care of all the troublesome logistics, the plotting and planning, making the rounds of officials or else going around them somehow, and whose services also helped his clients overcome their own inhibitions. The aristocrat stood to gain much more than he might forfeit by dealing with such a person, of whom he only has a faint picture anyway. The institution of the house-Jew, who feels tacitly permitted to cheat his master at every turn, was an ancient tradition within the feudal caste of the eastern lands. And ever since we met Solly Brill, and had tasted the delights of his amusing directness and admired his juggler's adroitness in all practical operations, we had nothing but understanding for such an arrangement.

But Săndrel Paşcanu was a peasant and a greedy rogue himself. A man who comes from severe poverty but manages to become a millionaire, and who associates with the great men of the world as with his own kind, is not so easily blinded by the audacity of a cheap crook.

Incidentally, Ephraim Perko casually resurfaced in Czernopol a year later as jaunty as ever. Not the smallest infraction could be proven against him, not even the knowledge that anyone else—much less himself—had ever intended to break the law. Nevertheless, coming back was a risky thing to do. Presumably he wasn't prompted to do so because of his utter innocence: So what did bring him back to Czernopol?

He wasn't poor. Counting the Paşcanu diamond with all his other jewelry, which he owned thanks to the misfortune of the Russian refugees, not to mention his cash holdings and the return from diverse transactions—he kept very busy—Perko must have acquired a fortune sizable enough to have allowed him to settle on the Riviera, for instance, where he could have had incomparably greater hunting, with more game in the preserve, so to speak. But he chose not to leave Czernopol. He belonged to this city, just as the city belonged to him. I'm certain that old Paşcanu realized this, and that he had counted on it.

Only in Czernopol was Ephraim Perko allowed to be exactly who he was; only here could he count on an utter and unchallenged acceptance. What need did he have of the déclassé duchesses of the Côte d'Azur, when the ladies of the Trocadero, which was owned by his friend Schorodok, were just as well (if not much better) built? Did the band leader at the casino in Monte Carlo launch into the tango "Ay-ay-ay" the minute Ephraim Perko walked through the door? Gyorgyovich Ianku never failed to do so, even if this meant interrupting the national anthem, which he was expected to play at three in the morning, as a signal that the official portion of the evening was over and the unofficial part could begin. And begin it did when Effi Perko arrived! What need did this diminutive playboy have for yachts in blue bays—he was afraid of water. A Rolls-Royce? Here he happened to be one of two or three people who could afford one if they wanted. But did he? He did not. He preferred the sweet, romantic carriages that swung back and forth, dipping deep into their long leaf springs, and the homey tang of the horses, the brittle old protective leather, and the musty smell of the coachman's coat. Although he was born in Odessa, Czernopol was Effi Perko's true homeland. He was attached to this town with a natural, gleeful dedication, a lucky boy in perfect, sunny resonance with the place that was both the source of his good fortune and its stage. And Czernopol rewarded his loyalty by providing him with a willing realm that blossomed forth like King Laurin's rose garden.

It was also the only place on earth where people could understand his speech.

Effi Perko spoke Russian, German, Romanian, Ukrainian, Polish, Yiddish, French, English, and Italian all in the same way: namely, gurgling, croaking, and choking—like someone dreaming that he's spitting out his teeth. You had to have a keen and well-trained ear in order to understand a single one of his sentences, and you had to have a similarly keen and well-trained spirit—the spirit of Czernopol—in order to fully appreciate the wit behind his words, both the intended as well as the accidental.

It wasn't so bad when he explained that he was an aficionado of opera, while his wife preferred comedy—at that time he had been married three times, and two more wives would follow, each more beautiful than the last—and sank his teeth into the sentence: "I likh verry mutch goink to opera, but my wife she prreferrs more the comedies." But it was quite a stimulating challenge to decipher, for example: "I shut go for makingk bisness vit Peshkaner? I shut vant for go making caca in bucket!"—by which he meant: People think that I got involved in some dealings with Paşcanu; do they think I want to get locked up in a cell where to relieve myself all I would have at my disposal would be a bucket? Even the metaphor he used—"making caca in bucket"—was not some regional turn of phrase but his own coinage, invented on the spot.

And the remarks he casually tossed aside were downright brilliant, as for instance his appraisal of a sensually languid—not languidly sensual—woman: "she snorrs vit de oygen"—she snores with her eyes.

The man clearly possessed great charm as well. No one who saw Effi Perko dancing at the Trocadero, with great abandon, agility, and grace, and with women two or three heads taller than himself—he only liked tall blond women with beautiful skin, ample bosoms, and long legs—could deny a certain admiration for this lucky dwarf with the character of a hyena. He deported himself with the elegance of a racetrack devotee: the high narrow collar of his silk shirts joined with a gold pin clasped beneath his narrow tie, a gray homburg with a bound edge and black band, tilting off his forehead onto the back of his neck, his jacket unbuttoned and opened to reveal his exotic belt of crocodile leather or snakeskin, his hands permanently in his trouser pockets, and more often than not sporting a toothpick in his mouth. He smelled of high-priced fragrances, like a harem beauty. One time he asked old Brill, point-blank: "Say, Brill, who wears such tidy *shmattes* vat you sell?" It was no wonder that Bubi Brill, for deeper reasons than "simply business," as he said, sought out Ephraim Perko's friendship. It was even less surprising that Herr Tarangolian found this highly amusing.

"If Tildy can be considered the only man in Czernopol with a true face," opined the prefect, "then we rightly have to concede to my friend Perko that no one else—not even Năstase—could boast such nerve."

As for Bubi Brill, we later had more than enough opportunity to get to know him as he was an avid member of the tennis club near our house, which we eventually convinced our parents to let us join. The clubhouse had been the officers' salon of the former Austrian military shooting range pavilion and was built in the classic style of the fin de siècle: it was too large to be a weather station packed with barometers, thermometers, wind vanes, and hygrometers, and too small for a bathhouse or public library. The old bullet trap could still be found behind the building: as high as a house, long since overgrown with the most beautiful meadow grass, and hemmed in by streets lined with nut trees—a paradise for the happy children who were allowed to grow up without much supervision, and for the soldiers from the nearby barracks, who on warm summer nights attempted to ravish the servant girls they lured there. The tennis courts were managed by an attendant, who also served as the municipal dogcatcher, or *hitzel*, setting forth in that capacity twice a week with a cage mounted to a cart and a wire snare affixed to a long pole, to reduce the prodigious numbers of strays that roamed the streets. He was only too happy to round up pedigreed dogs as well, and charged their owners a handsome fee for their release. The president of the Czernopol Lawn Tennis Club was Wolf Leibish, Baronet von Merores, Junior, who was quite devoted to the sport.

It was he who effected the connection between Bubi and Effi Perko.

It happened on the same morning as the altercation between Bubi Brill and his father, after which the father, Usher Brill, paid a visit on old Hirsh Leib, Baronet von Merores, Senior. What happened was as follows:

Bubi showed up at the tennis courts as Wolf von Merores—his middle name, Leibish, was usually suppressed—was winning his game against the director of the Anglo-Maghrebinian Bank, a certain Dr. Sudbinsky, with one final well-aimed overhead smash. Herr von

Merores was walking up to the clubhouse, a towel draped casually around his neck and half a dozen first-class rackets bunched beneath his arm, while Bubi Brill idly surveyed the tennis courts, still morose following the "scene with the old man."

"Good morning," Wolfi shouted, in English, in a comradely way. "What's new?"

"Morning," replied Bubi Brill. "Just the usual. Are you done?"

"Yes. I have to be in town at eleven. You missed an interesting game. I'll have to take away Sudbinsky's handicap if he keeps playing like this. He nearly beat me."

"I'd like to talk to you about a small matter," said Bubi Brill.

"Sure. Come on over here. I just have to take a quick shower." He carefully wrapped his towel around his neck. "Evidently there was another scandalous incident last night that everybody's talking about," he mentioned casually. "Have you heard anything more about it?"

"Not a thing," Bubi lied, since his mind was too focused on something else.

"People are talking about a Nazi demonstration on the main street. Your father's store was hit as well?"

"Oh, the usual slogans smeared on the shutters. Not worth mentioning," Bubi admitted sullenly.

"Wait just a minute," said Baronet Wolf, "I just want to tip the ball boy."

"It will just take a second," said Bubi, on the way to the clubhouse. "I'm sure you've read in the papers about the delegation from the Ministry of War coming to town."

"Naturally," said Wolfi von Merores. "Border security, so the story goes."

"Exactly. I've found out from a dependable source that they're going to contact old Paşcanu."

Wolfi looked up and smiled. "Interesting," he said.

"Supposedly it's about developing a preliminary contract for lumber consignments to the army." Bubi paused a moment. "I figured the information would not be entirely uninteresting to you, just as you said. Should the occasion present itself, I hope you will keep me in consideration?"

Wolfi went on smiling his fine smile. "Where does the information come from, if I may ask?"

"From a reliable source. By the way, have you thought of me in regard to the person we were speaking of yesterday?"

"Effi Perko? Yes, I *have* been thinking of you. Speaking of which, what are you doing tomorrow? Why don't you come up to my office for a few minutes. Let's say at eleven. Perko will just happen to be there. It's the perfect opportunity."

"Fine, I'll be there. Then I'll tell you more about the other business. In any case: old Paşcanu is still very active."

"Evidently," said Wolfi. "So, tomorrow at eleven. *Ciao*, my friend."

They each waved a friendly goodbye, and Baronet Wolfi disappeared into the clubhouse. Bubi Brill sauntered down to the courts and soon found a game among the young people there.

By the time Wolf Baronet von Merores had changed, shaved, and combed his hair, the Chrysler was already waiting out front. His chauffeur held the door for him, then climbed behind the steering wheel and gave an impressive blast of the three-toned horn—the signal he used to inform the members of the club of the arrival and departure of their president. At the same time, the vehicle surged forward.

The splendor of the trees in the Czernopol Volksgarten was without comparison. Seated in the back of the Chrysler, he had taken off his gray homburg and set it beside him, and the summer light floated down through the treetops onto the avenues like smoke spilling from a censer, occasionally flashing in the baronet's smoothly parted black hair. Wolfi von Merores was of less than medium height, a little on the chubby side, with a delicate bone structure. He carried himself with the distinction and elegance of a businessman at the peak of his power. With a hint of dreaminess in his dark almond eyes, he peered through the raised windows of the sedan into the park, which glided past him like a tapestry, the consummate background for a princely profile, but once the vehicle reached the officers' casino and the backdrop shifted abruptly from handsomely cultivated nature to the uncivilized doings of the main street, his manicured hands reached for the paper and he spent the rest of the drive into town reading.

In Neuschul Street the Chrysler gently braked in front of the von Merores' house. Baronet Wolf, who never failed to deliver a personal word of thanks to his staff, gave his chauffeur a friendly nod: "Thanks, Kozarishchiuk. I won't be needing you before five o'clock bridge."

He made a very lordly impression as he climbed out of the car, folded his newspaper, and stepped into his father's house, carrying his gray homburg.

The von Merores' house was well tended, with an air of patrician stability. In the nineties it had belonged to a very rich Armenian. The front rooms exhibited an Oriental sumptuousness, with mosaic floors and deep window niches. Corridors that were almost devoid of light led back to a variety of small rooms that once may have sheltered servants, or perhaps even harem wives—one never knew what kind of family arrangements prevailed among the Armenians.

A slender man who served as the Merores' secretary met Wolf in the corridor, which they referred to using the English word "hall," took his hat, and said: "You have a visitor. Old man Brill."

"Interesting," said Wolf von Merores. "Anything else?"

"He wants to speak to your papa. I told him he should wait until you came. Other than that, nothing unusual."

"Mail?"

"A few letters. I've set out everything that requires signing."

"Thank you, Seligmann," said Baronet Wolf. "I'm going back for a few minutes to wish Mama good morning. Then you can let Brill in to see me."

He set off into the dark labyrinth of the rear wing. Stopping outside one of the doors, he gave a careful knock, and when he heard someone invite him in, he swept open the door and bounded lithely to his mother and, as he was well bred, kissed her hand. The old lady in her peignoir was in the process of shaping her Eton crop with a curling iron. A few experiments with bleaching agents had given her hair a somewhat violet tinge.

"You are incorrigible, Mama," said Wolf, patting her on the hand. "How often do I have to repeat how happy I am that we can afford a hairdresser, thank God."

"Why should I give good money to that Figaro when I can do the same thing myself? Or is it maybe for making an impression on people? I'm telling you, I don't give a damn what people say. I'll do my hair the way I want and that's that."

"It's not on account of the people, Mama, please. Only, you'll burn the tips of your pretty hair. And the money you save on that you spend anyway on sweets you shouldn't be eating. So it's really on account of your liver. Emancipation is fine and good, but one has to consider one's health." He smiled and kissed the tips of her fingers. "Papa is doing well?" he asked.

"From what I hear he is."

"Now, there's a striking example of tender marital affection, by God, Mama," laughed Baronet Wolf. "That really makes me want to attend to your wishes."

"Stop it, you rascal. Papa is happy when I leave him alone, assuming that he'd even recognize me if I went in there. My behavior is only out of consideration, you impudent rascal. Actually, you should take it as an example not to marry too old. Look, you're almost forty. If you keep waiting another few years you shouldn't be surprised if you wind up with a young wife when you're seventy-five."

"Can we change the subject, Mama," said Baronet Wolf with cheerful tenderness. "You know there's no sense in trying to convince me. You know what my heart says."

"*Nebekh*," replied the old lady. "You make me sick with your sentimentalities, by God. Take my advice and put it out of your head. And you better be on time for dinner tonight. The Fokschaners are coming."

"With daughter, I presume?"

"Don't be difficult. She has twenty million—at least."

"If you need a new fur, Mama, all you have to do is tell me. You don't have to work so hard to earn it, Frau Marthe Schwerdtlein!"

Mama Memores playfully threatened to whack him with the hot curling iron, and Wolf once again laughed and kissed her rings.

"Don't be late, you cheeky thing!" she called after him as he hurried off.

In the hallway he paused in front of a dark mirror and carefully brushed his hair, then stepped into the study, where Usher Brill was waiting, visibly impatient.

"Please excuse my tardiness, Herr Brill," said Wolf von Merores kindly. "We weren't expecting you. May I offer you some cognac? My sympathies concerning the incidents last night, by the way. They should really take more energetic action. Kavalla cigar?"

Usher Brill observed him thoughtfully. "A fine *yingl* you've turned out, Leibish," he said. "Manners like a count." He rocked his pale reddish head. "That's an unusual development with young people these days. But don't go to any trouble on my account. I'd like to speak with Hirsh Merores."

"I'm sorry, Herr Brill," said Wolf. "You know that Papa hasn't been receiving anyone for years."

"And what is that? Too fine for everybody?" asked Brill. "Or does he have gout?"

"Papa has completely withdrawn from the world—it's been some time now, Herr Brill. Please take the feelings of an old man into consideration. He is given almost exclusively to pious thoughts."

"That's quite a trick, with his career," said Usher Brill.

"We don't hide the fact that thanks to my aged father's business acumen we have attained a certain wealth and standing," said Wolf with dignity. "So it's all the more praiseworthy if my old papa, following the faith of our fathers, expresses thanks for the blessings that have been bestowed upon us in such abundance. I assume that in an analogous case you, Herr Brill, would expect your son to exhibit the same respect for your feelings as I feel for my father's. He's a friend of mine, by the way. A very sympathetic young man."

"I can imagine you'd like that lout," said Brill, bitterly. "My whole life I've dreamt of having competitors that easy."

"I wouldn't know in what branch we might compete, Herr Brill," answered Wolf, not without a tinge of irony.

"Jews are always competitors, by God," Brill sighed heavily.

"Nobody is tougher than your own people. And toughest of all are your own children."

"How may I be of service?" asked Wolf von Merores, slightly irritated but controlled.

"I want to speak with Hirsh Leib, not with you, you jackass. It's information I need. This isn't a matter for little boys still wet behind the ears."

"As I said, I'm very sorry," stated Wolf patiently. "Papa isn't receiving. Incidentally, I've been familiar with the running of all the businesses for years now. Of course I don't have the experience of my revered father. Nonetheless, I am in a position to offer information that is at least more up to date. What is it about, Herr Brill?"

Brill looked long and thoughtfully at young Merores, who withstood his gaze casually and calmly, with just a hint of old, knowing melancholy in his almond-shaped eyes.

"I don't need any stock tips," Brill said at last. "I need some information, *yingl*, you understand! For tips and other *shmontses* I'm smart enough myself. But confidential information is a matter for old people. I want to speak with Hirsh Leib."

Wolf von Merores continued responding with his eyes full of old melancholy, while Brill went on: "Back then, when I was so young as you, we listened to the old people. We worked hand in hand and not against each other. The sons, they still learned from the experiences of their *tatehs*. From the old people they took the experience and put it into practice. These days the young people are quicker and brighter and more up to date than what their parents were, they're already like that while they still go caca in their nightshirt. So the old folks can just sit in their room and daven. These days they aren't worth anything anymore. The businesses are bigger and faster and everything is efficient. But for something solid, I, Usher Brill, still turn to the old people."

Wolf von Merores got up. "Be so kind as to wait a minute, Herr Brill," he said, before stepping out. "I'll be right back."

After a short while he came back. "Please come with me," he said.

They went through the dark corridor to the rearmost wing of the house. Wolf stopped outside a door and listened, his hand on the handle, for the length of a few breaths, and then carefully opened the door. "Please step inside," he whispered into Brill's ear.

Usher Brill entered a room that was almost completely dark and crammed full with the most diverse pieces of furniture. The air was stuffy. Hirsh Leib Baronet von Merores was sitting at the end of a long table, blind, a tefillin box strapped to his forehead and a fringed tallis draped over his shoulders.

Brill couldn't help but be gentle as he approached the old man, while Wolf carefully shut the door and stood there, waiting. Hirsh Merores mumbled a quiet singsong to himself, and after the two had waited for a while in vain for the blind man to notice them, Wolf finally went up to him, placed his hand gently on the old man's shoulder, and said: "Papa, Usher Brill wants to speak to you."

The blind man felt for the teffilin on his forehead and took it off. "Brill?" he asked, with a high-pitched, old-man's voice. "Where is Usher Brill. I'm listening!"

"*Zayt mir gezint*, Hirsh Leib Merores!" said Brill. "It's been so many years since we've seen each other."

"Brill?" the old man piped. "Where is Brill? I'm listening!"

"Here I am, Hirsh Merores, here!" said Brill, with urgency. "Here I am, standing in front of you, after many long years, to be asking a question, one old man to another..."

"Brill!" repeated old Merores, listening to the sound of the name. "Where is Usher Brill?"

"*Nu*, where is he supposed to be if he's talking to you right here!" said Brill, already a little impatient. He looked to Wolf Merores for help, but found only the same old melancholy in the younger man's eyes.

"Here I am, Hirsh Merores," he cried as loud as he could, "right here in front of you!"

Wolf von Merores placed a calming hand on his arm. "Please restrain yourself, Herr Brill. Papa is blind but not deaf."

"Brill!" said old Merores, fading away. He began to sing quietly.

Usher Brill looked to Wolf Merores.

"Come on," said Wolf. "Let's leave the old man alone."

He placed the tefillin straps in his father's hand. "I'll just turn on a little more light, Papa," he said tenderly, then shoved the table lamp a little nearer and switched it on—a senseless waste of electricity, Brill thought to himself, but which seemed to calm the blind man.

"Light," he mumbled. "Yes, light."

"What?" asked Brill, half out loud. "Is he completely..." He placed his index finger on his forehead and twisted it, as if boring inside.

Wolf signaled to Brill to walk out with him.

"God is just!" said Brill. "And not a day more than seventy years old..."

At the door he turned back one more time. Did he notice the beauty of the picture before him? The lamp with its dome-shaped shade of green silk. A flood of greenish gold, set upon by the heavy umber tones of the surrounding darkness, had taken refuge in the face of the old man, who had turned toward the light, his head angled upward as if blindly sniffing out a path, the one thing he could see, the mildly painful labor of a long search for God that is never fulfilled. His prayer shawl was draped over his shoulders, white with narrow black stripes, with folds and wrinkles that called to mind Oriental grandeur and opulence, and the curls of his white beard shone with a silken splendor.

"Usher Brill!" he said, his voice sounding like a child's, in a register from his head, and began to giggle. "The *bokher*!"

In the dark passageway Brill grabbed the young man by the sleeve. "As I live, I didn't know a thing about this," he said. "Just a few years back he was still a lively man..."

"It really is very painful," said Wolf. "I can remember the last time I went riding with Papa for a vigorous gallop across the fields of Klokuczka..."

"Riding!" said Usher Brill, mockingly. "On the office stool, I bet!" He pulled Wolf close to him. "Now you tell me: What's with old Paşcanu? Is he bankrupt or not?"

The eyes in front of him contained nothing but the same old melancholy. Brill was breathing heavily, almost panting.

"You are known and respected in the marketplace as a careful businessman, Herr Brill," said Wolf von Merores after a while. "Very cautious, impressively so. You may have heard of certain government business deals. You will also have heard of some payment difficulties involving the daughter, Frau von Tildy—most unfortunate. You should not expect any personal information from me about the individual in question. After all, if I am not mistaken you know him much better than I do. In short, Herr Brill: What is it precisely that you want me to tell you?"

"Old Paşcanu is a wolf," Brill gurgled. "A wolf is a dangerous animal." Young Merores couldn't help chuckling. "When it comes winter, and the wolf, he sees there's nothing more to eat, he turns into a tiger."

Wolfi Merores now smiled openly and full of kindness. "With this transformative illustration you're saying that under certain circumstances Herr Paşcanu is capable of anything... Well, Herr Brill," he shrugged his shoulders high, "I wouldn't deny the truth of that. The daring feat, Herr Brill, the measured risk—forgive me, but in our profession, among businessmen, that seems to be the Attic salt, and one of the reasons, just *en passant,* why I have not already retired to the country. Perhaps a man of your age—forgive me, but you do belong to the younger members of my papa's generation—perhaps a man of your age, in this time of tempestuous progress, which also has great impact on the financial world, really ought to leave the reins to the younger generation in order not to be overly taxed by the complexities of technical and scientific developments and so on."

"What do you mean, *tax*?" asked Brill. "What does any of this have to do with taxes, you *nebbokhant*?"

"'Taxed' in the sense of burdened, not in the sense of levies and tariffs. What I meant to say was that you shouldn't have to deal with the burdens of all the new technologies, that it might be better to hand the reins over..."

"You want maybe for me to hand the reins to you snotfaces!" Father Brill roared. "You little scamps? I'd sooner have a stroke right here and now..."

"That will inevitably happen soon enough if you keep getting so excited," said Wolf von Merores, in complete command of the situation. "You will permit me to have my secretary see you out, my time is sadly limited. Pleasure to see you, Herr Brill."

Herr von Merores himself regaled the members of the Lawn Tennis Club with the story of this visit, much to their amusement, and word soon spread across the entire city. What Herr von Merores did not relate, but what his secretary, young Seligmann, did convey a little later, was that Baronet Wolfi himself had been very distracted while looking over the mail that Seligmann had brought him in a special pouch made of calf's leather—the Merores were proud of having remained true to the religion of their fathers and of being one of few noble families of Israelite origin in the former Imperial-Royal Monarchy, and so they also kept their leather goods kosher. At that point Wolfi had once more gone to visit his mother. Seligmann, whose secretarial duties included obtaining a signature for any document that required immediate attention, had risked the danger of provoking his employer's displeasure and followed him. There he had overheard the old lady say the following:

"I'm telling you, the whole thing is a shameless rumor that old rogue Paşcanu leaked out so that people would think he still has some kind of deal with the government, so that under cover of that rumor he can make some lousy proposals. Why is old Brill interested in him? It's not for any contracts with the army—please, not with the goods he carries! I can tell you what he's after, and it's the same thing young Brill is after, too, namely some kind of measly commission and that's all. If I'm not mistaken, he'll want to sell the leftover jewelry he has lying around, otherwise why would he need Perko? By the way, you could give him a nod so he would show you first—there might be something for me there. Of course only the really clear stones . . . Go ahead and fix him up with young Brill, so he can be a *shlattenshammes* for old Paşcanu just like his *tateh*. Something like that isn't to be mentioned in the same breath with the likes of us, that's child's play. Don't rack your brains about the other business—I'm telling you, the delegation from the army has to do with Tildy, that *meshuggener*, according to what Constantin Tarangolian whispered to me yesterday in confidence. Evidently, Petrescu wants to conduct a purge so to make all the officers swear allegiance to the nationalist program. But under no circumstances will Constantin allow that; he says Petrescu can twist and turn as much as he wants as far as he's concerned, he can clean up the cavalry like the Augean stables and purge people like Turturiuk, but he can't start anything like that, or the prefect will undermine him. So you don't need to let yourself get mixed up in what young Brill says or break your skull over why the old man suddenly wanted to see Papa, not when I have information straight from the horse's mouth. Because what could those two possibly have with old Paşcanu? Listen to me. Especially seeing as Perko is getting mixed up as well. If they start talking about building border fortifications, then I'll let you know in time to send out feelers to the right people. All that's going on now is that the nationalists want Petrescu as minister of war so they can get their clutches on the army. That's why the whole business with Tildy is good for them, yes, but also not good for them, because it's still too early. That's why Constantin says he's dead set against the whole business—because where is he going to wind up if a scandal happens here, with more minorities than natives? He'll do what he can to see that Petrescu chokes on the whole business, and that they make the man disappear, so our prefect can go on working here in *dulcie jubilo* without their pestering him with things like that. So go ahead and let the Brills gather the crumbs from under old Paşcanu's table: by our standards it can only be a bagatelle of no import whatsoever, and it's more than likely that all anyone is going to wind up with is a crick in the neck from that old *ganef* of a sheepherder. With such a *punim* as he wears day in and day out, and nothing but debts front and back, I'm sure he can run around a long time playing the army supplier. Papa always said that the man was quick to grab the best bits of whatever deals they made together, but one day even he will have gone to the well once too often, especially if he's already starting to dump his load of jewels on the market. So don't work yourself up into a lather over that. Just make sure you're on time for dinner with Lily Fokschaner, you jail-breaker, you."

Against his usual custom, Seligmann, who had chanced to overhear the entire speech when he stood at the door (his knocking had gone unnoticed), felt obliged to share this information with Bubi Brill, who had been his friend since childhood. He was, furthermore, attached to Bubi's sister, Riffke; in fact, the two of them were discussing certain common intentions. Bubi listened carefully to what the secretary told him, and then answered: "That is outstanding! So my old man was so scared he wouldn't touch that deal with a ten-foot pole, you should have seen him running around the house and biting his fingernails because he was so scared it hurt. But what's the risk if old Paşcanu wants some security for the stone he's entrusting, that's understandable. I'll just sign over a few drafts in his name. And if he's under pressure, so much the better: then I can talk to him about all the expenses, and so on. That the whole thing is just a maneuver on his part was clear to me from the beginning, the moment I heard about this business from Mama. Wolfi Merores isn't the only Jew with a mother. What do I care how he's going to pay for the other stone? I'll be setting the whole thing in motion here once and for all. I'll take a commission from the gentlemen in Amsterdam, that's enough for me, I don't need one from him as well. And if he does shell out—look, he's capable of anything, what with the connections he still has, just between you and me—well, all the better. Then he'll pay me as well, you'll see. And Perko, I hear, is one interesting character, yes?

Bubi Brill had half a year's leisure to ruminate on that, since Herr Perko had helped him cross the border—and at least as far as he managed to get. Bubi didn't really have cause to complain about him.

"On the contrary!" he explained later. "When they grabbed me at the customs checkpoint, he very honorably intervened, until they told him they would take him in as well if he didn't shut up. So to this day I don't know where that little case really disappeared to, assuming one of the customs officials didn't take it. It's odd: I know Effi Perko quite well by sight, from Schorodok's place. I was just never able to introduce myself, because I was usually with gentlemen from the regiment, and now all of a sudden I'm supposed to believe the man stole my luggage, while all he had to do was wait until I came back and then he could have snatched both stones at once if he'd wanted to. Psychologically speaking, the whole thing is a mystery to me."

"When Jews are stupid," commented his little brother Solly, "they are *really* stupid."

In any case, the Trocadero once again united Bubi Brill and Effi Perko, and they remained friends.

What remained to be explained about the whole grotesque story was how old Paşcanu came to Perko in the first place, and how Bubi, instead of his father, found out about Perko's planned participation in the business.

The answer to the second question is easier than the first: Perko was never so sure as Paşcanu that old Brill would get involved in the deal. However greedy he might be, Perko didn't think the old man was that dumb. The "transaction" was "too good" and "too simple"—in fact, it stunk to high heaven. Old Brill had too much experience with Paşcanu's other business customs not to immediately suspect something and steer clear of it, no matter how much that might annoy him. But not so Bubi Brill, the youthful habitué of the Trocadero. Perko was a good judge of people; he observed them carefully—Bubi Brill, for instance, sporting with the ladies of the establishment, or enjoying the camaraderie of the officers of the cavalry regiment, in which he was allowed to serve, if not with a saber then at least with his pen, thanks to his mother's hefty contributions to Madame Turturiuk's pocket money.

So on the same morning when old Paşcanu received Brill, Perko sent his "feelers to the right people" and had Bubi Brill informed on in confidence, namely through a telephone call placed by their common friend Schorodok, proprietor of the Trocadero.

The answer to the first question—how old Paşcanu came to Perko, or vice versa—seems baffling beyond belief, unless one is able to empathize fully with the spirit of Czernopol. To wit: Perko had won the friendship and confidence of the castrato Miron, most especially in the church of St. Parachiva—through his acts of piety.

He had long ago been baptized in the Orthodox rite, and his religious fervor went so far that when he was with his friends in the Trocadero, no matter how advanced the hour, he categorically forbade any and all disrespectful allusions to religious or churchly matters. Moreover, after Paşcanu's death, he supported the *scopit* in the most generous manner, so that Gogeamite, the human mountain, whose voice was like the bright pealing of Easter bells, was granted a peaceful and carefree autumn of his life. Czernopol gained fodder for its laughter. Ephraim Perko was the hero of the day.

"I have to confess," said Herr Tarangolian, "I can't figure out how I can hang this person at the same time I'm supposed to build him a monument. For what he did to the unfortunate Russian refugees he undoubtedly deserves to be hanged..."

"Drawn and quartered!" exclaimed Uncle Sergei. "Every single bone broken, the nails slowly pulled off and the tips of his fingers immediately dipped in vinegar..."

"Of course, you are speaking from a very pardonable emotion, my dear Sergei Nikiforich. But for the business with old Paşcanu he deserves a monument. Not because he was able to out-trick the trickster—my friend Merores had already beaten him to that, and very thoroughly. But because in one stroke of genius he was able to dupe the swindler and in so doing taught Czernopol, this most intelligent city on the planet, a lesson, by showing that the man was basically as dumb, primitive, and foolish as on the first day he climbed down out of the woods. To show Czernopol that it had been taken in by a blockhead, that it had fallen for a masquerade, a legend, the old fairy tale about 'the chosen one'—well, that, my friends..." Herr Tarangolian muffled his voice into an ecstatic whisper; he shut his eyes appreciatively and rubbed the closed fingertips of his luxuriantly ringed hand under his Levantine nose, as if he were sniffing highly aromatic spices. "That, my friends, is magnificent. One of a kind. Brilliant. *That is something worth relishing.*"

14

Blanche Reports on the Insane Poet; Herr Adamowski Comes to Tea

MEANWHILE our appreciation for the sublime and magnificent comic spirit had yet to acquire the sophistication that Czernopol demanded. We looked at Săndrel Paşcanu's attempted diamond swindle as no more, and no less, than an adventuresome and exciting tale, made all the more colorful by the figure of the old man, who for us belonged to Tildy's retinue—one of the figures that surround the hero and provide a picturesque symbolism, like the shield bearers, unicorns, wild men, and lions on a princely coat of arms. And no matter how hard we tried, we couldn't bring ourselves to see Ephraim Perko as anything more than a scoundrel whom we would have happily and eagerly sent to his doom, if he had chanced to fall into our hands.

Our unworldly upbringing failed to educate us in many areas, but thanks to our friendship with Solly Brill we were able to catch up on what we had missed by making several forced marches. Nor did this friendship suffer because of our other one with Blanche Schlesinger. As siblings of different ages, with strong internal bonds, we had always been essentially self-sufficient, and at the same time open with one another in sharing whatever came from the outside, and as a result we were never in danger of succumbing to the isolating exclusivity of those exalted childhood friendships that carry within them the seeds of anger, where disloyalty takes root alongside jealousy. Moreover, what we called our friendship with Blanche Schlesinger was really the lightest contact: she had set herself down beside us like a butterfly, and we marveled at her and loved her and took care not to endanger her fragile tenderness.

Our closed, rounded world grew layer after layer—"*We were like an onion,*" was how Tanya put it later on, shortly before she died,

"*Whatever became of us?*"—and Solly burst into this world, raucous and robust, full of lively cheerfulness. Of course our dealings with him had no trace of the heavy disposition people so often mistake for "soulful." We have these two Jewish children to thank for the realization that the seat of the soul is found in the forehead and not the stomach, although we didn't quite know at the time they were Jewish.

At least, back then this was of no account to us. Doubtless after all that I've said up to now it sounds surprising to say the least, and yet it was true. At home we constantly heard remarks about Jews that were disparaging but also stretched into a grotesque or burlesque form that couldn't be taken seriously, and which left us with an exaggerated impression of their essential nature—a notion that was contradicted by the reality we were now experiencing, despite all of Solly Brill's characteristic traits.

Naturally we had known other Jews before, and not just from hearsay. Every day swarms of peddlers, so-called *hondeles,* descended on our house to buy up whatever junk we might otherwise throw away, and in our neighborhood there were also Jewish families who had sufficiently expanded our minds and freed our imagination from the cliché of kaftans, *peyes*, crooked backs, protruding ears, and unrestrained gesticulation. But we had never had any personal contact; to be sure, we had heard them speaking among themselves, but had never spoken with a single one of them. And so Jews, by which I mean the concept of "Jews," seemed like a species of clown, constantly on the move, devising their clever and comical—if also somewhat repugnant—plans to coax money from the pockets of Christians, but not humans with generally human traits. In his outward appearance, Solly Brill did indeed fit this image, but not in his character, which we found endearing. The fact that Miss Rappaport had been called "the Jewess," and more or less openly teased with the insinuation that she really was Jewish, always struck us as one of Uncle Sergei's ideas, as absurd as it was funny, and we never really believed it.

Nor did the speech of many of our classmates, in particular our friend Solly, startle us out of our innocent and unbiased amusement. In Czernopol every language was corrupted, and none more than

German: the communal barking of the ethnic Germans, their dreadful maiming of their mother tongue, sounded more unpleasant to us than the patter of the Jews, in which now and then an old, powerful, and wonderfully patinated expression or a richly picturesque turn of phrase emerged out of the linguistic sludge, and even the degradation of the language showed a spirit—admittedly a repulsive one, but a spirit nonetheless.

But, as I say, the most important thing was that we came to converse with our friends in the first place, and only later—quite a bit later—did we find out that they were Jews. So we didn't make the usual discovery *that Jews are also people*, but rather the reverse, *that people are sometimes also Jews.* This was one of the most beautiful of the invaluable discoveries that we owed to Madame Aritonovich and her Institut d'Éducation, as well as to our parents' temporary inattentiveness.

In this way we learned that what these people known as Jews shared was not so much a common character, but rather common forms of expression: in other words, that there were no "typically Jewish" traits, but rather a characteristically Jewish way of expressing traits that were simply human.

For the moment I'm not even talking about Blanche. Solly Brill with his shock of red hair, his freckles and protruding ears could have easily been the son of thoroughbred Prussian parents, the "bright lad" that would have occasioned much delight and a host of proud anecdotes. The only one thing likely to have gone missing was his sharp wit, which made common platitudes sound persuasive, absolute, and irrevocable, and which legitimized his cheekiness as a time-honored, effective means for probing and testing—and that is not only a characteristic of Jews, but also of other older peoples. Thus not a racial trait, but a character marker of specific races.

From earliest childhood we had been brought into contact with the concept of race, whether in connection with our dogs, horses, or the colorful fowl in the countryside, or else with the ingrained overestimation with which our family fed its feeling of self-worth, and we understood the idea of race as something that applied equally to all human types, as a collection of specific physical and mental peculiarities. Consequently a "thoroughbred" Chinese was more closely related to a "thoroughbred" Negro or European than to a compatriot of lesser breed. After we made the acquaintance of a few Jews of remarkable intelligence and beauty, we were inclined to think that Jews were considered a race apart because the specific characteristics of their race found more frequent and stronger expression than was usually the case among Christians.

Madame Aritonovich took care to cultivate our friend Solly Brill's cheekiness, coaxing it out of him but never failing to challenge it in some way, almost in the manner of a gymnastic exercise. We felt reminded of certain theories of Herr Alexianu.

"I can't help think, Fiokla Ignatieva, that you are raising this specimen precisely to help advance the anti-Semitic cause," said Uncle Sergei during one of his occasional visits to the Institut d'Éducation.

"You are mistaken," she replied. "I am treating this child exactly as I do the others. I myself had the unhappiest childhood, because people tried to give me an *upbringing.* Even then I knew that children can't be brought up. In the worst case they can be trained; in the best case their characters can be fostered. You can't implant anything, you can't develop anything that isn't already inside them; in fact, I am of the opinion you that can't suppress what they're born with, either. Even if I were to succeed in pruning this little boy, by clipping off his brazenness—and I consider the attempt hopeless—I would only break him in doing so. Then there would be one more ape in the world and one less character. And that would be regrettable. My children come to me so late that I'm never able to teach them what is known as good breeding. They either bring it from home or they will never attain it. Well-bred and embarrassed is a delightful mixture; ill-bred but happy and cheeky is the same. The combination of ill-bred and embarrassed, however, is a deadly one. Avoiding mistakes in life is not as important as not making something out of the ones we commit. In this matter you'll admit I'm right, my dear Sergei, won't you?"

Strangely—and to this day it's a riddle to us exactly why—Madame Aritonovich and Blanche avoided each other. Did Madame Aritonovich realize she was no match for this girl? Not that it would have ever come to a test of strength that she might have been afraid to lose. That was out of the question. The reason for Madame's reserve may have had more to do with the fact that she, too, couldn't help feeling secretly guilty about the girl—and Madame Aritonovich hated the very idea of guilt, as she expressed in no uncertain terms and with telltale vehemence. Whenever some anonymous prank or a question of responsibility triggered the judicial question "Who is the guilty party?" she would intervene forcefully and declare: "No one is at fault. It happened; it did not amuse us; let's forget about it!"

But perhaps the association between Madame Aritonovich and Blanche—which while not hostile did show a certain tense distance—was one of those inexpressible relationships, which if anyone had ever dared ask her to explain, Madame would have answered by glancing at Tanya and asking, "You understand, don't you, Tanya?" There was a furtive, mutual sizing-up, and not such as between teacher and student, or between grown-up and child—Madame once declared that the "envy that grown-ups have for the richness of childhood can never fully be eradicated"—but rather between two women. Tanya herself stayed silent on the matter, like any other woman.

Blanche had the tacit permission to withdraw or occupy herself with other things whenever "nonsense time" was declared—for instance, when Solly jumped up in the middle of the class and called out, "Madame, I know what! Why not let's have nonsense time?"

"What, Solly?"

"I can act out how Papa had another row with Mama because of Bubi."

"No, Solly. We know your family by heart. They're beginning to bore us."

"All right. Fine. I know something else. I learned a new song, a real hit."

"Which one? We've heard 'Die süsse Klingelfee' as much as we've heard Papa Brill. And that goes for 'Salomé' as well."

"Not 'Klingelfee' and not 'Salomé,' nothing like that. It's the brand-newest of the new, not even Bubi knows it from Schorodok."

"And how do you know it?"

"Record collection. I got it yesterday. Shall I sing it?"

"All right, if the others want to hear it as well..."

"Yes, please!" we called out in a chorus.

"Fine. Ten minutes nonsense time," said Madame Aritonovich.

"I think the words might be even better than with the other two. I'll say it more than sing it. We can practice the melody later on, it's a foxtrot. So here we go:

"You pretty girl,
it's pretty mean,
to be as pretty as you!"
"It's pretty clear
that's not enough
And pretty true I'm more than pretty—oooh no
—with you"

Solly started to sing:

"Every lady
likes-to-be-invited to the thé dansant,
but every lady
thinks-that-she's-the-only girl who's élégante
whenever trying on a dress
she causes tailors great distress.
Every lady
wants-a-look-that's one of a kind,
she won't be happy
unless-the-other-girls go out of their mind..."

We cheered like mad. When Solly came to the part—

"Buy the girl a dress,
she will climb right in,
and run-home-very-happy indeed.
But for a fancy hat
she'll climb... right out again..."

—we already knew the rhythm and enough of the melody that we could sing the second verse ourselves, with Solly conducting.

I turned to Blanche and found her sitting by herself on the last bench, apart from all the others, as usual. She returned my glance, which undoubtedly revealed how much I was enjoying the triviality of the satirical song, with a brave smile that was clearly pained, but also confident and illuminated, and signaled that she had something to tell us.

An hour later we went to see her. "I brought you something. It's a poem written by one of my father's patients. I should tell you that the man who wrote it—or, more precisely, whose words were written down, because he can barely write—is insane. My father is a doctor for the insane. This is a fantastic discovery. The poet is completely uneducated; his German is very bad, like with all the uneducated people here, and still he's created something incredibly beautiful. My father says if it were any more amazing it would be a religious experience. You want to read it?"

"Read it to us," we requested.

"It's called 'The Young Dancer,'" said Blanche, warmed and glowing with joy. Then she read:

Eine große Glockenblume
wehte fort vom Frühlingsbaum
lichtem Frühlingstag zum Ruhme
tanzt sie sich in sanften Traum.

Eine Wolke weißer Seide
spiegelt rauschend jeden Schritt:
mystisch wandeln unterm Kleide
Blut und Haut und Atem mit.

An des Körpers Blüten-Stengel
schwingt des Rockes Glocke sie,
und der Beine Doppel-Schwengel
läutet leise Melodie.

Eine große Glockenblume
wehte fort vom Frühlingsbaum:
lichtem Frühlingstag zum Ruhme
*tanzt sie sich in sanften Traum . . .**

"It's wonderful," said Blanche, when she reached the end. "The circumstances are just as remarkable: another patient, who is in the institution just for observation, heard it from the lips of the poor sick man. They aren't even in the same ward. The man who composed it is a former locksmith named Karl Piehowicz. He's been in the asylum for years and works in the garden, and the other, who is likely not even sick, offered to help with the garden work, in order to have something to do. He is an officer . . ."

"Is his name Tildy?" we asked, utterly beside ourselves with excitement.

"Yes. How do you know that? Do you know him?"

We tried to tell Blanche who Tildy was, at least who he was for us. We barraged her with stories about his wife, Tamara Tildy, about old

---

*Karl Kraus first published the poem in Heft 781 of *Die Fackel* (1928), and later returned to it with an extensive analysis of the language. A literal translation follows:

A large bell-flower
wafted off the springtime tree
to the glory of the bright spring day
and danced into a gentle dream.

A cloud of white silk
rustling by reflects each step:
mystic change takes place inside her garment
of blood and skin and breath

On her body's flower-stalk
she swings the bell of her skirt;
the double clapper of her legs
gives a quiet melody.

A large bell-flower
wafted off the springtime tree
to the glory of the bright spring day
and danced into a gentle dream.

Paşcanu, about Widow Morar, the dogs that always ran with his horse and about how one of them always limped out of sheer hysteria and how they had all been poisoned. We told her how he had been sent to the asylum, all the people he had challenged to a duel, and how he had smacked Herr Alexianu in the face...

Blanche looked at us with wide eyes and listened patiently. "You have to understand what a miracle it is that a mentally disturbed person can produce something with such beautiful order," she said. "My father told me that it isn't unusual for the mentally disturbed to find some wonderful form of expression, whether they are writing or drawing or painting—but that usually starts off beautifully and quickly turns confused and ends all twisted up in a painful muddle. There's hardly ever anything that's complete and can stand on its own, so full of light and clarity, so immaculate as this here. But the most amazing thing about Karl Piehowicz is that everything he composes is just like this, as clear as day. I have another poem here, called 'Springtime.'"

She wanted to recite it. We interrupted her, paying no attention to the pain in her eyes. We besieged her with questions about Tildy, and didn't let up until we discovered she didn't know any more than what she'd already told us, at which point we were disappointed, and even a little embittered. All at once a distance grew between us, and we were immediately tempted to attribute this sudden inability to understand each other to a more fundamental difference—precisely the one that purports to separate the Jewish and Christian "races." Was it not significant? We wanted to tell her all about our hussar, and she went on about a crazy locksmith who wrote poems. During those days we felt more inclined to stay at home than we usually did, as if we had ignored all the well-intended warnings about the weather and stayed outside too long, and now, frozen through and sopping wet, were grateful for the comfortable warmth of our parents' home.

It was at that time that Aunt Paulette brought Herr Adamowski to our house for the first time.

When she announced that she had invited Herr Adamowski to tea, no one said a word—a clear refusal to take any stand on the extravagant invitation—and so the decision either to disapprove or else to quietly acquiesce was left up to the mistress of the house, in other words, to our mother.

"I hear that Herr Adamowski has been looking after Tamara Tildy in a very commendable way," our mother said. "We should all feel a little ashamed that she has to turn so far for help."

No one chose to reply. So Herr Adamowski came to tea. No one—with the exception of Aunt Paulette, of course—had any idea that he was Tamara Tildy's lover.

It happened that on the same day some relatives had come from the country, on very short notice. They had come to town just for the day, so there was no way to avoid their visit. No one said anything more about the unexpected meeting, although it was to be feared that our relatives—an older couple given to country pursuits—and the editor would have very little to say to one another. On the other hand, their presence would also prevent it from becoming all too obvious how little anyone had to say to Herr Adamowski.

What made Herr Adamowski's entrance embarrassing was the fact that he had taken off his jacket. It was a warm day, and he was carrying it draped on his arm when he stepped through the gate by the *dvornik*'s hut and headed through the garden to the house, his beret slanting over his head and his monocle sparkling in his left eye. Everyone expected him to put it back on before entering the room, but he hung it up in the hall along with his beret, and brought his cane inside instead, though that could hardly be held against him, on account of his clubfoot. The man also exuded a fairly pungent odor, although that, too, could be forgiven, considering how much effort it took him to keep going with his physical defect. However, the dogs, which were always close at hand, refused to leave him alone, and he had trouble fending off their friendly attention. Once inside the room, he was introduced to all the relatives one by one, and made his rounds rocking from one side to the other, passing his cane from his right hand to his left in order to shake hands, and then taking it back with in the right, until he finally came to a place where he could sit down between our mother and the aunt from the country. At that point the dogs were energetically shooed away and he was offered a cigarette, which he politely accepted. With the stilted gestures of the newcomer who senses that he is being offered an opportunity to shed his awkwardness, he lit it and inhaled, but then immediately had a coughing fit. Everyone overlooked his clumsiness.

Meanwhile, he felt put on the spot, the focus of a deference that lasted too long and was at best ambivalent. Our country relatives were people happily filled with their own simple self-assurance, and although they were considered open-minded, in reality they viewed whatever was outside their immediate range of vision, or else what didn't have to do with the joys and limitations of their unpretentious life, with blank incomprehension, before proceeding along in their narrow way of thinking. They were devoted to each other in an entirely uncomplicated and somewhat coarse way, and were not at all shy about criticizing each other, or recounting the occasional vicious disagreement, so that a complete stranger had no choice but to feel excluded from the intimate sphere they never seemed to leave. The rustic isolation in which they lived, with no children, had led them to the habit of listening only to each other. When, for instance, Uncle Hubert said, "It's horrible how much time you waste in the city. We spent the whole morning running around from one place to another just because we needed a permit to import a new reaper-binder," Aunt Sophie paid careful attention to his every word, even though she had been present on this errand, which could not have been particularly entertaining—just in case she had to complete his report by reminding him of something he had left out, or even simply to paraphrase what he had already reported. "We set off at five-thirty in the morning, were in the city by nine o'clock, and even though we went straight to the permit office before doing anything else, by noon we still weren't done." As predicted, the couple paid little attention to Herr Adamowski. What's more, whenever our mother tried to fill this gap by interrupting Uncle Hubert's report with a question or comment, Aunt Sophie would cut her off: "Listen to what Hubi's saying, it's very interesting."

What Uncle Hubert was saying was not the least bit interesting, but it did have the calming effect of the straightforward narration of simple events.

"Now, I've ordered a gun rest for the stag season," he said, for example. "Because, well, it's like this: I can hardly see anything with my right eye anymore, since I was wounded in the war. So I ordered a telescopic sight from Zeiss so I could shoot with my left eye. Except I can hardly hear with my left ear. So when the gamekeeper locates a stag, he has to go to my left, to hand me the rifle with the sight and point it in the direction of the stag so I can see it. Then he has to step behind me over to my right, where I can still hear, and whisper how many points the stag has, because I can't see that while I'm hurrying to look through the sight. I mean, of course I see it when there's time to. Then I can give him a good looking-over, but mostly there isn't enough time, what with the thick underbrush out where we are, not like what you have, with those tall fir stands; but where we are it really is like a brush. So when I don't have enough time for a proper identification, the gamekeeper has to tell me what it is I'm shooting at. After all, you don't want to be shooting the wrong thing, do you? And then he starts whispering in my right ear, and as it is I can barely understand the man, what with his pipe in his mouth..."

"So now Hubi's told him he can't bring the pipe anymore when they're out together," seconded Aunt Sophie. "But that man always has something in his mouth—he's always either chewing on a blade of grass or a button or something..."

"And he stinks on top of that..."

"He stinks like you can't imagine. I've already asked Hubi if he doesn't ever bathe, but Hubi says the animals prefer it that way..."

"Well, they always say you're not supposed to scrub yourself too thoroughly when you go hunting, because soap stinks even more to the game than an unwashed man does to us. You can see that whenever you give a dog something that smells good—smells good to *us*, I mean..."

"That's right, and what smells good for a dog doesn't smell good to us, right? But you wanted to tell about that new shooting rest you're having made."

"Well, so if the man next to me stinks that much, the gamekeeper I mean..."

"And Hubi has a nose like a fox, I'm telling you, it's so sensitive that if one of our servant girls smells just a little bit I take care of it right away, though I can't be checking their armpits first thing every day or God knows what else. But you know what works best?" She turned past Herr Adamowski to ask our mother. "Permanganate. Make them take a permanganate bath because that takes care of things for a long time. Remember that, it's bound to be of value to you. I learned about it from Olga."

"Yes, of course, potassium permanganate, that takes care of it right away. But I can't put the gamekeeper in a tub of bichromate of potash. In the first place he doesn't have a tub at home, and in the second place the man is busy throughout the rutting season listening to the calls: he's been sleeping outside for days, that's a tremendous strain, the rut, for him . . ."

"Well, he stinks even outside the season. But never mind that, finish telling about your shooting stick, because we'll have to be on our way soon."

"Can't you stay for supper?" asks our mother.

"No, dear, thanks very much, but Hubi has to write tonight and in the morning he has to make it to the station because the new thresher has come in and he insists on being there while they unload it so nothing happens to the parts, we've already put a fortune into the thing. I'm telling you, if we didn't grow what we need to live off we'd starve to death, sure as shooting."

"Well, sooner or later we'll amortize the costs of the machine, right . . ."

"Sooner or later, Hubi, it will be amortized. But who knows if we'll live to see that day—in other words, we might just starve to death if we didn't have everything, at least to eat I mean, believe you me. But now go on and listen to the rest of Hubi's story about his new shooting rest . . ."

"So, like I was saying, when the man is whispering in my ear, and he always has something in his mouth, then I can't help turning my head to him in order to hear him better, after all, you get worked up in a moment like that, with the stag standing over there, ready to move off at any moment, or else he spots you and then he takes off, oh yes, that's happened to me a few times, that I've lost him from my sight, and you know how that is, when you try searching around with that, I can't send the gamekeeper to the other side to set up the rifle again, that would make too much noise, would take too much time, even the most trusting deer isn't going to stand there that long, of course..."

"He'd have to be tied to the ground. But go on, Hubi, otherwise we'll be late..."

"It's not that urgent, Sophie, just let me finish..."

"I'm telling you that you should finish now, because you know how much Janos dislikes driving on these bad roads. It's absolutely scandalous—where we live, you know—potholes two feet deep, you can imagine what that does to our axles, and Janos really is a careful driver, say what you will..."

"Listen to you! On the way into town he drove like the devil was breathing down his neck. Of course during the day it's a different matter."

"But tell us about your gun rest, Hubi. Pay attention, Elvira, because I'm sure this will interest you as well."

"So now we'll simply do this: once the gamekeeper has the gun pointed in the direction of the deer, I'll stick the gun rest in the ground and hold the rifle tight—then he can talk to me as much he as he wants with the straw in his mouth. That way I won't lose the deer anymore from my sight, and this also has the advantage that you can shoot with greater certainty, say what you will, but I'm no longer one to get embarrassed when I pass up a shot or anything like that. After all, I've shot enough in my life freehand, and fast, too, tossing them off with the shotgun..."

"Hubi can shoot from enormous distances, often up to four hundred yards..."

"Well, with the rifles these days you can do that..."

And so on and so on. They were always in the process of leaving, never had enough time, and still they would stay rooted to their chairs for several hours, then only to draw out the unpostponable departure.

"Well, we really have to be going, no two ways about it, but Hubi has a few new jokes you simply have to hear. Very quickly. Tell that one, Hubi, you know..."

"Which one?"

"The one you told me on the ride in—that Ferry told you..."

"Which one was that?"

"You know. Oh, it's slipped off the tip of my tongue right now, but it's really funny, it is, Hubi always has the best jokes, he can keep an entire company entertained."

"If only I could remember them at the right moment—right now I honestly don't know which one you mean. Really I should write them down immediately, because there are just too many to remember."

"It's a real pity, Hubi, that you can't remember this one, it was really good."

"No, there's another one that's a lot better, the one I told you the other day, except I can't tell it right now in front of the children—and there are ladies present as well. But you really can't remember which one?"

"Didn't it start like this: 'Two Jews are sitting in the train...'?"

"That's right, that's the one! No, no, it was a different one—give me just a moment..."

Strangely, we children didn't experience this as boring: that was simply how things were and therefore how they had to be. Despite their ridiculous traits, our two relatives displayed a very high degree of what Herr Tarangolian referred to as *haecceitas*. Raising his finger, he launched into an explanation: "A wonderful expression from the good Doctor Subtilis, my young friends, well worth noting!" In short: they were exactly who they were, in a manner that was absolutely and utterly natural; they were perfect in their own way and defied comparison, because they represented a world that was complete unto itself. And while this world might be questioned, especially when measured against other forms of existence, it could never be negated or denied. This gave them an added measure of representative authority, apart from their own powers of persuasion, in the same way that Johann Huber the farmer is greater than and stronger than Johann Huber the man, or sailor Hein is stronger than and greater than just plain Hein. Ten minutes in their company was enough to transport us to the peaceful and leisurely pace of country life, where the eternal repetition of natural cycles is perceived and welcomed as variety, so that ultimately all impatience is lulled to sleep by the rhythmic rising and falling of the Great Breath, and banal, everyday events acquire a kind of nourishing power. Aunt Paulette, who detested anything to do with the country, couldn't help giving one of her bitter-angry groans a biblical cast: "And breakfast and dinner and tea and supper were another day."

Of course that world afforded Herr Adamowski little room to maneuver. After he managed to break the spell of the first awkward moments, he changed his role from observed to observer, and began calling attention to himself, so as not to be left at a disadvantage. He laughed out loud at a joke or anecdote, and looked around seeking consensus, as if every person present could claim some of the credit for the general merriment, himself included. Finally he overcame his awkwardness and began interjecting an occasional word or sentence into the conversation being carried on by Uncle Hubi and Aunt Sophie, though of course he never had much of a chance, since any insights he might have were diminished by his being an outsider. So he grew increasingly uneasy, as if he had performed below expectations and didn't deserve the cup of tea and the anchovy roll that were set in front of him. But there was no way to get past the utter self-containment of our aunt and uncle from the country. Consequently he turned to us children, baring his teeth in a sawlike smile and winking to imply some secret understanding, as if coaxing us to join him in silent mockery of our relatives. All of these gestures set his monocled face into a circular motion like a wheel of fortune capable of producing a winning number at any moment, but which most of the time stops at a blank, only to continue undeterred onto the next spin, equally full of promise. He actually succeeded in attracting our attention, but as soon as he started to perform his magic tricks and suddenly pulled a piece of candy out of nowhere, just like that time at the gate, Aunt Paulette interrupted him with a "Would you please stop that," in a tone whose sharpness lingered in the room for several seconds.

Not until the end of the visit, as the relatives were searching for the joke that had escaped them, did Herr Adamowski get a word in. Uncle Hubert was apologizing for what we had missed, while Aunt Sophie promised to send the joke on by mail—"You know how it is: the minute you take your seat in the carriage it all comes back to you"—along with another one that was nowhere near as good as the one they couldn't remember, as both of them seemed vexed to admit. Herr Adamowski jumped in to take advantage of the opportunity and said: "But perhaps you haven't heard *this* one..." and finally had a chance to say something. He told a fairly boring joke, and then, without waiting to see its effect, which could hardly have been remarkable, quickly added: "And here's another, if I might..." and went on telling a second, third, and fourth joke, one after the other, until he finally noticed that enough was enough. Then he went silent, baring his saw-teeth, while Uncle Hubi said musingly: "Yes, that's a good one... But if only I could remember mine from this morning..." until a general silence settled, which Aunt Sophie put an end to: "Well, Hubi, I think it really is time for us to get going..."

"You're right," said Uncle Hubert. "I think it really is time for us to get going..."

Herr Adamowski wanted to leave with them, but his hosts asked him to stay, claiming they'd hardly had a chance to talk, though in reality they wanted a chance to see off the relatives undisturbed. The couple from the country—bright-eyes, iron-gray hair, clad in coarse brushed wool with thistly tufts, with large, dry, kind hands—seemed to anticipate the fresh air on their ruddy cheeks and the wind against their carriage. They quickly took their leave of Herr Adamowski with an alarmingly brusque display of cordiality and returned to their true element. Left to his own devices, Herr Adamowski ate two more anchovy rolls and soon went on his way. The impression he left behind neither disappointed nor exceeded what had been expected of him. No one said a thing about it.

By the time Herr Adamowski left, we had run outside. Aunt Paulette accompanied him halfway to the gate. He waved to us and gave a meaningful, smirking nod, which we returned with the reserved politeness that Miss Rappaport had drilled into us and which Madame Aritonovich had enriched with subtle shadings vis-à-vis people of "higher, equal, or lower rank." When Aunt Paulette came back, we were still standing in the same place. She walked right past us, but then all of a sudden turned around and smacked Tanya in the face as hard as she could.

It was so cruel and unexpected, so bizarre, that the resounding slap seemed like a trick of the senses by the time Aunt Paulette reached the stairs leading up to the house—like one of those eerily ephemeral hallucinatory events that are no sooner noticed than they are gone, such as when clouds open up and an angel drops out of the sky, or a sudden shifting of the planet, as though mountains were dancing: things we feared with a peculiar sense of excitement, and also craved, because they would have proven to us that the enchanted, heightened reality we so wanted to believe in, with the skeptical urgency brought on by our need to affirm our own identity, was real after all. But then we saw Tanya, shielding her face with her hands as if she had been blinded, still reeling under the brutal force of the blow, crumpled inward as if wounded. Not one of us had ever been hit before. We sensed that something critical had transpired, that this blow to the face had shattered something holy, something sacrosanct—a fragile mask of inviolate dignity, and now its splinters were being rubbed into our skin. I remember my pulse pounding in my throat while wishing to see a drop of blood trickle out from Tanya's hands, as if such a sparkling, ruby-red mystery might effect a mystical reconciliation, and rid the taint of that colorless blow.

Tanya uttered something that was half whimper, half panting groan. She turned and raced off to hide in the furthest corner of the garden. And we followed her, also concealing our hate and choking thirst for vengeance in the leafy thicket of the bushes. We were ashamed for her and even more for ourselves, that we hadn't been hit, too; we suffered because of her awful martyrdom. We stood around her in silence and waited with a terrible curiosity for her to take her hands from her face, and felt fear and seething rage when she finally did. She removed them slowly, holding them like the ruined shards of a bowl, and looked straight ahead with huge eyes, as if checking to make sure she still could see, her hands ready to spring back at any moment and cover her dead eyes. Then she let them drop, and we saw white welts from Aunt Paulette's fingers between splotches of bright red.

Tanya didn't look at us. None of us said a word. A desperate sense of helplessness overcame us—the seed of a sadness that would never go away: our childhood had been struck dead.

When we were finally rousted from our hideout, evening shadows were already bluing the garden. Her penance, designed to provide satisfaction, succeeded only in weakening our thirst for revenge while failing to put things right: Aunt Paulette was made to apologize to Tanya in front of us, and then to each one of us individually. Our mother forced her to do it.

I can still see my sister Tanya, accepting Aunt Paulette's apology with a silent nod, and it's painful to compare that image with that of the slender girl who scarcely a year before had taken the apple from the smirking Kunzelmann, every bit as immaculate as that beautiful green apple itself, with its smooth skin, and full of self-assured grace and the inviolable majesty of a child. I know that she died from that blow. She expired at the age of twenty from a passing cold that worsened into pneumonia. But I know that the seed to that early death had been planted inside her with that blow.

It had another, indirect, effect as well, that blow. When Blanche came to us a few days later, a little more shyly than before, and mentioned that her father had come into possession of a new poem by the insane locksmith, Tanya demanded to see it. She read it and gave it back to Blanche. "It's very beautiful," she said. "Would you please make me a copy? And of that other one as well, that you read to us first. It was very foolish of us not to see then how beautiful it is."

"And now you see it?" asked Blanche with a poignantly illuminated smile—we hadn't told her anything of what had happened.

"Yes," said Tanya.

Blanche put her arm around her neck and kissed her.

The new poem was called: "One Drink of Love."

Laß uns in dem Silberglanz,
mit des Blutes letzter Welle
so hinübermünden in den Strauch,
wie ins Wurzelwerk der Quelle!

Laß uns mit dem letztem Atemhauch,
den die Birken grün umhüllen,
unserer Herzen Krüge ganz,
mit der tiefen Stille füllen!

Alles Irdische muß wesenlos
ohne Trauer von uns fallen;
kindgeworden in des Waldes Schoß
*sind um uns nur Nachtigallen.**

Shortly afterward, the Viennese author Karl Kraus—the most significant German-language thinker and writer of his time—wrote: "Only at the highest peaks of German lyric poetry, where peace and quiet reign—only in a few verses by Claudius, Hölderlin, or Mörike, or today in lines by Trakl or Lasker-Schüler, does what a single heart and nature have to say to each other find such form, such sublime harmony of vision and sound. Lines such as *unserer Herzen Krüge ganz, /*

---

*From the same edition of *Die Fackel*. A literal translation would be:

Let us in the silver glow
that cloaks the birches green
fill the vessels of our hearts
with the deep silence!

Let us with our dying breath
and the last wave of blood
flow into the shrub
as into the roots of the source.

All that is earthly must fall from us
without substance, without sadness;
a child once more, in the forest's womb,
with only nightingales around us.

mit der tiefen Stille füllen; like this divine thought of nightingales surrounding us, *kindgeworden in des Waldes Schoß*—make up for entire libraries full of verse. The real miracle is that this force of nature, this insanity, to which one easily entrusts the act of birthing the vision, has also affected or permitted this unbelievable congruity: one could write an entire essay on the symmetry in alternating short and long lines, and the psychic effect that proceeds from this, for example about the great pathos reserved for the additional two syllables of this *final* breath."

And the miracle continued. Because it soon turned out that this poem, which was already a finished work of art with the closing verse about the nightingales, was even further elevated by the following magnificent addition:

.... Nachtigallen.
die uns über Raum und Zeit
über uns hinaus zu den Gefilden
Gottes wiegen in die Ewigkeit
wo die Engel mit den milden

Mutterhänden unsren Liebesbund
heiligsprechen und in Harfenchören
und von Mund zu Mund
*jubeln, daß wir wieder Gott gehören.**

---

*From the same edition of *Die Fackel*:

... nightingales around us,

that gently rock us past time and space
beyond ourselves, to God's fields
and eternity,
where the angels with their gentle

motherly hands beatify our bond of love
and rejoice to choruses of harps
from mouth to mouth
jubilant that we again belong to God.

"Of course it's hard to say," Karl Kraus wrote in a postscript, "whether we ought to bemoan the loss of the full caesura following the line about the nightingales, or be thankful for the magnificent resurrection contained in this relative clause woven from these two verses that lead straight up to God. No matter what the results of the investigation into the authorship, and even if it turns out that admirers of spiritual values have found and memorized a poet who has gone unknown for centuries—it cannot produce a greater miracle than the work itself, and editors around the world will remain shamed by the fact that the asylum is, if not the source, then the refuge and sanctuary of this creation."

The unresolved question of authorship had its own story: Czernopol was not a city to believe in miracles. After Blanche's father and one of his colleagues—the junior house physician Dr. Kipper—forwarded the poems of the poor mentally ill person to a publicist named Sperber, who published them in the *Tschernopoler Tageszeitung*, people began to treat the case "scientifically." The insane locksmith was then subjected to a cross-examination that yielded the following result:

> Karl Piehowicz, whose command of German is lacking, and whose transcription of the poems is so difficult it literally requires deciphering, is not capable of defining single words of his poems. When repeating certain dates from his life he commits inaccuracies and entangles himself in contradictions. Upon much questioning and urging he confesses that he spent time in Morocco in the Foreign Legion in the company of some Germans, who "together wrote poems with him," and his description of the origin of these poems is peculiar and not easily understood. The forementioned legionnaires evidently spent their free time trying to outdo one another composing poems, polishing and improving them, etc. Today Piehowicz is unable to identify with any degree of certainty the authors of the individual poems; he is sure of having composed only one of the poems himself. After much questioning, he ascribed the verse "The Young Dancer" to a certain Otto Berger, who comes from

> Stuttgart or Strassburg, and whose last address in Morocco he claims to know... Karl Piehowicz maintains that he possesses a notebook at home containing 1,500 (!) poems...

"My father is of the opinion that it doesn't matter whether his patient was really the author of the poems or not," said Blanche. "It would be miraculous enough if this entirely uneducated man had preserved them in his memory as the legacy of an unknown poetic genius and thereby saved them for us. Precisely at a time when, according to my father, all the keepers and custodians of German writing let this poet go undiscovered, the miracle is all the greater. By the way, my father speaks with great respect of Major Tildy, whom you admire so much. My father says that it's only thanks to his soothing and calming influence on Piehowicz that the man has been able to withstand all these terrible examinations, without having his condition made much worse. Of course, ever since they started he feels he's being watched at every step, so he looks for protection from Major Tildy, who seems to have a strange authority over him. Anyway, Piehowicz is devoted to him like a loyal dog, he does everything Tildy says, and is never at peace unless Tildy is by his side. Those are his happiest moments, in the little toolshed of the vegetable garden, where they both work, when he sits down with Tildy and can tell him his poems. Tildy is very conscientious about recording them. Piehowicz isn't always capable of inventing them or remembering them, you see—he needs inspiration. Because he has never felt it in all the years he has spent in the institution up to now, and my father is inclined to attribute it to Tildy's arrival, who apparently has had an influence on other patients as well that is quite puzzling but undeniably beneficial. Even ones who are raving mad grow calmer when Tildy, who is fearless, enters their cell. But then there are others who get worked up and angry at the very sight of him. My father says that he projects a force that no one can resist except people who are either completely without feeling or else depraved. So I owe you an apology." Blanche smiled her beautiful, poignant smile, which in moments like that could exude such delightful and beguiling charm. "I was being insensitive when I didn't understand why you wanted to hear about Herr Tildy more than listen to the poems. Imagine, Major Tildy is very happy in the institution. He's never said a word about the fact that he's being kept there with absolutely no justification. In my father's estimation, he is a cultivated man, though not particularly educated in literature, but still his taste is so uncompromising that he not only immediately recognized the genius of the poor locksmith, but when he and Piehowicz make their selection from among the poems that Piehowicz writes down for him or which he transcribes according to the locksmith's words, Tildy always knows which one to choose and how to tell the genuine from the false. My father says that Herr Tildy's sense of *justice*, which the mentally ill notice as well—because that's the first thing that anyone with any sensitivity notices about him—is so pronounced that it also guides him unfailingly in literary matters. Many of the poems Piehowicz produces contain verses borrowed from others, for instance there's one about a southern landscape that begins with Goethe's *Kennst Du das Land, wo die Zitronen blüh'n.** Much to the astonishment of my father and Dr. Kipper, Tildy had no idea it was a line by Goethe, though he immediately expressed his doubt. He felt it wasn't 'genuine'! Of course, even if he's never been interested in literary things up till now, he's bound to have heard that more than once. But his reaction was the same with other, lesser-known citations. One poem, which Piehowicz calls 'Life of a Legionnaire,' closes with the line *Auf ferner, fremder Aue*†... And another verse out of a group of Italian poems is from Schiller: *Prächtiger als wir in unserm Norden* ‡... Tildy, who didn't know the poem, said without hesitating that the lines seemed 'borrowed.' In the meantime, it's no longer just a question of choosing only poems that are entirely original—people are also demanding some kind of evidence that would establish to what degree the mentally disturbed locksmith might be the author of lyrical compositions. As I mentioned, Herr Tildy, Dr. Kipper, and my father all agree that it doesn't really matter,

*Longfellow translated this as "Knowst thou the land where the lemon-trees bloom?"

†"On a far-off, foreign meadow" [Johann Gabriel Seidl]

‡A 1902 translation by Forster and Pinkerton renders this as: "More dignified than in our northern lands."

because as long as no other author can be determined, Piehowicz is the source of the wondrous poems he has given us. But the more it becomes clear that he can't be the author, the more they should leave him in peace. And it seems more and more certain that he cannot have written the poems. After all, he completely lacks the education for that, he knows even less than Tildy—neither what he is quoting or whom—and his very low intelligence in general makes it questionable whether he could ever produce something original of such beauty. But that's a different issue. What I wanted to say is what a fine ear Major Tildy has for distinguishing what is complete from what is not complete. From the cycle of *Roman Poems* he picked two where he claims to recognize that Piehowicz is quoting poems from several authors:

Die Zypresse, die Olive,
Pinienwald und Berg und Au
tauchen in das himmlisch-tiefe
fleckenlose duft'ge Blau.

Um die Wasser, um die Lande,
Näh und Ferne, weit und breit,
legt der Himmel weitgespannte
*Arme der Unendlichkeit.**

"Tildy thinks that these verses couldn't possibly come from the same divinely gifted person who wrote a poem like 'One Drink of Love.'

---

*The lines come from the poem "Tivoli" by Friedrich Theodor Vischer, The literal translation would be:

The cypress and the olive tree,
piney woods and hill and meadow
sink into the heavenly deep
spotless fragrant blue.

Around the waters and the lands,
high and low and far and wide,
Heaven wraps the outspread
arms of eternity.

"The mark of culture in a man," Blanche concluded with her most beautiful smile, "is not his knowledge. I think I know why you are so taken with Herr Tildy. It's because he has a kind of perfection, as my father has confirmed. He is complete in his form, and so he is related to all other forms of perfection. He is the peak of what we can attain. I'm envious that you know him, and can't wait for the day he's set free so you can show him to me."

"Can't you ask your father to let you visit the institution just once so you can see him? You could speak with Tildy!"

"No," said Blanche. "That's impossible. I've always wanted to see the poor souls my father looks after, and to be just as brave as he is. But he thinks I wouldn't be able to stand the impact. I was very sick as a little child. I'm sensitive. It shames me to admit it, but it's stronger than I am."

A mark of forced concentration showed in her face that made her almost ugly. "Besides, I have to admit that at first I was put off by Major Tildy's intention of dueling with everyone. My father tried explaining to me that the resolve to kill or die for the sake of order and righteousness was worthy of respect. I don't approve of that view, since I detest any kind of violence. But when I started reading about duels I came across a very beautiful saying. You know that Pushkin was killed in a duel. He asked the doctor examining him to tell him frankly how long he had left to live, and when he was told 'Three minutes,' he closed his eyes and said, '*Il faut que j'arrange ma maison.*' That is beautiful. I'm looking forward to when you show Herr Tildy to me."

Tanya stroked her hair. "You once wanted to tell us a poem that was called 'Springtime' which you found very beautiful."

Blanche hesitated, almost a little embarrassed. "I don't want to repeat it," she said. "It would lead you down the wrong path. It was the first of the poems ascribed to poor Piehowicz and then proven to be not his. It almost pains me to see the miracle shattered like that. As for that poem, 'Springtime,' the one with the last stanza that so delighted everyone—

Alles Schwere sinkt
von den Dingen, die sich weiten

und die Erde trinkt
*Wunder der Entbundenheiten**

we now know for sure that it was written by someone else. He seems to be a gifted poet by the name of Count Karl Berlepsch."

She must have seen our astonishment, even though we tried to suppress it. "Do you know this poet?" she asked, amazed.

Indeed, we thought we did. In one of the old issues of *Gartenlaube*, which Aunt Elvira had subscribed to, we had come across a poem by Count Berlepsch and had learned it by heart, fascinated and wickedly delighted and simultaneously repulsed by the realization of what was wicked in our delight. Just as the hunchbacked figure of Fräulein Iliuț seemed attractive to me in a way that left me feeling guilty, so this poem acquainted us with a kind of forbidden longing—a longing for the opposite of beauty, and for what consciously and shamefully sets out to destroy it. We didn't know whether we should consider the piece a satire. It addressed the injustices suffered by cavalrymen deprived of their mounts, forced to dig trenches with a shovel, and was composed in a tone people generally referred to as "witty"—a genre our parents steered us away from in no uncertain terms whenever we encountered it. This was not due to the childish silliness of the writing, but because of something worse: a vulgarity of spirit that can infiltrate the soul and as such constituted a latent danger one must take pains to guard against. We had seen this deep-seated vulgarity in the smirking Kunzelmann, and every line of this poem brought him back to us; its bumpy rhythm and dreadful German called out to be recited in Kunzelmann's awful dialect, and we never tired of repeating the lines in his voice:

Not so long ago, it seems,
riding was held in great esteem.

---

*From *Die Fackel*, Heft 781, 1928.

All that is heavy sinks
away from the things that expand
and the earth drinks
wonders of release

It continued in that vein, with an orderly who springs "from wing to wing," and dragoons "who lost their jades," now consigned to the barricades, where "instead of being tossed off by their steeds," were digging dirt with mole-like speed.

Enough of that. We took our wicked delight in the jocose grotesqueries that struck us as even more bizarre for having come from the German war camp, from that terrifying world of earth caterpillars and fire butterflies. The verses brought the horror painfully close to the absurd, and what was fearful was brought into the soul-crushing proximity of the ridiculous. We would declaim certain lines in Kunzelmann's voice and intonation, using the raw Czernopol German dialect, lines such as:

> If they don't shoot him into tatters
> he'll learn that other weapons matter,

or

> See the army engineers
> deep in dirt up to their ears

but it was only much later that I realized we did so out of a particular sense of despair, which often seems far more painful when we are children than later when we are grown. These were idle hours spawning devilment, empty but for a nervous aversion we couldn't explain—not for the world that surrounded us, but for all the awful things that characterized life in this world that we were part of. In such moments we felt the malicious urge to destroy beauty, the craving for satire. And I would later learn that Czernopol's nasty passion for laughter, for mockery and scorn, stemmed from a deep-seated desperation, and probably sprouted from the vast emptiness of the countryside that besieged the city. The threat of this looming emptiness was what made the soul unable to resist the dreadful spirit of the satirical: instead of the little elves known as Heinzelmännchen, we had "Schmunzelmännchen, little gnomes, that by night in secret come," enlisting "all of

Satan's powers to erect a town with towers"—the town we would have to fend against our whole life.

"Satan is coming closer to us, and he is smiling, my little ones," Uncle Sergei used to say, himself smiling with his irresistible charm. And since we didn't notice Satan hiding behind all the smirking, we assaulted Blanche with rhymes from the dreadful poem, and added insult to injury by reciting them with the crude gesticulation that we had picked up from Solly Brill:

"Oh me, oh my
another shell comes flying by:
first we listen to the whine,
next it's Boom!
behind our line"

as if Blanche's lovely story of the insane poet and Tildy's noble strivings on his behalf had become a farce, a joke. Even Tanya couldn't refrain from laughing along, in a sudden disregard for Blanche that clearly let it be known that she, Tanya, had little regard for herself in that moment. "You're overexcited," she said to Blanche, using an expression the grown-ups applied to us whenever our enthusiasm tried their patience, because their souls could no longer summon the same unbridled fervor. Today I know that this act of cruelty came from a different source, a secretly concealed despair with deeper roots.

Because in actuality we were taking revenge for something beautiful that had been destroyed, something that had been the epitome of beauty in our childhood: that image of the hussar in front of the lance-leafed pickets along our garden. Tildy had become entangled in a farce, in a joke. He was attempting to coax beauty out of the mouth of a crazy person, and this beauty had been proven counterfeit; what's more, the true creators of this ostensible beauty were on the same level as the smirking Kunzelmann: they were his German brothers. We no longer saw Tildy on his horse: the line

And the hardest struggle in the battle
was easily solved atop a saddle

cruelly exposed a deeper meaning, replacing the hussar's beautiful feat of derring-do with the foolish act of a simple-minded cavalryman like the ones sitting in the Trocadero. The hussar had dismounted and was rooting in the mud. Tildy was mixed up in a *literary* quarrel, and consequently became the victim of ridicule, as a cavalryman.

Once more it was only much later that I would again encounter the tragicomic figure of a hussar lost in a world devoid of poetry—in a photo of the German crown prince, which I happened to see in the same seedy dive at the edge of town where Tildy's fate would be determined. But back then we were unconsciously taking revenge on Blanche Schlesinger for the fact that the poetic symbol of our childhood had been destroyed. We had no idea what had caused the destruction, only a vague intimation that this figure had been stripped of its poetry—the hussar had dismounted and had become the gambling buddy of the German count with the Kunzelmann-like verse ("*what makes men today are spades*") which added the macabre humor of the Ludenburg brothers floating off into the air to the absolute horror of the earth caterpillars exploding into fire butterflies. Tildy was caught up in everything that he had opposed as *the hussar*: his poetry had become embroiled in a literary controversy; his struggle for justice had been derided as untenable, he himself had fallen victim to Czernopol's dominant reality, which was that of the smirking Kunzelmann.

Unschooled in literary fairness, we didn't ask whether the conclusions we had drawn were false, whether the abstruseness of an occasional verse—that was clearly "witty," although perhaps out of desperation—gave us the right to pronounce judgment, as though its author were unworthy of producing anything more beautiful, whereas what came out of the mouth of the poor insane locksmith Karl Piehowicz had to sound like it issued from the wellspring of beauty itself, as in the poem "Springtime," ("All that is heavy sinks away from the things that expand") or if the desperate wittiness of that shoddy effort from the trenches should be allowed to call Tildy's noble efforts into question. In the poetic justice of childhood, which has its own laws, judgment had been passed on our hussar in the poem out of *Gartenlaube*, to which the great poet Karl Berlepsch had signed his name: "Into the dust, you proud rider!"

For that we took revenge on an innocent party—as always happens when taking revenge—namely Blanche. Only later did we realize this, and understand at the same time that our revenge was just, at least in the poetic, fairy-tale sense of childhood, because she had functioned as the *messenger* of the destruction of this poetry.

During these weeks two exciting events occurred, subsequently telescoped in memory in an odd and unsettling way due both to the turbulent events that followed and to our later illness. The first involved Herr Adamowski's second visit; this time he was received by Aunt Paulette alone, that is to say accompanied only by Aunt Elvira. Our mother, whose relationship to her sister had become strained after the awful scene with Tanya, had excused herself with an obvious pretext and arranged an outing for us children, which ended up being canceled because of an unusually violent storm. The intense tropical downpour made such a spectacle that we completely forgot our disappointment at the missed excursion, and when it started to clear up after two hours of pouring rain we ran into the garden to see the damage that had been done. The drains were all stopped up; the water was foaming past the sandstone plinth of the lance-leaf fence like a wild brook and had formed a small lake on the lawn in front of our house. Keeping our feet dry required all our skill and attention, so that we didn't notice what was happening around us, and didn't look up until we heard a high-pitched woman's laugh. Then we saw Herr Adamowski trying to navigate around the deepest puddles and streams, awkwardly on account of his deformity, while underneath the arc of water still cascading from the eaves of the *dvornik*'s hut was Frau Lyubanarov, leaning against the wall as usual, laughing out loud as she watched Herr Adamowski.

He appeared not to take offense at her rather tactless amusement, but merely trudged ahead, rocking from side to side, swinging his cork-soled boot into one puddle after the next. When he came close to where she was standing he stopped, leaning with his hand against the wall. She studied him with her golden, goatlike eyes.

"Well, old goat-hoof," she said in a guttural voice. "New paths to travel?"

"Your lack of shame is magnificent," he said. "You know that your blouse is wet and wrapped on you like a skin—that you can see right through? And you're not wearing anything underneath."

"That's why I'm standing here. I like it when people see me."

"I know. And who do you think will see you here?"

"Whoever comes by. I'm not picky—that's something you should know as well."

"And you never get enough?"

"Do you ever get enough?"

He bared his saw-teeth. "I never get enough from you."

"And from that fool who poisons herself and stumbles through the streets like a drunk woman—what about her?"

"Whom do you mean?"

"Come on, let's not pretend. You know as well as I do who I mean. I'm talking about my little sister, the fine lady. The major's wife, who's so far gone as to sell herself to you for a little pack of powder. Who's finally landed completely in the mud. How is she in bed? As good as I am? I can do it even when I'm drunk—but her? It's only you men who can't when you're plastered."

"They ought to tie you to a stake and burn you. If you had lived a hundred years ago they would have done it, too." He shoved his face right next to hers. "Where'd you come up with that?" he asked.

She gave a dark and throaty laugh. They stood there and looked at each other, face-to-face.

And suddenly the golden rain tree beside her parted, and a figure burst out and headed straight for Frau Lyubanarov.

It was the Widow Morar. As she later told us, she was on her way to us, and had arrived at the open gate just as the two had begun their conversation.

Like a fury she went after Frau Lyubanarov, screaming: "She's lying, the tramp, she doesn't know a thing—she doesn't know anything and pretends to know everything in order to coax it out and then broadcast it to all her studs and stallions, so that the filth will lust after her. You don't know a thing, you cesspit, who'll open your legs for any Gypsy's slime. In the mud, you say, you who are nothing but mud yourself. If it's mud you want, then I'll give it to you! Mud to mud!"

She clawed at the gurgling runoff and scraped up a handful of earth and gravel and leaf mold and hurled it at Frau Lyubanarov's head. We heard it rattle and slap against the *dvornik*'s hut. Frau Lyubanarov had shielded her face with her hand, but a stream of dirty water came flowing out of her hair onto her forehead. Before her opponent could reach into the gutter a second time, she shot forward and threw herself on the other woman. In the process she knocked Herr Adamowski's arm off the wall he had been leaning against and sent him tumbling. The two women grabbed each other by the hair, tangling themselves into a knot; they clawed each other to shreds and bit each other with a venomous rage, such as we had never seen before and thank goodness never would see again. Howling, shrieking, and screeching like cats, the two women rolled over each other on the ground until the coachman, who had heard the noise, came running up and tried to separate them the way you would separate fighting dogs, with a bucket of water. But that didn't help; they only became more and more entangled. Shaggy locks of hair clogged their mouths, bloody welts marked their faces, and their eyes rolled back into their heads out of pain and rage. All the household servants came running outside; the women's fingers had to be pried apart, their feet had to be held so that they wouldn't keep striking blindly at the other, and they were lifted or dragged away, Frau Lyubanarov returning to the *dvornik*'s hut, Widow Morar into the street. Their screaming and howling brought the entire neighborhood out of their houses.

Our mother and Aunt Elvira, who had also come outside, chased us back into the house. For the first time in our life Mama lost her composure in front of us; she shooed us in and threatened us with terrible punishments, even spankings, all because we had been involuntary witnesses of the horrible scene. We were locked in our rooms, had to eat supper late, and by ourselves, and were immediately sent to bed. The storm at home raged for days, bringing with it the dreaded arguments between our parents, behind closed doors that were suddenly opened and slammed shut. Our aunts looked at us as if we were to blame for everything that had happened. Uncle Sergei deliberately stayed out of the house as much as possible. Only Herr Tarangolian, who once again stopped by for some black coffee, treated us with the same affectionate and attentive politeness as always, and invited us, as compensation for the outing that had been canceled on that ill-starred day, to a long ride in his carriage, which was a great treat for us, especially as it was crowned by a lavish visit to the Kucharczyk Café and Confectionary.

We were the only ones who knew of the conversation between the two furies that had set off the fight, and we kept that to ourselves.

The second incident I have to report before I go on to events that also affected other people was so cruel it made the first one pale by comparison. It was not quite as violent, to be sure, but the pain was greater for having been inflicted on us in a blindly unfeeling and incomprehensible act of stupidity.

Clearly the preceding episode took its toll on us, though it would take a far greater shock before an actual illness manifested itself. Meanwhile it was only thanks to our school that we were able to withstand the psychological burden as well as the physical stress: there our friendship with Blanche Schlesinger and the irrepressible vitality of Solly Brill allowed us to escape the chaos at home completely for part of the day, and we felt liberated and very happy.

Madame Aritonovich decided that the school should put on a ballet performance for parents and guests; in later years the gratitude we always felt for her made us think that she came up with the idea just for us, and above all for Tanya, who danced with enthusiasm and talent. Nor can this supposition be entirely mistaken. Madame Aritonovich was too close to the prefect and Uncle Sergei not to know every detail of what went on in our house. She probably knew more than we did at the time, for instance about the heated arguments with Aunt Paulette, who stood accused, justifiably, of having opened the house up to Herr Adamowski. At the same time, no one had any idea of the content of Adamowski's conversation with Frau Lyubanarov, which was the actual cause of the fight between her and Widow Morar. But Herr Adamowski was mixed up in it somehow, and that was bad enough, according to the entirely proper view that even an innocent bystander at such occurrences bears some responsibility. In other words: "That kind of thing just shouldn't happen to you, regardless of whether you were involved or not." Naturally Herr Adamowski never came to our house again; instead, Aunt Paulette began to visit him.

In any event, the prospect of the school ballet recital excited us, along with all of our classmates. We began rehearsing the snowflake scene from Tchaikovsky's *Nutcracker.* Tanya danced the part of the Snow Queen, while a handsome and talented boy from a higher grade played the Snow King; Blanche, to our delight—and this seems to confirm our suspicion that the plan was devised with us in mind—was given the part of Clara, while the rest of us, as part of the *corps de ballet*, were to be plain snowflakes, albeit exceedingly eager ones. Solly was cast as a comical snowball with his own special choreography. Turning to her inexhaustible supply of assorted odd, highly original, and skillful acquaintances, Madame Aritonovich assembled a small orchestra. Other instruction was reduced to the bare essentials. Costumes were sewn; Tanya was given a genuine tutu. We were in heaven.

Our parents continued to insist that we never go to or from school unaccompanied. Until then, our coachman had always driven us in the morning, and Aunt Paulette had usually met us after school and walked back home with us through the Volksgarten. That had been very fun on occasion. But ever since she had hit our sister, Tanya, Aunt Elvira picked us up. Aunt Elvira was in her forties, and to us she seemed ancient and unbending. In addition, she had been "left on the shelf," that is, she hadn't found a husband, which also may have soured her. She was the oldest of four sisters—after her came, at significant intervals, our mother, our late Aunt Aida, and Aunt Paulette—and so she commanded a certain degree of authority in the family. We always considered her a terrible party-pooper. For like many unlucky women who have missed their natural vocation as mothers with families of their own, and who though not entirely without work lack much that is truly theirs, being forced to live with relatives, she clung to the illusion that our family was nothing more than an extension of her parent's home, and kept a jealous eye out to make sure that everything was done in the same way and according to the same views as had been practiced there. This led to frequent conflicts with our father—

so-called crises—that split the house into factions. At first glance, such divisions do much harm to family life, but frequently they are the only thing that makes us aware that there is such a thing as "family life" in the first place.

I have already mentioned that we didn't concern ourselves with the religion of our new friends—nor in fact that of most of our classmates—though it's hard to say whether this was intentional or an unconscious decision. But I would be straying far indeed from the truth if I were to claim we didn't know what kind of instruction we were receiving every week from a certain Dr. Aaron Salzmann. We had never discussed or planned our participation; we simply took it for granted that we would take part in that course, just like the majority of our classmates, and above all like our close friends Blanche Schlesinger and Solly Brill. There were so few Catholics in the Institut d'Éducation that the school did not offer special instruction for them. We had been told at the outset that one afternoon in the week we were expected to visit the priest of the Herz-Jesu Church, Deacon Mieczysław Chmielewski, who had a hard time ridding us of the Anglican notions we had acquired thanks to Miss Rappaport. Similarly, the larger group of Lutherans, the occasional Eastern Orthodox or Greek Catholic, the Armenians, and Calvinist students went to their churches for instruction every Wednesday afternoon, and kept away from Dr. Salzmann's class, which was the last one of the day at the institute. So it didn't really attract any attention if we took part in that course; besides, no one at home paid much attention to our schedule.

Only Solly Brill expressed his surprise the first time he saw us in Dr. Salzmann's class. "What's this?" he said. "I thought you were little *goyim*. You're not even circumcised. Well, so much the better. We'll sit through *cheyder* all together."

Blanche, however, appeared to see through our friendly deception. She said: "My father often talks to me about Christ and the holy symbolism of his crucifixion. I'd become a Christian myself if it weren't for the fact that as soon as you do that you get attacked from all sides. My father also thinks that people can feel Jewish and Christian at the same time."

Thanks to the short time we spent in Dr. Salzmann's class, we never thought otherwise ourselves. Because what we heard there and learned was a beautiful reverence for God and an equally beautiful tolerance, wise and smiling—in any case far more ethical than the relentless zeal of Deacon "Mietek" Chmielewski, who tried to convince us that we, as Austrians—in other words almost Germans, by which he meant Protestants—had little or no chance of ever truly being good Catholics, and that a good Catholic had the duty of being an even better Pole.

From Dr. Salzmann we heard about the only people—apart from the Hellenes—whom we felt had a legitimate claim to national seniority, a nation made holy both by the greatness of its religion as well as by a thousand years of martyrdom, that had produced the men we had learned to revere as our own patriarchs, and whose cruel persecutions throughout generations were no less than those suffered by the martyrs of our Church, and continued to the most recent times. We were shaken to hear about the atrocities committed during the uprising led by Khmelnytsky, whose name sounded so much like that of our deacon.

In portraying those events, or the persecutions of the Spanish Inquisition, Dr. Salzmann's intent was not to show how bestially the Christians had acted in their religious zeal. He mitigated their guilt as well as he could, with wisely resigned pronouncements about human nature, and by constantly demonstrating that stupidity or foolishness were more to blame than actual ill will—for instance when he told us that the reason Russian soldiers so much enjoyed enacting pogroms was because they had great fun slitting the feather beds with their bayonets. The fact that people who had been frightened out of their wits happened to have crawled under those same feather beds was, so to speak, a misunderstanding—"bad luck," as Miss Rappaport might say, who also responded to such situations with cool objectivity.

In talking about the agonizing history of the Jews, Dr. Salzmann was not simply dishing out the murky broth of nationalistic feeling by citing the hardships of the fathers; his goal was to emphasize the steadfastness of belief that had been handed down through the generations. Untold hordes of old and young, men, mothers, children had been tortured to death upholding the precept of *Kiddush Hashem*—in the praise of the one whose name cannot be taken in vain, according to the commandment that for us also was the first—and would continue to be martyred for their belief. They died confessing their faith with words that we, who also believed in a single God—the God of the same tribe from which our Savior came—happily repeated with conviction the *Shema Yisrael*: "Hear, O Israel, the Lord our God is one!"

But most of all we loved this class on account of the teacher. Dr. Aaron Salzmann had a captivating way of treating each of us as creatures that were at once human and all-too-human, whose understanding of the world, from the least things to the greatest, was limited solely by our lack of practice in clear and logical thought—in other words, in merely thinking. He accepted neither ignorance nor stupidity, which he considered mere excuses. Whenever he encountered a lack of understanding, he never lost his patience, but closed his eyes, arched his eyebrows, and repeated the question or sentence that had not been immediately understood in his soft, rich tenor, adding a sigh of ponderous contentment—for as long as it took until he finally came out with the explanation or answer himself, because it was part of his internal vision. His standing expression was: "I'm thinking out loud."

He was very fat—his stomach stuck out so far it seemed to push him backwards; his face had a glossy, reddish tinge with the olive undertone of his race, and he had sparkling black eyes and a thick, assertive mustache. His bearing was warlike. Embedded in the cushions of fat around his cheeks we could still make out the features of his youth: the face of a young David, bold, clear, and beautiful. His mouth was defiant, soft and sensuous, with finely molded scarlet lips. A profusion of oily ringlets formed a wreath around his neck inside his collar, which was always a little grimy.

He came into the classroom and said: "What am I doing? I am thinking out loud. I will speak about religious matters. So I step before God. Who am I to step before *Him* whom we do not name, out of respect for the first commandment—who am I to step before *Him* with my head bare, combed or not, just as I am? Am I subject to the order to cover my head? For the Orthodox it is imperative, and for the liberal, half-imperative—one doesn't have to, but one should. I'm thinking out loud. Maybe the liberal isn't wrong when he says that God sees his reverence even though he isn't wearing a hat. Because *He* sees everything that is over a hat and everything that is underneath. But next to me is maybe an Orthodox man who finds my uncovered state offensive to his religious feelings. In order not to offend his religious feelings, I therefore put on a yarmulke." He pulled out a round black silk yarmulke from his pocket and put it on. "There was once a man in Russia who saw an officer approaching with soldiers. The man thought to himself in fear: 'Now they are going to beat me. Because if I let them pass with my head covered they will yell at me: *Why didn't you remove your hat to greet us?*—and they will beat me. But if I take off my hat, they will yell at me: *Who are you to be greeting us by removing your hat?*—and they will beat me. Probably they will beat me to death. And if I die, I don't wish to come before *His* countenance, whom we don't name, with an uncovered head. So I keep my hat on my head.' In this way the man died for *Kiddush Hashem*... The Orthodox wants to be certain at all times and ready for all things, and so he wears both, a yarmulke as well as a hat."

Dr. Salzmann had a watch that always stopped. Several times during the lesson he would pull it out of a small pocket on his waistband below his enormous stomach—he never wore a vest—listen to it, shake it, knock it on the table, and listen again, all the while patiently speaking. The watch seldom seemed to run, and hardly ever on time. Because there was no bell to mark the end of this last period on Wednesday mornings, it occasionally happened that Dr. Salzmann kept us past time in the classroom. That would prove to be our undoing.

For one day Aunt Elvira, who had come to pick us up, no longer had the patience to wait for us outside the institute. She knew from Herr Tarangolian or Uncle Sergei how free and easy things were at our school, for instance that one could visit Madame Aritonovich during ballet class. So she ventured into the corridor of the Institut d'Éducation and asked "some woman"—whom she took for a cleaning lady—how to find our classroom. She was completely taken aback when this same woman accompanied her into our room: it was our mathematics teacher, Dr. Biro, who was on her way to fetch Dr. Salzmann, in order to walk home together, as usual. And, as usual, Dr. Biro was chewing on something—this time a richly buttered poppyseed bun that we called a "braid."

Aunt Elvira entered the classroom with the put-on smile of grown-ups who view children as half-dangerous, half-idiotic creatures. She nodded and uttered a semi-sour, semi-friendly "Good morning," which Dr. Salzmann answered with a sonorous-relaxed "Indeed it is!" Aunt Elvira's smile froze at the sight of his black yarmulke, which she stared at as if transfixed.

"If the ladies will be so kind as to wait one more minute," said Dr. Salzmann, shaking his watch and holding it to his ear. "I'm thinking out loud. The course—that is to say this class—in this *Institute Dedication* combines students from the *cheyder* as well as from the *yeshiva*. What is the *cheyder*? The *cheyder* is the basic religious study. So what is the *yeshiva*? The *yeshiva* is the place of advanced religious instruction. But what is this *Institute Dedication*? A private school with expensive tuition. The students of this institution are therefore children of rich people. Being rich doesn't make one grateful. The children of rich people are seldom brought up in the faith. I am the teacher of this course. So what is my duty? My duty as teacher of this course is to make up for what has been missed. What tells me whether the pupils of the *yeshiva* master the basic instruction of the *cheyder* or not? My presumption as well as my knowledge. My presumption that the pupils of the *yeshiva* in this course have not mastered their basic instruction from the *cheyder* is based on the experience that children of rich people will have paid inadequate attention to religion. What confirms this supposition? My knowledge of the students of this class confirms that my supposition is correct. I repeat: my duty as teacher of this course is to make up for what has been missed. So the students of the *yeshiva* will repeat the greatest of the prayers in the faith, the *Krias-Shema*. What is this prayer? This prayer is the *Shema Yisrael*. The *Shema Yisrael* is the only prayer that must be prayed in Hebrew. Other prayers can be prayed in Hebrew as well—they should be, but they don't have to be. This is half-imperative. That's why one of our assignments is *Taitsch*. What is *Taitsch*? It is the Germanization, the translation of the prayers. We will translate the *Shema Yisrael* as well, but we will pray in Hebrew:

Shema Yisrael adoshem eloheynu adoshem echad!

Taitsch—I'm thinking out loud... *Shema Yisrael*—Hear, O Israel. *Shema Yisrael adoshem*. What is *adoshem? Adoshem* comes from joining *adonai* and *shem*. What is *adonai*? *Adonai* means God. So what is *shem? Shem* means the word for name. But what is the name? The name is God. *Adoshem* means the name of God, both literally as a compound drawn together and symbolically. The class will repeat:

"Shema Yisrael—"

We repeated it as a chorus.

"Hear, O Israel. *Shema Yisrael adoshem—*"

We repeated: "*Shema Yisrael adoshem—*" and so on, with the translation in *Taitsch*, until the end.

Dr. Salzmann had not yet put his yarmulke back in his pocket when Aunt Elvira walked right up to him. "Excuse me," she said. "Am I standing before a teacher of this institute?"

"If you would prefer to sit down, ma'am, please," said Dr. Salzmann politely, "you may have my chair."

"And with whom do I have the pleasure?"

"Dr. Aaron Salzmann is my name. The lady here teaches mathematics at this institute, Dr. Margit Biro, née Wurfbaum."

Dr. Biro, who was in the process of biting into her poppy-seed bun, bowed to Aunt Elvira.

"I only desire to learn the nature of the course being taught here," said Aunt Elvira.

"You speak like a diplomat, ma'am. We are simple Jews. The course you have just attended was the Mosaic religious instruction."

"And is Madame Aritonovich cognizant of the fact that this instruction is being imparted to Christian children?" asked Aunt Elvira, indignant in the true sense of the word, that is to say, removed from her dignity.

"For that information you have to ask Lustig, ma'am."

"I have to ask *how*? said Aunt Elvira, sharply.

Dr. Salzmann closed his eyes and arched his eyebrows. "I use the word *lustig* not as an adjective, meaning jolly, but as a given name. Dr. Lustig is the professor in charge of this class, who takes care of the enrollment relating to religious instruction."

"In that case, one will have to turn to Madame Aritonovich personally," said Aunt Elvira, her non sequitur sounding painfully illogical to Dr. Salzmann.

"By all means, please do," he said, bowing to her, as much as his enormous stomach would permit. Dr. Biro followed him out, still chewing.

The revelation that the Institut d'Éducation was a "pure Jewish school" where classes were taught in Hebrew, was first met with disbelief at home. But when asked, we had to confess that we had been taking part in Jewish religious instruction. This set off one of the usual "crises." Our mother sought out Madame Aritonovich, who listened to her carefully and then said: "Didn't you know that I'm Jewish myself?"

Not a syllable of that was true—both Herr Tarangolian and Uncle Sergei took pains to rebut this claim as tactfully as possible, but even as they did, our parents remained resolute in their decision to remove us immediately from the school. We cried for days. It was only thanks to some strenuous intervention on the part of Herr Tarangolian, who openly declared that he hadn't expected his personal friends would disrupt his efforts to prevent the national, religious, and racist antipathies in this city from boiling over, that we were permitted at least to stay through the end of the term—naturally without further participation in the Jewish religious instruction.

As it turned out, we wouldn't even be able to finish the term. Meanwhile, our family's friendship with the prefect, which had lasted for decades, from that moment on began to chill.

15

Journalistic Activities of Herr Alexianu and Professor Feuer; Death of Old Paşcanu

A POPULAR ditty started spreading among the so-called *patchkas*, or groups of young flaneurs who swarmed up and down during their daily morning and evening promenades. It was in Romanian, and people attributed the authorship to Herr Năstase on account of its wit, as well as because of the undisguised allusions to the goings-on in the house of Tildy, and to the Germans in general. The catchy refrain went like this:

> *Poftiţi cu toţi acuma la balamuc,*
> *unde boeri de rasă azi se mai duc:*
> *comfort—guic-guic*
> *fără bucluc…*
> *poftiţi la balamuc…*

Balamuc is an idiomatic expression for asylum. In translation the song might sound like this:

> Just follow me to the nuthouse, please,
> where aristocrats come and go with ease;
> it's swank beyond dispute
> and no one gets the boot,
> so off to the nuthouse, please…

In reality this creation was taken from an article in the newspaper *Vocea* that focused on the discovery of the insane "poet" Karl Piehowicz.

As I have mentioned, the junior house physician of the municipal asylum, Dr. Kipper, had forwarded a selection of the transcribed poems to a certain Herr Sperber, who published them in the *Tscherno-poler Tageszeitung*, with some remarks:

> ...we are literally confronted with the mysterious revelations of a vibrant lyrical spirit that comes from another sphere and speaks through the medium of this broken mouth. What a font of words, what breath of the earth! Not since the days of Johann Christian Günther and the other noble Baroque poets has such a voice been heard. Am I exaggerating? Here is the proof.

This page found its way to the great critic Karl Kraus, who called it "by far the most respectable thing I have found in a journal in a long time, and certainly the most important I have ever discovered in a daily." He published the poems ostensibly authored by Piehowicz, along with what he knew of their origin, in his highly influential polemical journal *Die Fackel*, juxtaposing them against some poetic creations recently published in German newspapers, in an essay entitled "From the Editorial Desk and the Asylum." This was the focus of the article in the *Vocea,* which carried the headline "Voice from the Beyond":

> An apt old proverb states: For the jackal to admit his soul is black, think how black his soul must be...We are always happy to discover professions of ethnicity that serve to unmask a pose of national arrogance. Recently a particularly delightful example came to our attention. This particular voice comes from a nation that suffers more than any other from the flatulence of exaggerated self-opinion, and which misses no opportunity to rub the excesses of its discharges (which somehow never seem to bring relief) in the noses of other nations—to put it plainly, from the German nation, whose sons, down to the last stinky-foot, claim to be the descendents of Goethe and Beethoven—even in circumstances where intelligence (not to mention tact, which they don't possess) would counsel against claiming a binding legacy, namely when living in scattered groups as guests

> of other nations, where the validity of such assertions is easily checked by comparison. However, the voice that now surprises us with its revelatory insights, with all the gravitas of a voice from the beyond, does not hail from our local ethnic Germans—the *Volkdetusche,* whom alas we must count among our minorities—but from their own homeland, although it is connected with an occurrence in our city. The great German journalist feels compelled to proclaim: "My inquiries led me to discover that the greatest German poet is an insane locksmith by the name of Karl Piehowicz, a resident of the Czernopol municipal asylum. He deserves every literary prize that Germany has to give.

The author went on in the same malicious tone, lifting another sentence from Kraus's article with poisonous glee:

> I would particularly award him (Piehowicz) the Schiller-Prize, albeit without the bonus offered by the Odol Mouthwash Company, which has led the German people from literary Idol to literary Odol, a symbolic move that suggests their language is good for rinsing out the mouth.

Nor were the attacks confined to general targets. The writer went on:

> ...We have since made our own inquiries and learned that it is an officer of our own army who has particularly distinguished himself in helping the Germans acquire a new genius, insane though this brilliant poet may be, as has been clinically proven beyond a doubt. It happens that this particular Herr Major is in the asylum himself, where his own mental state is under observation following a series of lunatic acts that several weeks earlier sparked both laughter and terror in this city. The entire chain of events begs the question of whether we ought not pay more heed to leaders of the nationalist program who advocate a thorough purge of our army, and give them a freer hand to implement their commendable plans than hitherto...

This was an allusion to General Petrescu and openly dragged the case into the political arena. The article ended with a satirical verse:

> *—as proof that we are not ourselves lacking in lyrical gifts*
> *—even outside the municipal asylum—*

And was signed *Ali.*

The "stinky-foot" reference was all we needed to recognize that the pseudonymous author was none other than our former tutor, Herr Alexianu.

A few days later a response appeared in Herr Adamowski's *Tescovina German Messenger*:

> FERMENT OF DECOMPOSITION
>
> I hope the foreignness of this title won't be held against me; it does not come from a German pen, although it does stem from a German-minded one, as is well-known, and from no one less than the pure-blooded Briton H. S. Chamberlain, who thus for all time branded the essence of the Jewish race. The Jew: instigator of dissent, the little man who unlike the little men in Grimm does not roam the woods, but stands on crooked legs nevertheless, exactly as our wise Wilhelm Busch observed with his superb smirking acuity and the unerring discernment of his blue eyes, leaving all grinning aside in order to warn us:
>
> Too short trousers, coat to his toes,
> Crooked cane and crooked nose,
> Eyes pitch-black and soul of gray,
> Hat tipped back, with cunning gaze:
> Look, here comes Shmul Shievelbein
> (Not so handsome as our kind...)
>
> And there it is: little Shmul the bowlegged lackey and lickspittle, bent on currying favor with the German folk and sponging off the stock of our tree unless the hand of the watchful forester

scrapes it off the oak-bark in time. Because any whose eyesight has not yet been compromised by the mixture of races surely will not fail to see that behind the flatteringly feigned face of bourgeois decency lurks the hideous grimace of a creature whose natural purpose and national predisposition is to decompose, and destroy. Of course it's often hard to see through the tricks and intrigues of this dwarfish race; the blond and bright-eyed approach, with its straightforward thinking, clearly contradicts the Talmudic way of thought, and easily brushes aside any evil plans concocted by the vermin. Nevertheless, what was hardly an itch can still turn into a bad boil after the louse has been pulled off. Don't tiny mites cause the oak forest to die? Haven't you seen how the sheltering tree is felled by the worm? Therefore let us overcome our disgust, as all who are skilled in healing must, if they wish to strike at the pest. If the festering boil stinks, it's only because the destructive bacteria are eating away inside. One sharp cut will cause the pus to drain away.

Recently we read in a Jew-paper that a poet of the German tongue had been discovered in an asylum here, whose works were of a quality to overshadow Goethe—no, Schiller himself. Not since Agnes Günther, the Baroque nightingale, has such a voice been heard. Well now! Let's pass by the question whether Shmul Shievelbein is entitled to an opinion on that matter... but no, let us not! The sheer brazenness to meddle with the most German of matters—our poetry!—should raise our suspicion. Does the Jew ever undertake anything without a cunningly devised ulterior motive? Therefore beware! A Jew is always a Jew—so be on your guard. He is not out to serve the German drive for beauty, or to enlarge the German trove of art, but he is relentless in pursuit of his own goals.

This publication falls into the hands of one of the coffeehouse literati who are sadly all too common in the city on the Danube, that great stream of the Nibelungen. Did it blow in on the wind? No! Another Jew passed it to him. And the former, who publishes a monthly rag vilifying anything printed in the German language, is grateful for the opportunity to pounce.

He fancies himself a critic. Mere envy, you think? A pallid milquetoast and limp-loin, lacking any creative power of his own, and who therefore chafes at those who are brimming with life and bursting with song? Be on guard—because a Jew is always a Jew! Behind the appearance lurks a vile plan. And never does he point his poisoned arrows with more hate than against his own race. Presumably his aim is wide, too. So he just tears the jester's cap off the woolly head. What for? Simply so he can put it all the more smoothly on his own. He cloaks himself in the appearance of legitimacy in order to fulfill his task of decomposition all the better, all the more unchallenged. He takes the little verse of the insane man, lavishes the most outrageous praise, as if he were hawking the lines at some flea market, but why? Simply to sprinkle excrement on what is better, to widen a crack into a fissure that he may continue to wedge asunder. And in the guise of fair dealings and just desserts! Beware, the cards are marked! Where deceivers dwell no home is clean.

Is it any surprise that foreigners develop the wrong picture of the German race? Is it any wonder that another paper has taken up the matter, and gloating with derisive bewilderment, poses the question: Is the greatest German poet a madman? And is it at all shocking to see another case enter the discussion, which—however wrongly—connects insanity with Germanity, and raises fundamental questions as to how far the loyalty of national minorities should be trusted . . . ?!

We have nothing to reply to that except: Recognize the true pest! Observe his methods! Find him out in your own home as well! Clean house however you crave—verily it is necessary! Pick up the iron broom and sweep out those truly bad housemates! Do not overlook the fact that it was German diligence that created this flourishing settlement, as pretty a town as could be, so long as the Jew let it alone! Do not throw the baby out with the bathwater! German military might has served faithfully in many a foreign service, and has always fought bravely, indifferent to displays of gratitude as of thanklessness, concerned only to fulfill our sworn duty to teach the adversary the sharp bite of the German blade. Clean house, then! But with the proper sense of proportion! Do not the scales fall from your eyes when you examine the asylum, from which has emerged this threat to ethnic accord? And when you realize that out of seven medical assistants five are Jews, one is Polish, and one is Ukrainian? To work, then! We Tescovina-Germans will look on calmly, even with delight. Moreover, we offer you our energetic assistance. For we feel bound by the words of Luther:

Here I stand! I can do no other!
God help me!

Averse to hiding behind a pseudonym, and unafraid to sign his own full name:

—Professor Dr. Lothar Feuer,
Senior teacher at the German Boys' Lyceum in Czernopol

And a dreadful thing happened: the Jews of Czernopol, led by a couple of youthful pranksters, seized the issue of the *Tescovina German Messenger* in which Professor Feuer's article had appeared; they bought up the entire run, paying collector's prices to the German subscribers, and howled with laughter. They read Professor Feuer's article to one another with tears in their eyes and breaking out into spasms of laughter. They spoke among themselves in a lightly Yiddishized "flickering-Waibling-Wälsung" German, and it became fashionable among young people to talk among themselves somewhat like this: "*Sieg-Heil*, selfsame Sigi! Have you perchance perceived Luttinger's lascivious Lily? No, forsooth? Some foul fate has flubbed our flirt? Elsewise she twines about me like the ivy twines about the ash, *die sheyne shikse*! *Nu*, so now I'll have to wend my gleeful galosh-gait into the garden of the *Volk*. Are you pleased to plan to take your pleasure with another? Engage in a bit of racial defilement with a blonde, perchance?"

The reference to the "Baroque nightingale Agnes Günther" was a particularly delightful tidbit for connoisseurs.

All in all, the newspaper war enlivened the city. The *patchkas* in the circles around Năstase and Alexianu popularized the satirical verse about the *balamuc* that was soon put to music. Gyorgyovich Ianku played it for the habitués of the Trocadero, when the doors opened to let them in, with Ephraim Perko in the lead: the popular fiddler Gypsy first plucked the tune quietly on the strings of his fiddle, and little by little the entire orchestra joined in until they broke out in a thunderous march full of joie de vivre:

Just follow me to the nuthouse, please . . .

The flaneurs hummed it on their paths about town. The promenade pranced to its rhythm. Czernopol was in a champagne mood.

Only here and there were fisticuffs observed. Herr Alexianu knocked a Jewish lawyer to the ground because the man had inadvertently stepped on his feet in the confusing shuffle of the promenade. The leader of the Tescovina-German fraternity Germania struck a cadet of the officer's school and was locked up for two days. And Solly Brill received a resounding slap when he greeted Dr. Salzmann in the corridor of the Institut d'Éducation with the words "Greetings, O brave cuckold." He had not understood the meaning of the word and thought it sounded chivalrous, in the style of Professor Feuer.

During this time old Paşcanu died.

Herr Tarangolian never spoke otherwise about his death than as an important signal, a beacon.

"Explain such an end, if you can," he said. "Gather up all the possible reasons, place the circumstances in a cogent chain of causality, and you still won't be able to exclude an element of the demonic. No matter what people claimed to know after the fact, no matter what explanation they put forward—the failure of this venture or that, the catastrophe with Tildy, the attempted diamond swindle, how one thing led to another to exacerbate the mistrust that was already smoldering, and, finally, clear signals of a bad end—that's all wisdom after the fact. No, no: we must look elsewhere for the true cause of Paşcanu's ruin. Because ultimately the catastrophe did not affect him alone. Even if we can find sufficient cause in his own person—and that's not hard to do—it still falls far short of explaining the misfortune into which he dragged others. Believe me, we all think too rationally. The death of Săndrel Paşcanu was a *sign* . . ."

And, indeed, other ominous things occurred in those days which had nothing directly to do with Paşcanu's death. An ill star hung over Czernopol. We couldn't help but think of articles we had read about the holy hermits of India whose presence protects a land from floods and crop failures, pestilence and rapacious beasts—plagues that soon return when the sainted person leaves. Today, as the story of Tildy has become the myth of our childhood, it seems to me as if we had known back then whose beneficent being it was that had been taken from the city of Czernopol.

The day they arrested Bubi Brill was a Saturday. On Sunday Czernopol was seething with rumors. On Monday morning old Paşcanu was called in for a hearing

Monday in Czernopol was market day. The peasant carts began trickling into town while it was still dark. In the pale dawn the markets filled up with seasonal vendors and booth operators setting up their stands; the large vegetable market at Theater Square, near the synagogue, a funfair at the Turkish Fountain, and a flea market behind the provincial government offices all swelled with teeming life. Soon the cardsharps had coaxed the first farmers to try their luck at three-card monte, which they played by manipulating three aces—two black and one red—with bewildering dexterity, by the festering light of sunflower-oil lanterns. After plucking the farmers of a few quick leos, they raced off at the first sign of a policeman. By the time the day arrived, the trading was in full swing. Housewives, followed by their servant girls in colorful peasant dress, haggled with farmwives over vegetables and fowl. Above the flea market, the pungent smell of untanned sheepskins lingered like a poisonous cloud. Ancient horn-phonographs squawked out the disembodied voices of Caruso and Lilli Lehmann. Spectacularly ragged figures stood beside old scraps of newspapers strewn with crooked nails and rusty screws, waiting to make a sale. At the fair by the Turkish Fountain, barrel organs droned away, swings arced back and forth, and the carousels went round and round. Older farmer couples and soldiers on leave with their brides had themselves photographed against a picturesque cutout of a well, their hands awkwardly clasped together, stiff as wax statues. Gendarmes with fixed bayonets patrolled the lanes between the stands, while pickpockets worked themselves into a sweat behind their backs.

While old man Paşcanu was being questioned on the third floor of the courthouse, and the state prosecutor—a young, ambitious gentleman freshly transferred from the provincial capital, eager to earn his spurs and anxious to worm out a confession with whatever display of lawyerly histrionics it might take—was taking pains not to allow his opponent to respond with anything that was clearly innocuous... while this was happening, something unusual occurred: a crowd began to gather on the street and kept growing bigger and bigger. The vast majority consisted of peasants, coachmen from the country, raftsmen, grain dealers, all of whom crowded outside the bombastically severe façade of the courthouse and looked up at the dusty windows in silence or muted conversation: the countryside had come to witness either the downfall or the triumphant vindication of its great son... No, not his vindication, not his resurrection in the glory of innocence—it was his downfall that they wanted to see. The rabble of Czernopol mixed among the country folk, spreading their coarse jests and uncouth jokes. Peasants hunched over from hard work, with shoulder-length matted hair, shriveled by the wind and tanned by the heat of the sun like an old goat ham, with skin as dry as worn-out Gypsy fiddles, listened in earnest amazement to the tales being spun about the heroic feats and dastardly deeds of the man who had at last come to be judged inside that building—the man whose name they didn't even know, but whose magical powers had brought them there: a great man, a son of the mountains and forests, a son of the earth like themselves, born in the high bracken among the firs, a man whose countless adventures had brought him power and splendor and untold riches—whole lands had been in his possession—but whom the devil, with whom he had been in league, had discarded, and who was now on his way to the place of judgment. Would they hang him . . . ? Hang him? Outside the city they were already building a platform, first to impale him and then to saw him into quarters and show his limbs to the populace: those arms and hands that had raked in the gold: Jewish thalers and widows' bread money intended for feeding their hungry orphans . . . The rabble of Czernopol said all this and more—even as they cleaned out the peasant women of whatever they had in their meager belt pouches.

The examination dragged on for hours. Time and again the young prosecutor picked some new aspect of the attempted tax evasion to entertain extravagant speculations concerning the most unrelated issues, and time and again he would stop after a fruitless detour, slap the pile of documents on his desk, and say: "Your answers are insufficient and intentionally misleading, sir. But don't go to the trouble: everything about this case is watertight. The major fact—the active bribe—has been proven beyond doubt. For the moment I'm leaving aside gross embezzlement, extortion, fraud. The indictment will give you the opportunity to convince yourself of the soundness of my accusations. Herr Paşcanu, you are a cancer on the economic body of our nation. Your actions are tantamount to sabotage. The public figures incriminated by you will be called to account. The highest state positions have been compromised by your misdeeds. I consider it very likely, *monsieur*, that a special law will be passed just to mete out the justice you deserve."

Old Paşcanu didn't respond at all, but merely stared at the young zealot with his lurking, menacing, boarlike eyes. Behind his bushy white mustache it was impossible to tell if he was smiling contemptuously.

But when he then stepped out of the courthouse, he found himself face-to-face with his own kind, with his brothers who no longer believed in him. Even though Paşcanu had yet to be charged, the prosecutor had arranged—quite unlawfully—for the old man to be escorted by two policemen—an act that was all the more malicious as it had no other motive than simple spite. And so the moment he stepped outside, flanked by two minions of the law, people considered him already under arrest.

Had a single voice been raised, it would have saved his life. A curse, which was otherwise always quick to fly, or a stone, which was always at hand in Czernopol, would have aroused his old fighting spirit, his craftiness and his desire for revenge. But nothing like that happened. He looked into the eyes of his people—the people for whom he had become a legend—and saw that his star had fallen.

And old Paşcanu raised his arms toward heaven, turning up his palms like the two pans of a scale, and rocked them up and down before his people, meekly nodding and shrugging his shoulders; he was holding his case for them to see, the case of a bold and adventuresome life, holding it in his empty hands and weighing it before their eyes: a human life that had been the way it had been; the life of a man who had wanted the most and obtained much and still wound up with nothing more than his bit of used-up earthly self—an old body; a crippled, disappointed spirit turned brittle, tough, and mean; the ruins of frail desire, paltry fulfillment, spoiled wishes, missed goals.

It was a gesture both disturbing and strangely redemptive, a pitiful paraphrase of old man Brill's—and just as ridiculous—and it released the rising tension of the crowd, which ran the gamut of feelings from bloodlust to jubilation, triggering a great cackling laugh, a storm of roaring and bellowing laughter. The marketplace had understood: a legendary crook was confessing his failure. The weather-beaten peasants, whose last bits of brain had been singed away under their pointed sheepskin caps by the Podolian summer, and whose spirit had been stunted beneath their broad waistbands by the icy wind of the vast steppe—these peasants laughed so hard that tears came rolling down their jagged cheeks. They slapped their gnarly, rootlike hands against their scrawny thighs, raising the dust off their hemp-linen pants and scratchy shirts; they hunched over even more and bent back so far that their skulls rested in their necks; barked their laughter through the yellow stubble teeth of their rough mouths up to the heavens and down to the earth. The hoi polloi of Czernopol squinted until their eyes were mean slits, and bleated and bellowed with all their might; the Jewish hawkers gloated out loud in booming tenors; ethnic Germans come to market uttered short guttural sounds of disbelief because they could not comprehend; street urchins let out piercing whistles through their teeth; and from a group of young gentlemen flaneurs sauntering from the tennis courts came the cry: "So God the great is giving the *ganef* a good going-over. Let us leave leisurely from hence or else the mob will go *meshugge* and perhaps tear his head asunder."

Old Paşcanu looked on at this raging merriment for several minutes. Then he picked up his cane and began lashing out without mercy in all directions, laying into shoulders and heads, until he had cleared a passageway. He beat his way through the tangle of people as the laughter rose into a howling roar. Because it was not anger that drove him on: it was shame. Nothing could have a more comic effect in Czernopol. The two policemen followed the old man, knocked about this way and that like little jumping jacks as they attempted to ward off and return the jostles, thumps, and punches of the crowd.

Paşcanu's old-fashioned coach with the colossal horses was waiting a little ways off from the main entrance of the courthouse. The castrated coachman was dozing on the high box, a tower of quivering flesh kept in check by a bulging pale-lilac sash. He sat without moving, his expressionless, moonlike Mongolian face reminiscent of a pumpkin. Old Paşcanu woke him from his flabby, lethargic apathy by slapping his cane across the whale-sized back, and tore open the door to the coach. The crowd shoved and pushed him in, lifting in their wake the two policemen, who were striking this way and that, their faces red with fury. White-haired peasant patriarchs and mangy urchins clambered onto the springs and axles of the coach and pressed their noses against the windowpanes, and when the horses started up they tumbled off into the arms of the pushing mass, which knocked them down, trampled them, and jerked them up again. The howling and laughter followed the coach even after it turned onto Neuschulgasse, a glorious bouquet of unbridled jollity, rude and cruel, like the tail of a peacock being dragged along through the gutter, which shimmered with a metallic iridescence like its besmirched feathers.

But Săndrel Paşcanu did not drive home. The two addled policemen could hardly object when he called out to the *scopit* in a shrill, almost rattling, voice to drive to the house of his daughter, Tamara Tildy. Much later, Window Morar—who had been forbidden to set foot on our property after her catfight with Frau Lyubanarov—told us of the conversation between father and daughter, after we had sworn complete secrecy:

"... And you know, they hadn't seen each other ever since she left home to marry the major: at that time Tildy was a lieutenant with the Austrians and handsome as a young hero. They hadn't spoken in years, father and daughter, not since the death of her mother. She had cursed him whenever she said his name, and now there he was, standing before her and speaking to her of the same blood, the blood of the Paşcanus, that flowed in her veins as well. He reminded her of how he had cradled her in his arms as a child, and of a little pony he had given her on which she trotted along next to his coach wherever he went. Because back then she had loved him, her little father; it wasn't until later that her mother ingrained her own hate in her daughter, when the other woman came, the maid Ioana Ciornei, who produced the witch I tried to tear apart with my own two hands, and whose children I now feed from the work of these hands because she is also blood of her blood, and because evil should not be passed from one generation to the next, from the grandfathers to the grandchildren. That's how he stood in front of her then, shaking and sobbing, the old man, and his voice, whose power had once struck fear in the high and mighty of this world, was the voice of a whining woman. 'Do you want to let this shame cling to your name?' he howled. 'Do you want to be the daughter of someone who has been laughed out of town, chased out of house and fortune, back to the loneliness of the mountains from which he came? Do you want every churl to grin in contempt when he hears whose child you are? I will give you all the jewels, all the gold that I own, I'll tear open the coffins, not of your mother, but of the other. I'll take the rings off their decayed fingers and the stones from the necklaces that have fallen between their ribs and will give them to you—but you have to help me. You have to help me restore our honor...!' And he pushed his nose, that vulture's beak, close to her face and said, with crazy eyes: 'Let them see what they have gone and done. Let them find out who they are clashing with. May terror seize their hearts when they hear that I, Săndrel Paşcanu, have gone to my death. And then let them be horrified when I again rise up before them, may they fall on their knees in fear and regret and grovel for mercy... Because I will not die,' he said close to her ear. 'I intend to hang myself, and you are to come and cut me down at the last moment. I know a body can hang for a long time before it gives up the ghost, I've seen many people hanged, at the siege of Plevna and elsewhere: it can last up to five or seven minutes. I know,' he said. 'I know how long I can last. I can stand three minutes. You come inside after two minutes: the doors will be open. You can be praying at St. Parachiva and then be at my home in half a minute. I could order Miron to do this but I don't trust him, the dog, I don't trust anyone in the world except my own flesh and blood. This is not a servant's business, it's a matter for one's own flesh and blood. He'll be in the stable, sleeping, the way he always sleeps, the *castrato*. You are to leave me lying there and go to him and scream: *My father has hanged himself*, and tell him to go and shout it out in town! And he will do it, and you will see how terror will strike the hearts of all who will be ruined if I die and who I can save as long as I stay alive. And then how they will fear if I will still save them when they see I haven't died—resurrected like the Savior!' He said those very words: *resurrected like the Savior!* My blood froze to hear him speak them. And he said: 'You will see how they will cower. How they will crawl in the dust before me, from the greatest to the smallest in this country! You are to lock yourself up at my house and admit no one, and if they want to come in you will say: my father is dead—and so on until the next morning. I don't need a doctor to bring me back to life, I'll do it myself, I tell you: I know how. Once when I was young they tried it with me. I can last three minutes and don't need any doctor to help me afterwards... Will you do this?' he asked her. And she was as if transfigured. She said: 'Yes, I will do this!' 'Do you swear by the grave of your mother?' he asked. And she said: 'Yes, I swear by the grave of my mother.' 'So go to mass at St. Parachiva,' he said, 'and when they ring the bell, I will climb into the noose and kick the chair out from underneath, and you look at your watch and wait one and a half minutes. You need half a minute to my house. You can say you heard a voice telling you to go there while you prayed.' And she said: 'Yes.' 'Swear to me once more on the memory of your mother,' he said. And she said: 'I swear it on the memory of my mother!'—and was as if transfigured. And that's how she was the whole day, and when I came to her and told her: 'You have to go now, the mass at St. Parachiva is at six o'clock!'—she just sat there as if transfigured and didn't hear me, not even when I shook her shoulder, in her trance she was as if dead. And I shouted: 'You don't want to become the murderer of your father, think about your oath!' But she didn't move. And then I saw that she had smashed her watch under the heel of her shoe. And I ran out, and it's a long way to the Turkish Fountain, it was long after six by the time I reached his house, and I ran to the *scopit* in the stable. I ran so fast I could taste my own blood in my mouth, and I cried out to him that he should come with me. And he woke up and went with me. And all the doors were open that were usually closed on account of his treasures. And when we came inside, the coachman and I, the old man was standing on the top of the stairs and shouted: 'So she didn't come, eh! She didn't come, just like I foresaw. Did all of you think it would be so easy to let me hang myself?' And he laughed like I'd never heard anyone laugh before, the marrow froze in our bones, of the *scopit* and me. Only the devil can laugh like that. And up on the stairs he shouted: 'Run and tell the whole city how well Paşcanu knows people. Everyone who has laughed at me shall learn to fear me!' And he spread out his arms, brandishing his cane, and shouted: 'Because I'm alive, you see, I'm still alive!' Returning his cane to the ground he reached out too far, past the top of the landing, but he had already placed his entire weight on it and so he lost his balance. He fell down the steep stairs so hard that the house echoed and the landing splintered into pieces. And when he hit the floor at our feet he had broken his neck: his eyes were open and fixed in that last gaze, and his mustache stuck out in front of his teeth so that he looked the way a dog does when he wants to bite you. We carried him back up, and I tried to close his eyes, but they wouldn't shut, so I had to leave him that way, still seeing and looking like a dog who wants to bite. And above him was the painting of his two wives..."

It was the famous Titian. A completely inferior copy of the *Reclining Venus.* Some obscure painter had been commissioned to repaint the picture with the head of Princess Sturdza and the naked body of Ioana Ciornei. Paşcanu had had the red curtain installed so he could change his view according to his inclination, so that it sometimes covered the head and sometimes the body. The collected rubbish they found in his house didn't even pay for the costs of his funeral. The two colossal horses would have fetched the highest price, despite their age, but they were found the next morning dead in their stalls, grotesquely bloated. People said that the *scopit* had poisoned them out of some ancient hatred.

We never found out how Săndrel Paşcanu's funeral unfolded. And because no one ever looked for it, none of us knew anything about his grave.

The mausoleum of his two wives in the forest of Horecea fell peacefully into disrepair. When we visited it once years later we found it completely overrun by a rank growth of wild blackberries, pussy willow, and anemones. It was still bizarre, but quite romantic in its ruined state, made even more beautiful thanks to the decorative arts of a lush and rampant nature. The surrounding barbed wire had long been stolen to keep pigs penned in at some distant farmyard. Wild doves cooed in the tops of the old oaks that ringed the site. We had a picnic there and whiled away a moonlit night, telling ourselves the old stories.

16

Tanya's Generosity; Herr Adamowski Contemplates the Times

ALTHOUGH the cooling of our friendship with Herr Tarangolian meant that the prefect stopped coming to our house altogether for a long time, and after that only visited rarely, we did continue to see him whenever he called on Madame Aritonovich during the remainder of our term at the Institut d'Éducation. He hardly missed a single one of our ballet rehearsals, the success of which seemed quite important to him. He would sit in the corner like an old habitué, diagonally opposite the large mirror, observing our warm-ups *à la barre* and *au milieu* with the eyes of a connoisseur, and watching the rehearsals of specific scenes, while chatting with Madame in between. Once we happened to be nearby when the name Tildy surfaced in one of these conversations.

"Tildy sent me a letter," said the prefect. "But he isn't challenging his excessively long internment or petitioning me to use my influence to shorten it. No, he's writing on behalf of this insane locksmith, the 'poet' Piehowicz. He complains that they won't leave the poor man in peace. Apparently they're subjecting his poetic genius to a thorough grilling. That offends the major's sense of justice. He's beginning to get on my nerves, this knight of the overly upright posture. He wants to create order even in the insane asylum, after having created such a pretty mess for me here on the outside."

We were shocked. We had never heard the prefect speak in such a tone of voice. We asked Blanche if she knew anything.

After our callous reaction to the poem, Blanche had avoided speaking to us about the goings-on in the asylum. Now she showed that she had generously forgiven us.

"Unfortunately it's true," she said, worried. "They're torturing poor Piehowicz with these so-called cross-examinations, and what's more, they're keeping him away from Tildy. Because—I'm ashamed to tell you—people are so upset by the consequences of the publication of the poems that they're beginning to suspect Herr Tildy. The whole business sounds crazier than anything you'd expect to hear coming out of an insane asylum, but they think that Herr Tildy is in cahoots with Dr. Kipper and my father—and that they are secretly leaking the poems to the press or that they leaked the poems to Tildy so he could publish them as transcriptions of Piehowicz. Herr Professor Feuer calls it an example of devious Jewish scheming, and although the article doesn't say it outright, the implication is that Dr. Kipper and my father wanted to provoke a literary scandal that would damage the reputation of German literature, and enhance their own prestige among their peers. The same view is more or less openly stated by two new gentlemen who replaced two other physicians who were dismissed after Professor Feuer wrote an article denouncing the fact that five of the seven doctors at the asylum were Jewish. That created a lot of bad blood, and that's why those two were replaced, because of the pressure from the nationalists. But there's another reason for all the recent examinations, and one that runs counter to all the suspicions, voiced or otherwise. It turns out that he himself has put an end to the theory that he isn't the true author of the poems and that he just brought them from his poets' circle in the Foreign Legion—with a piece of prose that he could hardly have committed to memory back there. It's a letter that he wrote to Tildy complaining that he no longer sees him. And this letter uses such linguistic power and is such a shattering poetic allegory of pain and despair that there seems to be little choice but to once again assume that he's the author of the poems as well. If you're interested I'll bring you a copy tomorrow."

The last sentence pained us, even though we knew Blanche in no way meant to annoy us. Because the words "if you're interested," along with the simple fact that she hadn't thought it worth the trouble to inform us right away about such important events concerning Tildy, were certainly her way of getting even with us for the shameful way we accosted her with the pitifully shoddy poetic efforts of the author of "Springtime." Blanche was too outspoken for that. Rather, it was an indication of the distance that had crept, unbidden, between us ever since we had been discovered in Dr. Salzmann's class. I don't think that Blanche had consciously removed herself, though a certain tactful reserve may have played a role. But with Solly, who hardly knew the meaning of the word "tact," it was the same: ever since we were kept away from the Jewish religious instruction, an invisible wall had risen between us that would never have been there had we simply acted as declared Christians and never taken part in the course. We had contributed to the erection of this barrier ourselves, albeit unconsciously: we felt like renegades and traitors, and this secret sense of guilt affected our interactions with our friends. This had nothing to do with yielding to the attraction, or magic, if you will, of another religion—of being "partly in the clutches of Israel"—but was first and foremost a delicate matter of principle: loyalty toward our friends, a loyalty we were powerless to maintain. But in cases like that, powerlessness justifies everything but excuses nothing. Powerlessness is a condition without grace, tantamount to a state of indebtedness. Then again, it's possible that the real source of the new distance came from breaking the bond of common experience in such an essential matter as religion.

It is a tribute to Madame Aritonovich's pedagogical prowess that we were able to confide our worries to her. She responded with a coldness that we found inexplicable at the time, but whose wisdom we later learned to admire.

"Surely you don't want to find out what your friends think about you?" she said. "A question like that is a sign of cowardice. We all want to know the truth about ourselves, because every judgment we hear pronounced out loud seems more bearable than what we suspect is being kept concealed from us. And with reason. So you can safely assume the worst."

In this way we were left to our own courage to deal with the matter, which was dreadful at first but ultimately proved salutary. The fact that Madame had so unsparingly confirmed our guilt left us no way out, and we learned that when it comes to the soul there's no excuse for powerlessness.

Blanche brought us a copy of the insane locksmith's letter to Tildy, which went like this:

> ... And my pain is so great that everything good and most dear in the world can no longer heal my aching burning wounds. The sun cries, the wind is sad, the snow has turned completely blue, and the meadow is silent. The moon is deep in concern: everyone is suffering my pain. The concrete of the prison cell is cracked from my tears. The heavy iron is slowly eating through to my bones. Everything, everything feels, everything sees my suffering and my undeserved misfortune, living and dead things alike, only one human being does not. I am unhappy, indeed—the unhappiest among the unhappy.
>
> After I was imprisoned in deepest sorrow, my hound died, then right after that all my chickens, and right after that my cow. My child was born and the sun cried through his window about my undeserved misfortune, and a few days later he was sad for his father and a few days after that he left this hated world—and today he is being carried to his grave, with no father and mother, accompanied only by strangers. Because his father is being tortured and his mother has practically forgotten the entire world, including her child and his father. She lies quietly in bed, holding a candle, looking up to heaven. I have nothing more, nothing on earth.

Tanya read it and broke down in tears.

We could see how much our sister Tanya was suffering by the way she danced. Only the visitors who had no idea what was going on could come to rehearsals and say things like: "What's wrong with the girl? She always danced with such grace." "She probably has stage fright, poor girl. That will pass." "I don't think so. That's how it often is with talented children, they don't fulfill their promise." "Well, she's coming into a difficult age now."

Madame Aritonovich never wasted words on misunderstandings of that sort disguised as half-questions. She merely ignored them and smoked one cigarette after another, unmistakably nervous. During the rehearsals she had eyes only for Tanya. She evidently didn't care that our performance, too, was rather mediocre. Blanche failed entirely. The *corps de ballet* became a wooden chaos. Madame Aritonovich nodded and said: "Fine, that will do. But Tanya has to repeat it once more." We had the impression that she couldn't care less whether the performance succeeded or not, that everything was being undertaken solely for the sake of Tanya. The ballet hall, which presumably had been the main dining room of the private villa that now housed the Institut d'Éducation, became the arena for a daily struggle over Tanya's soul.

Madame Aritonovich didn't spare her in the slightest. We quit trying to understand her relentless criticism, although at first we, too, were surprised by Tanya's lack of fluidity. But as a consequence of the cruel repetitions, Tanya seemed to attain the peak of technical perfection. Her leaps and *battements* were downright acrobatic. Nevertheless, Madame Aritonovich kept interrupting: "That's an imitation of a stork," she said. "You're thinking, my child, you're thinking too much about what you've learned. Let it go. Forget everything except the music. Close your eyes and listen, listen. Nothing else."

She spun around sharply to Herr Tarangolian. "Can't you make this child's obtuse parents take her to Paris right this minute to show her some ballet? Diaghilev is there, Coco! Think what it would mean for her!"

"I'm not certain," said the prefect, "if Tanya's parents would be so delighted if she chose to devote herself completely to the ballet. It's sad, my dear Fiokla Ignatieva, but even if Diaghilev appeared in person to tell them that we have a second Pavlova, even if Pavlova herself confirmed it..."

"But that's not what I mean at all!" she interrupted him. "Don't you understand me either, Coco? I'm not trying to breed ballerinas here. Let me confess something to you: I've never really liked children. Of course I claim I do, and I persuade others as well as myself. The fact is, they torment me. I can't bear seeing their need. But what I can stomach even less is standing idly by, watching the way they're ruined while being processed into 'grown-ups.'"

"Of course," said Herr Tarangolian. "But where do you want to begin? The domestic circumstances in this case are a lot more difficult than you suspect... And don't you say yourself that children cannot and should not be spared anything?"

"My God, Coco, how thick you are today! An everlasting kindergarten is not my notion of an ideal world. Of course they should grow up. But in a different way."

"Don't you think that a good portion of the unhappiness we see here is because too much is being demanded, Fiokla Ignatieva?" asked Herr Tarangolian. "Excuse me, but surely you see the pain in her eyes each time you criticize."

"You're confusing cause and effect, my dear—just like everyone else. I can't do anything to help you, but I have to do something so *she* doesn't make the same mistake." She turned to Tanya and looked her over from head to toe. "Believe me, Coco," she said, nervously inhaling, "there is no other cure than this. I know exactly why I have my children dance. I assure you, it's not just fun and games."

"I know, my dear," said the prefect. "I truly admire you. You know that."

"I know you do. But you don't believe me. Even though we're true soul mates, you and I. You wouldn't be such a good prefect if you weren't so musically—or should I say, dancerly—inclined."

"Aha," laughed Herr Tarangolian. "You flatter me too much. My job might be better compared to belly dancing than to your harmonious choreographies."

"In any case, it's a question of hearing—of hearing that goes down to the blood and bones."

"Very beautifully put. That's what I do: I bend my bones to the harmony of my sphere."

"Now don't go senile on me, my dear Coco," Madame Aritonovich said drily. "You're getting sentimental. But I suspect you're simply being insincere—and always have been. You enjoy the tune you dance to, don't try and pretend with me!" She turned back to Tanya. "Come, Tanya, once more, all by yourself. All the others to the barre!"

The person clearly most bored by the constant repetition was Solly Brill.

"As far as I'm concerned you can take all this jumping up and down and stick it in a pipe," he said. "Anyway, I like soccer better. But this? Nothing but *shmontses*. Too much aesthetics and not enough athletics. From the pedagogical point of view, the whole thing is off target. What does it have to do with here and now? D'you hear about the game on *shabbes* afternoon? Makkabi over Jahn? Did they take a tanning or what? Seven to three—a nice embarrassment for the swastiklers. And then they wanted to get fresh on top of that. So they paid for it with a couple of teeth. Then they wanted to get at the referee. But he gave Strobel—that's the center for Jahn—such a blow it laid him out. And meanwhile the guy was one of them. Next Sunday it's Makkabi against Mircea Doboş. Well, I'm excited... And what are *we* doing?" he finished, morose. "Hopping around on our tiptoes in a hooped skirt. Am I some kind of dying swan or what? The whole thing is nothing but *shmontses*."

Then, one morning, Tanya had a breakdown. She fainted for a very brief moment, and had already come to by the time anyone could help her. She smiled, a little embarrassed and confused, but it was a smile—and we hadn't seen her smile in weeks. Then she said quietly: "It's nothing, I'm fine, I can keep dancing."

"Did you hurt yourself?" asked Madame Aritonovich. "Let me see you move your feet. Nothing hurts?"

"No," said Tanya. "Please, may I continue right now? And from the beginning, if that's all right?"

Madame Aritonovich helped her to her feet, face-to-face, and looked her in the eye. "Fine, from the beginning, then."

I've occasionally wondered whether Madame Aritonovich might have seen those first movements Tanya made by looking in the mirror, but that's impossible, because she was walking away from her, in the direction of Herr Tarangolian, who was sitting in his usual corner. In any case she had turned her back to Tanya and was heading toward the prefect with such a triumphantly relieved smile that I, a rather clumsy snowflake deployed close to that same corner, couldn't help being amazed. The prefect lifted his heavy eyes as she approached his chair, and said: "How did you do that, you sorceress?"

"It wasn't me," said Madame Aritonovich. "Could I please have a light, Coco?" I saw how her hands were shaking. She lit her cigarette with the match he offered, and only then did she turn around to look at Tanya.

"This is one of the few truly miraculous events I have witnessed in my entire long life," said the prefect. Madame Aritonovich did not respond. She was focused on Tanya's dancing.

"Ahh," said the prefect, gasping with glee. "Fiokla—such a *port des bras*! But don't pretend—that *was* you, you're the one who brought it out of her." He expressed his delight in an artificial excitement. "I admit, the child was always talented, we agreed on that from the very beginning, but this, this is brilliant. *Brava, brava!*" He applauded. "You see..." He played the awestruck admirer with such verve that he wound up being truly moved. "What balance, what elevation, what *ballon*!"

(*Ballon* refers to a special trick in dance, or better, the divinely given ability of a ballet dancer to appear to hold a position in the air, as if released from gravity. The effect is attained by the dancer's rapidity in assuming the desired position during a jump, which makes the flight seem more drawn out, relaxed, and full of élan.)

"She already had all of that," said Madame Aritonovich. "What she had lost, and has now regained, is herself."

"I admire you, Fiokla Ignatieva," said Herr Tarangolian. He kissed her hand ardently.

When the scene was over, Madame Aritonovich said: "Well done, Tanya. And the rest of you were excellent. Ice cream for everyone. Who would like to volunteer to go get it?"

We broke out in cheers. Herr Tarangolian got up, went over to Tanya, took the red carnation out of its buttonhole and presented it to her with a very seriously intended, exaggeratedly gallant bow.

"*Nu*, finally something worth hearing: ice cream for everyone," said Solly Brill. And then, to Tanya: "You could have come up a little sooner with the dance discipline and all that, you know." He sighed. "Whimsical creatures, these women, by God!"

He had planted himself in the middle of the room and watched Herr Tarangolian, who had righted himself after bowing to Tanya and was gravely prancing back to Madame. "Herr Coco, you have a button open!"

The prefect looked down at himself, dismayed and embarrassed. "No, on your left gaiter," said Solly. "Why? What did you think?"

That same afternoon Tanya was missing at home. They called for her but she didn't come. They went looking for her, increasingly agitated, but she was nowhere to be found. We were forced to ask at the neighbors, but she hadn't been seen there either. Uncle Sergei was sent into town to look for her at Madame Aritonovich's or at the institute. But she wasn't there, either. They were on the point of asking the prefect to contact the police when she came striding through the garden gate—accompanied by our father and Aunt Paulette.

Without paying any attention to our mother's worried expression, our father went straight to his room. That was the sign of a rising crisis, and everyone took pains not to say a single unnecessary word.

"Where were you?" asked our mother.

"She was with me," said Aunt Paulette, in place of Tanya. "I took her to visit some friends."

"Couldn't I have been told beforehand?"

"No," said Aunt Paulette, without any further explanation, and likewise retreated.

Tanya kept quiet about her adventure. Everything remained very secretive and enigmatic.

But a few days later, over the after-dinner coffee—to which Herr Tarangolian no longer came—Aunt Paulette asked: "Will it be possible for me to borrow one of the children this afternoon?"

"I don't know exactly what you mean?" said our mother.

"I need a chaperone. I'd like to visit some friends."

"And might we know what 'friends' you have in mind?" asked Mama.

"Herr Adamowski. Don't worry: the children's moral health will not be placed in danger."

"Wouldn't it be more appropriate if Elvira went with you?"

"I can't imagine she would much enjoy herself."

"But you think that one of the children might?"

The conversation was clearly growing sharper by the second. Only Aunt Paulette stayed charmingly casual, her head leaned lazily against the back of the chair. "One of the children can drink chocolate and browse through some of the picture magazines. But if you think Elvira would be satisfied with that..."

"I have no intention," said Aunt Elvira, poisonously.

And so I was chosen to accompany Aunt Paulette.

We passed through the Volksgarten the same way we went to school. Aunt Paulette hardly said a word to me, then stopped at a booth and bought me a bag of sticky candies, with the casual hint of contempt that was her way. But I preferred to go with her than with Aunt Elvira; she was eye-catchingly pretty with her dark-waved bobbed hair and wore her clothes with a natural elegance. She was tall and had beautiful legs, which she was already beginning to show back then—not past the knee, as later became common, but just enough to reveal the striking taper of her calves down to the ankle: when it came to fashion, Aunt Paulette was always ahead of the time, thanks to a certain intuition. Her flesh-toned silk stockings with the straight seam increased the appeal. I've always regretted that this seam, which connotes a slight disguise, has all but disappeared today. The overly thin hose-gauze looks like bare skin, causing the legs to appear naked. "Nakedness," Uncle Sergei used to say, "has no charm. It is always the covering that awakens the erotic."

Herr Adamowski lived on a side street off the Neuschulgasse, on the fourth floor of an ugly, dark apartment building. He had on a casual jacket of brown velvet with braid trim on the front. The homemade mixture of student-fraternity-jacket and Hussar uniform struck me as particularly revolting.

"Aha," he said. "A young man as an escort, a true cavalier from top to toe—noble, elegant—my congratulations!" He bowed before me, sinking down on his clubfoot, and then righting himself by exchanging his swinging leg for his stamping leg. He had bared his saw-teeth and his monocle was flashing. "Take your coat off, dearest," he said to Aunt Paulette, "and please step inside, the colloquium is all assembled."

We stepped into a kind of library that also seemed to function as his living quarters. All the tables and even some chairs were littered with piles of books, magazines and newspapers. Three men rose as we entered; a woman in a brown silk dress stayed seated and took in our greeting with a nonchalant play of worldliness. Aunt Paulette introduced me with a mocking undertone as her chaperone. Everyone laughed.

"Please, have a seat wherever you like," said Herr Adamowski, swaying from his long leg to his short one, and then straightening back up. "Of course the young gentleman will have some liqueur—a little glass of Cointreau won't harm anyone, am I right, *Herr Kavalier*? For who can reject a drop of respect!" The three men laughed loudly and tensely, all the while nodding to one another.

"Give him something to look at," said Aunt Paulette. "Then he'll sit in a corner and not bother us anymore."

"What bother, what bother!" exclaimed Herr Adamowski in feigned indignation, baring his teeth and flashing an embarrassing conspiratorial look at me through his monocle. "Who said anything about bother! We are delighted to have the young man's company. If you feel inclined to have another little glass, please, help yourself. I'll put the bottle here just in case." The three men laughed. "You have all the books you could wish for at your disposal, although I'll ask you to skip the ones on this particular shelf." The three men laughed. Herr Adamowski winked at me: "They're a little on the piquant side, *capito*? Only for collectors. But perhaps this one here: Greek vase paintings. It shows figures that are in their paradisiacal state as well, but they've been rendered harmless by their classical lines. Hellene goddesses and gods in contemporary portrait. And so on. Seek and ye shall find."

Aunt Paulette had sat down in her usual lethargic posture and said nothing in response to these fatuous remarks. One of the men lit her cigarette with exaggerated eagerness, cupping his hands around the matchbox to create a hollow for the flame, as if it there were a violent storm inside and the match were in danger of expiring at any moment. Aunt Paulette had to dip her face into this hollow: the reddish-yellow tinge of the flame spilled onto her mouth so that she seemed to be drinking fire from his hands.

Herr Adamowski sat down as well and stared at each of the guests, one by one. When no one said anything, he stated with an eager, smirking grin: "So, our gathering is complete. And how is the general health of the assembly?" The men laughed once more, this time accompanied by the woman in the brown taffeta dress.

I began leafing through a book, pretending that I was entirely absorbed in my reading. I was disappointed and alert at the same time. After everything I knew about Herr Adamowski, and the secretive circumstances surrounding both my visit and Tanya's earlier one, the last thing I expected was a group like this: boorish, gauche, and awkward despite the crude familiarity, where no one ventured to speak except the host, and everyone seemed to be waiting for some comment or observation that would relieve the tension. The three men sat there like lumps of wood: I found out that their names were Leutgeb, Fellner, and Kopetzki, but couldn't discover more about their background or occupation. The names alone sounded like a bunch of bandits. Fellner was still rather young, with a healthy, ordinary face and large hands, evidently very strong. He was the most awkward of them all; at every new outburst of nervous laughter he would squirm in his chair and look around and nod to the others, hiding his large hands between his knees, since he didn't know what else to do with them. Leutgeb was a middle-aged man, thickset, with a small mouth that displayed a hint of malice. Kopetzki seemed to suffer from a lung disease: he never stopped quietly coughing, though at the same time he smoked a pipe that gave off thick clouds of smoke. He had a finely shaped head, narrow and pale, with a dark Polish mustache. The woman in the brown taffeta answered to the name Theophila—evidently a nickname; her dress looked worn and its rhinestone embroidery gave a shabby appearance. On the rare occasions when anyone but Herr Adamowski said anything, they addressed their host as "Adam" or else by the less-than-elegant diminutive: "Adamchik."

I have to confess that it was my Aunt Paulette who gave this group a peculiarly macabre note. Her presence was like a last spot of paint, a bit of contrasting color that paradoxically fit the whole picture and made the group seem a little eerie, or even dangerous, like a secret alliance, a conspiracy sworn to fulfill some covert mission. In later years I would encounter in spiritualist circles a similarly tense atmosphere charged with a furtive intimacy, together with the same vapid cheerfulness and habitual shallowness in the conversational tone of the séance leader before launching into the parts of the program that were meant to be creepy.

"You laugh, Ladies and Gentlemen," said Herr Adamowski in his harsh-sounding German. "But these days one cannot be serious enough in inquiring after the health of every worthy gathering. You see, Gentlemen and Ladies, you are caught up in the course of the times, without realizing that this is more than just your personal progression—please consider the implications! All jests aside—the difference is a crucial one. For me the difference is quite clear, as a journalist with his finger constantly on the pulse of the times, I live with it every day, I experience this same discrepancy in all its tragic consequences, not only the direct effects that have already resulted, but ones yet to be seen, ones to be feared. It makes a tremendous difference if one chooses to view the times abandoning all claim to exclusive possession, in other words no longer as a phenomenon of personal episodes alone, but of collective experience. As a journalist I have a professional obligation to provide an accounting of the quality of the times, both for myself and for others. While doing this I have to bear two things in mind: first, that the quality of the times is shaped and molded by the sum of its details, a sum of purely personal experiences, which taken alone would be completely insignificant, and would lead to nothing but misleading exceptions divorced from the spirit of the times, but which in the aggregate, as I have said, help determine the general character of the epoch. And, second, that this specific general character in return has an effect on each individual fate, no matter how isolated, and shapes how each person passes their time, no matter how remote the activity. That, Ladies and Gentlemen, is perhaps the most interesting interplay in all of nature, the one that leads us closest to metaphysics, and one that demonstrates the difficulty of the journalistic métier... Yes, you laugh, but please bear in mind what our thankless task consists in. The journalist, Ladies and Gentlemen, does not have as congenial a profession as people are wont to think." The group laughed out loud. "He must, as my esteemed friend Professor Feuer would put it, act like the squirrel carrying discord up and down Yggdrasil, between the eagle in the canopy and the dragon in the roots. He must roust the privately minded man from living solely for himself, by ceaselessly calling his attention to outside his personal sphere—events that don't concern him at all, that don't apply to him in the least, as he sees it, but which in reality are of his utmost personal concern, whether it's a murder in the house next door or a change of regimes in Portugal, for instance, or an earthquake in Kamchatka. On the other hand, our conscience dictates that we journalists hold up this model of the private man to the so-called general public as an ideal form of being." They laughed. "Yes, my friends, that's the way it is. Who among us would deny the singular truth of the saying *beatus ille homo qui sedet in suo domo*, and who does not yearn for this very same thing from the bottom of his heart? Nietzsche was proud of not owning a house, but you ought to read sometime what he said about Epicurus..."

The room groaned with laughter. The woman known as Theophila said: "That was fabulous, Adamchik, truly fabulous. Where does he come up with all of that?"

"The happy isolation of the man," Herr Adamowski went on, after granting just enough time for the applause to play out, "*que sedet post fornacem et habet bonam pacem*—you laugh, my esteemed friends, but deep down you also feel envy for such a person. You would not be able to resist his powers of persuasion, as I myself experienced in a recent visit to Fräulein Paulette and the parents of the young man there in the corner who is reading so nicely and at the same time listening so intently..."

I now had to acknowledge that the laughter was meant for me and acted as if I was so deeply engrossed in my reading as to give the lie to Herr Adamowski's comment. At the same time I was ashamed of being afraid to openly admit that I had been listening in on the conversation—after all, no one could have held it against me. But we often lose our nerve in milieux that we disdain, and when that happens we easily lose our candor as well—otherwise the most reliable of our virtues. However, the embarrassing situation I found myself in did lead me to understand what Herr Adamowski said a little later about the "chemical" makeup of human relationships. Meanwhile he went on:

"The person, Ladies and Gentlemen, who *cultivates his garden*, has a certain unimpeachability, and indeed, I would feel as though I were ignoring my calling if I missed an opportunity to uphold this as an ideal worthy of the highest striving, to lay it as a charge on the general public—in all earnestness! And herein lies another contradiction: on the one hand, the genuine regret that such happy, modest people are harder and harder to find, and a certain indignation that such a lifestyle still exists—an almost criminal removal from the world, a selfish consumption of time that is actually antisocial, just like someone secretly nibbling from the common larder. I only mention it as one example among many..."

"Fabulous," said Theophila. "Truly, truly fabulous, Adamchik!"

"You will see, Ladies and Gentlemen," said Herr Adamowski, baring his saw-teeth, "that people show so little understanding for the difficulties of our profession, for the true dilemma that lies at its core, that they begin to mistrust it." Laughter echoed along the bookcases. "It is so grossly underappreciated that people are inclined to link our efforts to this cause or that—because they fail to understand that journalism is a cause in and of itself. And yet people will dismiss even its most serious attempts to convince the public exactly how great its own misfortune truly is." Laughter. "I see a time approaching when people will no longer speak of the *terribles simplificateurs*, but of the *terribles complicateurs*..."

"Magnificent," said Theophila, thoroughly exhausted. She nodded to Fellner, who wriggled uncomfortably on his armchair as he relayed the nodding and sighing on to Leutgeb and Kopetzki. "Simply fabulous."

"You see, Ladies and Gentlemen," said Herr Adamowski, "people reproach us for the fact that what we produce—i.e., the newspapers—is so open to dispute. Of course this criticism comes in various degrees, but that is the general accusation. I'm not talking about the loss that occurs between an idea and its execution, between the vision, so to speak, and the hand that gives it form—everyone knows that the best things are always lost in this process. I mean the fundamental misconception that someone who undertakes to put out a newspaper would ever be able to create anything but a newspaper..."

Fellner slapped his thigh and immediately hid his hands again, aware of his faux pas. Leutgeb grumbled, and Kopetzki coughed on his pipe smoke when he started to laugh. "This ought to be written down word for word," said Theophila, suddenly very serious.

I was watching Aunt Paulette. She was sitting opposite Herr Adamowski, between Fellner and Kopetzki, evidently unmoved. She did not take part in the bursts of applause that were elicited by every other word and came cascading down like loose scree sliding down a mountain. I could tell that she felt the same inner aversion for the surroundings as I did—that she, too, could not abide the peculiar atmosphere, the combination of slovenly comfort, unabashed abandon, and an extreme but nonetheless futile attentiveness. It was as if Herr Adamowski's gait were a feature of his words, in the stamping rhythm that resounded in all those present in the room: rearing up and straining excessively on the upswing, and then collapsing onto itself, as the ambitious stamping leg fell onto the careless swinging leg. We could even smell his sweat, for there was nothing comic to his remarks, which were clearly meant to be taken very seriously. The whole performance was like a feat of strength when the athlete is clearly straining and seeks to escape into the grotesque by clownishly exaggerating his own grimace. Herr Adamowski's own contortions, under a burden that made his forehead bead over with sweat, were repulsive. Today it seems to me that I must have compared his pitiful efforts with Herr Tarangolian's expertise, the juggler-like ease and fluidity with which the prefect mastered the most tangled trains of thought, evincing far more wit than Herr Adamowski was ever able to wrestle out of the angel of *esprit*. I'm not saying that I realized then that the Latin's intellectuality could best be described with the French word *lucidité*, for which there is no German equivalent, but certainly it was that moment that led to my ultimate understanding that the secret to such clarity of intellect lies in the power of discernment, the ability to differentiate the truly simple from the truly complicated—in other words a sense of tact that accords each person his own room to move.

I found Herr Adamowski's guests even more disagreeable than I did the host himself. They were delighted with his faux clown act, wallowed in his sweat, so to speak. The graceless laughter of the men, and Theophila's idiotic, vacuous enthusiasm were better suited to a fairgrounds sideshow than a kaffeeklatsch. In a word: I was in bad company, and, as usual, profited greatly from the experience.

For my own insights were immediately deepened and strengthened as he went on riding his hobbyhorse.

"Yes, Ladies and Gentlemen," he said, and I suddenly realized that his relentless holding forth was meant as a provocation for Aunt Paulette. "Yes, Ladies and Gentlemen, you don't realize how much of being a journalist is really about innate aptitude. Take, for example, our young colleague from the other school, so to speak: Herr Alexianu of the *Vocea*. This youthful firebrand has literally been dubbed a knight of the press, and by someone to whom we also have a certain connection ..." Laughter. "The slap that Herr A. received from this person—there's no need to mention any names—was an act of initiation, a rite of admission, so to speak. The vague inclinations that had merely seethed beneath the surface of this young man suddenly took shape after this painful introduction to manhood. As I say: we are not molded by ourselves alone, by the inner core of our being, but from the outside as well—for example, by the general quality of the times, isn't that right? The true man is revealed to himself and all others first by his enemies. Only when his hatred has a tangible goal does he come into his own, does he find himself. In this connection it is interesting to think of the theory postulated by the well-known Herr Năstase—I will spare a commentary." Laughter. "According to him there is among men a very definite, let us say, measuring stick, for ranking individual prestige. And widespread feelings of insecurity come from the fact that this—again, let us call it a measuring stick—is seen in its proper proportion where it pertains to others, but in our own case is almost always viewed from above, and so appears foreshortened. Only the condition of exaltation reverses this image, because the elevation to a horizontal plane brings one's own expanded capacity to view, while the optical illusion ceases to play tricks with regard to the other when the focus is on the other. But precisely in this state one should not underestimate the other..." Groaning laughter. "I don't wish to make this mistake. As a journalist I am duty-bound to be objective..." Enormous merriment. "Therefore I am full of admiration for the upright hatred exhibited by Herr A.... All joking aside, Ladies and Gentlemen, we cannot pay enough attention to our young colleague's journalistic success. His holy excitement has made him the guardian spirit of the entire press. His paper, the *Vocea*, which had the keen sense to hire him, is not the only one that has experienced an unprecedented upswing. I'm sure you know how much our own circulation has risen thanks to him, ever since my friend Feuer's response rekindled the general interest in reading newspapers..." Merriment. "Recently this stimulating effect has spread elsewhere as well. The newspaper of the Ukrainian minority, *Narodny Dym*, which you see lying here, has published an incisive piece examining the general legal state of minorities in light of the purge-concept propounded by Herr Ali—exactly what people want to read, my friends, a true example of the press as mouthpiece for the public..." Laughter. "Other ethnic groups won't be far behind, either. So you can see that the spirit that has filled our young genius is one of general enlivenment. And so please bear in mind that being a journalist entails a lot more than curiosity for events, joy in expressing yourself, and a certain talent for writing. You have to be animated by a specific will to assert yourself, rather like a washerwoman using indelible ink to number items of especially fine and beautiful clothing—all to make sure they are returned to the rightful owner..."

"Wonderful, Adamchik," groaned Theophila, "truly wonderful. Where does he come up with all of this?"

"And to think that this act of will can be conjured by a slap on the face!" Herr Adamowski continued, teeth bared and monocle flashing. "Yes, my dear friends, once we realize that true human relations occur as chemical reactions, outside all logic and even morality, then we land smack in the middle of alchemy. What spirit guided the hand that with one stroke made a hitherto chaste youth into a man, a human being full of the desire and distress of his hatred—with no apparent cause, mind you—it's impossible to have any delusion in the matter, this is not about motives, but a metaphysical rite of initiation, the meaning of which we are able to discern with increasing clarity as it plays out. I tell you, we live in a magical hour, and so it is our human duty to ask, and with the greatest concern: How is the general health of the assembly?"

"Fabulous, Adamchik," said Theophila. "Ready for print. Amazingly clever. You're outdoing yourself lately."

Disgust filled me with a restless despair. I was now looking openly at Aunt Paulette, no longer pretending that I was reading my book, and I knew at once that she was lost. I understood that what drew her here was a similar despair, although hers was far deeper and more relentless. Her self-contempt formed a bond of kinship with these people. The terrible act of exposure contained in Herr Adamowski's words must have transformed this contempt into lust. I recalled one of Herr Tarangolian's lines: "*Because if you live in a world so full of disdain and contempt, armed with nothing but your own scorned existence* . . ." and a terrible pronouncement of the smirking Kunzelmann: "*Humor is when people laugh in spite of everything* . . ."

At that moment the doorbell rang, and Herr Adamowski got up, saying, "Aha, she decided to come after all . . ." and rocked out of the room to open the door for a new guest.

It was Tamara Tildy.

She entered with a shy, apologetic smile, nodded to all present, and said, when I was introduced to her, "How is your sister?" She smiled as she explained: "I once wanted to give his little sister my necklace. If I had only done so—but I had mislaid it somewhere, back then. Now I no longer have it."

Fellner squirmed in his seat, and Kopetzki choked again and coughed prolifically. Aunt Paulette didn't move, and Theophila in the taffeta dress was also frozen in a mix of hostile defensiveness and gruesome curiosity that was evident in her hard eyes.

Tamara Tildy sat down in a chair that Herr Adamowski had wedged into the circle after freeing it from a load of magazines. Fellner came to his aid, brushing off the dust that had collected there with his handkerchief.

Madame Tildy smiled with strained grace, a little painfully, to each guest, one by one, and as she did so her head rocked slowly and slackly to the side, as if she had just woken up from a deep slumber full of happy dreams—a recuperative sleep following a long, strength-sapping illness. She was dressed in the trappings of a bygone elegance, faded and exceptionally feminine, with an abundance of silk scarves as delicate as veils, now frayed and torn. Her silver brocade jacket was now tarnished to a shade of black that hardly matched the hour, much less her delicate woolen dress, which was light-colored and summery. She was carrying a gold mesh purse, clutching it somewhat frantically, as if she were afraid someone might take it from her; its long chain was forever getting caught in the fringes, corners, folds, and bulges of her overburdened attire.

"It's nice that you could make it after all, my dear," said Herr Adamowski, staggering around to set a glass of liqueur in front of her. No one seemed astounded at the embarrassing way he addressed her.

"Yes, my friend, I have come to you," said Madame Tildy gently. "You know that. I always come to you, day after day..." Below her sharp hooked nose, her doll-like mouth expressed a tender irony.

"Here, I have a present for you," said Herr Adamowski, placing a delicate, high-stemmed glass of rare shape on the table in front of her.

"A Murano glass," said Tamara Tildy in a cheery voice that was agonizingly distant. "From Venice... I'll put it in my room, in the middle of the floor. It will be very beautiful there, all alone in its beauty."

She stared at it for a while, and no one said a word.

"It will be very beautiful there," she repeated. "All alone..." She reached for it and squeezed it to splinters in her hand.

"Oh, I've cut myself," she said, and looked at her hand, which was dripping blood.

"I'll bandage your hand," said Herr Adamowski. He tottered to a chest covered with magazines, and fished a little bottle of tincture of iodine and some bandages out of a drawer. The general silence was so horrible it hurt. It made me hate everyone in the room, including Aunt Paulette.

"This will burn a little," said Herr Adamowski, as he first blotted the blood with some cotton wool and then pressed another piece that had been dipped in the iodine against her fingers. He exuded a fatherly, if also awkwardly transparent, authority.

Once he had cleared the shards of glass off the table, she said: "You can do magic. Why don't you make it whole again?"

"I'm not allowed to perform magic in the presence of Fräulein Paulette," he said, with a toothy smile that was meant to be charming.

"But if I want you to..." said Tamara Tildy, looking at my aunt. Aunt Paulette met her stare with a similar coolness and indolent calm.

"Yes, yes, I know..." said Madame Tildy, lost. She got up. "I'll be going again."

"But why? You just got here," said Herr Adamowski.

"I have something to do. Something important. Something very important." She seemed very anxious. "I had forgotten about it when I came. I have to... My dress is full of blood. I have to change." She left the room without saying goodbye. Herr Adamowski followed her out. We heard him stamping as he walked her to the door.

"Well, *Herr Kavalier*, how about another little glass of Cointreau?" he asked me when he came back, and brought me the glass that Madame Tildy had left untouched. "Not a drop of this noble drink should go wasted."

The three men, who had been sitting there, dumb as blocks, laughed once again. Herr Adamowski returned to his seat and launched into a long anecdote of excruciating wit that began with the words: "By the way, do you know the story of the two Russians who go to their priest..." Like all bad mimics he grossly exaggerated the Russian accent, going from the highest head note to the deepest bass, and back up to a high-pitched squeal, going so far as to say "saltpyotr" for "saltpeter"—which elicited a new burst of applause. I was relieved when Aunt Paulette was finally ready to go.

We spoke even less to each other on the way home than we had on the way to Herr Adamowski's. We were just crossing the street between the officers' casino and the entrance to the Volksgarten when a caravan of vehicles drove up that we had to let pass. There were several families of Galician Jews, who were coming to town in small horse-drawn carts piled with their meager possessions. Their melancholy dark eyes looked on us as strangers.

At home, my mother said: "My heavens, the boy is completely pale. Aren't you feeling well?"

I said I was fine, although I really felt awful. Tanya steered clear of me and avoided being alone with me for the next several days.

As a result it wasn't until much later that I learned about Tanya's own visit to Herr Adamowski's:

During the night, she hadn't been able to sleep. She was so restless and upset about her clumsy dancing that she was crying. Finally she got up to go to Mama. As she passed Aunt Paulette's room she heard our father's voice, very worked-up: "If you go to his place one more time there's going to be hell to pay. Believe me, I'm not joking. This time I'm serious."

Tanya had fled back to our children's room. In keeping with her romantic nature she began to hatch a plan for getting back at Aunt Paulette for hitting her—the revenge of the proud: magnanimity.

She was so animated that the next morning she seemed to "melt" into the ballet music. She never realized how beautifully she danced that day. But from then on she danced with the same dedication, until the dancing came to a sudden end.

That afternoon she had lurked about, hoping that Aunt Paulette would go to Herr Adamowski despite all threats—Tanya had no doubt as to whom she wasn't supposed to visit again. And Aunt Paulette did go.

Tanya kept an eye on our father. When he left the house a little later, she went to warn Aunt Paulette. She had planned everything carefully, going so far as to find out where Adamowski lived. She had taken money out of her savings box to pay for a cab—much too little, as she later told me, it would have never been enough. But she couldn't find one. So she ran, very afraid lest our father should get there first. By the time she reached Herr Adamowski's she had half fainted. God knows in what situation she expected to find Aunt Paulette there. In any case, not in the company of Messrs. Fellner, Leutgeb, and Kopetzki, and Theophila in the brown taffeta dress. Utterly taken aback, they let her in; naturally she didn't explain why she had come. It wasn't until the general astonished merriment had subsided that she was able to tell Aunt Paulette in a few awkward sentences what had driven her there. Aunt Paulette stared at her a while with cold attention, then tilted her head back and laughed out loud.

Nevertheless, she was considerate enough not to tell the others what she found so funny. Tanya was deposited in a corner with some books and a glass of Cointreau, just as I would be later on, until Aunt Paulette decided to leave.

They met our father on the corner of the street, where he was standing and waiting. He was very dismayed to see Tanya together with Aunt Paulette. But he said nothing about it. Aunt Paulette shot him a mocking glance and said, casually, "I took Tanya along to visit my friends. She was an excellent guard of honor."

They went back without a word, along the way that Tanya had run in great fear, alone for the first time in her life. Later she told me that she had felt a deep sympathy for our father, a practically excruciating love, almost more than she had ever felt before.

She also knew then that Aunt Paulette was his lover. I wasn't to find out until later. And then I would also learn the bitter truth that for all those years we had been living off of her inheritance: hers was the only one, of all our mother's sisters', that had remained intact.

Tanya later smiled at her childish adventure, which had had none of the expected drama. But she was never able to recall running to Herr Adamowski's apartment with complete calm. She told me that the worst thing was how artificial her emotions had seemed to her—because all her fears were riddled with doubt. She didn't know for sure if our father's threat had really been meant in earnest, if Aunt Paulette even needed to be warned—she even doubted the reality of her immediate fear that she would be missed at home; or that they'd look for her and find her before she made it to Herr Adamowski's; or that the policeman who saw her running might mistake her for a thief and chase her. Until then she had strolled through life smiling, as if through a garden, and it wasn't the discovery that the garden also contained terrors that erased the smile from her face—every terror had only made it seem more wondrous—but rather the discovery that the colors of all its flowers, from the tender, gently gleaming ones to the ones that glowed with dark mystery or the terribly garish ones, seemed to have acquired a false sheen, and all because of some mysterious fault of her own. It was the same thing, she said, when she saw that the roses surrounding the Madonna in the Herz-Jesu Church were made of dusty, faded crepe paper: then, too, she had cried, because she knew that she was only acting her passion, and that in reality she had lost her faith long before. In Herr Tarangolian's words, her existence had become *literary*.

The only thing that had remained real was her deep, sympathetic love for our father on the way back. The two of them had to wait for one of the caravans of wandering Jews to pass, just like the one Aunt Paulette and I would meet a few days later. And they, too, felt oppressed by the stares of unfamiliar eyes. Tanya noticed that our father avoided meeting their eyes, and that his doing so made him angry and irritated. She realized that he was avoiding contact because he didn't want to give up an animosity of his own making. And in this way she recognized how people create enemies out of their own despair: our father's pride was clinging to what he could despise so that he would not despise himself, and his anger was setting the stage for his hate, and insuring that these people were worthy of his detestation.

Tanya had taken our father's hand and held it tight until they were at home, "bleeding in contempt for my own generosity" she said.

17
Many Eyes: A Sports Fest in Czernopol

LONG AFTER we had left Czernopol, whenever we thought about the Jews in those surroundings, what always came to mind, from all the myriad faces and figures, was the otherness of that gaze. The Jews were *many eyes.* We told ourselves that for them we were probably also *many eyes.* Because nothing gives a more painful demonstration of how far apart we humans truly are than eyes peering out at us from the mask of a different race.

Their gaze hits us like that of a prisoner looking through the bars of his cell. We consider ourselves free, and view others as free as long as we *can see through their faces,* because they have been shaped in the same way that our face, which we cannot see, has been shaped. But where a different world has left its imprint to obstruct our vision, we recognize just how much we are trapped behind our own masks.

In fact, we never truly love the other, but merely the different world he represents.

Back then I loved in the way all children love: greatly and with passion, and in no way childishly but with all the desires and hopes, all the disappointments and pains, and all the tensions of Eros, though still removed from any sexuality. But the ardor of desire never treats physical proximity as anything but an allegory, and can neither be stilled by an embrace nor by a kiss, although it plunges into such contact like a thirsty man cooling not only his lips but also his eyes, forehead, cheeks, hands, and heartbeats in the reflection of a fountain. Our appetites expire. But those who maintain an inner need for tenderness past childhood will end up among that select unhappy group of those who will always and forever love.

Like all children and tender lovers, I also loved not just one, but many at once. I loved Tamara Tildy on account of her excruciating inner turmoil and the feminine tawdriness of her lost and faded elegance, and I loved Frau Lyubanarov because of her honey-colored eyes and the glory of her naked shoulders, because of her ample breasts bobbing in the near-transparent embroidered peasant blouses that she favored, and on account of her smile so full of shameless enticement, sweet and beguiling like the sound of a flute. I loved Aunt Paulette for her dark, lazy brittleness, the strong eroticism of her large girl's body and the cold mockery in her eyes. From time to time I also loved—though guiltily and secretly distraught over it—the seedy charm that emanated from Fräulein Iliuț's misshapen body, her clear scent of womanhood, and also her beautiful eyes. And I loved Blanche.

I dreamed about them all, held each of them in my arms, let them engage me in the ever-alluring game of being ignored and then noticed, overwhelmed by their sudden acknowledgment, after which *they would give themselves to me.* This didn't take on any concrete sensual image in my mind; what I experienced was the foretaste of a certain bliss, of unity not only with the beloved person but with the universe, a rising and setting, a kind of sensual death, which scared me and immediately made me wish that my beloveds would marry me and live with me a long long time.

Not that I was unaware of how absurd and embarrassingly comic the idea was that Frau Lyubanarov or Aunt Paulette might love the boy I was in any other way than one loves a child. But as the actors of our waking dreams, we are both their most extreme abstraction and their most distilled essence: we are *I* to the very core, ageless and sexless as the angels, but for the innate wisdom and stupidity of our sex. Never is our self-awareness more pure than in these images that our fantasy fashions from our desire, and at no time is our knowledge of ourselves more clear. Because in the staking and claiming of the world that is our childhood, everything remains image and parable. Including the plunging together of lovers, which produces nothing more than itself—the image of love.

When I thought about Tamara Tildy, this image of love was full of enigmas, of unrest and torments, but it was also ready for a redemption that superseded all reality—a combination of deep bewilderment and Easter-like promise. If I thought of Frau Lyubanarov, it was of a pagan sweetness, of the spirit of the flesh smelted into the scent of honey and the crimson haze of sensuality: my breath basked in the grassy acerbity of her hair, my arms and hands surrendered to the deliciousness of smooth skin pulsating with sunlight. When I embraced Aunt Paulette, it was with a fighting, destructive passion, an angry ardor that opened wounds until our foreheads leaned together out of exhaustion; sometimes I dreamt of both of us dying, of an acknowledgment that came too late, as we expired. When I dreamed of Blanche, however, I was torn by the ache of eternally unresolved difference, the need of two great solitudes meeting only in the gaze of a single yearning. She was the most painful and the most beautiful, the most knowing of all my loves.

I can picture her face, in which only a few, barely discernible differences of proportion, of expression, of lines, caught my eye, kept me from seeing through her mask. It was without a single disharmony, unlike, say, in Tamara Tildy's face, whose hooked nose shot out of the doll-like oval as if of its own accord, razor sharp. And still there was an awe-inspiring otherness in the relation of her broad and not very high forehead to her narrow cheeks, of her fine, long nose to her large, overripe, and expressive mouth, in the beautiful almond cut of her eyes and the alarmingly rich framework of her firm black and very curly hair—an otherness that she seemed to recognize in herself and which evidently caused her sorrow, and threw me back into my own otherness causing me a similar sorrow.

Even in my dreams I never dared touch her. If my mouth moved close to hers to kiss her, her countenance would dissipate like breath on a mirror. I was only able to imagine her from a distance, and always alone: I pictured her in the flowery meadows of a gentle landscape—a German landscape, the East being too garish for her tender magic.

She was not of the willowy slenderness that you see alongside an oasis, a gracefully angled arm propping a tall jar. I know nothing about her body; today I can't picture how she moved and probably could not do so back then: she would sit or stand in a German world of gentle hills, flowery village greens, distant spired cities, in pale shades like one of Dürer's early silverpoints—lonely, sad, but accoutred with the quiet and delightful certainty of our love.

For I took care not to conjure the pain of the enormous otherness; I removed it from me, so as not to fall into the abyss of the much larger distance that already lay between us. Not the distance imposed on us by race—that, too, was only a metaphor—but the one that is revealed by love.

We suffered because of how badly she danced. This great-granddaughter of Judith and granddaughter of Salome was incapable of moving in rhythm to the music she so adored. She was too much like a jar herself to carry in her blood the ancient wisdom of the swaying gait under the elongated burden of bulbous jars and the beautiful flow of arms to prop them. Nor did her skin display that saturated ochre sheen that seemed to reflect the terra-cotta vessels she carried on the head. Her skin was opaline, almost transparent, like the fragile sides of delicate Chinese porcelain, sprinkled here and there with a tender hint of sepia—at the bridge of her nose and on her shoulders and upper arms, pale like the tint of an eggshell. Although her lids were a bit on the thick side, they released a bluish shimmer whenever she lowered them; the wreath of her lashes cast a pale shadow on the matte, freckled skin of her gently vaulted cheeks. And another, darker shadow, precursor to a delicate down, could be seen around the corners of her large, knowing mouth. All of that was very exposed and at the same time very static. She was filled with something that weighed her down and threatened to explode at any moment. She couldn't dance because she didn't take herself lightly. We had read that angels could fly *because they take themselves lightly.*

Of course not too much was being asked of her as Clara in the snowflake scene from *Nutcracker.* As well as she could, Madame Aritonovich confined her part to a few decorative poses. We rehearsed one last time with the full orchestra and in costume. The performance was to take place in the hall of the institute. The orchestra was seated in the gallery. The spectators were seated on both sides of the hall, next to our classrooms. Madame proved a very ingenious director—she thought of everything. There was a cold buffet and punch for the grown-ups, ice cream and sweets for the children. The last week of preparations was enchanted. Dr. Salzmann, who was surprisingly strong, performed miracles transporting furniture. Even Fräulein Zehrer lent a hand; she also contributed greatly by monitoring the precision of the *corps de ballet.* We feverishly awaited the Sunday evening when the performance was to take place.

The final game of the league championship, between Mircea Doboş and Makkabi, was being held that same afternoon. Even among the residents of our rather remote villa district, the tension over the outcome was palpable. Colonel Turturiuk, the honorary president of Mircea Doboş, was picked up by a delegation from the club and an escort from the national student fraternity Junimea, traveling in a long column of coaches. By noon Frau Lyubanarov was standing at the gate, waving and greeting acquaintances. Even Herr Kunzelmann, who came rattling up on the *taradaika* pulled by his Kobiela to deliver fruit from his garden, was on the way to the playing field. He was wearing a dark Sunday coat and a gray felt hat with a black band, but hadn't been able to part with his riding pants and leather gaiters. Whip in hand, he explained to us why he had to be there "without fail": Makkabi had beaten Jahn a few weeks earlier because the referee "hadn't been as objective as he should have been" and now he had a craving "to be a witness to the revenge" that at least Mircea Doboş was going to have on the Jews, because this time it simply wasn't possible that the referee would side with Makkabi. Raising his finger, Herr Kunzelmann also quoted the warning of his great wise man Wilhelm Busch:

If someone climbs with difficulty
So high up into a tree,

And thinks that he might just be a bird:
He is absurd.

—and left us with the task of reproducing the smooth original from the embarrassingly ruined rhythm.

Just before four o'clock, Fräulein Riffke Brill showed up on our street, in a coach festooned with blue-and-white banners and the Star of David, together with her fiancé, young Seligmann, to pick up the young ladies of the Grünspan family, who lived not far from us. Bubi Brill was unfortunately still in custody, and the president of the Lawn Tennis Club, Baronet von Merores, remained true to his racket sport.

But Ephraim Perko had loaded a fiacre with half a dozen exquisitely beautiful, long-legged blondes, and was lounging in the cushioned carriage, beaming, his arms wrapped around their blossoming voluptuousness, his short legs crossed and resting on the jump seat, his jacket open and his homburg tilting back onto his neck.

A little later we heard the first roars of the crowd greeting the players as they ran onto the field; the din came bursting over the canopies of the trees in the Volksgarten like a dark cloud of passion.

Despite their animosity toward Madame Aritonovich's Institut d'Éducation, our mother and even Aunt Elvira had agreed to watch the ballet, for our sake. The performance was to begin at seven o'clock, but Madame had told us to be in the institute no later than five, to give us enough time to put on costumes and makeup. Uncle Sergei had promised to come later, and to persuade Aunt Paulette to join him. Our father had left town to go hunting with Uncle Hubert.

We loaded the costumes into the carriage and set off. In the main boulevard of the Volksgarten, which was open to traffic, we ran into various packs of people on foot—mostly adolescents. They whistled as shrilly as they could to spook the carriage horses. One voice outshouted the others: "Yossel, what's the score!" "Four to three for us!" was the answer. "Fight's broken out. Better not waste any time getting there."

The noise from the playing field had become constant, tumultuous, disquieting. Outside the officers' casino a platoon of gendarmes was being sworn in. A man with a badly bleeding head passed by, kicking and screaming and struggling against the two companions who were escorting him. Someone called out: "I can't believe that the gentlemen in the casino won't let a person use their phone even in a case like this. I'm going to report this. A scandal, that's what it is!"

We turned off the main street and stopped in front of the Institute. Solly Brill pounced on us, very excited: "Haveyouheardanything? Anynews? What's the score at halftime? A stroke you can get from all this worrying, on account of this stupid ballet! Mama brought me here but she left right away to tell Riffke to stay away from all the passions running high and such what a *nebekh*—what's it going to hurt her if Jacky Seligmann gets a bump on the nose. Oy, am I sad that Bubi's in jail! He'd have a good chance of losing his spleen—they'd sooner slap him as look at him. I can't tell you how worried I am, really."

Aunt Elvira remarked pointedly to Madame Aritonovich: "This young man seems to regret missing the opportunity to see his family killed."

"Not exactly," replied Madame. "He's merely behaving like the farmer who prays for a few drops of rain to fall on his field when he sees it's pouring at the neighbors'."

"Very well put, since we come from the country," said Aunt Elvira, with an alkaline smile.

"Really!" said Madame Aritonovich. "I know some very charming people from the country."

Our mother looked at Dr. Salzmann. Madame Aritonovich introduced him. Mama spoke a few half-friendly words about how she hoped our inadvertent participation in his course had not wounded the sensitivities of any of the other pupils' parents.

"Absolutely not, *gnädige Frau*. Jewish parvenus are usually quite tolerant."

"Well, that's reassuring," said our mother, nodding to Dr. Salzmann.

"Not for me," he replied, ignoring her gesture of parting. "Among the better-off members of the Mosaic faith, at most sixty percent still believe in a personal god—the remaining forty percent do not. The truth lies somewhere in the middle, as usual. Those of us with convictions would prefer to see a better proportion."

He reached below his mighty stomach into his waistband pocket, pulled out his thick watch, glanced at the face, wound it, held it to his ear, knocked it against the back edge of an armchair, and listened once again. His jocund, awe-inspiring face was redder than usual, and his thick mustache bristled warlike over his scarlet lips.

We were shooed into the bedroom that had been designated as our dressing room. A few latecomers arrived and reported that the soccer match had been broken off because a tumult had erupted just as the second half was beginning—at which point the game was tied four to four. The fighting was still going on and had spread into the city. Reinforced squads of police and gendarmes were trying to restore the peace.

They started getting us into costume and applying makeup. The theater barber and his assistant applied scented creams to our foreheads and cheeks, dusted us with powder that tickled our noses, and under the careful supervision of Madame Aritonovich, shaped Tanya's and Blanche's eyebrows into the wingtips of demonic butterflies. We were enjoying ourselves immensely, and performing every conceivable nonsense. In fact, Solly had to be reined in; he had fashioned a ball out of a bundle of stockings in order to show how Moishe Eisenstein, the center-forward for Makkabi, dribbled.

Meanwhile, more disquieting news continued to filter in about what was going on in the streets. Evidently the police, heavily reinforced by the gendarmerie, had managed to restore order outside the playing field. However, it was time for the daily promenade, which usually filled Iancu Topor Avenue—and, at least on Sundays, the paths in the Volksgarten as well—with alarming masses of people. But today it was positively frightening to find out how many inhabitants Czernopol really possessed—and what kind of people they were. Apparently the entire rabble from the outlying districts had formed a mob. The *matchyorniks* from around the train station, accompanied by hordes of streetwalkers, the *burlaks* from the settlements around Kalitschankabach, the *huligans* from Klokuczka, and whatever the other particular groups might be called, roamed across the avenue so that even the spacious Volksgarten was practically overflowing. Even the fashionable *patchkas* of young flaneurs had armed themselves with sticks; individual groups of Junimea had taken important strategic positions at specific corners and intersections; the ethnic German fraternity Germania—wearing the colors of their club, with ribbons and caps and provocative glances—approached anyone coming their way, and the Jahn Athletic Club was in the beer cellar of the Deutsches Haus, ready to spring to action as a man to the cry "*Brothers, come out!*" And finally it was impossible to overlook the throngs of young Jews—including some who were practically children—who were streaming in from all sides. The police had been ordered to disperse groups of more than three people, and performed this task—at least the older watchmen among them who recalled their "German" from the Austrian days—by saying the words: "Either go where it is you're going or stay where it is you're staying but don't be making any *kupkis*!" which, in their mix of Polish, German, and Ukrainian, meant, quite simply, "Either move on or stay where you are, but do not defecate."

Mama Brill hadn't returned to the institute. "What do I care if she runs after Riffke," said Solly. "What I want most of all is to be out on the street myself—but no, it's a snowflake I have to be playing, the one time something fun is going on outside."

We asked Blanche about her mother. "I don't have a mother anymore," she said. "You couldn't have known. She died two years ago."

"And your father? Is he here?"

"No, he wanted to come, but he was called to the asylum. I'm all by myself."

We began to grow apprehensive. Report after unsettling report alarmed us to the point where we lost our joyful anticipation of the ballet. Seven o'clock came but Madame Aritonovich gave no sign to begin: Herr Tarangolian had yet to appear, and she didn't want to start without him.

Uncle Sergei arrived late and unaccompanied—Aunt Paulette had turned back when she saw the seething crowd in the Volksgarten. Giving his most charming smile, he said: "The mood on the streets is just like before a revolution. I saw someone almost beaten into mincemeat."

At seven-thirty, Madame Aritonovich asked Dr. Salzmann to go to the corner apothecary and telephone to see if the prefect would be able to attend—unlike today, back then it wasn't a given that a private school would have its own phone connection. Dr. Salzmann set off with eyes ablaze and martial mustache twitching—and never came back. Frau Dr. Biro (née Wurfbaum), who had laid out the cold buffet and was chewing on the remnants, set off to find out what had happened to him. After a very long while she came back and informed us that Dr. Salzmann had been to the apothecary—which incidentally was hastily closing its shutters despite the official after-hours service—but had disappeared in the direction of downtown. In any event, Herr Tarangolian could not be reached; she herself had tried, in vain. Nevertheless, her trip wasn't entirely for naught, because she was sucking on a gumdrop with great relish and satisfaction.

"So we'll start without him," said Madame Aritonovich. "All right, then, children, to your places!"

But the parents had already decided to put off the performance to another day. The way things were, it was time to get the children home as quickly as possible.

"Please," said Madame, "consider the fact that right now is the worst possible time to be driving through the city. At least wait till after the promenade. Besides, I don't believe that anything serious is going to happen. There's no reason for..." She interrupted herself.

"What was that?" someone asked. "Those were gunshots."

For a few seconds all of us in the festively decorated Institut d'Éducation were deathly silent. We heard the same roaring crowd that we had heard in the afternoon coming from the playing field—except now they sounded much closer, just down Iancu Topor Avenue. We heard a noise as though a handful of beans were being tossed into a bucket. After that it went quiet for a moment, and then the noise broke out again, louder and higher by a whole tone. We could now make out individual voices, very agitated, shouting.

"A salvo," observed Uncle Sergei, gleefully.

Panic broke out among the grown-ups, though not among us children. They threw coats on top of our costumes, grabbed our clothes, and fled to the carriages.

"What you are doing is insane!" Madame Aritonovich cried out. "Don't go out onto the street right now while there's shooting going on. It's bound to be over very soon."

"That was just a warning," one of them countered. "If things don't calm down after that, then the shooting will really start in earnest. And we want to be home before then."

That point of view was compelling and ultimately proved correct. Madame Aritonovich's request to spare the children the sight of the pandemonium was ignored. After all: there was property and furnishings to protect.

Our mother was inclined to stay in the institute until the worst was over. But Aunt Elvira said: "I wouldn't take the risk of waiting in a school like this. The bitterness is clearly directed toward Jews."

Uncle Sergei also thought it would be better to return to the villa district, which would be relatively free from danger.

"I beg you, think of your husband," Aunt Elvira added. "I refuse to be held accountable if anything happens."

"If you do decide to go," said Madame Aritonovich, "please take little Brill and Blanche Schlesinger and see that they get home. They're both on their own here."

"Yes, but you have teachers from your institute at your disposal," said Aunt Elvira. "For us it would mean taking a long detour through downtown."

"That's true," said Madame Aritonovich. "But we don't have a carriage. Please, do it for the sake of your children's friendship with them."

"Of course," said our mother. "After all, we have Sergei to protect us."

Our coachman was a long-serving, reliable man, whom we had brought from the country. "*Ach*, that's nothing" he said. "People beating on each other like at the fairgrounds, knocking out windowpanes, firing into the air to chase everyone away. We'll put up the cover so we won't catch a stone on the nose, that's all. I'll see that everyone gets home." Uncle Sergei sat heroically next to him on the box. And in fact the noise seemed to have passed in the direction of the Volksgarten.

We made a loop through several streets that were completely deserted, and crossed Iancu Topor Avenue just before the Ringplatz. The pavement was strewn with shards of glass, but otherwise empty. At the main street, however, we ran into the commotion. Our coachman charged so fiercely into a mob of suspicious characters that a few of them barely escaped getting run over. One stone hit the cover of the carriage.

Solly Brill was fidgeting between us anxiously, as much as the cramped space allowed. "There's our shop," he called out. "Look at what they're doing, the pigs!"

Some of the rabble was in the process of systematically demolishing the Brills' store. The roller-shutters were torn off, the windows shattered. A few men had crawled into the display window and were tossing the wares to the others outside.

"Look at the robbers!" Solly cried. He jumped up and clambered onto Aunt Elvira's lap, stuck his head out the window, and shouted, full of tears: "Why does it always have to be us! Aren't there any other Jews?"

He was pulled in as quickly as possible.

But then we saw something that made us shout with jubilation.

From the darkness of the chestnut trees in front of the provincial government offices, a troop emerged and fell upon the plundering mob like a flock of avenging angels. They were muscular young men dressed in white linen pants covered with flour; their shirts were open, and their heads were covered with little visorless felt caps—apprentices from the numerous kosher bakeries. Swinging their long wooden peels like double-edged swords, they mowed their way through the streets like threshers.

And leading them into battle was a Jewish Mars, a stout god of war, powerful and glorious in his ecstatic rage, his fat face flushed red like David when he became a man, his black eyes flashing behind the high cushions of his cheeks, his mustache bristling furiously over his scarlet lips, and a greasy wreath of black ringlets on his neck:

It was Dr. Salzmann in his hour of greatness.

We turned away toward Theaterplatz. Around the synagogue we could see the glow of fire. Evidently a real battle was under way there. Soldiers with fixed bayonets were running diagonally across the plaza as if attacking.

Our coachman drove calmly ahead in a quick, steady trot, then turned onto a side street that led onto a somewhat elevated lot where circuses set up their tents, but which now was empty. Just before the small rise, the coachman brought the horses to a gallop and had them take the embankment in three bounds. We were shaken through and through, but soon the carriage was again rolling smoothly on the hard-packed ground. The shortcut was cleverly chosen, since it allowed us to avoid the streets that might be jammed with soldiers, and we approached the Brills' house from the rear.

Uncle Sergei leaped from the box and helped Solly out. "Don't worry about me," Solly said. "Just keep driving. I'll make it home on my own."

But my mother insisted that we wait for him. We stood parked for a few minutes in the shade of the bare firewalls that stood around the garbage bins. Then Uncle Sergei came back.

Solly's mother and sister weren't yet home. "The father cried when he hugged his son. You are a saint, *ma chère cousine*."

We drove back across the empty circus grounds. Blanche was sitting between Tanya and me. It was the first time that I had been so close to her and could feel her body against my own. Tanya and I had our fingers clasped over one of her hands. The sky above the empty lot was dark—outlined only in the background by the lanterns along Wassergasse. Blanche raised her other hand, laid it around my cheek, and pulled my head to hers. I felt her thick, hard, curly hair; our cheeks touched just briefly, then she withdrew her hand.

I was overwhelmed by the sweetness of this chaste, almost holy touch. All the bottled emotions of my dreams suddenly seemed like pale shadows of an almost painful irreality—although this, too, was only a dream, as it happened so unforeseen and passed so quickly and so irretrievably.

At the embankment the coachman held the horses back: we eased down the incline at a walk, but then resumed our former speed. At that point a man ran diagonally across the street, and we heard two or three shots ring out behind him: the man flung up his arms, stood for a moment like a black cross, then staggered ahead, stumbled, and collapsed on his face, and the wheels of our carriage rolled a hairsbreadth away from his legs, which were still twitching. Tanya cried out. I could feel Blanche trembling. But the coachman kept the horses at a constant steady trot.

We drove up to the Herz-Jesu Church, whose stone towers jutted hypocritically into the violet sky. Outside the nearby police headquarters we saw helmets gleaming under the bright light of the arc lamps that formed a whitish bell as it illuminated the forecourt, where an officer was shouting commands.

Blanche and her father lived in a building behind the Ukrainian high school. Blanche jumped up as soon as we turned onto the short street. The apartments were all fronted by narrow, fenced-in garden beds. Only one of the buildings—the one where Blanche and her father lived—appeared to have been vandalized, but thoroughly: even the cast-iron fence had been torn out of its base, the pieces scattered on the street like giant waffles. Both windows on the second story had been shattered; bed linens were hanging out of one, and a ruined chair was caught in a shrub in front of the other. All manner of household goods lay strewn about—mostly books. At one place they were piled into a heap that had been set on fire, before other people had doused it with water that was now running into a black puddle. A group of men stood facing the devastation; one of them was wearing a tattered coat and a torn shirt and his face was bleeding.

"Father!" cried Blanche. She had jumped out of the carriage even before it could come to a stop, and threw herself in his arms. Dr. Schlesinger had a gaping wound above his temple, with a moist handkerchief pressed against it. His eyes were bruised and practically closed shut; one corner of his mouth was torn; even his hands were hurt and bloody—he could barely move them.

"My child!" he said. "How good that you're here. I was just about to go looking for you. Now everything is all right. There, there, it's all over. We'll put things back to order."

One of the neighbors standing by stuck his head in our carriage. "One is ashamed to live in a world like this," he said. "They beat him half to death and threatened to hang him. If we weren't so close to the police station they might have done it, too. But the police are content just to look on, or even take part if possible."

Dr. Schlesinger came to our carriage. "Thank you for bringing my daughter home safely," he said.

"You're wounded," said our mother. "You and Blanche should come to our home and spend the night. The child can't be left in this devastation. And you need looking after."

"Thank you, *gnädige Frau*, we have kind neighbors that have offered to take us in. I'm sure you'll understand that I first want to put things back in order as much as possible. Some scientific works that mean a lot to me have been destroyed. You are very kind, and I thank you."

"But you are clearly the person they are targeting. The violence isn't over yet. You may still be in danger."

"I'm sure I'm not, *gnädige Frau*. They did what they set out to do. Now it's all over. We'll be putting things back in order now." He stroked Blanche's head. "Once again, I thank you from the bottom of my heart."

Blanche broke away from him to come to us, but then turned around and ran into the damaged building.

Dr. Schlesinger nodded to our mother. "You should take your children home, *gnädige Frau*. As you see, I have help. Blanche and I are not alone."

"And I know every single one of them," one woman said. "I can name each one by name. They should be publicly whipped, the lot of them."

Dr. Schlesinger smiled, resigned. Our mother signaled the coachman to drive on.

Our street was empty: nothing had happened here; the whole commotion had passed by almost unnoticed. We were given a cup of tea with a good dose of rum and sent straight to bed. Uncle Sergei came to our room to wish us good night.

"Was he dead, the man they shot?" we asked.

"What man, my hearts?"

"The one who fell next to our carriage."

"No, never. He just stumbled. I saw how he got up and happily went on running."

"That's not true, Uncle Sergei, you're lying to us."

Uncle Sergei was quiet for a moment. "Would you rather believe the alternative?"

We didn't know what to answer. No and yes.

"Does it hurt when a person gets shot to death?" we asked.

"Not a bit. You don't feel any more than when you get thwacked with the finger—*tuk*—and it's all over. It's no fun at all to shoot someone dead."

"The children should go to sleep now," our mother said. "We'll be right nearby and will leave all the doors open."

Behind the gardens outside our windows, the darkness was rocking the treetops in the Volksgarten. The song of the nightingales rose from there and echoed off the walls of the night. Apart from that, there was no sound.

The next morning we were running a fever and stayed in bed. Toward evening Tanya had a big reddish patch on her forehead and cheeks. The doctor was called. He diagnosed scarlet fever.

"No wonder, in that Jew school," our father said, who had just returned from his hunting trip and had yet to hear what had transpired.

18
Farewell to Childhood and to Herr Tarangolian

HONEY-golden like a pastoral goddess, Frau Lyubanarov stood at the garden gate, against the saffron and sandalwood tones of the autumn foliage, a life-mystery pulsing with warm-blooded corporeality, encased in her skin, breathing, peering, profoundly alive amidst a barren splendor, vast and translucent, woven of light and air and color, in which those earthiest of birds, the crows, gathered in flocks as if plowed up from the fields, cawing their gray, brittle, crumbly cries. She stood there in the perfected glory of the fruit, the late sunlight falling through the thinned-out leaves, glazing her face with the thinnest coat of pure gold before drowning in the warm amber of her skin, as though the fires of an ancient sun were raining onto the surface of a pond that lay concealed within a reedy secret beneath some oaks. Her thick black hair curled into a firm wreath above her topaz goat-eyes, her pale, full lips peaked at the corners into a smile full of sweet enticement, and melted into a delicate, sharp clarity like the tone of a flute—that's how she stood there, while the chestnuts came drumming down from the trees, their prickly, ball-shaped hulls bursting apart to release the shiny kernels, which rolled in front of her feet like a cornucopia of peasant offerings: the bright, tenderly yellowing leek-green husks, wrapped around a whitish membrane tinged with shades of violet, like fresh sheep's cheese swathed in a burdock leaf; the eye-catching brown of the tough kernel, sharp with tannins, with a luster rich as old beeswax that refracted the ruby hues of congealing lamb kidneys into a warm and sparkling rusty red, exerting a tangy, satisfying attraction like the smell of woodsmoke; and the bright, pinkish mushroom-and-shell colored blemishes on her skin—a shellfish in the rainbow opalescence of unspoiled purity, with all the slothfulness of the autumn encapsulated in its pearl.

I gave her names such as *Mother of Corn*—because of the glory of her shoulders and breasts, or *Stallioness*—because she struck me as the mythic mate of that sinewy steed the hussar had ridden, or else *Thetis* or *Nereid*—on account of the gritty curliness of her hair, which contained the churning swish of waves. But the most beautiful, the most divine of all her names was the one bestowed on her by Herr Adamowski: *magnificently shameless*...

I eyed her through the window, yearned to go out to her—all the while secretly conspiring with my fate, grateful that the wall of glass panes separated me from her and cut me off from the reality outside, which I would have lost had I ventured out—just as every reality is lost as soon as we enter with a mind to act: just like the air in which we breathe is not visible to us. In my room I was fully transported, and also removed from her, therefore fully gifted with her presence: the window of my room was set before the transparency of the bright October day like the facet of a prism, refracting its image into a spectrum without disowning its structure; it focused my visions into a perspective whose vanishing point was the woman at the garden gate—a sparkling equilibrium of correspondences, which showered me with riches, weightless like the joy of forgetting oneself while dancing.

I took this being separated from the world by a glass pane as a kind of pictorial correspondence—a reflection of the transported condition my sickness had left me in. It happened that I was sick longer than my siblings, and my case was more threatening: the scarlet fever led to a completely abnormal case of pneumonia and pleurisy that kept me laid up for weeks with aches and fever while the summer simply passed by.

And it was only reluctantly that I recovered: I had no intent or desire to return to the loud, crude, and tumultuous world of the healthy, with their ruddy cheeks, where one robust thing alters another, and connections of a base nature cheapen the worth of everything. That world possessed nothing of the floating interchangeability of all that is perceived, a quality I had learned to love, thanks to the fever and the exhaustion, like a delicate intoxication. As the care and attention I was being shown began to taper off, I responded with a kind of charitable scorn, which I wielded like a dagger, either turning the point inward toward myself or out and away—at least for as long as I was visibly sick. As I recovered, I could feel how I was being cheapened, how my senses—which my ailment had honed to a fine, excitable edge—were again getting sucked into the undertow of a life that struck me as full of fake cheer, that seemed artificially packed with pointless actions and gestures, and overflowing with wholesome precepts—all aimed at deliberate deception. And the harder people worked to peddle this concept of worthy *life*, the more they aroused my suspicion, just as if they were hawking one of the Dobrowolskis' more dubious goods. Consequently, while I hated the dishes that were designed to make me stronger, and which with every meal were meatier, spicier—more masculine, so to speak—what disgusted me even more was the fact that my appetite for them was growing. And as much as I despised the eager voices full of anticipation, and modulated to cheer me up, as if wanting to transfer their own impatience onto me—"Just a few more days, then you'll be able to go out and get some fresh air and play with the others. I'll bet you can't wait, can you?"—I detested the excitement that I felt against my will, and which was all too closely related to that uncouth cheerfulness.

I had the feeling as though now were the time for me to leave my childhood once and for all. Because what was expected of me, this ideal of "being healthy and taking part in all of life's joys and duties," meant renouncing the earnestness I had developed in the great unconscious tension of my unmediated confrontation with the world. It meant exchanging the inscrutable autocratic splendor that accompanied each new thing as it *entered* that world for a routine interaction with the all-too-familiar, where things were ascribed functions merely as needed—thereby *manufacturing* a world that was falsely acted, instead of *experiencing* a world full of mysterious play.

Not that the reservoir of things to be experienced seemed depleted. Had that been the case, I would have had no cause to lament any loss: I was sensing that my own ability to experience things was diminishing as I recovered. There was clearly a limit—not of the wonders that surrounded me, but of my strength to perceive them, as if my soul, which had once again been exiled to my body, possessed only a limited facility to comprehend, an unalterable capacity that could contain a finite quantity of basic images and not a single more.

Hesitantly, then, and with an anticipatory sadness, since I was growing out of my childhood anyway and registering the renunciations that this entailed, I took leave of my sickroom, within whose walls everything had been calibrated to my sickness, with gentle consideration and tender care, and which was filled with the echoes of heightened perceptions that had grown in time and space, and which I had savored to the fullest, just like my aches and pains. For years I wasn't able to pick up a book or look at a picture that I had studied then without feeling the vague stimulus of a deeper recognition, an impact that strikes the core of our being, the sense of déjà vu mingled with nostalgia that comes when we reencounter motifs from our childhood and we regret having lost the power to experience the world in a way that brought us closer to the essence of things. Because we never again experience the world with the same thoroughness as in the stillness that fills us when we are completely alone and close to not-being, the tranquility that is either the echo of the not-yet-being that precedes our birth, or of the no-longer-being that follows death. The other states of rapture we encounter—love and intoxication—merely borrow this proximity to not-being, and are therefore merely reflection and illusion. They do not entirely come from us, do not spring out of that same enigmatic element from which our life arises, and into which it ultimately descends. Neither love nor drugged exhilaration can be attained without assistance: they require other means to transport us and connect us to their qualities. Only the most lethal narcotics or the most feminine—that is to say, the most changeable—woman are able to temporarily create the illusion of the truly lived life, owing to their deadly effects. And the despair into which they plunge us is the voice of our innermost conscience, which opens our eyes to our illusion and reveals the underlying fact *that we turn to surrogates to still our true desire—the desire to be extinguished.*

In the autumn air, the morning frost was sharp, pungent—like a mild odor of fire and mold. I went out into the garden and joined my siblings. I felt estranged, no longer able to follow their games. What's more, they had acquired new friends—or rather reacquired old ones: the two Lyubanarov daughters had come home, shy and a little feral after their long stay in the country, where they had acquired the exaggerated and somewhat clumsy manners of a God-fearing household, amid the black-bearded and unctuous patriarchy of their clergymen kin. They even smelled like church candles, like the spice cakes laced with icing and adorned with almonds, and the aromatic brandies of baptismal celebrations and wakes; their hair still contained the shady cool of the untended corner of the parish garden where the blue glint of jays with their rosewood breasts squawked away. They were suntanned and hardened and wore sleeveless summer dresses, and I felt mollycoddled and awkwardly dandyish in my scarf and coat, like a scholarly bookworm confronted by peasant beauties.

Looking through the lance-leaf fence, which once again appeared indisputably slender and erect against the trembling gold of the leaves on the bushes, we saw the prefect's shiny black coach approach, the gleaming brass and polished lantern panes like heraldic emblems, towed behind a whirlwind of red spokes and horses' legs blurred in movement. The carriage stopped at our gate. The batman jumped off the box; the martial eagle on his heavily polished spiked helmet gleamed above the silver buckles of the chinstrap, and Herr Tarangolian leaned heavily on his shoulder to climb out of the carriage. Then he stepped into the garden with the mincing gait of a bon vivant, a red carnation flaming in his buttonhole. Without turning his head he walked past Frau Lyubanarov, who was leaning against the wall of the *dvornik*'s hut, giving her a restrained greeting by placing three fingers of his gloved right hand to the brim of his stiff hat and barely lifting it. His heavy eyes, however, rolled out past the twirled ends of his mustache in a meaningful sidelong glance and sank inside the depths of her topaz gaze. She leaned her head back and smiled, without changing her overall expression—except for a barely perceptible narrowing of her eyes, and a tiny upward tilt to the corners of her mouth. But her shoulders and breasts smiled from under the hem of her colorful embroidered blouse; her crossed arms smiled as if they wanted to open up to receive a guest; and the curve of her full hips smiled with provocative irony. The prefect's bon vivant gait seemed to pick up a mechanical whirr. His knee action—as the horse experts call it—increased, and he started to strut like a peacock. The immaculate white linen spats above his dainty shoes showed a vain display of carefully aligned buttons; his collar and cuffs were flashing; his tie was a billow of silk beneath his pompous chin. His arms, slightly angled at the elbows, rowed alongside his flanks, which seemed to shrink, so that his gloves suddenly appeared too large, as if he were shoveling the air in front of his silvery gray vest like a clown, or securing a path for his virility through a tangle of unwelcome advances. He seemed to sense how silly they looked and so he gave them something to do by twirling his ebony cane between his fingers and then rapping it against his left palm. We were expecting him to pucker his lips under his executioner's mustache and whistle a few tense, jaunty bars from under his bulbous Levantine nose, while his jaundiced eyes bulged more than usual above their heavy bags, and his pupils stayed as rigid as archers' targets.

Frau Lyubanarov glanced at him tenderly as he passed by, then focused her smile on the batman, who was following the prefect with a large bouquet of flowers, loosely wrapped in crackling tissue, along with several unwieldy packages tucked under his arms. Her goat-eyes took in his strong neck and strapping legs with appreciation. He pulled himself together like a soldier snapping to attention, turning red underneath his spiked helmet; he seemed on the verge of hot manly tears, humiliated, emasculated, and ashamed at having to perform the duties of a maid in carrying such fragile trumpery. With great effort he kept his eyes fixed dead ahead, his heavy boots stamping defiantly on the gravel.

And so they passed, one after the other, the master and his servant, dancing like marionettes on the string of a woman's smile, until they reached the house and were safely removed from the singeing gaze on their backs.

Herr Tarangolian had come to say farewell.

"Take this visit," he said, "which may seem somewhat premature, in the spirit in which it is undertaken—namely as an expression of my inner need to thank you, and to bid you adieu before all others, and not at the last minute. I may be recalled tomorrow or a year from now—I confess that I have only been informed in confidence, albeit from a highly reliable source, that this is something I must reckon with. I don't need to tell you how painful it will be for me to take my leave of this city, and especially of you. I am being moved, as they say, up the ladder—*hélas*—and I would be lying if I were to say that weren't some solace. But believe me: it is a very weak consolation. Even if I have no desire to hide my pride at being granted a chance to serve my country in a position of greater responsibility than hitherto—perhaps yet as a minister—you realize that my heart is here, and here it will stay forever."

He handed us his abundant gifts, and I received what I considered the most beautiful of all—the unabridged edition of *A Thousand and One Nights*, which was immediately taken into safekeeping, for when I would be "mature enough." Herr Tarangolian was served some of his favorite walnut liqueur. He lit a cigar with delighted meticulousness, crossed his legs, and leaned back in his chair. Giving one of his black eyebrows a diabolical arch, he let his eyes wander from face to face, meeting each of our gazes and then moving on, in one quick, intelligent sweep, as if they were registering once and for all the fixed points of furniture, the corners of the room, the windows and doors, arranging them in a linear plot that would serve as an abbreviated diagram, like a stenographer's shorthand, until finally, glassed over in a kind of blank meditation, they came to rest at the glowing tip of his cigar. The smoke rose in a fine perpendicular thread, billowing into a veil-like ribbon that trembled in tender, wrinkly grooves. All of a sudden we felt the space surrounding us, the room where we had been with him so often in the commonality of the old friendship we took for granted, a powerful presence, a spatial reality we had never fully appreciated—as if it had never been real. And, strangely, this freshly produced reality imparted something peculiarly false: it was as if the curtain had risen dramatically on the last act of a play that had begun with the same set, and as if all of us—supernumeraries and principals alike—found ourselves arranged exactly as at the beginning, tasked with working out some inner drama—a highly effective director's trick that had the immediate consequence of seeming untrue. We became sentimental: in other words, we supplied an artificial melancholy with the first motivation we were able to summon. We thought about our hapless Aunt Aida, whom God knows we had missed too little hitherto: now her death acquired the significance of a practically spiteful martyrdom, and seemed to us like an irreplaceable loss that demonstrated how hopeless life had become, and how the connections between us had been torn once and for all.

Herr Tarangolian was clearly the instigator and moving force behind this dramatic effect, its director and lead actor in one and the same person, and when he launched into one of his entertaining philosophical monologues, his words also struck us as deceptively meaningful and spruced-up for effect. Not even our usual pleasure in hearing his euphonic voice—the Latin love of hearing oneself speak that we so enjoyed in him—could release us from the unease we felt that everything he was saying, everything he was alluding to and everything he was concealing—and thus the entire situation in which his speech proceeded—was only for appearance, alleged and pretended, and in a way that twisted reality to such a degree it could no longer be grasped. This uncanny feeling went to the root of our being, calling it into question, as if it were merely an assertion, a claim, as if our existence could be replaced by some other at any time—although without altering the inevitable course of events. In this way its essence acquired a deeply ironic character.

"Indeed," said the prefect, "it is so difficult for me to part from Czernopol that I don't know whether I should be grateful to my friend Petrescu or hold it against him. Because it's to the general himself and no one else that I owe my upstairs plunge. In any case, I am bound to him—in the true meaning of the word—bound by fate, as rivals always are. But I have my own understanding of this rivalry, which couldn't consist in anything other than our love for Czernopol. I sincerely regret that such a capable man must atone for a mistake with a banishment that cannot possibly advance his outstanding qualities. For my part, I have complete understanding, even the highest respect, for his foolishness. His rash decision, which was unilateral and against my express orders, to unleash his troops during that wretched night—supposedly to restore the order that was never seriously endangered—the spontaneous and fateful stupid act of an otherwise intelligent man, I beg you, can only have one cause—jealousy. And not political jealousy. No, no! It was General Petrescu's jealous love for Czernopol that we have to blame for most of the forty deaths that night. And it fell to me to play his rival. Not that I would have given him any reason to begrudge my clear affection for this city. Oh no! For that, Czernopol is far too loose a mistress, who is so generous with her love that it would be petty to attempt to hoard it. A mistress somewhat like Madame Lyubanarov there, leaning so charmingly against your garden fence. Who—apart from a fool like Tildy—would forget himself so far as to be jealous of someone like that? But don't forget: we are in large part Latins and Orientals. Our jealousy is directed less at a particular *person*, the given favorite of a mood or of an hour, and more toward the *impulse* to love that which we love ourselves. As a result this blinding passion also sharpens our sight. We suffer whenever we sense that someone else understands how to love better than we do. We expect so much from our love that love tendered by someone else always seems better than our own. Well..." Herr Tarangolian smiled his most inscrutable smile. "I may flatter myself that in my love for Czernopol I conquered even a general. I simply knew the better way to love. My friend Petrescu wanted to be master over this city. He wanted it the way a soldier wants his mistress: wild but submissive, untrue but devoted, contemptuous but full of admiration for him. I, on the other hand, love her the way she is: moody, because she cannot find release, because she is unreliable, because she is helpless and crafty and treacherous, because she is fundamentally *chaste.* You don't believe that—you are smiling at my remarks. I won't be able to convince you. But love doesn't make one blind, as people say—on the contrary. It concentrates all our attention on one object that we see with greatly increased focus, because it is we who *discovered* it. Our love is an expression of our having perceived things in that object that no one else sees. Its monomaniacal character might make us blind to the rest of the world, for a while—but it only seems that way, because in fact we never do see more of the world than its surface, anyway. In love, however, we see *the essence* of the object of our affection. Because I believe that the only true love is the approving kind, the kind that lets something be the way it is. I have never wanted to change Czernopol in any of its qualities. The idea of order as perceived by the military mind strikes me as inapplicable, both in regard to women and to the world at large—and especially this world right here. To force it would require violently changing its nature—and that would be tantamount to destroying it. To create order in Czernopol would mean to kill Czernopol. It would mean strangling its spirit in the name of some imagined, abstract form. You may have your own thoughts about the spirit of Czernopol, but permit me to declare how much I revere it—that's right, revere it—because I see our infamous street-character as one of the primal forms of the great Eros, as the wellspring of all living spiritual fertility. I see it in what I call 'the drunkenness of the sober': in a nagging, alert skepticism toward everything, and, above all, itself. Nowhere fully settled, nowhere secure outside of this skepticism—and therefore without any respect, fear, or awe, ready to get mixed up in anything and prepared for nothing—*that* is impressive... You might accuse me of loving chaos. That's not true. I merely believe that nature's idea of order is stronger than that of human beings. And I owe this insight not least to Czernopol. You consider its spirit corrosive. I do as well. Except that I consider it a kind of destruction that is more economical than our measures to guard against destruction. General Petrescu's praiseworthy attempt to spare the city a bloodbath, which would in fact have been satisfied with a few broken noses, cost forty lives. The spirit of Czernopol seized these forty deaths—you can call it corpse-robbing as far as I'm concerned—*and made a joke about it.* That sounds despicable, but may I remind you how much sorrow, what abundance of painful experience is required to produce a joke? Generations sink into their graves before the grotesque quality of a particular human situation that might have been the original cause of their torments, or even death, becomes clear enough to be expressed in humor. While the laughter it triggers cannot cause a single tear to become unshed, it does forgive all fault. For Czernopol it only took forty dead people to create a *symbolon*—an allegorical seal for the grotesque of a human, all-too-human situation. A story is making the rounds that on that night a giant policeman—in other words, a defender of order, sent in to protect the Jews against the anti-Semites—raised his rifle butt high and started lambasting away at a small Jewish man, who cried out 'Stop! What's going on? *I'm* not a Nazi!' To which the policeman replied, 'But *I* am!'"

With the exception of Uncle Sergei, no one laughed, but Herr Tarangolian didn't seem to have been looking to elicit merriment at all.

"I can't think of anything more characteristic for Czernopol," he said. "This joke, filtered through forty dead people, seems like an ideogram of our city—a single image containing all the elements of its spiritual structure. It calls to mind the strange alternative posed by Tildy, by which I mean his *either/or*—whether the solution is about justice or about a joke. Nowhere is the deadly comic quality of the grossly unjust made so clear as here, but only as a joke, in the moral function of wit, in its lightning-flash illumination of the one true and incontrovertibly genuine reality in the paradox. What does it mean, then: destruction, decomposition, decay? I recall finding a leaf that had decayed down to the veil-like veins of its ribs. And in that state of decomposition it had become uncommonly beautiful, a natural work of art, reduced to its most essential, highly ordered and compacted into an idea. But again, it was only a paradox of itself, in the uselessness of those same ribs that no longer held anything together, the joke of a leaf, so to speak—rather in the way a skeleton is a macabre joke of a human being. And still it seemed to me that the greatest possible justice had been done to the leaf, by the manner of its destruction into this basic sketch..."

Herr Tarangolian studied the intact ash-cone of his cigar, lowered it carefully to the ashtray, and tapped it off.

"Please forgive my boundless chatter," he said. "I'm letting my emotions get the better of me. *Partir, c'est mourir un peu, n'est-ce pas?* Because you are always parting from yourself... Perhaps everything I think and say is wrong. Perhaps"—he arched one of his magician's eyebrows—"my thinking is intentionally wrong and my speech a deliberate lie—in order to deceive myself. I am leaving this city and have to hold myself accountable for the state in which I leave it. Perhaps"—he smiled broadly, so that his all-too-perfect teeth appeared under his blackened mustache—"perhaps I am removing myself from all accountability by claiming that our human idea of order doesn't exist at all except in our minds, in our thinking, in the artificial sketch—in other words, not in nature but only in art. That leaves it to whim whether we act in one way or another, depending on how serious we are. Because what I truly believe is that we are not capable of comprehending the world, but merely of interpreting it—and, to be sure, the simpler our interpretation, the better. The more resolutely our interpretations vanish into one point, whether it carries the name of God or is merely some symbol for relative nothingness—the more stable the earth is under our feet. It is the privilege of the dumbest as well as the wisest to have firm ground beneath their feet. Both live in the blessed state of simplification. And it makes no difference whether they inhabit the center of this world—which we are told is a sphere—or the outermost surface. After all, this sphere may also be conceived negatively—not imagined, but conceived—so that the periphery may just as well be considered the middle, and the center its surface..."

Herr Tarangolian took his leave, and remained in Czernopol for years, without ever revoking the legend of his imminent recall—and without renewing his former friendship with our parents' household. From then on we saw him only rarely; he no longer mixed among the people like Harun al-Rashid disguised as an idle bon vivant. In time his appearance acquired a legendary quality: we would gape in wonder at our close friend from a long-vanished past whenever we happened to catch sight of him, driving by in his elegant black barouche, with the gleaming brass-crowned lanterns and the cinnabar whirlwind of spokes, the batman seated gruffly and martially beside the coachman on his box. And when once or twice he did appear on some extraordinary occasion in his full presence, it truly was as if he came riding in from some distant place, paying the honor of a special visit that seemed to demand appreciation. From then on he was removed from his old sphere into a new and higher one, and over the years he acquired an unusually high—and, for Czernopol, essentially unique—prestige. After that we never referred to him anymore as our friend,

Herr Tarangolian, or even disrespectfully as "Coco," but reverently, as *the prefect.* But later on, shortly before he left the city to become a government minister, he had become such a popular figure and public institution—a figure so steeped in legend it was impossible to imagine Czernopol without him—that the gently ironic nickname had become common currency. Even the newspapers took the liberty of referring to him as "*Our Coco*" in the headline of an article on the occasion of his sixty-fifth birthday.

"Perhaps we should all let ourselves be 'recalled,'" said Madame Aritonovich once—incidentally the only person he visited with any regularity, albeit at greater and greater intervals. "Because sooner or later the hour comes when our lives want to step into a new phase, completely of their own accord, and all previous connections are rendered null and void. Why not give fate a little help? One day all the old meadows are mown and we have to look for new ones—the same nomads we always were, incapable of cultivating our field."

And as before, on the winter days when the prefect would come to visit and we would peep through the feathery patterns of the frosted windows as he climbed back onto his sled, eerily swathed in blankets and furs, and drove off into the white-and-gray snowy landscape—so now, with his parting from our lives, we felt the emptiness racing in, as though we had been abandoned to the merciless elements, to an all-powerful nature where humans, and with them all measure and order, had moved on, never to return.

19

Frau Lyubanarov Goes to the Asylum; Tildy Shoots at Năstase

WITH ITS profligate smile of spun light, which was both captivating and a little suspicious, like Uncle Sergei's sentimental charm, autumn scattered its deceptive riches, dusting the profane tin roofs with its cheap gold leaf, and sprinkling its chromium-yellow, blue, and ochre-brown hues on the streets like confetti from a carnival, a parade of paradoxes—a motionless riot of color, a silent din, as dramatic as an *attitude en pointe*, and just as the ballet position becomes transformed by the cryptlike emptiness behind the sets, this autumn display acquired an unreal dimension, under the glass dome of the blue, silken skies where the crows were gathering.

Frau Lyubanarov stood at the garden gate day in and day out, filled by her own sweet idling, her sumptuous presence like a piece of fruit ripening away in some secret understanding with the late sun. We saw a man wearing a large gray hat enter our yard and pass her by; his posture was ramrod-straight, and he exuded a pallid, grim determination that seemed manic. Ruthlessly he passed through the force field of her honey-smile and emerged unscathed, then approached the house with decisive steps. The ingrained tautness of his bearing reminded us of the artificial vigor in the gait of our hunchbacked seamstress, Fräulein Iliuț; the steady output of energy had become second nature by dint of cultivation and habit, just as her misshapen body had mobilized its reserves and developed unexpected powers, even a certain degree of grace. The tortured correctness of his clothing seemed provincial. His summer suit was tastefully understated in its cut and pattern, but its ironed surfaces and creases were so immaculate and pristine it looked like it had been hanging in the closet for a very long time. His smooth brown leather gloves were carefully buttoned at the wrists, and his broad-brimmed felt hat sat upright on his head with a defiant ponderous formality that showed through despite all intention to appear casual. A brooding earnestness and a knee-jerk pride—compensation for the visible discomfort with his own person—lent him an air of macabre absurdity. I caught myself thinking that it was the hangman in civilian clothes, en route to a quaint and wholesome little spa where he intended to spend his vacation—incognito, of course. Full of curiosity, we strained to see below the brim of the travel hat that had been arranged on his head with an angry attention to detail: it shaded his eyes and was underscored by the parallel lines of a vigorously trimmed mustache. Our gaze perceived nothing except for the impression of something alien, so far removed in time as to be anachronistic, or from another world entirely. And only after he had passed did we realize, more as a result of a slow, inner dawning than a clear and precise recognition—*that it was Tildy.*

Will it sound off-putting if I say that we weren't the least bit dismayed to realize who it was? But this was not because our other image of the man had faded; on the contrary, it had long ago acquired a life of its own, inside us, unfettered from his person, forever free and independent—the hussar in his dazzling uniform that threw off sparks of blue and gold, his stallion and saber transforming him into a dangerous hornet, the menacing protector of his lady who glided alongside, at rest in the shell of her sleigh, the dogs dancing around like a pack of mythic guards . . . It's true that this image had flashed by in an instant, straight into the enigmatic depths of the past, where it was entrusted to our powers of imagination before our eyes scarcely could take it in. But that doesn't mean that it had become a dream with no correspondence to reality—no, that wasn't the reason we remained unmoved when confronted with the actual man. In fact, it was precisely because we *recognized* him, because our vision of the hussar was a perfect, seamless match with the somber stranger in his well-preserved travel suit—that is to say, *the reality was so convincing it left us no room for baffled amazement.*

Because this reality was inherently transcendent, made plain to us by a gently persistent illumination, a dawning sobriety, which although it did not originate with this reality and in fact barely touched its skin, much less its core, did offer an intimation, like the distant echo of a sounding, *that all reality occurs in this way*: not merely in the sense that our expectations of life might find fulfillment—albeit only as it is granted or rather fated—so that we only acquire late in life what anticipation has long divested of its true value, but also because the reality never really affected us directly. However, even if the world was removed in a way that made it impossible for us to truly experience it, we nevertheless clearly felt how much it molded us from without, from outside ourselves. No refraction by the prism of perception can diminish the power of the events themselves. Tildy had come to talk to Aunt Paulette about his wife, since he knew our aunt was a friend of Herr Adamowski's. Because Tamara Tildy had left the house in our neighborhood and moved in with Herr Adamowski.

Naturally we never found out anything about the conversation he had with our aunt. He left half an hour later and cut through the aura of the woman at the garden gate, his countenance unmoved, his back flat and straight as a board. Overcome with curiosity, we ran into the house and ascertained what we could. All we were told was that Tildy had finally been released from the asylum, but was going back one more time—presumably to fetch his things. As for his future, they simply shrugged their shoulders. Given the party now in power, there could be no talk of his being rehabilitated.

"Won't he duel with any of the men he challenged?" We posed our question in all innocence but they didn't understand that and dismissed it as inappropriate and silly.

That same afternoon, Frau Lyubanarov vanished from the gate.

"If you didn't know who she was waiting for, day in and day out," Widow Morar later told us, smiling with eyes closed in a state of ecstasy, as if blinded by the joyful truth coming out of her golden mouth, "if you didn't know before, then now you do: he was the one she was waiting for. And every man that passed by was his herald. Because she has evil in her blood. She was conceived in sin and born and nursed with her mother's hatred, the hatred of a common maid. She had to wait for him in order to annihilate him, out of hatred for the other who is her sister and is not her sister, a princess so delicate and so unique that in this world she is like a butterfly in a thunderstorm."

But the strange thing was that our old friend's oracular whisper now struck us as vapid. The biblical intonation, part curse and part annunciation, which used to cause our eyes to gape and filled our hearts with an almost holy awe, no longer held us in its spell. The monotony of her interpretations began to bore us. Their mythic oversimplification no longer sufficed to explain all the incomprehensible things that life now offered.

Another strange thing happened: our interest in the fate of our hero declined—or you might say became more abstract—just as his dramatic situation was approaching its pointed end. Much later, while reading *Dorian Gray*, we would be upset by a cynical remark of Lord Henry concerning the suicide of Sibyl Vane: namely, that he felt younger by years upon hearing that romantic gestures of that magnitude, which no one really believed people actually did, truly happened. Our experience was just the opposite, although it did not completely contradict that sentiment: namely, that living through a genuine drama only amplifies its incredibility; in other words: that the loss of reality stands in direct proportion to the intensity of the experienced reality. The appearance of Tildy shorn of mystery only touched us on the outermost surface because it was so irreversibly real; and in that same way, the news of his death and the circumstances surrounding it merely struck us as a distant echo. It took a long time for his story to *become absorbed in us*—a long time and much travel until we regained the wondrous world of the *literary existence* of our childhood.

As for Frau Lyubanarov's disappearance from the garden gate, which would set off subsequent events, we heard yet other commentaries.

"*Que voulez-vous?*" asked Uncle Sergei. "The fact that she went after him is the most basic female psychology. He almost fought a duel on her behalf. What can convince a woman more about her man than his willingness to die for her? Read Leskov..."

Aunt Paulette, to whom he was speaking, remained unmoved for some time, and then said, slothfully: "Yes, I will read your poet in order to better understand women. But I think there's a simpler explanation: He was the only one who never paid attention to her."

"How so?" Uncle Sergei was getting worked up. "Are you saying that a man wouldn't even notice the woman for whom he is willing to risk his life, not even with a small corner of his fantasy? Ah, *chère cousine*, you consider us men to be less coquettish than we really are."

"No. I think you are every bit as exaggerated."

"It only speaks for the unfortunate Major Tildy that he was willing to duel for a principle," Aunt Elvira chimed in quietly. She didn't have to swallow the rest of the sentence, since her meaning was written clearly on her face: "—and not for a woman like that."

Conversations that we chanced to overhear—or, better put, monologues of this sort that were directed against each other—left us irritated, and we responded by being willful and recalcitrant. Against our great reluctance, they exposed us to the entirely new field of stupidity, full of hidden snares. We didn't encounter the dangers they posed until much later, and even then it's possible we never fully understood them.

Much later we had an opportunity to hear Herr Tarangolian's view of the events back then. By that point he had long since removed himself from our world, so we had to remind him of certain specifics surrounding the case before he could recall it in any detail.

"You may rest assured that Tildy wasn't the only one immune to the charms of this woman," the prefect said, with dignity, adjusting the flaming red carnation in his buttonhole. "And of course there might be a kernel of truth in the theory that his evident indifference provoked her to follow him all the way to the asylum. But not much more truth than Sergei Nikiforich's version or the one espoused by your macabre Widow Morar. Or even in the view of Fiokla Ignatieva, which, if I remember correctly, was far more plain and simple: namely, that no other man came down the street that afternoon. Believe all of it and none of it. In general, you should always believe everything and nothing at the same time. This formula is particularly recommended in psychology, which is the reason why that field is so popular, and why it is always correct in the general application and never in the specific case. So always take hold of the most obvious interpretation, while at the same time searching for the most remote."

"And what would that be?" we asked, resigned to an answer we thought we knew in advance.

"If you're asking for my own interpretation," said the prefect, "it would be this: it had to happen, because it happened in Czernopol. Admittedly, there's no logic in that explanation, but at least it has as much truth as all the others. Because no matter how much you might learn by studying a fateful chain of events: you can never escape from the notion of *Providence*—if you understand what I mean by that."

He nodded majestically, taking his leave, and was about to turn to someone else, but then suddenly stopped us with his old, familiar smile.

"I often used to wonder," he said, "what it really was you saw in Tildy. At times I thought I understood. I also thought I ought to warn you against it. Because what you presumed to see in him—or what you yearned for—is something, my young friends, that does not exist. Our vulgar world lacks the *form* that a human could adopt so perfectly that it would become transmuted into the heavy core of a magical force field. Those are legends, like that of the Grail, where the absolute ideal of chivalry is endowed with mystical significance. Very nice, of course, as a rough draft, a desired ideal—but only as a utopian one—in other words, as the hope of fools. At the same time"—and here the prefect's expression became terribly contorted in the failed attempt to conceal his utter hatred behind a façade of joviality—"there is still a powerful difference between Percival, the savior, *who is, in that he is, in coming,* and a monomaniacal fool who pigheadedly opposes the world with his rigid principles. Clearly much was lost with the passing of the black-and-gold glory of the Austrian double eagle, much that we who are robbing its corpse, so to speak, mourn and miss. But the code of honor espoused by its booted and spurred cavaliers isn't worth shedding any tears over. We can be thankful to Tildy for showing us exactly how ridiculous it was... Farewell, and please give my best to your esteemed parents."

That was our last meeting with the prefect, and it took place at a fête that Madame Aritonovich gave to celebrate the tenth-year anniversary of the Institut d'Éducation; she could hardly foresee that it would soon be shut down under pressure from the nationalists, because she was a Russian. So we once again found ourselves among our friends from that brief episode when we had been her pupils. To be sure, Blanche Schlesinger was missing: shortly after the night of the "Petrescu-pogrom"—as the unfortunate events were called—her father had been called to Heidelberg, and she was living with him there. She had written to us how extremely happy she felt in Germany; for the first time in her life she felt free from fear. Sadly, after just a few letters back and forth the correspondence trickled out. But now I want to tell without interruption what happened on the day Tildy came to see Aunt Paulette, and in the following night:

Tildy had returned to the asylum, presumably to take care of the formalities regarding his dismissal, or perhaps to spend a few more days there, since he had no roof over his head, as the saying goes. In any event Frau Lyubanarov followed him, whatever her motivation.

I've often pictured the two of them on their way: the landscape at the edge of town, a belt of fields opening onto the vastness steeped in melancholy, and the figure of the man, in his stiff, ramrod-straight, tin-soldier daintiness, marching unwaveringly ahead, followed at some distance by the woman in her colorful knit peasant blouse, moving in a lazy saunter, swaying her beautiful hips, her topaz gaze fixed ahead, lethargically and dreamily, an aster stem between her teeth, barely touched by her lips. I imagined her passing the gardens with no apparent purpose, as if the sweetness of doing nothing were pulling her into a violet-blue Somewhere. I pictured her lazy, voluptuous gait in front of the bizarre architecture of the Feuers' house, whose absurd Nordic ornamentation seemed practically Chinese, and I perceived the melody of both, that of the house and the woman, a *Nouveau* Arts and Crafts Wagnerian motif together with a flute theme distilled into ever higher spheres of sensuality—both tinged and intertwined with the sounds of a Jewish fiddle shifting between major and minor keys in a resigned, ironic melancholy, bowed by an old beggar who sat in the dust of the curb on the outskirts of town, in front of the poor simple little houses that looked as though they had been constructed by schoolchildren, with white-and-yellow walls, their pitiful lamps emerging against the pigeon-like blue of the twilight and igniting within ourselves our common forlornness, and the great sense of humility that entailed: an old man offering his poverty to God, rendering his meekness in tones and colors; a blind man whose smile was turned inward, whose pallid skin was patinated with hunger and verged on pistachio green, whose archaically and beautifully curled iron-gray sidelocks cascaded below the brim of his cracked and worn lacquered Galician cap, trimming the threadbare violet of his old coat with the sumptuous purple of inalienable human dignity. And in my mind I also always added the distant stamping of the musicians on the dance floors in the outlying districts, drifting on the wind, as they filled the tedious emptiness of a Sunday afternoon playing their music for homesick soldiers and their girls: the endlessly repeated and monotonous *rum-ta-ta* which now and then was drowned out by a single trumpet like a cock's cry that faded with the frailty of all yearning, giving way to the dull, muted explosions of the cymbals amid the double basses and drumrolls. In later years nothing came so close to recalling the city of Czernopol as this image composed of themes, colors, and sounds—and movement that was deeply meaningful and extremely sparse. It was as if I had captured its essence in a kind of logogram, an equation elevated to a mathematical formula, and perhaps it is due to this abbreviation and abstraction of memory that today I no longer know whether the city of Czernopol existed in reality, or merely in one of my dreams or drafts.

The large and repulsively desolate brick building of the asylum lay strictly isolated toward the front of large area that stretched back toward the open country and was enclosed by a wall taller than a man. I can still clearly feel our horror at discovering the razor-sharp bottle shards embedded in the mortar of the top of the wall, apparently to hinder people from climbing over. At the same time, the entrance gate was constantly open, and it was hard to guess which of the people loitering about and chattering the day away might be the gatekeeper. Later we learned that it was never shut at night, either. Why should it be? The dangerously insane couldn't be let outside without supervision, and the harmless crazy people who worked in the garden or helped out in the kitchen were said to be as used to their surroundings as pets and showed no inclination to leave. Of course one could only imagine what took place behind the securely barred windows of the cells inside. We had always contented ourselves with a glance through the gate at the sober, rectangular barrack with bricks of an unhealthy, almost feverish red that reminded us of the shades of scarlet in the raw meat at butcher shops. Still, there was something pleasantly dapper about the sharp contours beneath the flat tin roof, and when we looked further, to the plain rows of vegetable beds, we saw men dressed in the gray uniforms of the institution moving about—their figures made tiny by the perspective, just as the entire grounds seemed smaller and more distant, and all appeared neatly isolated, as if we were looking backwards through a telescope, or as if they had been painted with the dilettantish precision of so-called Sunday painters, as part of a daintified scene for a raree-show. It was exciting first to imagine Tildy entering the toylike simplicity of the enclosure with his unwavering tin-soldier march, shrinking as he stepped further away, a tiny particle of the whole, until he suddenly disappeared inside, swallowed up as if he had never belonged anywhere else but there and had only gone out for a brief walk, and then to picture Frau Lyubanarov pushing her way inside, bringing the hitherto still diorama into motion with her golden, swaying gait, causing the sleepwalking figures to dance around her peasant beauty so full of life, their faces tilted toward heaven, their eyes agape like seers, as they sought to follow and fix the odd thoughts and random insights that darted around their heads like magpies, occasionally responding with a blinding, empty laugh or a black storm of anger that was quickly sent off into the void.

Only in such a dreamlike roundelay could Frau Lyubanarov's honey eyes lose sight of Tildy as they did, drifting deeper and deeper into that magical world of unmoored connections that also spawned the frightful thing that occurred. According to what we were later told about what happened next, the repercussions were too momentous for us to content ourselves with a sober chronology of events. We needed to delve further into the tale of our sad childhood hero, in order to understand what forever remained unspoken.

Plain and simple, what happened next was that Frau Lyubanarov did not follow Tildy into the building of the asylum, but kept on going to the large vegetable garden in back. And in the furthest corner, by the glazed cold frames and the early beds strewn with straw, a man was working all by himself in a dilapidated toolshed beside the wall—the insane locksmith, the "poet" Karl Piehowicz.

Tildy soon finished all the formalities and went once more to his protégé, perhaps to say goodbye, perhaps to calm the man down and promise that he would continue to look after him. He didn't find his friend at the vegetable beds, and since he heard some horrible gurgling and animal-like groaning coming from the toolshed, he rushed over there. We were only given embarrassed hints at what he must have seen there, and it took a long time before we understood—or, more precisely, before we found the courage to understand. Tildy saw the gruesomely contorted face of the gentle poet, gazed at the cavity of his foaming mouth, the mouth that had spoken to him of beauty, in humility and shyness and stammering with the rays of illumination, and whose tongue was now unleashing gurgling cries from behind his bared teeth. Tildy looked at the pitiful insane man in his frenzy. And in his arms lay Frau Lyubanarov, in rapture.

No one was ever able to explain what Tildy had in mind when he left the asylum and headed into town. The notion espoused by some that he meant to find Professor Lyubanarov in order to inform him of what had happened and to remind him of his duty as a husband is highly unlikely, given Tildy's character. His motive for leaving will remain a riddle, a secret we didn't need to unlock because we believed to understand its sense.

There was also much speculation as to whether Tildy purposely picked up a weapon or whether he always carried one out of military habit. To what special end he might have put it in his pocket was never clarified.

In any event, he went straight back into town. By then it was late afternoon; the pigeon-blue veils of twilight were still meshed together in the bright sky. It was the hour of the daily promenade. In the former Herrengasse, now renamed Iancu Topor Avenue, the *patchkas* of flaneurs were gathering. Tildy strode past them, bolt-upright, his face expressionless, his eyes fixed steadfastly ahead, until he reached the Trocadero, whose arc lamp was already lit. There, among his disreputable pack of friends, stood young Herr Năstase.

All witnesses agree that not a word was spoken. Năstase supposedly neither smiled nor laughed; in fact, not a trace of added irony could be seen in his naturally haughty and mocking expression. He simply stared blankly at the man wearing the upright travel hat, as did all the others who were standing there idly. And Tildy, who was in the process of walking right past him just as he did the others, suddenly took the pistol from his pocket and shot him right in the face. Năstase collapsed on the spot.

A dismayed hue and cry followed several seconds of horrified paralysis, but then something happened that set off a flood of raucous laughter—laughter that even as laugh-craved a town as Czernopol hadn't heard for as long as anyone could remember, laughter that spread like the wind across the entire city and lasted for days, long after the rest of the story had played out: Năstase, who had been lying there, lifeless, started to move. With the help of his friends he pulled himself to his feet and stood there confused, wobbling on unsteady legs, blood streaming down his face and the back of his head, without knowing what had happened to him. He looked around at his friends who were propping him up, hoping for an answer. The bullet had hit the middle of his forehead one inch over the bridge of his nose and had exited through the back of his head and shattered the glass of the display featuring the lovely girls from the Trocadero, and nevertheless he was standing there, upright, and asking what had just happened.

The explanation was simple if unbelievable: Năstase had an unusually flat, backswept forehead. He also tended to carry his head at a proud height, tilted back on his neck. So the bullet had entered his forehead at such an acute angle that it glided along his skull without breaking any bones, just beneath his scalp, and came out several inches behind. At first glance it must have looked like it had passed through his brain without inflicting any damage. An anecdote as unheard-of as that made Czernopol howl with joy.

Several humorists were equally amused by the fact that in the general commotion no one thought to arrest Tildy. The surprised passersby, who had simply heard a gun go off but had no idea who had fired it, and who first directed their attention to the victim, would hardly have noticed the man marching calmly ahead. They must have expected to see someone running away, or already caught, and wondered where the man might be.

When a policeman was finally called to the scene, there was little he could do, first because of all the gawkers, whose backs formed an impenetrable wall and who had no idea what was going on themselves, and especially when the great laughing groan began to spread from the middle of the crowd. In short: Tildy went on his way unchallenged, past Kucharczyk's Café and Confectionary, on to the Ringplatz, until by the time his name was mentioned and people started searching for him, he had disappeared into the ever-more-tightly-woven veils of twilight.

It remains to be determined whether his encounter with Professor Lyubanarov was by design or mere chance. Uncle Sergei assured us that nothing would have been more natural, even for a man as disciplined as Tildy, than to need a drink after having fired a presumably fatal shot. With that in mind, he stopped at the seedy dive near the train station—where he may have been heading in order to take the evening train out of town. It's entirely likely that he knew the establishment from earlier days, and it was such a part of Lyubanarov's daily routine that it's highly unlikely their meeting was mere coincidence. But all of that is shrouded in mystery, as they say—and no new light was shed on the matter until Tildy was sitting with Lyubanarov and the story of his short and passionate love for Mititika Povarchuk began.

20

Love and Death of the Ermine

I AM AWARE that I am breaking all the rules of good storytelling by introducing a new character so late in my tale, especially insofar as she has an important role to play—that of my hero's only beloved. But as I said at the very beginning, those of us who want to tell you stories are really simply always talking about ourselves, and in such a way that the stories become *our stories*—which doesn't simply mean how we experienced them, but also the way they became ours in the telling. We were children when our heroes appeared to us as a vision, and we lost a wondrous world when we recognized its reality and when we realized it had died. And all we gained was the awareness of progressing one step closer to our own death. From that perspective, seen from the threshold of death, the figures that appeared last are the first: they cast their shadows over everything that went before—and so they were part of the story from the beginning, though invisible.

I am speaking about a girl Tildy met in his last night, in the dive near the train station. People say he loved her, and from all indications that was the case. We first heard about her after Tildy's death, and didn't lay eyes on her until much later. She was a streetwalker named Mititika Povarchuk. Around the train station she was known as "the American girl." I want to describe her briefly.

She was very young—younger than she seemed at first glance; and there was no doubt she was extraordinarily pretty, even beautiful. But the delicate features of her face, the tender, girlish curve of her cheeks, her dainty nose, her alarmingly large gray eyes set so far apart, her magnificent chin and delightfully cut mouth were covered with a mask of makeup so rigid and artificial it was frightening.

"I am not exaggerating," Herr Tarangolian once said to us, "when I say it took courage to look at her—in any case, more courage than is usually required to return a person's gaze. Any type of mask is a reduction, an abstraction of the human face into its most general and most impersonal, elemental form, simplified into four fixed points: the eyes, the nose, the mouth. It is the utmost banalization of the human countenance, and, like all banality, it gapes at us blankly—with the emptiness of death. And death was clearly showing through the mask of this young prostitute: because a mask is not something that conceals; on the contrary, it reveals, it lays bare—which is why a mask is so erotic. The root of its demonic power, however, lies in the shamelessness, the horror of the *lost face.* The mask is a vessel turned inside out that can accommodate countless faces, though for just an instant, with no one face ever able to achieve permanence. From what I know about Tildy's love—that is, from what I have managed to understand—it most likely consisted in fixing a face within the turned-out vessel of the mask, in other words, *creating a content from the form.* It must have been a heroic struggle against the horror that emerges from the banality of nothingness."

By the time we encountered the girl Mititika Povarchuk, she had entirely lost her face. Hers was a doll's mask, its beauty displaying all the cheapened and distorted features of some banal fashion, not one of them unique.

But when she met Tildy, her mask was presumably still full of the promise of countless faces. According to the fashion of the times, she kept her face framed between a nearly brimless hat that was pulled far down, and a high, flattering collar that reached up nearly to her cheeks. Her pot-shaped hat seemed to enlarge her head and shrink her body, and as a result her rigid mask of makeup gave her a childish appearance. She wore her hair short, with two curls under her hat clumsily and coyly teased across her temples. Her narrow shoulders were hunched together as if they were cold and seeking warmth in her collar, and her eyes seemed timid, lost, and distraught, appealingly bashful: her doll-like appearance concealed a nymph poised for flight. But then again she was all siren—dangerously and even triumphantly aware of her own allure. The timorous way she clasped her collar beneath her chin called to mind a woman attempting to cover her breasts when surprised naked. Her elbows angled sharply into her body, pressing her garment to her skin so that it offered no protection. Her dropped waistline hardly suited her knee-length skirt; it lengthened her torso and shortened her hips, and what was meant as a mincing step on her very high, thin heels was clumsy and ponderous despite all her svelte enthusiasm, and made her look like a wingless bird with a human head. On top of that, her hands were unusually ugly. They must have suffered frostbite at one time because they were bluish-red, with brittle, chapped skin and ruined cuticles, from which her long, painted nails grew out crooked, like claws. Her voice, too, was raw, cackling, and shrill. She was Ukrainian and hardly spoke more than a few words of any other language. The rough, thudding speech came as a surprise from her mouth, which despite all the makeup was still that of a young girl, so that at first she was difficult to understand.

Thus everything beautiful about this girl was offset by something ugly, and what was undeniably attractive—and that was limited to her figure—was also banal, because it was too much merely in vogue: she was too young, too poor, too uneducated to have a feel for quality. Her jewelry was tawdry and cheap. But it is an old theatrical insight that the best effect is achieved with the paltriest means, and I can only imagine that many women with everything elegant at their disposal except a brilliant sense of style must have secretly envied her, however much they may have disparaged her showy shoddiness.

People mockingly called her "the American girl," because she claimed to be the daughter of an elegant man who had been forced to emigrate to America on account of some scandalous love affair but had managed to make a fortune worth millions, which she would someday inherit. I never made the effort to discover how much truth, if any, there might be to that claim. Because among all the phantasms we paint on the cell walls of our existence in an apparent effort to expand them and break through to greater things, it is the image of a secret, highborn ancestor that vouches for the nobility of our own character. It is a metaphor, the most obvious interpretation and reinterpretation of our sense that we are of different blood than the masses, or even a pious representation of this, which aims to legitimize the feeling of special distinction through the grace of one's birth. If we still had gods, those among us with a need to feel extraordinary could claim divine ancestry.

I have imagined Tildy's meeting with this girl no less often or thoroughly than his path to the asylum, when he was followed by Frau Lyubanarov, and in some mysterious way the one never fails to strike me as a paraphrase of the other: two scenes from a ballet about the proximity of death in which the dancer-like figures of life and death have been reversed: the one scene consisting of constant motion, taking place within the empty nothingness of insane visions, against the translucent, petrified tumult of colors of the autumn countryside, culminating in the violence of animal-like copulation and a killing without death; and the other a motionless set piece, a study in forlornness—three figures sitting, stiff and ailing, amid the vulgar carnival of a seedy dive, while intense love pours forth from them in barbaric beams, like the jewel-studded halos of Byzantine saints.

The dive, which fate, in its merciless staging, had chosen as a backdrop for this final picture, was called the Établissement Mon Repos and was a holdover from Austrian times, frequented back then by the excessively bored lions of the garrison. Since those days, however, the place had turned shady and somewhat slimy. Apart from a regular clientele of pimps and smugglers, it hardly attracted anyone—at best a few traveling salesmen from the louse-ridden hourly hotels of the neighborhood, and stray packs of drunken students, as well as the paymasters, veterinarians, and staff sergeants of the new regiments, who brandished their sabers and rattled their spurs, boasting and roaring while playing at being officers.

Heralds of a new age had arrived in the grottoes of crude provincial merriment, and the grotesque twist of the Charleston challenged the supremacy of the waltz: rubber-limbed Negroes with large, raftlike feet—only their outlines moving stealthily in a world of reversed light as in a photographic negative, the tortoise-colored Moorish scalps merging with the nighttime umber, so that above the hard chalk-white of the high collars could be seen only the milky half-moon of teeth and the perforated full moons of eyes shimmering like the luminous numbers on a travel clock, and hands invisible when dangling from the sharply turned-back, flapping cuffs—then popping into view when they splayed across the silver sea-horse saxophones like spiders crawling through a shaft of moonlight. Amid the poisonously colored cocktails and liqueurs, against the self-important typeface of the yellowed police regulations pasted next to bouquets of garishly colorful paper flowers at the tarnished mirrors, in the deceptive light of the fly-specked milk glass lamps, above the cracked, faux-marble counter with the constantly dripping and oozing nickel taps, and among the shabby, matted plush of the seating booths, the dubious world of pugilists and flappers was revealed in all its seediness. But at the Établissement Mon Repos, along with the coarse clientele came something tangibly rustic. At the bar they had set up an iron grate for the snacks known as *zakuski*, something to bite into while drinking hard liquor. Braids of garlic and red peppers hung from the lamps, and the syncopated jangle squeezing out of the curved funnel of the gramophone was drowned in the coarse, throaty rumble of Romanian curses. The crude toughness of the godforsaken province was colliding with the victory parade of the *moderne*, and as an abandoned trading post is quickly reclaimed by the jungle, the ineradicable peasant merriment spread over the vestiges of former half-elegance. The only difference between the Établissement Mon Repos and the countless Jewish taverns and coachmen's inns of the disreputable neighborhoods was its shabbily pretentious name.

Yet nevertheless... later on, when I was a young man, I often visited the place in order to imagine Tildy's last night as vividly as I could, and on one of these occasions, over the door to the steps that led to the rooms upstairs that were rented by the hour, I discovered the picture of a hussar.

It was the photograph of the German crown prince wearing the uniform of the Danzig "Totenkopf" Hussars, a color print, evidently cut out of a journal and set in a cheap mahogany frame with no glass.

He sat his mount with his legs extended, with long thin tube boots casually stretched into the stirrups, with fully slackened reins. His horse was long-necked, with spidery legs as in the engraved portraits of earlier derby victors, idealized to the point of caricature: with its neck flexed to the point of overbent, and its barrel showing a shark-like taper, its small head reaching past the loose reins into the land-scape, saying nothing. The prince looked lost on this horse: aloof in the saddle in his Attila-cape, which was as festooned with knots and braids and tassels as a Turkish crescent—and, above all, his fur-trimmed collar, which seemed too tall and too tightly strapped below his chin, made him look like something between a gingerbread horse-man and an organ grinder's monkey. The prince's alarmingly narrow and overly long face was turned completely toward the viewer. From beneath his ponderously heavy fur cap, adorned with the pirate skull and crossbones, the prince's gaze was gentle and calflike: shy, inti-mate, tender and surprised, exactly as if he had emerged from the depths of a fairy tale or risen from the fabled waters of some unusual form of existence to appear in this strange world of humans—a child of the Merman and Mermaid Rushfoot, sticking his head out of the pond's reedy overgrowth, curious but hesitant, uncertain whether to dive back into the water or jump into the lap of the unfamiliar crea-ture suddenly standing before him, asking for love.

The enchanted aspect of this fairy-tale calf had a somewhat repug-nant effect that called to mind Professor Feuer's neck straining out of his Byronic collar—the sight of which once led Uncle Sergei to note that while people of other nations are moved by the sound of the songs they sing, the Germans are moved by *themselves singing.* The crown prince seemed silenced forever, as if by a spell, but there was something offensive about his desire to communicate in such a tender, familiar way, by jumping right into one's lap. It seemed like a betrayal of his princeliness; it suggested that he wasn't entirely without a self, that he wasn't one hundred percent *the Crown Prince*, that his unas-sailably superior surface could be marred by the impurity of being hu-man. As a result, even the ultimate expression of his princely character —his undeniable elegance—seemed oddly fake, becoming a gesture somewhere between escape and devotion, between the self-renunciation of pride and that of love, which clung to him like a kind of secret need. What was imploringly shy and vulnerable in his forget-me-not gaze seemed painfully intensified by the overly tall collar of janissary-like splendor, which seemed to crown all the braids that joined at the breast of the cape: he looked like a child in carnival costume who has been shaken out of the happy magic of the disguise by some brutal event.

Neither then nor today can I believe that it was mere coincidence that Tildy's last night and the love that made him *human* took place beneath this picture. The more I studied it, the more it seemed to be a vanishing point, the place where all the lines of my hero's story converged. And I studied it with a degree of thoroughness I had retained from my childhood. No matter how passionately serious and conscientiously we pursue our later occupations, nothing can compare to the patience—and therefore the evenhandedness—we show during childhood, in the raw process of assimilating the world. Childhood is pious in the true sense of the word, *because to be pious is to be patient while gaining awareness.* As children we refused to let go of what we observed until we had completely assimilated it. This was not a logical process but rather some kind of metachemical one: we grappled with what we saw, grappled with ourselves in our attempt to understand, we took the time to absorb what we observed, in an act of layered copying that left it intact and whole, but nonetheless dismantled it into its constituent elements. And so it remained deposited within us, in a different aggregate state, a kind of labile composition of molecules, until some stimulus—some related image, a sound, the tone of a similar voice—precipitated a kaleidoscopic cascade of corresponding images. It was always an act of *musing*, in the true sense of the word, when we observed something, focusing all our senses on the secret essence that all connections and all things possess.

With some pain I recognized in the photograph of the German crown prince our *hussar*, albeit distorted, caricatured to fairy-tale proportions, but for that reason eloquent—a revelation of his *essence.* I glimpsed once again the lost poetry of our childhood and realized what had brought about the loss: our defense against the despair that lies at the root of existence, a defense undertaken in the spirit of Czernopol, of the world, against the threat of the void. My eyes had begun to see, they had ceased dreaming in the presence of the dreamed; they recognized their vision as fantastical and now smiled at it with the envy of the impoverished, and opposed it with the weapon of the poor: irony.

I also saw that this impoverishment had been bequeathed to us along with what was German about our childhood dream—that peculiarly German fairy-tale quality, bewitched and enchanted, split between dream and nightmarish reality. Our reluctance to view Tildy as a German matched our unconscious struggle against what was German within ourselves. We were more deeply related than we wanted to admit to our comrades-in-arms, the caterpillars that exploded into fire butterflies, and we were closer than we would like to their self-destructive being, so full of despair. We had seen their other face in the hussar, and were forced to recognize it as the figment of a German fantasy, which was dashed not so much by the contemptuous reality of Czernopol but by the worldly-wise smile of Prefect Tarangolian.

The curtain of darkness that had fallen after Tildy's shooting of Năstase, and his subsequent disappearance into the twilight, now rises on a new scene, when his eyes meet the eyes of the streetwalker at the side of the drunken Professor Lyubanarov, in the smoky half-light of the Établissement Mon Repos. I never made the effort to find out what had driven him there. With the conscientiousness that for years bordered on an affliction, I gathered what information I could about his last night, I never thought to look for a reasonable explanation for that. The most obvious was that he followed Professor Lyubanarov to that place. But this—like all obvious things—was misleading. Where else could our hussar have met those eyes, and where else could he have met his death than here, under the picture that surrendered its *meaning* to me? He met her eyes in an unguarded moment—when they were observing him. He couldn't know that she was very short-sighted. The unfathomable enigma found in all eyes that are wide open and set far apart was magnified by the veil of her myopia, and that must have affected him as it did every other man who met her gaze directly. Between these eyes, the base of her nose seemed a little broad in relationship to the fine tip and the delicately flared nostrils—so that she looked short and childlike. The girl had turned her doll's face in the potlike hat toward Tildy, from the side, in a gesture of lazy curiosity born of boredom. She only understood Ukrainian, and although her attention was openly directed to the room and the men who were drinking and roaring, she made an effort not to appear impatient, out of a kind of professional courtesy, as long as she was afforded a place at the table of the enormous drunkard Lyubanarov, where she entertained herself attempting to decipher the effect of the professor's speeches—German interwoven with snippets of Latin quotes. The high collar of her coat was snuggled against her cheek, with its shabby yellowed bit of ermine fur. Her young girl's mouth, smeared with lipstick, was slightly open, in an expression of the gentle, almost tender irony with which one listens to the sound of boastful words in a foreign language.

Because Professor Lyubanarov was spouting languages she did not understand, in the unmistakable, pathetically high-flown speech of the chronically inebriated. The diatribe of habitual drunkenness flowed from his trembling mouth, punctuated by facial twitches and wild fits of laughter, which he slurped back in with rattling sobs; by visionary gestures; by grand, overarching gesticulations and sudden moments of glaze-eyed stupefaction. Full of torment and desire, he delivered his confession, replete with self-accusation and self-humiliation, with the embedded rage, scorn, megalomania, and orphic tones—the nonsense and profundity of a blind seer, who gropes through the purplish surge of dissolved connections and suddenly uncovers a brilliant insight for which he first finds wondrous words that then dissipate in confused speech. He had taken hold of Tildy's arm and gripped it tightly as he spoke with manic, desperate urgency:

"... Are you the man I think you are? Can you understand me? If you are, then you're bound to understand... *Omnes, unde amor iste, rogant, tibi? Venit Apollo: Galle, quid insanis? inquit: tua cura Lycoris, perque nives alium perque horrida castra secuta est... Ecquis erit modus? inquit...* And listen to this: *Amor non talia curat. Nec lacrimis crudelis Amor*—Are you listening?—*nec lacrimis crudelis Amor saturantur.* So, despise me! All of you! Look down on me! Who can claim to understand me? Virgil—the great Virgil! Did you even comprehend the words? *All ask: 'Whence this love of yours?' Apollo came. 'Gallus,' he said, 'what madness this? Your sweetheart Lycoris has followed another amid snows and amid rugged camps. Will there be no end?'* ... To which he replied: 'Love recks naught of this.' You hear that? *Love recks naught of this: neither is cruel Love sated with tears.*" He was shaken by more sobbing. "I know, I know, I am despicable, the most despicable of the despicable. I am the town cuckold. I am not Gallus, you hear, and she is not Lycoris—she is a whore." He laughed. "*As soon as his wife perceived that her husband was asleep, this august harlot,* ha-ha!—august harlot!—*was shameless enough to prefer a common mat to the imperial couch. Assuming a night-cowl, and attended by a single maid, she issued forth; then, having concealed her raven locks under a light-colored peruque, she took her place in a brothel reeking with long-used coverlets. Entering an empty cell reserved for herself, she there took her stand, under the feigned name of Lycisca, her nipples bare and gilded, and exposed to view the womb. Here she graciously received all comers, asking from each his fee; and when at length the keeper dismissed the rest, she remained to the very last before closing her cell, and with passion still raging hot within her went sorrowfully away. Then, exhausted but unsatisfied, with soiled cheeks, and begrimed with the smoke of lamps, she took back to the imperial pillow all the odors of the stews* ... O help me, help me in my shame! But who will show compassion? Perhaps yourself? Didn't you have her as well? Tell me, haven't you had her as well—ha-ha! You don't let yourself be taken aback, sir, my compliments! You don't let yourself be baffled. Allow me to introduce myself: Dr. Lyubanarov, formerly professor at the University of Sofia. It is my habit to baffle the students, in order to catch their ignorance off guard—except for the one who answers immediately: Book Two, Second Satire of Decimus Junius Juvenalis, the Martial of the Eloquent, *facundus,* verses two hundred sixteen to two hundred thirty-two ... It is a satire, sir. Life plays out in satires ... But you, sir, let us speak of you—*let us speak of pride.* A pride such as yours, does it not come from the fact that you despise yourself every moment you are not proving yourself? But what do you know about that, sir! This dog with his tail cut off: people point at him, ridicule him, and he is ashamed to show himself, and not ashamed that he is ashamed... The core of his character remains undestroyed—you know what I mean—the core of the character of this dog... Base creatures bow to higher ones and exact their revenge as best they can... But you, my brother? Come closer, I want to tell this to you, because you are my brother-in-law... I don't have the honor of knowing you, sir, except from seeing you and hearing about you and I know that you are my brother-in-law—I want to tell this to you: that, too, is a satire, an indirect and droll satire, a satire meant for laughing. The world is made of laughter: the angels laugh at humans; the archangels laugh at the angels; and God laughs at everything... He even laughs at the anguish that stems from your pride just as he laughs at the anguish that stems from my love. *Omnia vincit amor; et nos cedamus amori*... And God laughs at that. She fornicates with the whole city—they're all whores—*trahit sua quemque voluptas*—and He laughs. But you do not! You refuse to change your expression. You lack those two common lines that laughter cuts on either side of the mouth—no, not laughter, nature cuts them there, because she is ashamed, because she wants to place parentheses around the meanness of the human face... But not you. You could be beautiful, you know that? But you are not beautiful, Mr. Brother-in-law, you do not have a face; you have pasted a decal above your collar and in back of that, where everyone else, all the base ones, have a soul that bleeds, you have one that we see sweating... Is that why you came here? Did you want to see if the mongrels still step out of your way, Herr Major? Permit me to introduce myself, I am your brother-in-law. You were so generous as to risk your life for the sake of my honor, we are brothers—but it is the brotherhood of Cain and Abel. Did you ever think how much your generosity would drag me through the mud? Now everyone knows, now the mongrels on the street step out of *my* way. But see: I laugh. I am humiliated, and therefore I can laugh. I laugh, you see—I am a god! I am a god... I am a god..."

The girl at his side had turned to Tildy, her mouth hinting at an ironic, patient female smile. He was completely unknown to her; she knew nothing about him, and particularly nothing of his relationship to Lyubanarov, and she hadn't understood a single word of what the professor had been saying, although she was well acquainted with his monologues. Nor did she notice any dismay in Tildy's face, only that he seemed extremely exhausted, and she felt a mocking pity for the unruffled patience with which he withstood the pathetic surge of words, the terrible boredom, that—as she knew from experience—drunken diatribes unleash. But when her shortsighted eyes brought his image into sharper focus, she observed that beneath the very properly trimmed black mustache his mouth was completely helpless—the mouth of someone who has delivered himself up to the mercy of others. Nonetheless, his bearing remained that of a polite listener; his face showed no sign of suffering. She saw that his short sideburns had turned gray, and her half smile gave way to a soft, thoughtful expression. She found herself facing a man of better background and breeding than she had ever encountered. This was an elegance she did not know but immediately sensed and understood. And like everyone endowed with a greater sensitivity and a quicker mind—no matter what they might call, or to what they might attribute, such dubious advantages—she felt a kinship with the elegance. The fable of her better birth and future riches had given her a keen sense of human qualities; it made no difference where it came from, whether her mother had fed her the lie in desperation, spinning the promise of a bright future for her own consolation, thinking that the hope it would awaken would become her own; or whether people had made it up out of scorn, to ridicule her for being different, for being so maladroit and unskilled when it came to everyday life, the profane accomplishments at which those of more robust constitution so excel. She was still close enough to being a child that the first impression she gave was of a highly sensitive, quickly unsettled creature, happily dreaming away—an easy target for the hate of petty people. The aura of this childhood had made her oblivious to the absolute scorn with which people called her "the American girl," poking fun at her background; she accepted the moniker as a distinction. She was entirely spared from reflection on her current existence. She lived in the future, the future that had been promised to her. She was not fallen. The indescribably shabby elegance of the Établissement Mon Repos still represented the big wide world to her, even though she realized there was another, larger and more luxurious, one. But that's exactly what was headed her way, exactly what she was expecting here. It was natural for her to give herself to the men; it suited her playful, feline coquetry and her great tenderness, and the fact that she received money for doing so caused her even less concern. Now and then she referred to it as her "profession"—with the earnest sincerity of a child absorbed in play—and she kept an account of all her income and obligations. Despite all these traits that might be called infantile or backward, however, she possessed a deep femininity, which found its most visible expression in her brilliant sense of fashion, and which ran through her entire being. When Tildy looked up and their gazes met, it was this sense that allowed her to *recognize* who he was, and that recognition was written clearly in her eyes.

He looked through the mask of cheap makeup and saw her face, saw the beauty of a young woman not only in the tenderness and delicacy of her features, but in the expression of deep, intimate connection with the world, arising from her gentle breathing, the intimations and experiences of her body, the ancient innate wisdom of her senses. Later he would discover other faces in her, faces that would cause him torment—but at this moment he was delighted by what he was seeing. Because he looked into her eyes and *recognized* her as well. Through the deeply mysterious veil of her shortsighted eyes he believed he saw *her*, the core and substance of her unsettled, unfathomable being, her very identity—that *I* that sees itself within the conscious and unconscious interplay of the psyche as something fixed and constant. That was what he believed he loved when his emotion surged in her direction, and he realized that he loved her when the echo of her presumed answer brought first the happiness, and then the first sharp pain of disappointment. And I must say: he behaved heroically. He wouldn't have been Tildy, the knight, Widow Morar's armored angel, if he hadn't shown such extreme and patient resolve to love her core and substance, and not the promise of one of her fleeting faces. The report I received of the last horrible scene of that night, when he slapped her, has been corroborated, and therefore I know for sure that he must have expended whatever energy he had left, his last resistance, against the horrors of love. He was clearly not an extraordinary human being, certainly not the hero that our childish fantasy had wished him to be.

He was obsessed with duty to the point of being obstinate, a pedant with monomaniacal traits—a true oddball, if you will. His one great virtue was something beyond his own control; it was the legacy of the world he came from, a vanished world. In Czernopol they would have said he was on the slow side, someone who has a hard time grasping the fact that times change. He was so slow at understanding this that he had to die: there was no other choice except to understand. Assailed from the outside, his surface was invulnerable. It had remained unscathed up to this last night, despite all he had been through. It shattered only when tainted by his humanity. It shattered with his love, his love that was bound to be his downfall, since love is only possible in a world of forms. Because he was prepared to love something without a form, he gave himself away. As a character determined to carry every decision to the extreme, he therefore chose to die.

Professor Lyubanarov ranted on, weaving the purple mists of his desperate intoxication into language. Tildy offered the girl a glass of wine. She declined: she never drank. Then she asked, with timid courage, whether she might have an orange. Tildy didn't understand right away. His Ukrainian was weak; he only spoke as much as any officer needed to know in order to make himself understood to the motley soldiers under his command, which invariably included some Ukrainians. She pointed to a basket of oranges on the counter, and when Tildy immediately gave his consent, she called to the proprietor to bring her one. The innkeeper nonchalantly grabbed the closest one, set it on a plate and nodded to the greasy waiter to take it to her. At that point Tildy's innate aversion to the baseness of the establishment broke out. He lashed out at the proprietor, ordering him to offer her the entire basket and let her choose for herself. The waiter placed the basket on the table in front of the girl.

She clapped her hands together in delight. "Are they all for me?" she asked. Tildy had no choice but to nod to her, noting that he was rather moved by the unconventional and rather awkward gesture he had resorted to in his temporary embarrassment at her naïve question. He bit his lip. But he immediately found his emotion validated. She sat there a while, her hands clasped beneath her chin as if at worship, in enraptured study of the basket filled with bright balls of fruit, picked one up and weighed it in her hand, her fingers touching the peel almost with awe, stroking the pored surface, with its sparkling, oily sheen. Then she carefully returned it and arranged the others around it, once more sating her eyes with the sheer abundance. Her performance seemed exaggerated; he couldn't tell if these were mere antics, if her coquettishness wasn't meant to be deeply ironic, if she wasn't playing some refined game to accentuate the contrast between her fashionable getup and her evident childishness. But her delight was so genuine that he realized he might be underestimating her in two equally dangerous ways, and the potential of danger put him on guard while heightening his feeling of manliness, which made him happy. For this he was grateful to her, and insofar as he found himself willing to accept both challenges, he immediately respected her as his worthy opponent. He no longer needed to be ashamed of his sentimental impulse; it was part of a legitimate cause: a contest, a duel. Apart from igniting his emotions, which had already turned somewhat brittle, she had provoked his desire to prove himself, to perform a knightly task. From that point on he followed her game with the attention of a fencer *under assault*, and sensed that the attack was directed immediately at him, and his delight was ignited by her own. Once again she picked up one of the bright spheres and gave him a questioning look. And once again he nodded, smiling in the bargain. And she responded to his smile as if she were accepting a challenge: with one barbaric, cruel motion she sank her fingernails into the thick peel, pulling and tearing it off in huge furry scraps, oblivious to any possible damage to the fruit. Her fingers were dripping with oil and juice as she separated the wedges; she bored deep inside the sopping flesh to dig out the seeds, picking it apart into little pieces. But she didn't eat any. In a fit of nervous restlessness, a kind of disturbed compulsion for order, she arranged the sections along the edge of the plate, around the growing pile of discarded peels. She tore apart three or four of the fruits in the same barbaric way, piling the pieces on the plate, and finally, when the mountain of ruins threatened to collapse, she took them and stuffed them alternately into Tildy's mouth and into the mouth of Professor Lyubanarov, who was blindly driveling away.

Tildy parried when with dripping claws she unexpectedly shoved the torn-up piece of orange under his mustache. But her wild, almost primal gesture of maternal feeding was overpowering; against his will, he opened his lips to accept the first piece and then offered only weak resistance to the next one, and the next after that. She seemed to find more pleasure in taking care of Professor Lyubanarov, whose stream of words had suddenly been halted and who with a glassy gaze swallowed whatever was shoved into his mouth. All the while her bearing was suspiciously serious. Tildy had no sense for how hideously ridiculous the whole scene was. The fact that he, too, had become her victim only sharpened his tense vigilance. He realized that he had lost the first round, but was unable to explain how; the contest did not follow any of the rules he had expected. While inclined to think himself duped, led on, and made a fool of—a suspicion that gnawed at him, because it was unchivalrous and would have turned his "cause" into a farce, he was immediately ashamed of his mistrust. Because after the girl had fed the last piece to Lyubanarov, she let her hands—dirty and sticky as they were—sink into her lap, and stared at the mountain of discarded peels, thin and lost before the picture of senseless waste like a sorrowful child, and this was no pose. A deep sympathy for her poverty, her youth, her bad breeding, and the loneliness of her existence overcame him, as strongly as a sense of guilt. She stared helplessly at her hands, and he handed her his handkerchief. It was made of fine batiste, large and unadorned, and she touched it with the same sensual rapture she had displayed while touching the fruit. Then she held it to her mouth, closing her eyes, and inhaled its pure scent.

"I love you," she said, as if in jubilation. She stood up, letting her light coat slide off her shoulders. She was wearing a sleeveless dress of a very plain cut, which despite its cheapness seemed on her as elegant as a chiton on a young Greek woman. She came mincing over to him on her high heels, and sat down in his lap, with such a natural lack of inhibition that he did not resist. He let her drape her bare arms around him and snuggle her face against his, allowed her to kiss him, cover his forehead and cheeks with a shower of tender fleeting kisses like the warm droplets of a fine spring rain. Her display of affection showed a brilliant gift for avoiding routine opening gestures; she was able to elicit desire that went beyond the merely immediate and touched on the sublime; she knew how to draw things out into an ongoing play that was at once innocent and sinful. She touched the tip of his nose with her own and opened her eyes very close to his, and he gazed into her large, fixed eyes, ringed by the dark makeup, and saw the mask of death and yielded to the temptation of that ultimate sinking-away, that final act of relief, of becoming a child in the lap of nonexistence. And she tossed her head back and took a deep breath and laughed a mute, enraptured laugh, then nuzzled her temples against his mouth, and rocked her head as if falling into a happy, restorative slumber. Overwhelmed by this tenderness, Tildy found himself touching her with a sensual delight he had never known, as his hand caressed the beautiful curve of her head, clasped her neck with a warm, firm grip, and guided her blissful child's head close to him. A dark feeling of happiness engulfed him, clouded by an inexpressible sadness that was now finally free of all constraint.

Professor Lyubanarov again took hold of his arm. "No," he said, with glazed eyes, as if making a great mystic proclamation, "the curs no longer step aside for you, they rub their mangy fur against you, they lick your boots—soon they will bite you, brother-in-law. And yet you have also gained something: now the butterflies are alighting on you . . ."

And then Tildy sensed the hornet-flicker of a uniform hovering over the head of the girl. He looked up. Standing in front of him was a sergeant from his former squadron, who had been in the service for years: vulgar, mustachioed, brutal, his eyes empty and mean. "You will permit me a dance with the lady," he said in a voice dripping with scorn. And before Tildy could reply she had jumped up and was reclining in the arm of the mercenary, playing the same brilliant game of erotic delay, as she danced with him in the sliding, choppy rhythm of the tango—except her movements were more undisguised, blatantly routine, with a hypocritical coldness that did not lessen her pleasure, but on the contrary appeared to arouse it.

Tildy felt the raw, deadly sharp stab of disappointment and averted his gaze, eager not to meet the eyes of the brute in whose arms she was cradled. His courage commanded otherwise, to meet each and every scornful glance with his unruffled "English" countenance. He found himself once again deceived, because the sergeant no longer cared about Tildy but was simply staring at the girl, crudely lusting into her eyes. Nor did she pay Tildy any notice.

The tango seemed to go on forever. Its flat musical motif kept curling out of the monotony of rhythmic thrusts and shoves, twining into a primitive arabesque and tapering off with no real resolution into a banal loop of endless repeats. Professor Lyubanarov let his head droop from his pulled-in neck like a befuddled steer. "Bear it, brother-in-law," he croaked. "Here all pride has an end. I know all too well, believe me." He shook Tildy's arm vigorously—"Believe me," he shouted, "I know the arrogance that poisons the ear with phrases like 'even though I've treated you as my equal you're still far from being my equal.'" He sobbed once again, the tears running down his spongy cheeks. "Words! Their poison eats away the heart like the eagle gnawing on Prometheus's liver. But they don't help you in the least. Not at all. *If you are honestly uxorious, and devoted to one woman, then bow your head and submit your neck to the yoke. Never will you find a woman who spares the man who loves her; for though she be herself aflame, she delights to torment and plunder him*... Nothing will help you, and least of all words, words, words! *Subter caecum vulnes habes sed lato balteus auro praetegit ut mavis da verba et decipe nervos si potes*... Mere words, once again! *Admovit iam bruma foco te Basse Sabino iamne lyra et tetrico vivunt tibi pectine chordae mire opifex numeris veterum primordia vocum atque marem strepitum fidis intendisse Latinae*... Yes, soon the winter frost will coax us to the Sabine fireside—the Sabine fireside we do not possess... the winter frost... The world, I tell you—are you listening to me? You don't wish to hear what I'm saying, brother—you don't want to hear me in your hurt pride, sir, but nonetheless I am offering you a great and deep truth: the world, dear sir, is dark, wet, and windy—just like an old man's ass—yes that is a great—deep—wisdom."

Tildy was sitting, unmoved, when the girl came back. He did not look up when she picked up an orange and peeled and ate it; he saw only the barbaric motions of her clawlike hands, now less hasty, and he surmised that her face was as calm as he wished his own were. Then he rediscovered the same groping humility in her hands, and against his will he followed the one that was lifting the torn pieces of orange to her mouth, and he saw how she kept her eyes closed and chewed with an expression of inner gratitude, how she swallowed as if exhausted, gulping down that first, longed-for draught. He shuddered at the terrifying notion that she must have known or would yet know true hunger. At once, all thought of himself, all mistrust, all caution, all hesitation to become involved, was erased. He knew he had been called to protect her and save her from her dirty existence. He was flooded with self-confidence: for the first time in his life he felt how powerful he could be. He again sensed a deceptive amplification of his capacity to feel, and transferred his gratitude onto her, and as she faced him once again full-on, he sensed that her gaze was now more probing, and he believed that he saw in her eyes a tentative hope responding to the certainty that he was pouring into her.

"... In fact, brother-in-law, we never truly love the other," Professor Lyubanarov intoned, "but merely the different world he represents. Each of us wants to break out of our self and join with the other, but we never arrive, never. We are prisoners—do you hear, sir? prisoners—and we never even come close to the border of that unknown world we love with such yearning, we bounce back off its walls as an echo, and that is what we love, as a report from the other side: *our beautiful echo.* What do we see in our beloved? Does she really exist—does she? *A thing is not seen because it is visible, but conversely, visible because it is seen; nor is a thing led because it is in the state of being led, or carried because it is in the state of being carried, but the converse of this. And now, Euthyphro, is my meaning intelligible.* Do you understand, brother-in-law? *Neither does it suffer because it is in a state of suffering, but it is in a state of suffering because it suffers. Do you not agree?*" He shook Tildy by the arm. "*Do you not agree, Euthyphro? And is not that which is loved in some state either of becoming or suffering?* But what do you know about that, you philistines? See how I weep! Ha-ha-ha!" He laughed the crazed, empty pathetic laugh of the great tragedian. "I shed my tears out of cunning. *Lacrimae prosunt. Lacrimis adamanta movebis. Fac madidas videat, si potes, illa genas. Si lacrimae—neque enim veniunt in tempore semper—deficient, uda lumina tange manu.* Ha-ha-ha!" In one large gesture he wiped the table clean, sending the bottle and the basket of oranges tumbling to the floor and shattering the glasses. The greasy waiter came and picked up the fruits and shards of glass. Lyubanarov's heavy head sank onto the table. Just as earlier the girl had nuzzled her head against Tildy's, he now rolled his back and forth on the besmirched tabletop and repeated: "*Quid faciam? Monitis sum minor ipse meis. Quid faciam! Quid faciam . . .*" until his murmuring stopped and he fell asleep.

When the sergeant returned to ask the girl for another dance, Tildy placed his hand firmly on her arm and looked at the other with such authority that the man automatically clicked his heels together and pulled his shoulders together, just as his face filled with a dark-red rage. Meanwhile the girl withdrew her arm from Tildy's grasp and rose from the table. "What do you want?" she said, in her ugliest voice. "It's my profession."

She stepped, erect and resolute, up to the sergeant, who put his arm around her. After only dancing a few measures, he said something to her. Then they disappeared through the door to the stairs that led to the rooms on the second floor.

Tildy found himself driven to a desperate act of rumination. Here people fenced by rules he didn't know. He waved the waiter over and asked irritably what apart from bad wine there was to drink, and ordered a bottle of cognac. Following the time-honored custom of the officers' casino, he filled and drained his glass in one motion, several times in a row. With a dull sense of gratification, he felt the alcohol entering his blood and making his limbs heavy; this gave him the illusion that his spirit was being lightened. The delayed reactions of his nerves led him to believe he had gained some perspective. He followed this process with a kind of schadenfreude, a rage directed against himself. Once he had sufficiently numbed the wound within, he set out on his daring feat of thinking.

Yes, here people fenced according to rules he didn't know; what's more, it was clear that no one knew the rules apart from the person called on. Consequently there were no rules. In the end it was a duel in the dark, even if only figuratively—it was Tildy's misfortune that it was only figurative, because had it been real, he could have stood up to his opponent, even if it meant resorting to the same underhanded tricks: a duel in the dark with all conceivable weapons, tooth and claw. But even this image was false; nothing could convey how helpless he was against feints and thrusts like these. And yet he felt an ungrounded conviction, an inner certainty, that there were certain rules, and that this contest was chivalrous like no other, because it posed the most difficult challenge to his knightliness. He could have made it easy for himself and despised the girl. But he wasn't capable of despising her. Because he loved her. Not that his pride would have permitted him to love what he secretly despised. But it forbade him to despise what he loved. And he loved her because he could not despise her.

He tried to put a temporary halt to his thoughts. He was confused by what was coming out; it bordered on wordplay, on the tangled platonic drivel he had just heard from the drunkard Lyubanarov. He, Tildy, had a deep mistrust of wordplay, which came alarmingly close to wittiness—that is to say, it wasn't pure, wasn't fair. Wordplay was clever, analytic. He wasn't used to analyzing. He was principally opposed to anatomizing a matter, because matters pressed for decisions. Dissecting them lessened their true weight. He was no lawyer. It was not his profession to talk things to death, but to face them. Astonishing as it might be, he loved this girl, and it was equally amazing how and why and in what a short time that had happened. Something inside him had called on him to love her, something like an order. But ours is not to reason why: orders are meant to be obeyed without grumbling. Nor did he have any cause to do so. He saw her face. If he closed his eyes, he saw her face before him, the beauty of a young woman, a beauty fashioned not only by the tenderness and delicacy of her features, but also by the grace of a deep-seated connection with the world—here again a raw pain sundered his thoughts, drowning them in a sharp, dark anguish. But even despite that pain, her face emerged unscathed, and her eyes focused on him. Never would he be able to extinguish this grace that was indelibly stamped onto his innermost being, the beguiling charm of this face. Its imprint would cover and erase any other face he might peer into. There were no words to say what lent it this power. It was the reflection of a creature he loved, or rather of that creature's substance and core. Because even if she were unstable, labile, one moment brimming with kindness, the next inexplicably cruel, even if she didn't know herself and was a plaything of demonic drives—indeed, even if her face itself were merely the mask of some crafty quick-change artist—he knew that it contained a core and a substance fashioned from the same material as his own.

So it was the essence of the face that made the mask, and not merely its surface. Any discussion about its expression was simply a sham. Everything that Lyubanarov had spoken was nonsense; he was drunk, and didn't himself believe in what he was saying. Of course there was no way to reach the core of the creature we love that does not pass through the creature. And she places herself between this core and us, and takes us prisoner. Whoever does not wish to suffer as a prisoner must love his prison. Love the forms that hold us captive, the forms that lead us to surrender... Tildy recoiled from the word. He was a hussar, and a hussar does not take surrender lightly. But he realized that he, too, had become ensnared in a game of words. *Love the forms that hold us captive*—that was an unambiguous statement, let's forego everything else. So, love the creature that conceals her own substance and core. Love the *creatures*—all the unstable forms that merely signify the unrelieved torment of the core from which they spring. Did he not even love her ugly, spoiled hands, her barbaric movements, the fuzzy hair on her forearms that bespoke a low origin? It wasn't that he forgave her faults and flaws because he loved her; it was precisely these faults and flaws that he loved, because *they revealed her to him,* they *gave her away.* He didn't love her *despite everything,* but simply because she was. He loved what she was and the way she was. Did he therefore also have to love what she called her "profession"? No, rather the manner in which she practiced it. He loved the courage with which she acknowledged it.

The simple fact that she spoke of it as *her profession* was beautiful, it elevated her above the despicable activity. And exactly what was so despicable about this profession? Any more than, say, that of the professional murderer—the soldier—so clearly marked by the garb known as his "dress of honor"? It was a question of perspective, of point of view. To be sure, he, Tildy, was still ready to exact blood for the slightest sign of contempt for his profession, and he hoped, in fact he was certain, that he was prepared to stand up for hers as well. He now realized that his attempt to deprive her of the decision whether to follow the other man or not was foolish and less than chivalrous, and he believed he would have had less respect for her, seen her as less than equal, had she stayed when he wanted to force her to do so. It was her *profession* to follow men, and thus also her *duty* to do so. Her *honor* forbade her to stay. The ferocity with which she had retracted her arm from his grip when he wanted to hold her, matched what he would have done had she attempted to keep him from performing the *duty* that his *honor* commanded. He loved her for this toughness. She was his equal.

When she returned he stood up, as was his custom before a lady. She didn't understand, and gave him a frightened, hostile look, but once she realized he had risen out of respect, she sat down, placed her hands in her lap, assumed the same lost expression she had shown in front of the extravagant waste of the plate full of shredded orange peels, and said: "Forgive me. I won't do it again."

Professor Lyubanarov raised his head and uttered a malicious, soundless laugh, as if he hadn't slept a moment and had followed every vicious and moving detail of the grotesque proceedings, while discerning all of Tildy's reflections. "*Docta, quid ad magicas, Erato, deverteris artes?*" he said, full of scorn. "What for? Don't they believe you otherwise?"

"Whatever you do," Tildy said to the girl, "won't change anything between us. Don't be afraid."

"I know," she said. "We understand each other *po dusham*—through our souls."

Professor Lyubanarov grabbed the bottle of cognac and hurled it at the mirror above the counter. The glass shattered. The proprietor came to the table, spewing curses at Lyubanarov. Tildy curtly told him to bring a new bottle. The proprietor sized him up with an impudent glare. "Will you pay me for the mirror?"

"Bring the bottle," said Tildy.

"We will be rich!" said the girl. "We will be happy. I love you."

"I love you," said Tildy. "Don't be afraid."

She shook her head. "If you love me I'm not afraid of anything." She offered him her hand. Tildy took it, clasped it, and held it in his own.

"I saw a fur coat," said the girl. "I wanted to buy it, but it's very expensive. Do you want to give it to me?"

"I will give you everything I have, and do everything in my power to give you what you desire."

"We will be rich," said the girl, happy.

"We will not be rich. But that doesn't matter. Don't be afraid."

"You are noble," she said, smiling, "and therefore you are rich."

The proprietor came with a fresh bottle, followed by the waiter. "First pay the bill," he said. "I'm not bringing you anything until you've paid for the mirror and everything you've eaten and drunk."

"Where is the bill?" asked Tildy.

"In my head," said the proprietor. "Do you know what that mirror cost? And two bottles of French cognac? And a basket of oranges, at this time of year? You owe me"— and he named a fantastical sum.

"I don't have that much money on me," said Tildy. "I'll give it to you tomorrow."

"He'll give it to me tomorrow," the proprietor said to the waiter. "Do you hear that, Aurel? He doesn't have that much on him. You don't have a penny, sir, either on your person or anywhere else where you might fetch it to bring me tomorrow. You are that major who was booted from the cavalry regiment, and evicted from your own house. Your creditors are combing the town for you. You are well known here, sir. There are people in this Établissement who know everything about you. You act like some kind of boyar, and meanwhile you don't have a penny to your name, just a sack full of debts."

Tildy took his signet ring off his finger. "Take this ring as a deposit."

"He's a good one, isn't he, Aurel!" the proprietor turned to the waiter. "Making deals like his father-in-law, that old crook who bankrupted half the city. Look at what he wants to give us on account. You call this a ring? It's so worn down you can practically see through it. You can find a stone like that in any brook. Is this a joke, sir?"

"What do you demand of me?" asked Tildy.

"What do we demand of him—just listen to that, Aurel! We demand that you pay your bill. No more and no less. And now get on with it if you please."

The sergeant stepped up and shoved his broad, smirking face between the waiter and the proprietor. "If I pay your tab, *Herr Major*, may I take your lady upstairs once again?"

Tildy leapt to his feet.

"Watch yourself!" the proprietor shouted, brandishing the bottle like a club. "If you make one move we'll turn you into a cripple. There are three of us right here and even more nearby, do you hear? And every single person in my Établissement would relish the opportunity to beat your skull in. So, on top of everything else he wants to start a fight!"

"Let him, Mihai," said the sergeant. "Let him try. I'm enough of a match for him. By far!"

The girl, Mititika, stood up. "Come," she said to the sergeant. Up to then the sergeant had been hunched forward, with his arms dangling like an orangutan; now he straightened up triumphantly. "Good!" he said. They went off.

"I will give you half an hour," the proprietor said to Tildy, "to decide what to do."

"Give me something to drink!" roared Professor Lyubanarov. "Something to drink, you dogs!"

"Shut your drunken mouth," the proprietor yelled. "Aurel, show him the door."

With remarkable agility and strength the waiter grabbed the enormous man by the collar, pulled him to his feet, and shoved him, staggering, out the door.

"You see, we don't let anyone play jokes on us," the proprietor said to Tildy. "So..."

Tildy reached in his pocket and gripped the pistol. "Put down that bottle of cognac," he said. "And open it."

The proprietor lost his composure. "I'm warning you, sir," he said. "We don't let people jest with us."

"I said—put down the bottle and open it. And give me back my ring."

"Fine," said the other. "As you wish. The police will be here in half an hour. As you wish."

The door of the Établissement flew open with a crash and Professor Lyubanarov tumbled in. "Give me a drink!" he bellowed, tossing a handful of coins and banknotes into the room. "Here you have it, the bread of my children—but give me something to drink!" He stumbled over to the proprietor. "What's got into you, you cesspool? All of a sudden you're afraid. Of me! You're afraid of me! But I don't intend to do anything to you, little one. I never lay a hand on the pupils. *Quem taurum metuis, vitulum mulcere solebas*—there's no need to be afraid." He brushed him aside with a swipe of his hand, stepped toward Tildy, and collapsed massively on the chair next to the major. "I'm drinking away the bread of my children, you hear, the bread of your little hungry nieces. Despise me for that, spit in my face, I can see from your cold expression that I'm too low even for that, too inconsequential... But I, too, even I, once lived in a glorious city—a city beautiful and orderly as you wish to see erected around you—and it came to an end just like yours, her glorious inhabitants rotted and dead, sintered corpses with gaping mouths stuffed with ashes, nothing left but a few mucky bits of wall—and on it goes, the swarm of base peoples, the rich fall to ruin, temples crumble to dust, while the mongrel race endures, building their filthy huts from the wrecked marble columns of the sun gods, and whoring on the graves of the poets whose mouths were blessed by the sun... And we realize that we, too, belong to the mongrels, and yet we dare to emulate the children of the sun, appropriating their gestures as if they could become our own, presuming upon what they designed; if they were not mute shadows in the realm of Orcus, the world would shatter from the laughter we elicit from them. But I can hear it, you know, I hear it when I am drunk, because their laughter causes the bell of my intoxication to reverberate as though someone were furiously ringing the clapper, crushing me into that which I truly am—a nothing, a worm, one of any million swarming maggots that have been feeding off the cold golden body of mankind's one-time glory for two thousand years, and have consumed it entirely down to a few measly remains. The same celestial bodies that stand above it stand over us, the same riddles of the world, the same eternal questions, the same torments, multiplied by one thing only: namely, by the fact that our mouths have not been loaned the honey of speech so that we might call them by names of our own invention. Apes learned to speak and jabber away in countless tongues. And behold: they love each other, they caress each other, they pick fleas from each other's behinds and bite them in two, they sling their arms around each other and hold each other tight, their eyes filled with the anguish of loneliness, the primal mother fear that sets them in a frenzy so that they bite each other when they couple. Because love is guilt, it promises salvation and then swindles us out of it—Eros the charlatan, the quack, the barker, the thief, the con artist—Eros laughs! Laughs at the apes! People say that in India, the apes even build cities—are you listening, brother?—the city you wish to envision around you, the apes will build for you in India, yes . . . That is a deep thought, understand what I'm saying, better than the manure from which it sprouted. In India they will erect your city—hahahahaha . . ."

Time crawled slimily to the verge of endurance. Finally it passed, and the girl returned. She sat down, her hands in her lap. "Our debt is paid," she said.

"Come!" said Tildy, standing up and taking her by the hand. She followed him. Near the door that led upstairs she stopped and looked at him. He realized that she had misunderstood; he didn't want to go up to the rooms with her, he wanted to take her with him, out of this place. "Come!" he said once again and tried to lead her away.

"Where to?" she asked, hard—and he grasped exactly how she meant it: this time she had clearly understood him.

"I will take care of you. Don't be afraid," he repeated.

"Do you have a house for tonight?"

"We will find one."

She stood very close to him. "My father is a millionaire in America," she said quickly and quietly. Then she burst out laughing. "How gullible can a man be? What a joke!"

Tildy saw her coarse, mean laugh and slapped her face.

She stood for a second as if blinded. "Kiss me, to take that away," she said, and held her face up to him, with closed eyes and a smile woven with pain.

He drew her in and kissed her like a holy object.

"Come!" she said.

Professor Lyubanarov came staggering after them, nearly running them over at the door; he stumbled with them onto the street and tottered away in front of them. "*Nempe haec assidue iam clarum mane fenestras*," he sang, "*intrat et augustas extendit lumine rimas . . .*"

The morning was dawning. On the street by the station Lyubanarov tapped with his cane to find the tram tracks. He poked it into one of the rail grooves and let himself be led uphill as if tethered to a pole. Tildy and the girl, Mititika Povarchuk, were no more than ten yards away from him.

By one of those inexplicable coincidences that we call fate, the driver of the streetcar whose brakes failed was the Widow Morar's eldest son, the one who worked for "the line." He later maintained that he had recognized the vehicle's defect days earlier and reported the same, and had been assured that the malfunction would be corrected overnight in the streetcar shed. So on that morning he had climbed aboard his streetcar in good faith and during the level stretch of the route had had no occasion to learn that the repair had not been made and that the vehicle was still unfit for service. After he had rounded the loop at the Ringplatz and arrived at the incline where the Bahnhofstrasse ran into the Volodiak Valley, he reduced his speed, according to regulations. At first his brakes held, but the second time he applied them they failed entirely.

Fortunately there were very few passengers: apart from the ticket-taker, who jumped off as soon as he realized what was happening, just a few drowsy railroad men, a woman with a basket of eggs, and the director of the Klokuczka Horticultural Academy, who having spent the previous day taking care of official business in Czernopol, was planning to catch an early train back home. Widow Morar's son, who was the first to notice the general danger, could have also been quick to abandon the car, but his sense of duty pinned him to the driver's seat like the captain of a ship—even though there was nothing he could do in the circumstances—a fact that was justly emphasized in the press. He maintained there was nothing for him to do except pray that the tram not jump its tracks as it went careening down the steep slope with an alarming acceleration, and that it not collide with anything so solid as to shatter the car to pieces—which was hardly the case for the group of three people that made up the only obstacle along its hell-bound path.

It was Tildy who first saw the wagon racing toward them. He and Mititika Povarchuk were on the sidewalk along the Bahnhofstrasse, so the only person in danger was Professor Lyubanarov, who was moving along the tracks. Tildy raced in to yank him back, but Lyubanarov was too drunk to react rationally. He felt Tildy grab hold of him, and presumably in a dim recollection of his recent eviction from the Établissement Mon Repos, he fell into a blind fury and hurled the much smaller man right in the direction of the oncoming streetcar. This caused the professor to lurch away from the tracks, so that he himself escaped being hit. But Tildy stumbled, and as he fell, the fender of the racing vehicle struck him right in the face.

Mititika Povarchuk covered him with her coat. The ermine collar covered the bloody mess that had once borne his "English" expression.

Herr Kunzelmann, who began his tireless activity early in the day, and was already making his rounds, came rattling up on the *taradaika* that was pulled by his brave mare Kobiela, and saw, as he put it, "a fine kettle of fish." They loaded Tildy's corpse onto the cart and slowly drove it up to the Ringplatz, while Kunzelmann sat on his box, holding a sadly drooping whip. The girl walked behind. Professor Lyubanarov had long since tapped his way back to the groove and was taking his usual way home along "the line."

It fit the insatiable appetite of the city of Czernopol for dramatic effects that Tildy's pitiful cortège on the Ringplatz collided with a pack of nocturnal revelers, led by Ephraim Perko, who had filled the

Trocadero with his bubbly joie de vivre and was now on his way home, escorted by his friends and admirers.

"Tear out my heart!" he called, when he recognized the girl Mititika. "Now you are a widow? *Viens avec moi*, sweetheart, I'll pay a thousand leos for the hour. No need to play the *malakhamoves*."

And when the girl walked on without hearing him, he pursued her with a stubbornness his friends and admirers found highly entertaining, and raised his offer: "Two thousand, Mititikele, twenty-five hundred—can you hear and see!—three thousand, Mititika! . . . Thirty-five hundred. Going once, going twice . . . four thousand for half an hour! It's time to pamper the *kurvehs*. Well, Mititika, five thousand!"

But the girl went on walking behind the little cart carrying Tildy's corpse, unmoved. "My respects," said Herr Kunzelmann. "That's what I call character!"

There's still so much I ought to tell you: how Tamara Tildy separated from Herr Adamowski, who later to our painful embarrassment married our Aunt Paulette, and how Baronet Wolf von Merores confessed the love he had long borne for Tamara Tildy in secret and showered her with luxury and all the trappings of a respectfully shy, melancholic chivalry till the end of her days, when she died as his wife, destroyed by her addiction, on the Riviera, and how Frau Lyubanarov came to a gruesome end during a spring storm in the little woods of Horecea when a wall of the Paşcanu mausoleum collapsed on her and struck her dead—some claimed it was during a tryst, others maintained she was searching for her mother's jewels—and, finally, how Widow Morar of the golden mouth took in both of the half-orphaned Lyubanarov daughters after the professor wound up as a complete wreck in the municipal infirmary, and how in her macabre hands these girls blossomed into beauties who smiled their way through life as though through a garden. But that is another story.

OTHER NEW YORK REVIEW CLASSICS*

J.R. ACKERLEY Hindoo Holiday
J.R. ACKERLEY My Dog Tulip
J.R. ACKERLEY My Father and Myself
J.R. ACKERLEY We Think the World of You
HENRY ADAMS The Jeffersonian Transformation
CÉLESTE ALBARET Monsieur Proust
DANTE ALIGHIERI The New Life
WILLIAM ATTAWAY Blood on the Forge
W.H. AUDEN (EDITOR) The Living Thoughts of Kierkegaard
W.H. AUDEN W.H. Auden's Book of Light Verse
ERICH AUERBACH Dante: Poet of the Secular World
DOROTHY BAKER Cassandra at the Wedding
J.A. BAKER The Peregrine
HONORÉ DE BALZAC The Unknown Masterpiece *and* Gambara
STEPHEN BENATAR Wish Her Safe at Home
FRANS G. BENGTSSON The Long Ships
ALEXANDER BERKMAN Prison Memoirs of an Anarchist
GEORGES BERNANOS Mouchette
ADOLFO BIOY CASARES Asleep in the Sun
ADOLFO BIOY CASARES The Invention of Morel
CAROLINE BLACKWOOD Great Granny Webster
NICOLAS BOUVIER The Way of the World
MALCOLM BRALY On the Yard
MILLEN BRAND The Outward Room
JOHN HORNE BURNS The Gallery
ROBERT BURTON The Anatomy of Melancholy
CAMARA LAYE The Radiance of the King
DON CARPENTER Hard Rain Falling
J.L. CARR A Month in the Country
EILEEN CHANG Love in a Fallen City
NIRAD C. CHAUDHURI The Autobiography of an Unknown Indian
ANTON CHEKHOV Peasants and Other Stories
RICHARD COBB Paris and Elsewhere
CARLO COLLODI The Adventures of Pinocchio
IVY COMPTON-BURNETT A House and Its Head
BARBARA COMYNS The Vet's Daughter
ALBERT COSSERY The Jokers
HAROLD CRUSE The Crisis of the Negro Intellectual
ASTOLPHE DE CUSTINE Letters from Russia
LORENZO DA PONTE Memoirs
ELIZABETH DAVID A Book of Mediterranean Food
L.J. DAVIS A Meaningful Life
VIVANT DENON No Tomorrow/Point de lendemain
MARIA DERMOÛT The Ten Thousand Things
DER NISTER The Family Mashber
TIBOR DÉRY Niki: The Story of a Dog
ARTHUR CONAN DOYLE The Exploits and Adventures of Brigadier Gerard
BRUCE DUFFY The World As I Found It
ELAINE DUNDY The Dud Avocado
G.B. EDWARDS The Book of Ebenezer Le Page

* *For a complete list of titles, visit www.nyrb.com or write to:*
Catalog Requests, NYRB, 435 Hudson Street, New York, NY 10014

MARCELLUS EMANTS A Posthumous Confession
EURIPIDES Grief Lessons: Four Plays; translated by Anne Carson
J.G. FARRELL Troubles
J.G. FARRELL The Siege of Krishnapur
J.G. FARRELL The Singapore Grip
KENNETH FEARING The Big Clock
FÉLIX FÉNÉON Novels in Three Lines
M.I. FINLEY The World of Odysseus
THEODOR FONTANE Irretrievable
MASANOBU FUKUOKA The One-Straw Revolution
MARC FUMAROLI When the World Spoke French
MAVIS GALLANT The Cost of Living: Early and Uncollected Stories
MAVIS GALLANT Paris Stories
MAVIS GALLANT Varieties of Exile
GABRIEL GARCÍA MÁRQUEZ Clandestine in Chile: The Adventures of Miguel Littín
ALAN GARNER Red Shift
THÉOPHILE GAUTIER My Fantoms
ÉLISABETH GILLE The Mirador: Dreamed Memories of Irène Némirovsky by Her Daughter
JOHN GLASSCO Memoirs of Montparnasse
EDMOND AND JULES DE GONCOURT Pages from the Goncourt Journals
EDWARD GOREY (EDITOR) The Haunted Looking Glass
A.C. GRAHAM Poems of the Late T'ang
WILLIAM LINDSAY GRESHAM Nightmare Alley
VASILY GROSSMAN Everything Flows
VASILY GROSSMAN Life and Fate
VASILY GROSSMAN The Road
OAKLEY HALL Warlock
PATRICK HAMILTON The Slaves of Solitude
PETER HANDKE Short Letter, Long Farewell
PETER HANDKE Slow Homecoming
ELIZABETH HARDWICK The New York Stories of Elizabeth Hardwick
ELIZABETH HARDWICK Sleepless Nights
L.P. HARTLEY The Go-Between
GILBERT HIGHET Poets in a Landscape
HUGO VON HOFMANNSTHAL The Lord Chandos Letter
RICHARD HOLMES Shelley: The Pursuit
ALISTAIR HORNE A Savage War of Peace: Algeria 1954–1962
WILLIAM DEAN HOWELLS Indian Summer
BOHUMIL HRABAL Dancing Lessons for the Advanced in Age
RICHARD HUGHES A High Wind in Jamaica
RICHARD HUGHES In Hazard
MAUDE HUTCHINS Victorine
YASUSHI INOUE Tun-huang
HENRY JAMES The New York Stories of Henry James
HENRY JAMES The Other House
HENRY JAMES The Outcry
TOVE JANSSON Fair Play
TOVE JANSSON The Summer Book
TOVE JANSSON The True Deceiver
RANDALL JARRELL (EDITOR) Randall Jarrell's Book of Stories
DAVID JONES In Parenthesis
ERNST JÜNGER The Glass Bees
KABIR Songs of Kabir; translated by Arvind Krishna Mehrotra

FRIGYES KARINTHY A Journey Round My Skull
HELEN KELLER The World I Live In
YASHAR KEMAL Memed, My Hawk
YASHAR KEMAL They Burn the Thistles
MURRAY KEMPTON Part of Our Time: Some Ruins and Monuments of the Thirties
ARUN KOLATKAR Jejuri
DEZSŐ KOSZTOLÁNYI Skylark
GYULA KRÚDY The Adventures of Sindbad
GYULA KRÚDY Sunflower
SIGIZMUND KRZHIZHANOVSKY The Letter Killers Club
SIGIZMUND KRZHIZHANOVSKY Memories of the Future
MARGARET LEECH Reveille in Washington: 1860–1865
PATRICK LEIGH FERMOR Between the Woods and the Water
PATRICK LEIGH FERMOR Mani: Travels in the Southern Peloponnese
PATRICK LEIGH FERMOR Roumeli: Travels in Northern Greece
PATRICK LEIGH FERMOR A Time of Gifts
PATRICK LEIGH FERMOR The Traveller's Tree
D.B. WYNDHAM LEWIS AND CHARLES LEE (EDITORS) The Stuffed Owl
GEORG CHRISTOPH LICHTENBERG The Waste Books
JAKOV LIND Soul of Wood and Other Stories
DWIGHT MACDONALD Masscult and Midcult: Essays Against the American Grain
JANET MALCOLM In the Freud Archives
JEAN-PATRICK MANCHETTE Fatale
OSIP MANDELSTAM The Selected Poems of Osip Mandelstam
OLIVIA MANNING Fortunes of War: The Balkan Trilogy
GUY DE MAUPASSANT Afloat
GUY DE MAUPASSANT Alien Hearts
JESSICA MITFORD Hons and Rebels
JESSICA MITFORD Poison Penmanship
NANCY MITFORD Madame de Pompadour
BRIAN MOORE The Lonely Passion of Judith Hearne
BRIAN MOORE The Mangan Inheritance
ALBERTO MORAVIA Boredom
ALBERTO MORAVIA Contempt
JAN MORRIS Conundrum
JAN MORRIS Hav
PENELOPE MORTIMER The Pumpkin Eater
YURI OLESHA Envy
IRIS OWENS After Claude
ALEXANDROS PAPADIAMANTIS The Murderess
BORIS PASTERNAK, MARINA TSVETAYEVA, AND RAINER MARIA RILKE Letters, Summer 1926
CESARE PAVESE The Moon and the Bonfires
LUIGI PIRANDELLO The Late Mattia Pascal
ANDREY PLATONOV The Foundation Pit
ANDREY PLATONOV Soul and Other Stories
J.F. POWERS Morte d'Urban
J.F. POWERS The Stories of J.F. Powers
J.F. POWERS Wheat That Springeth Green
CHRISTOPHER PRIEST Inverted World
BOLESŁAW PRUS The Doll
JULES RENARD Nature Stories
JEAN RENOIR Renoir, My Father
GREGOR VON REZZORI Memoirs of an Anti-Semite

GREGOR VON REZZORI The Snows of Yesteryear: Portraits for an Autobiography
TIM ROBINSON Stones of Aran: Labyrinth
TIM ROBINSON Stones of Aran: Pilgrimage
MILTON ROKEACH The Three Christs of Ypsilanti
GILLIAN ROSE Love's Work
TAYEB SALIH Season of Migration to the North
GERSHOM SCHOLEM Walter Benjamin: The Story of a Friendship
DANIEL PAUL SCHREBER Memoirs of My Nervous Illness
JAMES SCHUYLER Alfred and Guinevere
LEONARDO SCIASCIA Equal Danger
LEONARDO SCIASCIA To Each His Own
LEONARDO SCIASCIA The Wine-Dark Sea
PHILIPE-PAUL DE SÉGUR Defeat: Napoleon's Russian Campaign
VICTOR SERGE The Case of Comrade Tulayev
VICTOR SERGE Conquered City
VICTOR SERGE Unforgiving Years
SHCHEDRIN The Golovlyov Family
GEORGES SIMENON Act of Passion
GEORGES SIMENON Pedigree
GEORGES SIMENON The Widow
CHARLES SIMIC Dime-Store Alchemy: The Art of Joseph Cornell
VLADIMIR SOROKIN Ice Trilogy
VLADIMIR SOROKIN The Queue
DAVID STACTON The Judges of the Secret Court
JEAN STAFFORD The Mountain Lion
STENDHAL The Life of Henry Brulard
ADALBERT STIFTER Rock Crystal
THEODOR STORM The Rider on the White Horse
JEAN STROUSE Alice James: A Biography
HENRY DAVID THOREAU The Journal: 1837–1861
TATYANA TOLSTAYA The Slynx
TATYANA TOLSTAYA White Walls: Collected Stories
LIONEL TRILLING The Liberal Imagination
IVAN TURGENEV Virgin Soil
JULES VALLÈS The Child
MARK VAN DOREN Shakespeare
ELIZABETH VON ARNIM The Enchanted April
EDWARD LEWIS WALLANT The Tenants of Moonbloom
SYLVIA TOWNSEND WARNER Lolly Willowes
SYLVIA TOWNSEND WARNER Mr. Fortune
ALEKSANDER WAT My Century
SIMONE WEIL AND RACHEL BESPALOFF War and the Iliad
GLENWAY WESCOTT The Pilgrim Hawk
REBECCA WEST The Fountain Overflows
EDITH WHARTON The New York Stories of Edith Wharton
PATRICK WHITE Riders in the Chariot
JOHN WILLIAMS Stoner
EDMUND WILSON To the Finland Station
RUDOLF AND MARGARET WITTKOWER Born Under Saturn
FRANCIS WYNDHAM The Complete Fiction
STEFAN ZWEIG Chess Story
STEFAN ZWEIG Journey Into the Past
STEFAN ZWEIG The Post-Office Girl